# BLOOD SO BLACK
## FAE OF THE SUN AND MOON

JEWEL JEFFERS

Copyright © 2022 by Jewel Jeffers

All rights reserved.

No part of this publication may be reproduced, distributed, or transmitted in any form or by any means, including photocopying, recording, or other electronic or mechanical methods, without the prior written permission of the Author, except in the case of brief quotations embodied in critical reviews and certain other non-commercial uses permitted by copyright law.

The characters and events portrayed in this book are fictitious. Any similarity to real persons, living or dead, is coincidental and not intended by the author.

Cover design by: Yanie Cadwell of **Real Life Design Covers**
www.reallifedesign.site

Edited by: Zainab M of Heart Full of Reads
www.heartfullofreads.com

# TRIGGER WARNINGS

*Blood so Black* is a Dark Fantasy that contains **mature language, explicit sex, graphic violence, physical assault, murder, sexual assault** (not major and not shown), **self-harm** (not major), **and suicidal thoughts** (not major). The relationships within this story are **toxic** and should not be misconstrued as a depiction of healthy relationships.

**This story is tragic as fuck. You have been warned.**

# BLOOD SO BLACK PLAYLIST

**Spotify:** https://spoti.fi/3CXfy1Q

**1. Sweater Weather By The Neighborhood**
Marie - Theme Song

**2. Everything I Wanted By Billie Eilish**
Corivina - Theme Song

**3. Chance With You By Mehro**
Marie - Chapter 5-8

**4. Moral Of The Story By Ashe**
Corivina - Chapter 6

**5. Lemons- Demo By Brye**
Corivina - Chapter 10

**6. Lovely By Billie Eilish Ft Khalid**
Corivina - Chapter 10 & 13

**7. Boyfriend By Dove Cameron**
Marie - Chapter 5-22

**8. Lights Down Low By MAX**
Corivina - Chapter 17 & 21

**9. If I Killed Someone For You By Alec Benjamin**
Marie - Chapter 19

**10. Cry With You By Jeremy Zucker**
Marie - Chapter 20

**11. Dandelions By Ruth B.**
Marie - Chapter 23

**12. Happiest Year By Jaymes Young**
Corivina - Chapter 25

**13. Play Pretend By Margo**
Corivina - Chapter 25

**14. Always Been You By Jessie Murph**
Marie - Chapter 26-31

**15. Remember When By Wallows**
Corivina - Chapter 28

**16. Lose You To Love Me By Selena Gomez**
Corivina - Chapter 30

**17. This Is How I Learn To Say No By EMELINE**
Corivina - 30 & 32

**18. Paris In The Rain By Lauv**
Corivina - Chapter 32

**19. Seamless By Chris Grey**
Marie - Chapter 33

**20. Middle Of The Night By Elly Duhé**
Marie - Chapter 39

**21. Stupid By Tate Mcrae**
Marie - Chapter 42-47

**22. Please Notice By Christian Leave**
Marie - Chapter 50

**23. What A Time By Julia Micheals**
Marie - Chapter 51

**24. If We Have Each Other By Alec Benjamin**
Corivina Chapter 53

**25. Infinity Piano Version By Jaymes Young**
Marie - Chapter 55

**26. Look At What You Made Me Do By Taylor Swift**
Corivina - Epilogue

To Shyonna

Just keep trying.

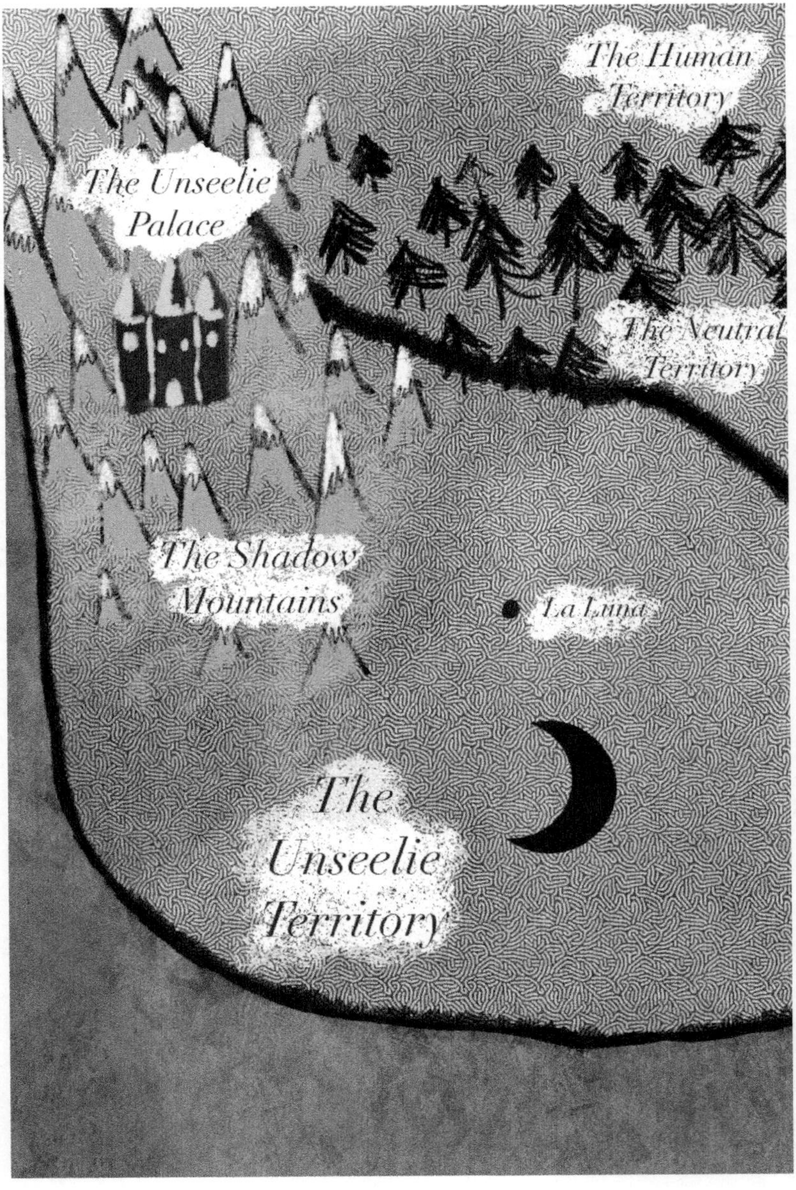
The Human Territory
The Unseelie Palace
The Neutral Territory
The Shadow Mountains
La Luna
The Unseelie Territory

The Wildlands
Lightwood Forest
Charlotte Manor
Lightwood
The Seelie Palace
The Diamond wall
The Seelie Territory

# PROLOGUE

CORIVINA
200 YEARS AGO.

*I* hated the sun. Here it always shined, and it was always hot. There was no regret for the first twenty years of my life I spent away from it because it was a horrid thing.

This place was my new home; hopefully, temporarily. It had been a little over three years since I was forced to come here because my blood bled gold. *Gold*. It was still unbelievable. I did not belong here. Everyone here had bronzed skin and looked to embody the sun. Where I was pale and personified the moon.

*Just one more year.* In a year, I could be rid of this place, and its forever shining sun that left burns on my luminescent skin. In a year, my training would be over, and I would marry Markos.

Markos and I had been together since I was seventeen. When I found out that I was a Seelie fae, he promised that he would marry me when my training was over. I was his one. He'd have no other. To prove that, he claimed me with his mark.

His promise was all I had to keep myself from going crazy in the wretched Seelie Territory.

I'd been walking for days just so I could get a few hours with him tonight. The journey from the Seelie Palace was only a portal away, but costed more than I could ever afford. Even though it took me three days to arrive here, he was worth the blisters that were starting to form on my feet.

Letters and a handful of hours on the lunar eclipses were what had become of our relationship. I had spent many nights with only my fingers for company. My sexual frustration fueled me with the power to keep moving my aching legs.

The amber sky that had accompanied the last hour of my journey had finally set. Stars poked through the indigo sky, the temperature dropping and cooling my skin. Soon, the beautiful moon appeared, full and white. My shoulders relaxed at the sight of her and my lungs exhaling a relieved breath. In a couple of hours, she would be painted in red, and I could finally be with Markos.

Arriving at the forest that bordered the diamond wall that separated the Seelie from the Unseelie, I listened for the light trickling of water. Kicking off my shoes, I let the soft plush grass tickle my feet, and used the sound as my guide to traverse through the woods. A small stream soon appeared in view, and I stripped my clothes off, dipping my body into the shallow pool and washing away the day's accumulation of sweat and dirt. I called upon my magic to dry myself and my long black hair that flowed down to my waist. A sinking feeling settled in my stomach as I watched the gold blood stream through my veins.

Shaking off the doom that always seemed to permeate the air when I used my magic, I grabbed the pink sundress with a plunging neckline out of my bag and pulled it on. I had saved it for tonight, hoping it would immediately draw Markos's eye.

I headed toward the gate that opened up to the Neutral Territory. Found a stone to perch on and rest my legs as I waited for access to the entrance. Others waited around the area, too. Some came to see their old loved ones and friends, but most came to party and fuck. Their chatters of small talk filtering through my ears. Normally, I joined in, but I wasn't in the mood tonight. Instead, I stared through the diamond wall, taking in the coloring change of leaves that decorated the trees outside of the civilized fae territories.

My foot tapped on the dirt floor as the moon traveled through the sky. Toying with my claws, my muscles ached for the world to move faster so the sun could color her with blood.

"Nervous?" A voice that sounded like fire on a calm summer's night floated through my ears.

The voice sang to my taut body, making it loose and pliant. Squeezing my legs together to stifle the throb that was settled there, I ignored its sensual purr.

A flask being uncapped chimed. "Care for a drink?"

I looked over, only to see the erotic voice was matched with an unbelievably handsome male. His skin was a light tan; his hair a toffee brown. He had a small close shaved beard that would just lightly tickle a soft face. If I wasn't promised to Markos, I would definitely love to have a tumble in the sheets with his muscular body.

"How do I know you aren't trying to poison me?" I queried.

"Why would I poison a female I don't know?"

"You could snatch me up," I said, voice slightly husked.

He chuckled softly, each roll of laughter vibrating through my skin. "You certainly think highly of yourself." He smirked as he took a drink, and I couldn't help but smile back. "You're born Unseelie?"

"Yes, how could you tell?" My reply dripped with sarcasm.

"Who are you visiting?"

"Why would you want to know who I am meeting tonight?"

He stepped close, blanketing me with his warm vanilla scent. My breath hitched as the heat of his body sizzled my skin.

"I want to know if the fae who has marked you is Seelie or Unseelie," he said, brushing the hair from my neck to reveal the mark.

I shivered under his touch, closing my eyes to revel in the feel of his calloused fingers.

Breathing in a shuttering breath, I hoped he couldn't smell the little bit of arousal that had gathered in between my legs. It'd been too long since I last been touched by a male, so the slightest stroke of his fingers had my body heating.

I sat back, moving from his inviting aura, my eyes connecting with his. I couldn't really tell the exact shade, but they were light in color. "I am meeting my male tonight, yes."

"Hmm." He looked up at the moon that was starting to blush. "Well, it's almost time. It was nice to meet you…"

"Corivina."

Bending, his hand found mine, and he brought it to his soft, full lips. "It was nice to meet you, Corivina." My stomach tightened at the sound of his smooth voice singing my name. He let go of my hand, turning and walking toward the gate, leaving me aching to the mystery of him. Before I was forever lost of him, he stopped and looked back. "Oh, and *Corivina?*"

"Yes?" I breathed.

"Let your male know his claim is fading. Wouldn't want any others to snatch you up." He winked, then disappeared through the crowd of people.

# ONE

MARIE
PRESENT.

*A* strand of my curly brown hair wrapped around Kolvin's fingers. They traveled the length until they reached the end that was bleached blond from too much time spent in the sun.

His hand moved up to repeat the action, but I snaked the curl behind my pointed ear.

Honey-green eyes locked with mine, anxiety flowing in their depths, reflecting what I was sure shown in mine.

Ignoring the fear that permitted the air, Kolvin's lips formed into an easy smile. His hand came out to grasp mine, offering a light comforting squeeze. "Everything is going to be fine."

I stared at our joined hands; my skin much darker than his—a light caramel. A product of my biological father's dark skin and my mother's lighter one. My fingers adorned with black pointed claws, wrapped around his larger fingers.

I have held this hand a thousand times, normally feeling the comfort that it offered, but today, my thundering heart didn't calm, nor could my mind stop racing. "You don't know that."

Kolvin lifted my chin. "Marie, you shine brighter than the sun. Your skin literally shimmers gold. The gods wouldn't make someone who looks like you Unseelie. That just wouldn't make any sense."

"When has anything regarding the fae made sense? We are—"

"Creatures of chaos." He rolled his eyes. "I know, but they wouldn't do something that wicked. You were made for the sun."

Chewing on my bottom lip, I nodded, trying to let the words soothe my fear. "What if you are Unseelie? What if I lose you?"

"Then I will do everything in my power to make it back to you—to my family. Even if I have to take the shittiest job under the king. I'll find a way back."

The thought of being separated from him for that long made my heart squeeze painfully. Kolvin and I had been best friends for as long as I could remember; I was pretty sure we even shared a crib at one point. Our fathers were both in the Seelie Army—my father being the commander, and his the first lieutenant. I had hardly ever spent a day without seeing Kolvin and couldn't bear to imagine it.

Anxiously, I studied the room. Everything was non-descriptive and bland. The walls were white with no decals. Simple brown chairs laid out on each side for us to sit. The windows weren't even covered with drapes, showing the graying sky outside—a product of the moon just beginning to shadow the sun for the solar eclipse.

This wasn't what I'd expected. I knew this building was only used for the Sorting Ceremony. An event that took place on a solar eclipse every three to five years. The ceremony had been going on for thousands of years, only ever here. In the Neutral Territory. In this room. One would assume that the room would be more eloquent. Grand. That both territories, Seelie and Unseelie, would chip in to make it look extraordinary.

The Sorting Ceremony was one of the most crucial days in a young fae's life. Magic wasn't dependent on your heritage, or I would be Seelie, like my parents. It was chosen by the gods at random, and seemingly without a rhyme or reason to it. The ceremony was held to determine what magic ran through your veins. Gold—Seelie. Black—Unseelie. Fae aging from eighteen to twenty-three were required to come and discover what color their blood ran to identify what race of fae they were.

Fae were creatures of nature. Their magic was bound to the world's elements, mainly the sun and the moon. Nature was fickle, brash, chaotic, and so were the fae. We were beasts who walked among humans, causing havoc everywhere we could, not sparing ourselves either.

If fae did live in harmony, once upon a time, I doubted it had lasted very long. The fae have had more civil wars than any other species. The Seelie and Unseelie constantly trying to gain power over another, like the sun and moon fighting to rule the sky. Each war ended with the same result—Light fae couldn't live without the dark, and Dark fae couldn't live without the light.

But we were quite volatile beings, too stubborn to fully try for peace. The two races only merged when the sun and moon shared the sky: dawn and dusk, and the eclipses. The eclipses were the only time when common fae were allowed to mix—the lunar eclipse for partying and the solar for the ceremony.

I removed my hand from Kolvin's, my thumbs twiddling with another as I waited for the conductor to begin. The room was loud with chatter as more faelings piled in, everyone pretending that they weren't scared shitless to leave their home and join an unknown territory.

They only talked about the positives of today: visiting the palace to learn magic for the next four years, freedom of adulthood, getting to meet new people if sorted. The excitement might be real, but my elevated hearing allowed me to listen to every hitch in their breaths and every slight stumble over their words.

My knee bounced in tandem with the rapid beating hearts. Trying to calm myself, I counted the fae sitting on the Seelie side of the room. Twenty-three. None of whom I knew since I was homeschooled, but Kolvin knew a few and chatted among them.

I turned my head to the Unseelie side—a sea of black, not one wearing an ounce of color. Forty-four of them, most half-fae like myself.

Fae were beautiful, almost flawless beings—in appearance. Full-blooded fae were often naturally tall, slender, and ethereal. If one was half-fae, they held some sort of difference to them, smaller ears that didn't come to a dramatic point, shortened height, or they held more of a curve to their body. I had all three. Half-fae were looked down upon but not because of the differences in appearance, but because one shared blood with a lesser being such as a human.

Looking over to the Unseelie side, it seemed it was more frowned upon in Seelie to be half-human than in Unseelie, or it was because the Unseelie had more human 'servants' and were known to indulge in their darkest desires.

In the back of the room, I assess the only four wild-fae who bothered to show up. Wild- fae were required to come, but they were also lawless creatures who wanted to live freely with nature and without running water.

As I was studying the wild-fae and their lack of clothing, my eyes locked on to an Unseelie male who'd just entered the room. His hair was a tumble of short, silky black curls that framed his face. A steel circlet formed into branches, gently rested on his brow. He walked with a powerful grace toward the front. Every step assured, but still somewhat rushed.

My head cocked to the side as I studied him. The movement somehow drawing his eyes directly to me in the cluster of Seelie fae. The connection of his black eyes meeting mine sparked a feeling within me, the sweet sensation traveling from my middle to my toes and back. All the tiny hairs on my body stood up on end. My heart rate sped up so fast that all I could hear was its pounding pulse in my ears. An opening settled in my chest, like a magnet drawing me to him. The pull was strong enough to force me upright, but then he looked away, breaking the connection, and leaving me feeling hollow.

"He's the prince," Kolvin whispered in my ear.

"The prince of the Unseelie Court? Is he the heir?"

"Yeah."

"What if his blood is gold?"

"Then he will be Seelie." Kolvin shrugged. "It probably would suck to be a prince and lose all that power because your blood is the wrong color, but fate is fate." The heir to the throne of either territory inherited the magic that had been passed down from king to king. If the prince was Seelie, he'd lose all of that and may even be shunned from his family—something that was common for many fae to face, not just royalty.

Swallowing roughly, dread started to seep into my pores. While I was evaluating the prince, I had momentarily forgotten why I was here.

Kolvin bent down and pressed a kiss on my temple, his arm coming around me in sympathy. "I will always be here for you, Marie, always."

I leaned up to press a kiss to his cheek. "Me too."

He smiled tightly. His eyes meeting mine, churning with an intensity as he stared into me. His gaze flicked to my lips for just a brief second, and I thought he might kiss me. I wanted him to kiss me—he was my best friend—but I had always wanted more. At times we'd have moments like this. We were fae, and fae loved to fuck almost more than anything. At this age, with our magic coming in, our hormones were aerated, but nothing ever happened between me and Kolvin. Well, except when we were twelve and we shared our first kiss, but I don't think that really counts.

Before anything could have become of the moment, the conductor stepped up to the podium, reinstating the panic in my lungs.

"Happy sorting day," she chimed in her sweet voice. "We only have so much time, so we won't waste. You are here to see what type of magic is in your blood. Are you a child of light, life, and growth? Or are you a child of dark, death, and decay? Today, your blood will decide. You may find you are neither, that you are just a child of this world and wish to just be a part of her. Either way, today, you will discover."

She gestured to the colored bowls—black, green, and gold—in the middle of the room. "You will line up according to age, the eldest first. Then each one of you will drink the elixir that will manifest the magic in your blood. Once your blood is drawn, you will drop it in the corresponding bowl and pledge yourself to that territory. If you choose to become wild, you will drop your blood in the middle green bowl."

Then she called all the ages up until we were all standing in line waiting for the elixir. Three fae walked into the room, two of which were carrying a huge bowl of purple liquid and the other a ladle and cups.

I stood in line, fidgeting with my claws. Kolvin was twenty-one, so he stood ahead in the line. While I waited alone, closer to the back, sandwiched between two Unseelie fae. I noticed that at a few heads from me was the prince. He must be the same age as me. Nineteen.

With his head turned, I got a good look at his back. He was tall, like most fae. He was wearing black like every other Unseelie. There was nothing about him that was interesting. I mean, he *was* beautiful. He had angled cheekbones and a sharp jaw that could probably slice through any female's heart. There was a darkness around him, not of one born to the moon, but of someone who you shouldn't fuck with. Yet, that feeling in my chest was pulling me toward him, telling me to move from my place in line and walk up to him.

His head turned back toward me, causing me to avert my gaze. I could feel his stare burning into my face. The caresses of it had my mind screaming to turn my focus back on him.

He looked away when he was handed the elixir by one of the servers. Soon after, I was handed mine. The citrus flavored liquid stained my tongue, and a buzz settled over me. The creature inside me stirred, my body standing alert as the blood in my veins changed to the color of my fate.

A chill filled the air after everyone had received the elixir. The boom of more fae carrying trays of ceremonial knives through the side doors crashed through the taut silence.

"Well, it is time," the conductor spoke. "Take a knife. State your name. Cut your palm. Then drop your blood in the bowl that matches. If you are Seelie, you will join the Seelie side, and if you are Unseelie, you will join the Unseelie side. If you decide to be wild, you will drop your blood in the green bowl and sit in the back. When the ceremony is over, if you are of the same blood, you will return home, but if you are of different blood, you'll get one day to say your goodbyes and then you'll have to join the territory you belong to." She motioned to the first person in line. "Let us begin."

The clinging of metal as each fae pulled a knife off the tray was all I could focus on for the beginning of the ceremony until it was Kolvin's turn.

Chewing on one of my claws, I watched as he grabbed a knife before stating his name. The gush of metal slicing into flesh pinging in my ears. Terror jolting through my body.

He pulled back the knife. Gold.

More fae went.

Black.
Black.
Gold.
Gold.

Mostly everyone was sorted to their respective territory, but there were a few half-fae born Unseelie who sorted Seelie, but none of them looked sad about leaving. Some even looked relieved.

"*Prince Levington Shadawn.*" His voice was like rough gravel, but it rolled over me like silk. Butterflies filled my stomach at the sound, adding to the already thousands of beetles rolling around in there.

The prince pressed the blade to his hand, everyone sucking in an audible breath. The first heir to the Seelie throne, Prince Karnelian, turned out to be a hybrid. The Seelie King promptly birthed a new son to be his heir after the discovery. Hybrids were extremely rare, but the chances of sorting Seelie weren't. The prince could lose everything, and we would all be here to witness it.

He pulled back. Black.

Collective sighs of relief permitted the air, but the prince's jaw ticked as he held his hand over the black bowl.

Three fae went and then it was me, grabbing a knife with trembling fingers as I walked toward the bowls.

"Marie Foxglove." I brought the knife to my palm, a slight zing of pain coasting through my nerves as I broke through flesh. Then I hauled my hand back, my heart sinking at the liquid dripping from my palm.

Black.

# TWO

## MARIE

*A* drop of black blood hit the floor as the earth fell out from underneath me. My throat closed as tears burned my eyes. I stood there frozen, taking in the black liquid streaming from my palm.

*Unseelie, a child of the moon.*

"Marie?" My head snapped up at the conductor's voice. "Your fate?" She gestured toward the bowls. I took them in. My choices were either to live wild or Unseelie.

A whimper escaped my mouth as I lifted my trembling hand. Tears spilled down my face as my blood dropped into the black bowl.

I turned slowly, walking toward the Unseelie side. My eyes found the prince, his black irises boring into me, slicing me open in an uncomfortably vulnerable way.

I ripped my gaze from him and found a seat, becoming the only color in the sea of black.

All the Unseelie fae were staring. Their eyes taking in the girl with skin that shimmered gold and curly hair dyed from the sun. Shocked just like I was.

Biting my lip, I smothered the sobs that wanted to break free from my mouth. I stared down at my palm, black blood staining my skin. My wound closed and my fate sealed, solidifying me to live a life of death, darkness, and decay.

Wrapped in Kolvin's warm embrace, we stood in the treehouse my stepfather built me when I was six. He really wanted me to like him when I was little, so he went all out. Instead of a cute little treehouse, he built practically a small cottage. The place was grand—furnished with a bed, sofa, and kitchenette. The icing on the cake was the illusion spell placed outside to make it look like a normal treehouse.

Kolvin's arms tightened around me. He was so warm, so Seelie, and I... wasn't.

The reminder was like a splinter finding its way to my heart, joining the thousands that already resided there. I buried my head into his chest, sinking further into his warmth.

"It won't be permanent." Kolvin's voice was clipped, almost harsh even. I could tell he was trying to hold himself together for my sake, but each one of his breaths was a suppressed shudder, showing his true emotions. "You'll visit on the sabbats. Mabon is only a few weeks away. After training, you can find a job in the court. The king employs Unseelies who are willing to make a deal with him. I'm sure your father can pull some strings. If not, then... we'll marry."

Another splinter joined the many as I pulled back to look at him. Tears trailed in a stream as I replayed his words. "I... don't want to marry you... marry anyone, just for a way to stay in

Seelie." Marriage, a human custom, was kind of a big deal for the fae. We often took multiple lovers or never stayed committed long enough to match our almost immortal lifespans. That being said, some did get married because of financial or regency gain, a difference in race, or a deep life committing love—like my parents. If I were to get married, that's how I would want it to be.

Kolvin wiped the tears from my face. His eyes boring into mine before he leaned down and pressed a soft kiss to my lips, shock rendering me frozen to the spot.

Kolvin waited for a brief second before deepening the kiss. His hands wrapped around the back of my head, pulling me closer and pushing all the raw emotions he felt into me.

My brain finally registered what was happening, and my hands found their way around his neck. My lips parted as I gave it all back to him tenfold.

My heart fluttered then ached. I tried to enjoy the moment, knowing this was probably just that. A moment.

After savoring the taste of him, I pulled away, meeting his honey-green eyes. "You don't have to pretend that you…"

"Marie, I fucking love you. I've been in love with you since we were babes."

"Why didn't you tell me?" I never outright told Kolvin I wanted to be with him, but I left clues at every turn, hoping he'd get the hint. He went to primary school, so he had plenty of options. I thought either he was just totally blind, or he wanted someone else.

"My mother told me I should probably wait to do anything with you until we were sorted because… Well, because of this."

Because we could be separated.

"So…" I nervously chewed on my lip.

He gave me a smug smile, the glint in his eyes telling me he knew exactly what I was thinking. "I'd never want to live a day without you, Marie. You're everything to me, and I honestly want no one else. I'd marry you right now if our parents wouldn't freak out about it. *So...* we'd have to wait till we're done with training."

"Truly?" I said with disbelief.

"Truly." He pressed his mouth to mine. Slow and tender, intensifying the ache in my heart.

Our kisses turned from gentle and loving to carnal and heated in a moment. I walked backward, pulling him with me until my legs bumped the bed.

Kolvin's weight settled over me. The scent of his arousal tickling my nose, and his cock pressing against my core. He traced the hem of my dress, drawing circles on my thighs. I couldn't think about anything but the feel of his fingers on my skin. How they were slowly inching higher, pulling my dress with them.

Raising the bottom of his tunic, I broke our connection to pull it over his head and connected with his heated gaze.

"This is what you want?"

I nodded. "You?"

"Every gods-damned day." *Kiss.* "Every hour." *Kiss.* "Every minute." *Kiss.* "Until the day I die." *Kiss.* "I will want you."

Before I could reply, his mouth was on mine again. The tension between us grew heavier, our breaths labored. My fingers fumbled for the ties on his trousers as he kicked off his boots and then pulled my dress above my head.

We took a second to take each other in. My eyes trailed over the tight muscles, starting at his broad shoulders, all the way down to the sculpted V that accentuated his cock. The sight of which had me licking my lips.

He pulled my legs apart and lined himself up, leaning down to kissed me softly, before entering me gently.

A small sting of pain speared me, but then he began to move his hips and the pain morphed into pleasure. The sounds of our joined moans, groans, and grunts filled the room. His subtle thrusts sending shocks of ecstasy through my body, but I wanted more of him. My hips moved on their own accord. I wanted him deeper, harder, faster.

The action sent him off. He grabbed my legs, raising them and spreading them wider as he began to pound harder into me. The pleasure intensified and drawled a guttural moan from my throat.

Feeling my muscles begin to tighten, I dug my claws into Kolvin's flesh. He winced, but I couldn't think about how I might be hurting him as my toes started to curl. He changed his angle ever so slightly, hitting that sweet spot that had me exploding into a thousand pieces.

Kolvin slowly continued to thrust into me, inspiring my climax to last a bit longer. He lowered himself, pressing a kiss to my lips as my legs wrapped around his body. As I began to relax, the tone of our sex changed. Everything was slower and deeper, our bodies flushed like we weren't close enough.

Kolvin's mouth left mine as he peppered kisses down my neck. "Can I?"

I knew what he was asking. He wanted to mark me, to claim me as his only. He wanted to sink his canines into me—the four sharpened teeth every fae had, that reminded other species of the beast that prodded under the façade of our beauty—Kolvin wanted to let his venom slow my healing, causing my skin to scar and create a mark. The mark would create a subtle bond between him and I, alerting others that I was his. I would be his until the claim faded or was removed.

"Yes, if I can you."

His response was to sink his teeth into my flesh. My back arched as the pain registered in my neck, but it was quickly replaced with pleasure as his venom spread through my veins. The effect like liquid glory had filled me. It heightened my senses, making everything feel extra sensitive, and better, so much better.

I was more aware of Kolvin than ever before. My walls became receptive to his thrusts, sucking him in and not willing to let him go while this exhilarating pleasure pulsed through me.

With my blood—still black—dripping down his chin, he brought his mouth to mine. I sucked in his bottom lip between my top two canines and sank in. A groan vibrated into my mouth; his hips thrusting a little harder as my venom weaved its way into his veins. Stars exploded behind my closed eyes, and I cried into Kolvin's mouth.

He quickly pulled out and spilled himself over my stomach. I was thankful he didn't come inside me, because my human blood made it more likely for me to get pregnant.

We laid in bed for a while, letting our breaths settle. Eventually, Kolvin got up and grabbed a towel from the kitchenette. He cleaned up his mess, then laid back down and pulled me into his chest. He held me tight, lightly stroking my back.

"I don't want to be without you." He kissed my temple. "I want to be with you and only you for the rest of the time."

A smile formed on my lips before I pressed a kiss over his heart. "You'll grow tired of me one day," I joked.

"No, I won't." He pinched my side playfully.

"Oww." I giggled, slapping at his chest.

"We could be mates," he said, his voice filled with hope.

To some, having a mate sounded like the most amazing thing in the world, while the rest of us saw it as a curse.

It had its ups—you love someone so much you would die for them. Mind-blowing sex with someone who was made to please your every need. But the cons outweighed the pros.

Many fae have gone crazy over their mates. They were possessive and extremely protective of each other. Once you found your mate, it was like every other person around you seemed to lose color and only your mate mattered.

That person had complete control over you. Your mate was not your equal. Your mate was the person who balanced you. Most of the mated pairs were often from different races, since their magic balanced another, but it was not always the case. One could be extremely powerful and the other weak, creating a power imbalance in the relationship.

You could end up being someone's slave. You'd kill for them. Wage war for them. Mated pairs almost always caused carnage. Almost all the fae wars started with a mated pair.

The only reason they were valued at all—besides inspiring true love—was for breeding children. Mated pairs can have about ten to twenty children. It was hard for regular fae to even have one in their lifetime. Luckily, mating was rarer than a fae babe. Most fae didn't have to worry about it. Currently, there wasn't a known pair in existence.

"Don't you think if we were mates, we would have mated by now?" I gestured to our naked bodies.

"Maybe we both just need to declare ourselves to each other," he prompted.

I grinned wickedly. I hadn't said 'I love you' back, but before I said it, I wanted to toy with him a little. "Declare ourselves?" I raised a brow. "Do we need to host a ball to tell everyone we fucked?"

"No, uh..." he stammered, shifting slightly, obviously embarrassed.

A sudden laugh escaped me as gold blood crept into his cheeks. "Of course, I love you."

He smiled against my lips, deepening the kiss for a second before pulling back and looking out the window toward the pond that laid a few feet from the treehouse. "You want to go for a swim before..."

A pang of sadness hit me. Before I had to go home and pack up to spend the next four years in the Unseelie Territory.

Sighing, I said, "I should probably wash your scent off as much as possible before I see my parents." Kolvin stilled under me. My father was the commander of the Seelie Army, trained to kill a man with his bare hands. My mother... Well, she was scary to everyone but me, and super protective.

Kolvin sat up, running his hands through his hair. "Fuck!"

I couldn't help but giggle. "Trust me, I doubt they will do anything. They'll be distracted from the fact that I'm leaving tomorrow night," I said, voice void of emotion.

I slid off the bed and pulled him with me. "Come on, we don't have much time till I'm expected back."

We walked toward the pond naked and slipped into the pool. My legs wrapped around his waist, and I ran my fingers through his blond hair.

"It's not fair," he whispered.

I trailed my fingers down his neck and drew little circles on his chest. "I know." He opened his mouth to speak, but I cut him off. "There's nothing we can do about it. Can we just be here right now?"

"Yeah." He kissed me softly, and I kissed him back with everything I had left. Our kisses deepened, and he entered me yet again. We took our time getting to know our bodies because it was the only time we really had left.

The second I entered the manor, my parents stood from the sofa and made their way toward me. I tried not to show any emotion on my face, to be strong like my mother, but I was never good at that.

My father—*stepfather*—held out a knife. The simple watch he always wore reflected the lights in the room as he pressed the hilt into my hand. His toffee brown hair was groomed today, and he was wearing his commander's uniform. My eyes found his warm blue ones, love churning in them. My stepfather, Darius, was my father in all ways but genetics, and he always tried to make me feel like I was truly his.

My eyes flicked to my mother's hard black orbs. In appearance, we were nothing alike. She was the typical fae, tall, thin, and celestial. She was born Unseelie and was sorted Seelie, and ironically, her blood was gold, but everything about her screamed Unseelie.

My human traits were more prominent. I was short even to a human, and I was in no way thin, but all of my fae traits mirrored in my mother. My shimmer was from her, but where my skin shimmered a bronzy-gold when reflecting light, hers was blue, making her look like a living ice sculpture. My claws were from her, but my human genes made them smaller. They were like longer than average fingernails that just happened to be naturally black, but they were still sharp, and if I had to, I could harm someone. My mother's were the real deal, long and deadly.

As I stared into her black eyes, like mine but hers carrying a coldness that gave others a chill, my heart started to tear. I loved her more than anyone else in the world. She appeared cold toward others and she wasn't fluffy, but my mother had always been my rock and she made sure I knew how much she cared for me. When I wasn't hanging out with Kolvin, I was spending my time with her, and if I was dealing with something, I could always talk to her.

Swallowing back my emotions, I took a deep breath as I dragged the knife across my hand and showed it to my parents. Seeing the black pool in my palm, I wondered how long the elixir would last until it returned to its normal scarlet red.

For a moment, everything was silent, and I was back at the sorting ceremony, frozen in disbelief, but then I was brought back when a sharp cry rang out.

My mother's tear-stained face came into my view as she fell to the floor. I'd never seen her cry; she always appeared poised, regal, and put together. Seeing her as a mess on the ground, crying like I had ripped her heart out... I didn't know what to do. I looked to my father for help, but his eyes were wet with tears too.

"Mother." Sorrow laced my voice as I placed a hand on her shoulder. Her fingers wrapped around my wrist, and I was pulled down into her arms.

I crumbled and let it all out, knowing she'd keep me safe as the pain of the situation cut through me. My father joined, adding his warmth and support to the mix. These two people meant everything to me, and now, I was being ripped away from them.

We stayed there, crying for what felt like hours, until I fell asleep from the exhaustion of today.

I awoke later in the night in my bedroom. The moon's glow illuminated the room, and I cuddled in my mother's arms. Closing my eyes, I curled deeper into her, hoping for the first time that tomorrow's sun wouldn't rise.

# THREE

## CORIVINA
## 203 YEARS AGO.

*I*t wasn't often I got to see the sun like this. Dawn and dusk were really the only times. Sometimes, I rose early enough to catch an hour or so before it set, but I never saw the sun like this—high in the clouds, streaming brightly.

I stared through the windows as Markos pounded me from behind, his fingers digging into my skin, his pace relentless.

The second the sorting ceremony was done, he brought me back to his room and started fucking me like a crazed animal. Normally I would be into it, but I knew what this was. It was goodbye sex. We'd—*he'd*—been going at it for an hour now. While I tried not to break down in tears.

My claws gripped the sheets as an orgasm threatened to build. I didn't want to come. If I came, he'd stop, and we would be over. If I came, I wouldn't be able to hold back the ocean's worth of tears building behind my eyes any longer.

"Come for me, Cor," Markos grunted behind me.

Gritting my teeth, I tried to hold off. This couldn't end. We couldn't end.

He thrust harder, his cock casting waves of pleasure over me. *Gods*, why does he have to know my body? This would be easier if he didn't.

As I tightened around him, there was no hope for me when he angled himself to hit that spot that shattered my soul.

The tears fell as my climax crested, and I buried my face in the pillow underneath me, sobbing heavily.

Markos pulled out, his arms coming around to comfort me, but I pushed him away, getting out of bed. I couldn't be here anymore. I couldn't stay for the end.

*But you have nowhere else to go. Not tonight.*

My parents said that I shouldn't even bother to come home if my blood ran gold. The Snows don't bleed gold and I was no daughter of theirs if I did.

Hurriedly, I picked up my clothes from the floor. I had some coin. I could maybe get a room at an inn. It didn't matter as long as I wasn't here.

"Cor," Markos whispered, despair dripping from his tone.

I ignored him, trying to flip my shirt right, but my hands trembled, and my claws threatened to cut the garment.

He was going to break up with me. He just wanted to get in one last fuck before he did it. I didn't really feel like staying for that part.

"Cor." Markos grabbed the tunic I was struggling to pull on. "What are you doing?"

I didn't answer, instead reaching for my shirt.

He held it out of my reach. His shoulder-length black hair shone blue as the sunlight hit his loose waves. "I won't give you the shirt until you tell me what you are doing."

I glared into blue-black eyes. "I'm getting dressed. Now, give me my shirt."

"Why are you getting dressed? Did I do something wrong?"

"No." Fruitlessly, I reached for my tunic. "I just want to leave."

He straightened his shoulders, his eyes glistening. "Why?"

The look threatened to ruin everything inside me. My world was tilting, and I just had to go before it came tumbling down. "Markos! Give me the fucking shirt!"

He dropped the fabric, pulling me into his warm embrace. I tried to push him away, but he held on, enveloping me in his love. His chestnut and snow scent wrapped around me, safety encircling me, making me feel at home.

For a moment, I surrendered to him, breathing him in for the last time. It was stupid of me to fall in love with him. I knew this could happen, but I just had to hope.

Letting out a breath to gather myself, I broke away.

"Corivina, talk to me," he pleaded.

"There is nothing to say, Markos, or nothing that needs to be said out loud. Just let me get dressed and I'll leave and be out of your hair."

He draped me in his arms again. "I don't want you to go," he whispered into my ear.

"Did you want me to finish you before?" I bit out.

"Corivina, why are you acting like this?" He grabbed my face and searched my eyes.

"Markos, I know you are going to break up with me. Why else did you need to fuck me like that?" I said, gesturing to the bed.

"I'm scared to lose you. That's why I needed to make love to you like that." He took a deep breath. "I wanted to prove to you that I'm the male you need."

"Oh."

He snorted. "Oh?" He brushed some hair behind my ear. "I told you I'd love you forever when I gave you that necklace." He pointed down at the ruby pendant around my neck.

I chuckled through my tears, burying my head into his chest. "We were eighteen. I thought you just said that so that you could get into my pants."

"Yes, I desperately wanted to make love to you. But I meant what I said." He pulled my head from his chest. "I will love you for the rest of my days." The last of my walls deteriorated, and the damn of tears burst. Markos led me back to the bed where I cried into his chest for what felt like hours as he whispered sweet affirmations into my ear.

*Home,* my heart sang.

When the sun began to set, I finally calmed down. We laid in silence, Markos rubbing my back, soothing me as I listened to the rhythm of his pulse.

I wished we could stay here forever, but we couldn't, so I sat up, and he followed suit. "You should probably go tell your parents," I said.

He shook his head. "They probably demanded to have the pledges read to them hours ago." He brushed my hair from my shoulder, lightly pressing a kiss on my neck. "They will also know that you are Seelie. They'll understand why I haven't told them."

"I bet they will be jumping with joy when they find out," I said flatly.

"They know how I feel about you. They respect it. If they didn't, they would have never let me give you a precious family heirloom." He played with the stainless-steel necklace. The rough callouses on his fingers making me shiver.

He stopped abruptly, his eyes scanning my neck. It had been bare throughout the whole three years of our relationship. He had asked me many times if he could mark me, but I always refused, wanting to wait until we were sorted.

Markos's focus zoned in on me, his eyes clouding with lust. "The sorting ceremony was today."

"Yes, it was."

His tongue trailed over my neck, his mouth tasting my skin before his teeth scraped across my flesh. "Can I now?"

Heat flared in my core, causing me to take in a shuddering breath. "Markos, I'm leaving in the morning."

"More reason for me to mark you now." He continued to pepper kisses up and down my neck.

"We are going to break up eventually. We should just—"

"Didn't I just tell you how much I love you? Why do you doubt it?" His lips moved across my jaw to press a quick kiss to my mouth before moving back down.

I tried to think rationally while he tortured me with his luscious tongue. "You know why I doubt it. Love just isn't enough, not with you."

He stopped and cupped my face. "I won't take another. I want you. My parents will see that."

"Will they?"

"Yes."

"How could you prove that?"

He moved in as if to go in for another kiss, but then stopped centimeters away from the destination. "Marry me," he whispered against my lips.

In shock, I wrenched back. My eyes going wide, scanning his for the jest, but there wasn't one. "You're serious?"

"Yes." He gently pecked my nose.

"But I leave tomorrow…"

"I don't think we can get around that. We can see each other on eclipses and maybe a few sabbats. You go and learn magic, and when you're done, we will marry. I promise."

"Oh, okay." Doubt clouded my brain. He wanted me to hope that his parents would approve, which would probably never happen. They didn't approve of me before, and I doubted they would ever let their son marry someone of gold blood.

I looked down at my hands, tears building in the back of my eyes. No matter what Markos said, we were doomed.

His fingers gently raised my chin. "There is no one else for me, my raven. We *will* marry. I can prove that to you."

"How?" I sniffled.

His lips brushed my neck. "I can mark you as mine." His tongue languidly circled my skin. "Show everyone who you belong to." His hand slid up my side, finding my breast so his fingers could tweak my nipple. "Let me, my raven."

Markos *loved* me. He loved me enough to try to make it work. He could just cut his losses and find another. Everyone wanted him, and he could have anyone, but he chose *me*.

"Okay," I whispered.

His canines sank in. The pain was short before his venom coursed through my veins, everything becoming clear and yet still foggy, my whole body alert and sensitive.

I moaned as he slowly pushed more venom into me, controlling the amount that was released. It was common knowledge that too little, and the mark wouldn't stay for long; too much, and I could pass out from the effects.

His hand slipped down my body, his fingers playing with my skin, creating extra little whispers of pleasure throughout my body. His hand stopped right before my clit, lightly pressing a finger down, making my entire body fracture.

He held me as I climaxed. Letting the effects of venom carry me into bliss. When I settled, I relaxed against him, feeling safe and ready to face whatever was to come, knowing Markos's love for me was unbreakable.

# FOUR

## MARIE

$\mathcal{T}$he sun did rise the next morning, and I awoke alone in my room.

Pulling the yellow bedding around me more, I looked over to my birth father's portrait hanging on the lilac wall. Dark brown skin and a shaved head. A pure smile that reflected mine, along with those coffee-black eyes I inherited. My mother never spoke of my birth father, but through the exquisite details of the artist's work, one can feel the rage of positive emotions she felt for him. I've studied each brush stroke a thousand times, and all I can gleam is that he smiled without care, something I think I might have adopted from staring at this portrait so many times.

*Maurice.*

For once, I was glad I didn't get to know him. He'd just be another person to say goodbye to.

Throwing something comfortable on, I walked downstairs to the kitchen where my parents were making breakfast. They could afford to hire a cook and an entire kitchen staff, but my mother loved to cook just as much as she loved to grow herbs. She said gardening and cooking helped keep her mind free of wandering thoughts, and today, I could guess what had her making a five-course meal for just our little family of three.

My father sat at the kitchen island cutting vegetables. When I approached, he stopped and pulled me into a loving embrace. He gave the best hugs. He was always warm and comforting. I would have never believed he killed my birth father if he wasn't the one to tell me.

We prepared the meal in silence. I helped chop; each crunch reverberating in my ears. I understood why my mother found peace in the kitchen. There were no thoughts, just silence, and for that moment, nothing existed except me and the food. I had helped my mother prepare a thousand meals, but it was not until this day that I ever truly understood why she loved it so much.

My father suggested we move to the library after we ate. We relaxed on a sofa, my legs resting on his as he read, and my head on my mother's as she played with my curls.

Her black eyes tracked the movement, sorrow reflecting in them. Normally, there was a wall up with her. I could never really tell what she was thinking, but today, she let it down, or the events of the past hours had shattered it.

The smooth harmony of my father's voice and the comforting caresses from my mother soon had me drifting off. When I awoke, it was to my parents discussing me.

"She can't go there," my mother whispered. "They will tear her apart."

"Vina, she will be fine," my father replied.

"How would you know! You never lived there," she snapped. I knew my parents loved each other deeply, but I had driven a wedge between their marriage. It was common for fae to have many lovers—even at the same time. It was not common for fae to have many children. In my mother's two-hundred and twenty-three years of life, I was her only child. She had been married to my stepfather for a hundred and eighty years before she met my birth father. My stepfather was okay with her being romantically involved with a human, but when he found out his wife's only heir was not his, the creature within him flipped and he impulsively killed my birth father.

It took my mother years to forgive him, and even though she said she did, it felt like she still didn't trust him. Mainly because my father wore my mother's mark, but she didn't return the notion.

"She has us. We will give her what she needs and support her. She is going to the palace, they have guards. She will be perfectly safe," my father supplied.

"The palace is where all the monsters reside."

"Vina, I know you hate the Unseelie, but she has to go."

"She doesn't have to. You could do something. You could petition the king. It's the least you could do."

"Do you not think I would if I could? I don't want our daughter going there as much as you. But it is out of our hands. She has to go. In four years, she will either marry the Denmor's boy or I will find a way to keep her here."

"What if she wants to stay there? What if she wants to be Unseelie?"

"Then that will be her choice, Corivina."

"She is my daughter, Darius. She's all I have."

My father sighed. "Vina, you have me."

My mother didn't respond as she lightly brushed the hair out of my face. "I don't want to lose her."

"You won't. I'll make sure you won't," he stated, before getting up and leaving the room.

I continued pretending to sleep, feeling my mother's gaze on my face. She kissed my forehead before waking me. My eyes opened to hers, both of us just staring at another for a moment.

My mother wasn't the cuddly type. She held me as a babe, but when I got older, she was less physically affectionate. My father was the one to hold me when some faeling pushed me down and scraped my knee, while my mother was always the one to go to the parents' house and yell at them for hurting her child. She had a fierce soul, and it always inspired strength within me. If I needed to be uplifted, she was the person I would go to.

"I love no one more than I love you, my flower." She told me that every day.

"I love no one more than I love you, mother."

She gave a light smile that didn't reach her eyes. "Go upstairs and start packing. I'll be up there in a minute."

Getting up, I walked upstairs slowly, my movements slow and hesitant. All I wanted to do was run back into my mother's arms, a place I never remembered to be so warm. I hated that look in her eyes, it was so broken, filled with so much pain. Pain I didn't know how to soothe, but I wanted to try, though I knew she'd never let me.

I packed light, knowing none of my clothes would fit in the Unseelie Territory. My clothes were bright and represented life, and I was going to be in a court that celebrated death.

My father came in to give me some coin so I didn't have to worry about money while I was there. When my mother joined, the tension between the two was thick. My father's shoulders tense, my mother staring daggers at him, eyes screaming at him to leave. I stayed silent. They were like this a lot when it came to me. My mother being domineering, my father just trying to be there, and eventually, him giving in.

He stood, walking over to give me a kiss on my temple. "I'll see you down there, flower. I love you."

"I love you too," I replied, hugging him.

He moved over to my mother, pressing a gentle kiss to her head. "I love you," he whispered so low I could barely hear it.

She pulled his face to hers and kissed him with passion. "I know," she whispered back.

When he left, she stood, blinking profusely before she drew out a bag of tea from her dress pocket. "Here, I don't want you to get pregnant when you aren't ready."

My eyes widened as I recognized what it was—contraceptive tea. It was something that existed, but fae rarely used it because with fertility so low, there was really no need.

Blood filled my cheeks as I realized she—and my father—had smelled Kolvin's scent on me. "Thank you, I... It just happened," I stammered, embarrassed.

"Then you'll be prepared for when it happens again." She sighed. "I should have told you about these things. I just thought I would have more time."

"Mother—"

"No." She raised her hand. "I will be fine. I will see you again."

"Maybe just one more hug? For me. I don't think I'm strong enough to leave."

Her lips pressed together. It was uncomfortable for her to be soft, especially around me. She let out a breath, her hard black eyes softening as she pulled me into a hug.

"You are strong. You're stronger than me in many ways."

My arms tightened around her. "I don't believe you."

She tilted my head up, smiling sadly. "Marie, what fae with an army commander for a father, and me as a mother, would dare sneak out with her best friend, go across the wild lands into the human lands, so she could play with the humans?"

"Yeah, but I know you would never hurt me."

"But I did make you do all the garden work that summer, right?"

I smiled. "Yes."

"You are strong, Marie. You have to be. For me. If anything, *anything* happens to you while you are over there, I will burn that horrid place to the ground. Do you understand?" Her eyes bore into me.

"Yes, I will be strong to save the lives of all Unseelie."

She took in another deep breath. "Listen, you love freely and trust blindly. That is okay here where I am there to protect you. But, the Unseelie are bastards of darkness, and you cannot trust anyone there. Am I clear?"

The Unseelie were not eviler than the Seelie. All fae were wicked and cruel, but my mother hated the Unseelie more than a regular Seelie fae. I think it had to do with the fact that she was from there, and her family rejected her after she was sorted.

"Yes."

She kissed my head. "Good."

Soon, the day edged its way to night. I said goodbye to my parents, then I made my way to Unseelie.

Kolvin met me at the edge of my father's manor. "So... did your parents say anything?" he asked wearily, his eyes scanning my neck.

"About you deflowering their flower? No, but they know. I wouldn't go near them over the next few weeks if I were you." I paused to think. "And I would sleep with a knife under my pillow. My mother is definitely pissed that you marked me, and that could send her over the edge," I teased.

Kolvin shivered, and I put my arm around his waist, tucking myself into him. "Hope it was worth it." I grinned.

He looked at me and smiled. "Of course, though I wish I could have lived just a little bit longer."

"You still got time."

"You're right. I should probably start working on my bucket list."

We walked to the wall that bordered the Seelie and Unseelie Territories. The wall was one of the few things that the Seelie and Unseelie agreed upon. It was fifty feet tall, made of diamond with steel portcullis stationed throughout for trade and travel.

It was made of diamond because the stone was nearly impenetrable and refracted magic. It was also transparent so you can get a view of the enemy patrols.

As we approached it, I turned to Kolvin, tears welling up in my eyes.

"It's going to be fine." He pulled me into his arms, kissing the top of my head. "We will see each other in a couple weeks."

"For one day," I protested.

"And we will make the most of what we have." He stepped back from our embrace. "I got you a gift." He beamed, pulling a pen out of his pocket.

"A pen?" I said, awkwardly taking it from him.

He chuckled. "It's enchanted. I have a matching one. If you write something, my pen will copy it, same for yours. We can communicate without waiting for a letter to come."

A smile graced my lips. "I love it. This is probably the best thing you could have given me."

"Really, you couldn't think of anything better for me to give you?" he said seductively, bending down to kiss my neck where his mark lie, the act sending shivers down my spine.

"No," I fibbed, pocketing my pen.

"Sure," he said before giving me a breathtaking kiss. I wrapped his tunic in my fist, tugging him closer to deepen the embrace.

The sound of metal clanking pulled us apart. Fear spiked through my body, seeping its way into my bones.

Kolvin cupped my face, pressing a soft kiss to my lips. "I love you."

My kiss back was harsh and desperate. "I love you too."

"Tell me when you make it to your room."

I passed through the gate, shivers wracking my frame as my feet crunched against the snow of the Unseelie Territory. My body going into shock at the abrupt change in weather.

The Seelie Territory was in a perpetual summer, warm and full of life. The Unseelie Territory was perpetually winter, cold, and lifeless. I had only experienced winter when I ventured into the wild fae woodlands to play with the humans, but I didn't remember it being this cold.

I wore a brown cotton dress that went down to the toes. The straps were as thick as a twig, so I wore a white long-sleeved tunic underneath. Over my clothes laid a royal blue cloak my father got me a few winter solstices back, which was way too thin for this weather.

Walking down the road, snow finding its way into my boots, I passed the fae who were lugging goods in through the gates. Until I stumbled upon a black carriage with the Unseelie Crest.

"Hello?" I called as I approached.

"Hello." A human walked from out behind the carriage. "You the Seelie turned Unseelie?" he said as he rubbed an apple against his black cloak before biting into it.

The Unseelie were most likely to have human 'servants.' Human slavery was illegal among the fae, but human servitude wasn't. Fae often acquired a 'servant' by making a deal with a human. Some servants were treated well like the ones employed by my father. Others... Well, they were slaves, but they entered the deal willingly. Humans were not the brightest creatures. They seriously thought that we couldn't lie and that iron hurt us. Everyone knew Unseelie's biggest export was steel, which was made of iron.

"Yes. Are you my escort?" I asked.

"No, I'm just the driver. Your escort"—he looked around—"was here."

"Do you know when they'll be back?"

He shrugged. "I don't know. He told me to stay here and watch the horses."

He finished his apple and chucked the core on the ground. "Here, let me take your bag. You warm up in the carriage. It's spelled." I lit up with his words and hurried into the cab.

A moan slithered its way out of my mouth, heat coating my skin and warming up my body. Yawning, I snuggled myself into the plush seat. The warmth in here and the cold out there had me feeling sleepy. It shouldn't be that long as we rode through the portals, maybe an hour's ride. I decided I could probably get a good nap in during that time and closed my eyes.

I was almost asleep when the door to the carriage swung open, and I came face-to-face with the Unseelie Prince.

# FIVE
## MARIE

Cold air brushed past him, chilling my cheeks, and freezing my mind. My pulse quickened, my breath shallowing as I stared at the prince.

*Beautiful.* Everything about him was beautiful. His midnight eyes cut into mine. Those irises mesmerizing me, swirling my mind and putting me into a trance. Their color was a bluish-black, like the gods couldn't decide whether to give him blue or black eyes, settling on a mix of both. His face was angular, framing those eyes perfectly. His black silky strands formed in soft loose curls that covered his brow and almost hid those eyes—eyes that felt like home for my soul.

*Mine,* my heart sang. *Mine.*

The thought was a splash of cold water pouring over me. Mine? No, he was not mine, Kolvin was. My fingers brushed my mark, the act drawing the prince's eye. His expression went from curiosity, to confusion, to cold within seconds. When he met my gaze again, all I saw was hate—deep and burning hate.

"You're marked." His voice was low, dripping with malice.

It was not a question, but I still replied, "I am."

He studied me for a second, thoughts churning in his mind. His eyes flicked back to my neck, his nostrils flaring slightly, then they met mine once more before he got into the carriage.

He took the seat across from me, scooting as far away as he possibly could.

The jolt of the carriage moving had me breaking the tense silence. "What about my escort?"

"I am your escort," he growled.

"But you're the prince. Don't they have someone, I don't know, of a lower rank to escort me?"

He refused to look at me as he talked, instead peering out the window. "I volunteered."

"Why?"

A shrug. "I had nothing better to do."

I didn't know what to say to that, so I glanced down at my claws, my thumbs circling another as my mind whirled. A small part of me was hoping he might say something different. Our interaction so far felt off, like this wasn't how it was supposed to happen, like the universe wanted me and this prince to get along. The pull toward him was still there, settled in the middle of my chest, urging me to make this better.

The feeling was so strong that I found myself speaking again. "What's the palace like?"

He didn't react to my question, continuing to look out the window.

I couldn't tell if he was ignoring me or if he was just lost in his thoughts. "Uhh, Your Highness? Did you hear me?" I cringed inwardly. *Your Highness?*

"My name is Levi, and I heard you. I just chose not to answer," he replied, not even gracing me with a glance as he talked. Instead, he kept staring out that stupid window.

I tried not to let this bother me, but it was really fucking annoying to be ignored. "In my letter, it said if I had any questions, to ask my escort and they would be *happy to help*."

"You must be fully human if you believe a fae would be happy to help."

I grimaced, almost rolling my eyes. "So, are you going to answer my questions?"

"I prefer if you didn't speak."

Closing my eyes, I took a deep breath. Fuck this feeling. I didn't want to be friends with this prick. "You know I thought you'd be a dick when I saw you at the ceremony."

He finally looked at me, and I smirked in victory. He stared at me for a long while, long enough for me to remember that I just called a *prince* a dick to his face.

Just when I was about to drop my smirk and start apologizing, his resolve broke and he chuckled. The sound was low and barely a laugh, but it sent sparks trickling down my spine.

"I thought you'd be some stuck-up Seelie. I see I was right," he countered.

I scowled at him, and it was his turn to smirk. A gleam lit in his eyes, screaming for me to challenge him. The beast in him edging mine to divulge in mayhem.

"Look, *prince*, I'm too tired and emotionally exhausted to play your stupid prince games. Are you going to answer my questions, or should I just wait to ask someone else when we arrive at the palace in an hour?"

"We won't be arriving in an hour, *princess*."

"*Okay*, when will we be arriving?" I asked with fake politeness, ignoring him calling me *princess*, and how I liked it.

He pondered for a long moment, stretching the silence, and aggravating me. "About a night and a half's ride."

Astounded, I asked, "Aren't we riding through the portals?"

"No, they are used for imports and exports only."

"But you're the prince."

"The portals are overloaded with imports from the eclipse right now. It would probably take more time."

"So, I'm stuck with you for the entire ride?" The second the words left my mouth, I realized how harsh they sounded, and I wished I could take them back.

I bit my lip nervously, his gaze dropping to the action before coming back to my eyes. A muscle in his jaw twitched, and he took a deep breath in before replying, "I guess you fucking are."

He turned to the window, dismissing me. A hollow feeling settled over me. For some reason, his dismissal felt like a punch to the gut. I tried to shake the feeling off. I didn't know this male and I didn't really need to. I just needed to get through the next two nights, and I would be rid of him and his grumpy attitude. In next three weeks, I could see my family again. Then after the next few years, I'd be rid of all of Unseelie for good and never have to turn back.

That thought made me feel slightly positive, but then I glanced at the prince and my mood instantly soured.

# SIX

## Corivina
## 200 YEARS AGO.

*N*erves built in my stomach as the clinking sounds of the gate rising vibrated through my ears. I last saw Markos on Imbolc—a minor sabbat—and that was months ago. He wrote to me every week, sometimes twice a week, but seeing him—*feeling him,* was a thousand times better than the sweet letters and gifts he sent me.

The second the guards nodded for us to enter the Neutral Territory, my feet were moving. Cold air encircled my body, the crunch of dried leaves sounding with each step I took. I frantically scanned the Unseelie fae who had begun to filter in. Shoulder-length obsidian hair caught my eye, then I was sprinting into his arms.

"Markos," I breathed, and it felt like my first in a long time.

"My raven," he whispered into my hair.

I pulled back enough to smash my lips to his, groaning at the familiar feel of his tongue against mine. The kiss lasted for a few moments before I began grinding myself into him, wanting more, needing more. I was already soaked from the encounter with that male before and all I wanted was for Markos to fill the ache he'd created.

"Can't you wait until we rent a room, my love?" He laughed. That hymn was my favorite sound in the world, my heart squeezing whenever I got to hear it.

"No." I smiled.

He grinned from ear to ear. "Soon."

"I wouldn't be in such a rush if I could have my way with you every day." I pulled him in for another kiss, which he returned half-heartedly.

His smile was tight, an emotion I couldn't read swirling within his eyes. "Tell me about how you are on our walk?"

"Horrible," I replied before quickly stealing another kiss.

He chuckled over my mouth. "It can't be all that bad. Have you made any friends?"

I wrinkled my nose. "Why would I make friends if I am going to leave that wretched place?"

"It is not that bad. It must be nice not to be so cold all the time," he said as he put his arm around my waist, guiding us toward the inns.

I peeled back my dress to show him my burned shoulder. "You have not spent all your time in the sun trying to 'connect to the light' as my professor puts it."

"They have to have some type of salve for that." He examined my shoulder, his touch gentle and loving.

Embarrassingly, I looked down at my worn sandals. "It costs more than I can afford."

His eyebrows drew together. "Why didn't you tell me? I can give you as much coin as you want. I told you I'd take care of you."

"I don't want your parents to think I only want you for money."

He took a deep breath, a muscle twitching in his jaw. "They do not think that way of you."

"Oh Markos, how you lie so sweetly." I poked his nose.

He clutched my hand and kissed it. "They know my love for you is real and that is all that matters."

"And if you can get me knocked up…"

"It would help with them liking you more," he teased.

"Well, I won't get knocked up if we spend all our time tonight *slowly* walking."

"I want to hear your voice."

"There are many different ways to hear my voice." My eyebrows raised, eyes suggestive.

He snorted. "I'm starting to think you only love me for my skills in the bedroom."

"They are some pretty good skills."

"You're not so bad yourself."

I slapped his arm playfully, and a frown constructed on his lips. "What was that for?"

"For saying I'm anything less than perfect," I cooed, smiling so hard my jaw hurt.

He pulled me into him. "My raven, you are better than the moon."

The statement gutted me, tears attempting to weld in my eyes. I blinked, trying to keep them down. "I will not cry tonight," I whispered.

He brushed away the tears that threatened to fall. "You'll cry tonight, just in a completely different way." His voice was husky, sending shivers down my spine. "Come on. We don't have all night!" He sprinted, dragging me toward the inns.

"Yes, because I was the one holding us back."

The second we entered the room, our clothes were off. Markos picked me up, laying me on the bed while smashing his lips to mine. He peppered my neck with kisses, stopping at the mark that ached for his canines to penetrate, and teasing the area with his tongue. He continued on to my breast, sucking each nipple into his mouth, causing moans of relief to emanate from me. Moving lower, he pressed a kiss right above my clit. Skipping my entrance that dripped for him, he moved his mouth down to my thighs.

"Markos." I squirmed as he continued to torture me. "Markos, please."

"Tell me what I want to hear, my love." He lightly brushed a kiss on my clit.

"Please," I cried.

"That's not it." His thumbs massaged my inner thighs. His fingers coming right up to my center but never touching where I needed him to.

His torment made me groan in frustration, my claws digging into the bed as his mouth neared me.

"Tell me what I want to hear, my love." His hot breath cascaded over my core.

"I love you," I breathed.

"I love you too, but you know that's not it. I want more than just your love." He grazed a finger across my clit, my back arching at the slight pleasure.

"I'm…" I gasped as he did it again. "*Yours, only yours.*"

He sucked my clit into his mouth in reward. A scream bubbled out of my throat as he made little circles with his tongue. My body wriggled under the pleasure as he continued to lick and suck at my clit. His fingers soon joined the mix, pumping until my muscles were tightening around them, and explosions flared within.

He removed his mouth as I came but continued to slowly thrust his finger inside me as my orgasm faded.

"Beautiful," he whispered. "You are the most beautiful creature I have ever seen. You are even more beautiful when I make you come."

"Then do it again."

He climbed on top of me, slowly stretching me with his cock. "Gods, I missed this," he moaned.

His thrusts were slow and torturous, and I groaned in tandem with them, loving the feel of him filling me. Our mouths locked together, our tongues sliding over another. My claws grazing along his back, his hands holding my legs around his waist.

My kisses roamed down his chin, the scruff of his stubble tickling my lips. My canines scraped across his neck and Markos shuddered, pushing his hips harder into me.

"You can't," he moaned. A sharp sting of rejection sliced through me, but I pushed it away. I knew why I couldn't, but it hurt to be marked by him and him not to wear my mark in return.

Feeling a little petty, I removed my teeth, but instead used my tongue to torture him for denying me.

He thrust harder, signaling he was moments away from coming. His mouth found my neck, pressing a light kiss before his teeth sunk in. My body flushed with elation, my walls clenching around his cock as the venom coursed through me. I wrapped my legs around him as I climaxed, my reality ripping apart. He gave one more powerful thrust into me, before he came, releasing his seed deep within.

Markos collapsed on the bed beside me. We laid next to each other, panting, taking a moment to regain our breath.

"My father is retiring," Markos breathed.

A chill formed over my body and I sat up in alarm. "What? Since when?"

He rose, his blue-black eyes meeting mine. "He told my mother and I two and a half years ago."

My mouth went dry, and it took a few moments to regain my bearings. "Why haven't you told me?"

He got up, reaching for his pants. "Because," he said with his back to me.

I stood and grabbed his arm, turning him toward me. "Because why?"

"Because I love you." His eyes filled with that emotion I couldn't read earlier, but now I realized it was guilt.

"What does loving me have to do with you not telling me your father is retiring?" I snapped.

"Cor." He moved his hand to cup my face, but I smacked it away. My world painting itself red.

"Just fucking say it, Markos."

"I can't marry you," he whispered.

There was a pause, the air in the room holding itself taut. For two and a half years, he'd known this. For years, he had pretended that everything was fine. That he would marry me and that we would live happily ever after. I trusted that. I trusted him. I believed every second of every day that we would marry.

I could feel my heart starting to shatter, my gut turning like I was about to vomit. A storm of tears built behind my eyes as they connected with Markos's.

*You'll cry tonight, just in a completely different way.* Fucking liar.

I wiped my face, rage replacing the sadness as I stared at the bastard. "Why not."

He wiped his face in frustration. "You are Seelie, Cor."

I raised a brow while crossing my arms. "So…?"

"You know what it would look like if I married a Seelie fae."

"Oh." Of course, no wonder he would never let me mark him. I gathered my clothes and hurried to put them on. "How could I be so fucking stupid," I whispered to myself.

"Cor." I ignored Markos as I tried to detangle the straps on my dress, remembering how I was exactly in the same place three years ago.

"Cor."

He walked over and grabbed my face, forcing me to look at him. "Cor, that doesn't mean we can't still be together."

I pulled his hands from my face. "What? As your whore?!"

"Concubine, my love."

My head cocked to one side as I stopped to look at him. "You can't be fucking serious."

"Corivina, please hear me out," he pleaded.

"What? You want me to be your whore? You want me to be yours and only yours while you can go around and stick your cock in anyone you please?"

"It won't be like that."

"You won't sleep with someone else?" He looked away from me, giving me the answer I needed. "Yeah, that's what I fucking thought." I got my dress untangled, slipping it on easily.

"Just until I have an heir, then I promise I won't. Hopefully, you will bear my child."

"Oh, fucking sure! It could take hundreds of years until that happens. I'll be your Seelie whore for a hundred years and hope that I bear your child, only for you to knock up someone else and marry her." I turned to walk out, but before I could get to the door, he blocked it with his huge frame. "I'm leaving, Markos."

"Cor, I love you." Desperation dripping from his voice.

"Not enough to marry me." I made sure my eyes revealed nothing. Not that I was dying inside. Not that I had no idea what I would do when I walked out that door. Not that I still loved him even though he lied.

"Dammit, Corivina!" he snapped. "The King of the Unseelie Court cannot marry a fucking Seelie fae! You know how that would look."

"No, I fucking didn't know. You said you'd marry me three years ago! You said you wouldn't choose another! Now, you're telling me you can't marry me, and you've known this for the last two and a half years? Why are you just fucking telling me this now? I could have not wasted the last three years of my life waiting for you to keep your fucking promise. Do you know what

I could have done over that time? I could have paid more attention to my studies instead of just coasting by. I could have found a job for the Unseelie Court. I could have married someone—"

Markos grabbed my upper arms. His grip bruising enough to have me squeal in pain. "You are mine." His eyes scored into my soul. I just stared back, shocked by his outburst. When he realized he was hurting me, his grip loosened. He didn't let go, pulling me into him, pressing a kiss on my head before he spoke. "I was going to marry you, Cor. I just thought I would have more time to figure out how. I thought I'd marry you as a prince, then in a hundred years, people would forget you were Seelie when I took the throne." He pulled back and brushed my hair from my face. "You are my world. I can't live without you. If you come back with me, I promise I will make up for not being able to marry you." His fingers caressed my cheek in a placating manner.

Burying my head into his chest, I breathed in his chestnut and snow scent. I took a second to remember the way we fit together. Then I stepped away from him, my eyes turning cold. My claws found his mark on my shoulder, and I sliced through, severing the claim he had to me.

His face contorted in pain. "Cor—"

"No, Markos. You wasted my last three years. Don't waste another second of it." He stood there, stunned from the shock of having the claim broken.

Walking around him, I grasped the doorknob. "Have an unhappy life, *Your Majesty*." Then I left, slamming the door behind me.

# SEVEN

## MARIE

*W*e didn't speak the rest of the night's ride. The prince read a book while I played with my claws, bored, trying not to stare at him.

Despite my effort, my eyes kept drifting to him. He just sat there, looking smug, reading his fancy book. The title read, *Unseelie Magic: Decay Volume II*. Nerd. Lessons hadn't even started, and he was on volume two.

"What," he barked, eyes still on his book.

"I didn't say anything."

He turned the page, continuing to read. "You've been staring at me for the past hour."

"No, I haven't!" The high pitch of my voice revealed my lie.

He looked over his book and smirked. Fuck, if it's not the sexiest smirk I'd ever seen. "Sure."

Gritting my teeth, I looked away from him. The smooth chuckle that followed seeped through me, coating my body with an alluring heat.

The carriage slowed, coming to a stop. "Where are we?" I asked.

"La Luna, a trading town."

I slid over to the window, looking out. The town was loud, busy with people. Stands lined the streets, fae shopping and bartering for goods.

The prince stood to leave. "The driver has to park the carriage."

I was reminded of how cold this place was the second I got out of the warmth of the cab. It was the type of cold that went straight to the bone. It wasn't long before I began shivering uncontrollably. I tried to think about warm things, fire, my parents' arms, food, but nothing could ever trick me into thinking this place was warm.

"Give me your cloak." My head snapped up to the prince standing near me with his hand extended.

I pulled my cloak around me tighter. "No."

"Your cloak isn't made for this type of weather. I'll trade you; mine is much warmer." I searched his eyes and saw he was being sincere, but I still hesitated. "Do you really want to stand here and freeze?"

Biting my lip, I removed my cloak and handed it to him. "Did you not bring gloves?" he asked.

"Gloves?"

He wagged his fingers and I noticed they were covered in fabric. "They keep your hands warm."

"I've never seen anything like that."

He removed his cloak, and instead of handing it to me, he wrapped it around my shoulders. This close to him, I could breathe in his scent. Burnt pine. The smell was so captivating, I wanted to move closer so I could breathe in his enticing aroma.

He gently tied the ends around my neck and pulled up the hood. Our eyes connected, my heart skipping a beat, breath hitching.

*Gods*, he was so beautiful it hurt.

He broke the connection, an ache settling over my heart to see those eyes again. He brought his hand to his mouth and pulled off a glove, then the other, and handed them to me. "You can use mine for now. I'll buy you some new ones at dusk."

I took the gloves, deciding not to question his sudden change in mood. They were made for bigger hands than mine, but they, like his cloak, were also fur lined and instantly warmed up my frozen fingers. "Thanks," I mumbled. "Won't you be cold?"

"I've lived through this weather my whole life." He shrugged and threw on my blue cloak, which was way too small for his tall frame.

I grinned at how ridiculous he looked in it. He caught my expression and smiled back. It was the type of smile that inspired artists to paint. His cheekbones tilted up, causing his eyes to sparkle with stars, his canines prominent and sharp. A part of me wanted to take his smile and keep it forever, but I brushed the thought away, knowing I shouldn't have thoughts like that about him.

The driver went to get keys for our room while the prince and I got food. The town was just shopping stalls and inns so when we found a place serving stew.

We finished eating and met the driver outside an inn. He handed a key to the prince, the prince's brows pinching together. "We need two rooms."

"They only had one," the driver replied.

"Did you try a different inn?" the prince asked, irritated.

"They are sold out. Looks like most travelers are traveling back from the eclipse."

The prince huffed, stalking into the inn and up the stairs. I followed him, having no idea what to do about this situation.

He reached the room, fitting the key into the door, and barged in. "One. Fucking. Bed."

He glanced at me, his jaw set tight. I avoided his gaze, and scanned the room. It was small but comfortable, a fireplace lining the wall, a bed big enough for two.

The idea of sharing a bed with him made me squirm and not in the way it was supposed to. He was beautiful and sexy as fuck. I may be with Kolvin, but I couldn't deny that the prince was probably the most attractive person I had ever met.

"I can sleep on the floor. It's okay." The floor was covered in rugs and didn't appear that uncomfortable.

"You are not sleeping on the floor," he gritted out before leaving.

I moved about the room and found a notepad on the bedside table. Pulling out Kolvin's pen, I scribbled a note.

*Not at the palace yet, taking the long way. It's cold. I miss you.*

I stared at the notepad, expecting a reply. I hoped he would be awake at this hour. It was almost morning but not quite.

The prince came back to the room with a set of blankets. Laying the blankets on the ground between the bed and the fireplace, he aggressively began to make a sleeping pallet.

I walked over, kneeling, and taking the blanket from him. "I can do it."

He yanked it back and jerked his head toward the bathroom. "Go get ready for bed."

"I'm fine sleeping like this." I tried to pull the blanket from his hands again. "Look, you don't have to make me a bed. I'm fine."

He stopped, cocking a brow. "This is for me."

I blinked. "What?"

"I told you, you weren't sleeping on the floor."

I looked down at the faux bed he made. It was really just two thin blankets and a pillow on the hard floor. "Yeah, but I didn't think that meant you would sleep on the floor." I made eye contact with him. "You are the prince."

"If you were anyone else, I'd make you sleep on the floor."

*What does that mean?* "You can't sleep on the floor."

We stared at each other for a few moments; the prince's eyes demanding I yield. I held his gaze, trying not to give in. Why won't he just let me sleep on the floor? What did he mean if I was anyone else?

I looked over to the bed and blew out a breath, hoping I would not regret the words that were about to come out of my mouth. "I'm marked, nothing will happen. The bed is big enough for both of us."

He cocked his head to the side, his eyes narrowing on my mark. His nostrils flared slightly before he grumbled a "fine" and started toward the bed.

I began to remove my shoes and wet socks as the prince took off my cloak, his shoes, then his shirt. I sucked in a breath, my eyes locking on his pale body. He was all sculpted lean muscle, and fluid in motion.

My eyes stayed locked on him, ogling him, until he looked over to me, forcing me to quickly look away.

He turned out the light, leaving the fire to cast an orange glow over the room, and we climbed into the bed, sliding under the covers. My whole body was alert with the knowledge that there was an incredibly gorgeous male only a foot away from me—half-naked. The fact had made me stay fully clothed, not even taking his cloak off. Heat pulled between my legs, and I tried not to move so he couldn't detect the change in my scent. My brain kept playing out scenarios where that body ended up pressed into mine, and he stripped off all of these clothes slowly, one by one.

This entire situation was agonizing. Moving my hand to grip the sheets and release the built-up tension, I accidentally brushed his hand. A shock flared on my skin at his touch, causing me to quickly pull away.

I was a terrible person. Not even twenty-four hours away from Kolvin and I was already thinking of taking another male. What was wrong with me? Why did the prince have to look like that?

*He's a dick,* I reminded myself.

*He was nice too. He gave me the cloak that I'm currently wearing. It smells like him, and he has the most alluring scent.*

*Kolvin is your male, Marie. You love him. The prince is just new and shiny, but Kolvin is the one.*

I stared at the ceiling for a while, repeating the phrase *Kolvin is the one* over and over until I found sleep. The more I had to repeat it, the more it felt like a lie.

I woke cuddled in someone's arms, feeling safe and at home. A smile painted my lips, and I snuggled deeper into the person behind me, my bottom brushing something hard.

My eyes flung open. I took in the cozy room, soon realizing that the person I was cuddled into was the prince. Either I drifted over to his side of the bed during my sleep, or he pulled me over, but there I was, wrapped in his arms on his side of the bed.

I didn't move for the next hour. Eventually, the prince stirred, and his arm clutched me tighter. He ground his hard cock into me, and I had to bite my lip to hold back the moan that wanted to escape.

The prince realized who he was grinding his cock into and stilled. I assumed he opened his eyes, but mine were closed. I decided pretending this never happened would be the best way to deal with this.

The prince pulled me closer, surprising me and burying his face into my curls and breathing in my scent. My heart squeezed at the action and warmth filled my body. He held me for a few moments, arms tight but embrace tender before letting me go and getting out of bed.

The prince shifted around for a bit before I heard the bathroom door close. He stayed in there for a while, long enough for me to fall back asleep, and when I woke back up, he was gone.

Getting up, I went to the bathroom to freshen up. He still hadn't gotten back when I was done. I slipped on my boots and dry socks before seeing that Kolvin had written back.

*I miss you too. If you were here, I'd never let you go cold. In fact, I'd permanently warm your bed for you. Love you.*

The note would have made my heart swell if not for the note underneath.

*Went out. -Levi.*

Not only did he read my note, he also wrote a note to Kolvin. I knew Kolvin wouldn't want anyone—especially a male—to see this note. He would probably be super pissed at me for letting it happen.

Sighing, I chose to worry about that later, knowing there was nothing I could do about it now. My stomach grumbled, and deciding to not wait for the prince, I set off to find myself something to eat.

The sun was starting to set when I walked outside. Sadness fell over me as I took in his dying light. This was my new life, a life away from my beautiful sun.

As I walked around the city that was just starting to stir with life, I found a fae selling porridge. It was bland, and the fae didn't even sell honey, but it was warm, and I didn't feel like wandering around to find anything else.

I explored the city a little before deciding on heading back to the inn. The carriage was parked outside, the prince leaning against it. My cloak wrapped around his shoulders, and him reading that book, not paying attention to anything around. Something about seeing him brought a smile to my face.

He didn't so much as look up at me as I approached or even acknowledge my existence. "Good morning."

He continued to read his book. "*Good evening.*" He pulled something out of his pocket and shoved some fabric at me. "The gloves."

The gloves were black with a silver trim, and silver swirling designs all over them. They were thick and made of fine material and the inside was coated with a fur lining. "Thank you," I said, taking them from him.

"Yeah, well, if you lose your fingers, it makes magic hard to do. Then coming here and making me suffer sleeping with you would have been pointless," he said, still not looking up from his book.

I gritted my teeth. I wanted to pretend that his words didn't sting, but they did. I thought he was done being a dick, but clearly, he can do good deeds, like buying me nice gloves and lending me his cloak, while also being an asshole.

I brushed it off and tried to gain a good rapport with him. "Do you know when we are leaving?"

"Whenever the driver is ready."

"Do you know when that will be?"

"Look." He glanced at me with an icy stare. "I don't know. Why don't you talk to him and stop bugging me?"

I gawked at him, irritation crawling its way up my spine. "What is your problem?"

"You," he replied before walking away from me and entering the carriage.

The carriage ride was boring. There wasn't much to look out the window except snow and trees, and the prince read his book the whole time, not paying me any mind. When we finally arrived at the palace, I was actually happy to see the place.

The palace was huge, or it appeared that way. It was nestled in between three mountains in the Shadow Mountain range, looking like it was a part of the peaks. Snow adorned the many towers, the stones a dark gray. The gate to the palace was nothing fancy, steel painted black, but inside of the gate, there was a long road that led to the palace with dozens of ice sculptures lining the way. There were sculptures of fae dancing and ice skating. Sculptures of Unseelie emblems, like the moon and the snowflake. Black rose bushes were scattered about. Evergreen trees were decorated with fae lights, making everything seem quite whimsical. It was breathtaking. I thought that Unseelie would be all about darkness and despair, but this place looked joyous.

It was late at night when we arrived, not many people were moving about inside the palace. I followed the prince, assuming he was going to take me where I needed to go. He was much taller than me and his pace was relentless, so I was basically running to catch up with him. I didn't really get a good look at the interior of the palace. Everything was either black, brown, or beige. Warm fae lights lighted the space, adding a cozy aura to the place.

Finally, we reached the academic wing. I was informed in my letter that this part of the palace was closed off for the students. Of course, the prince didn't give me a tour of the wing, nor did he say anything the entire time we walked.

He finally spoke when we stopped at a room marked with the number 12. "This is your room. Class begins the night after morrow just after dusk. The laboratory is down one floor, first door on the left. The cafeteria is on the same floor. They serve from dusk to dawn. Someone will come by and help get you books and a uniform." He handed me a key, then walked away without another word.

I opened the door and took in the small room. It was dark, like everything else in this palace. There was a bare bookshelf by the door. Next to that was a small desk, then a small wardrobe, and a door which I assume was the bathroom. Across from the bathroom was a bed, dressed with black sheets, big enough for a normal fae body, which meant it could probably fit two of me. The bed was pushed up against a window, lined with thick black velvet drapes.

Dropping my bag, I climbed onto the bed and pulled the drapes open. This part of the palace was carved straight out of the mountain. My view was nothing but the mountainside, snow, and evergreen trees. Moonlight sparkled over the snow and winter birds were starting to chirp, alerting the world of morning soon to come.

A fire magically roared to life in the small fireplace next to the bed, startling me. The realization that I was here suddenly dawning on me. Here I was, in the Unseelie Territory, away from my family and friends.

The fear that climbed up my throat had me scrambling out of bed and walking over to the desk, fishing out a pad of paper and Kolvin's pen.

*I'm here. I love and miss you.*

Tears lined my eyes as I made my way back to the bed. I laid down, not bothering with the covers—the fire made the room warm enough and I still had on the prince's cloak. I let my tears fall as I breathed in his scent. Even if the prince was a dick, his scent made me feel more at ease. I pulled the cloak tighter around me and let his aromatic scent lull me to sleep.

# EIGHT

## MARIE

*A* calm snowy day greeted me through the window when I awoke the next day. Climbing out of bed, I grabbed my bag and unpacked my stuff into the dresser. An uneasy feeling settled in my stomach as I unpacked. I had never stayed anywhere that wasn't my home; I didn't even sleep over at Kolvin's when I was little.

I took a deep breath, glancing over at the desk to see if Kolvin had written back.

*Who is Levi?*

I had forgotten the prince wrote to him by accident.

*You're such a male,* I wrote back, a smile lining my face.

He didn't take long to reply. *I just want to know why some male is using my female's pen.*

A laugh bubbled from my throat, settling my nerves. *Your female?*

*You know what I mean...*

*You're such a dork. He was obviously leaving me a note. He was my escort to the palace, but I'm here now and he's gone.*

I left out the fact that he was the prince. I didn't want to give him anything else to be jealous about. I think that even Kolvin could agree that the prince was gorgeous.

*Okay, I have to go. Write to me later and tell me of your first day. I love you.*

*I love you too.*

With a sigh, I started to get ready for the night. It was a couple hours before sunset, and someone was supposed to come later to show me around. The prince didn't give me a certain time, so I bathed and dressed, wrapping his cloak around me. The fire did an okay job at warming the room, but my body was having a rough time adapting, so I decided to keep it on.

Soon, as night claimed the day, a soft knock sounded on my door. I answered and was greeted with a female about the same height as me, meaning she was half-human. Her hair was dark as night and was cut just above her shoulders in an angled bob. She had sky-blue eyes that tilted up slightly and soft rounded lips that were painted red. Her skin was light, but she had a bit of color to her that was probably genetic.

My eyes trailed down her body. She was wearing a long sleeve black dress that cinched around her waist, then flared out at the bottom. The dress had a low cut in the front that showed just a bit of cleavage, and she had thigh-high stockings that flashed just a bit of her creamy thighs. Her body was curvy, not as much as mine, but gods was she beautiful.

I realized I was staring at her and quickly looked back up. When our eyes met, she smiled, making my heart skip a beat. I understood in that moment that I was attracted to this female. In the back of my mind, I was thinking about undressing her. It wasn't uncommon with the fae for us to have partners of the same sex, but I had been in love with Kolvin forever, so I never thought about it. This female, though, seriously had me thinking about it.

"Hi," I said shyly.

She blinked as if she was just lost in thought. "Hi, sorry, you're beautiful." Her voice was soft and seductive, causing my palms to become clammy with sweat.

Blood rushed to my cheeks. "You are as well."

"I'm Jessamine. Sorry I'm late. I just found out this dusk that I was giving you a tour. I was supposed to escort you, but the prince volunteered, taking it from me. Of course, in typical Levi fashion, he didn't want to finish the job. If you know what I mean."

It took me a second to get it, then a smile stretched across my lips before I burst into laughter.

"Good, you laugh at my jokes. I like you already." She extended her hand. They were soft, and I wondered if all her skin was this soft too.

"I'm Marie," I said, holding onto her hand a little too long.

"I know. I was at the sorting ceremony. No one is going to forget the Seelie girl with skin that shimmers gold, the embodiment of light itself, has black blood dripping from her veins." The smile she plastered on my face faltered. "Oh, bunny." She stroked my arm in comfort. "I promise you'll like it here. The Unseelie are known for being cold bastards, but we are cold bastards who like to have fun."

"If you were at the sorting ceremony, then why are you showing me around? Aren't you new to the palace as well?"

"Oh, my father is a part of the court, so I've lived here my whole life. I know this place like the back of my hand." She showed me said hand, her nails painted red, then she gestured toward the hall. "Shall we?"

"Lead the way."

We walked down to the cafeteria. Wood tables were spread about with Unseelie fae—who I recognized from the sorting ceremony—seated among them. In the middle, there was a long table with various breakfast food lining it. Huge glass windows lined one of the walls while three fireplaces were placed on the opposite side.

Jessamine and I grabbed some breakfast and found a place to sit. "So how was your journey here?"

"It was boring. The prince just sat there reading his book. I don't even know why he volunteered to escort me. He barely said a word to me on the whole ride that wasn't coated in disdain." I took a bite of the tasteless cafeteria food. "Is that something he would normally do?"

"What spew words of disdain? Yes, all the time. He is a prince; they are insufferable and always unhappy."

I shook my head, trying not to laugh. "No wonder."

"I've known Levi my whole life and I still can't figure the guy out."

"Are you two friends?"

Her head quirked to the side as she thought of what to say. "He is more of a loner. He hangs with us faelings sometimes, but he's distant." She leaned in close, dropping her voice to a whisper. "I honestly think his father forces him to hang out with us. He never stays more than an hour unless he wants to get laid."

Before I could respond, a beautiful male with long black hair, one side buzzed off, sat next to Jessamine, and another male with short black hair sat next to me.

"You showing the Seelie girl around?" The male with the shaved side said before shoving a piece of toast into his mouth.

Jessamine looked at the male and rolled her eyes. "She has a name, Gregor."

He looked at me with a cocked brow. "Marie," I offered.

"Marie. That is such a Seelie name," Gregor replied.

Jessamine playfully slapped his arm. "Greg, don't be mean."

He wrapped his arm around her, kissing her on the neck. "What will you do for me?"

"Greg, stop. We are eating. You can get your dick wet later," the male next to me said. He glanced at me and nodded. "Finch."

"Finch, you are just upset because Serene is Seelie," Gregor said.

Jessamine removed Gregor's arm from her and placed it on the table. "Gregor, one, stop trying to claim me. I'm not yours. I told you that when you tried last week. Two, if you keep being an alpha male asshole, I will never let you fuck me again."

Gregor huffed and looked at me. "Are you going to the springs with us tonight?"

I looked at Jessamine, puzzled.

"We are having a party down in the hot springs after the king's assembly. The prince will be there."

"Ugh, she wants the prince?" Gregor grumbled.

"No," I replied quickly. "I'm marked." I moved the prince's cloak over to reveal the mark on my neck.

"Like that means anything."

My brows furrowed. "I'm pretty sure the whole point of the mark means I'm taken."

Gregor sat up straighter, his elbows hitting the table. "Your mark is fresh?"

I covered it back up. "Yeah?"

"I'm guessing your male only marked you because you were leaving, since I don't remember that mark on your neck when you were sorted."

I stared at his black eyes, not really understanding what he was getting at.

He sighed. "Hate to break it to you, Seelie, but you and the Seelie male won't last a year. The whole 'I got sorted so I'll let you mark me' thing is cliché and doesn't work out. Everyone knows that." He brought his toast to his mouth to take another bite, but it was slapped out of his hand. "Hey!"

"Gregor, you are an ass!" Jessamine turned to me. "Ignore him. He does this thing where he thinks every thought he has is valid and needs to be spoken out loud. And you're coming to the party. I will make sure we pick you up a swimsuit when we get your uniform."

I nodded and took her advice to ignore Gregor's comment because I definitely didn't need that added to my plate right now. "Great."

"I know some super sexy ones that will make your body pop!" Her eyes lazily trailed down my frame causing me to blush.

After breakfast, Jessamine gave me a tour of the academic wing. The top three floors were student housing. The first floor held the library where we picked up the necessary books I would need for class. The second floor housed the gym and a store for student needs. The third floor housed the cafeteria and main laboratory where lessons would be held. When we were done exploring the academic wing, we headed back to my room.

At the students' store, I grabbed a couple uniforms and some everyday clothes. My shimmer made it impossible for me not to stand out among the Unseelie, but I didn't want to be known as the Seelie girl my entire time here, so I would try as hard as possible. I changed into a black closely fitted turtleneck and black trousers. A new pair of lace-up boots that were fur-lined and sturdy enough not to have snow seep in if I was outside. I pulled my curls back into a loose braid and drew the prince's cloak around me. It was way warmer than the ones in the student store, and in this place, no matter how many fires seem to be burning in a room, I still remained cold.

"Is that the royal crest?" Jessamine asked, pointing toward the back of my cloak.

I angled myself so I could see what she was looking at. Two roses that overlaid a moon were embroidered in black on the back of the cloak. It was big enough that if you were looking for it, you'd see it, but small enough to overlook.

"Oh, I guess that is," I said, trying to dismiss her.

She didn't let it go. "Did the prince give that to you?"

"Yeah, it's his. My cloak wasn't made for this type of weather, and he let me borrow it."

She walked over and ran her fingers over the velvet outer layer. "Gods, that is soft. I wonder how many more blow jobs I have to give him for him to give me a cloak this soft."

My nostrils flared slightly and lava filled my veins. I pulled the cloak from her grasp, wrapping it tighter around me. "I thought you said he was bad in bed?" My voice held a bit of edge that Jessamine didn't seem to notice.

She studied her nails and then said nonchalantly, "That was a joke. The male is great in bed."

The room was silent while I internally battled with this weird sense of jealousy that came over me. I didn't want the fact that she had slept with the prince to bother me, but it did, and I really didn't want to analyze why.

Jessamine, not reading anything into my silence, spoke up. "Should we finish the tour? I am supposed to show you the whole palace, at least the areas we are allowed, but"—she leaned in, her hand rubbing up my arm—"we could just stay in here."

The tone of her voice made my core clench and brushed away my jealousy. I bit my lip, looking away from her lust-filled eyes. "Uhh, I think we should finish the tour, if you don't mind."

She smirked, giving a lazy shrug. "Okay."

# NINE
## MARIE

The assembly hall wasn't very large, but the room was exquisite. Metal flowers decorated the walls. The lights hung in a fashion that made it look like stars were falling from the ceiling. Chairs sat in the center of the room all pointing toward the throne made of steel.

Jessamine and I took seats next to Gregor and Finch. Gregor immediately wrapped his arm around Jessamine as she sat. She grumbled but didn't remove his arm this time, leaning into him.

What I had heard of the king was mostly Seelie propaganda. He was a heartless male who ate babes and loved to cook humans outside during a barbecue. I was pretty sure the Unseelie didn't do barbecues because it's fucking freezing outside, but seventy percent of what Seelie says about Unseelie was untrue and stemmed from generational hate.

The other things I had heard were that he was a laid-back king. Arrogant and charming, and as long as you didn't fuck anything up too badly, he wouldn't remove your head. He was made king at quite a young age, about thirty when he took the crown. Most kings didn't rise until they were at least a hundred years old. Since he was so young, he loved to party and fuck. He was dubbed the Slut King on the Seelie side. He had never been married and refused to marry the prince's mother before she tried to assassinate him, so she could rule through the prince—which resulted in her death. He attended many parties at the Seelie Palace with the Seelie King, King Dominick. Their relationship had resulted in the Seelie and the Unseelie having one of the best relationships in quite some time, and even though he spent a lot of time at the Seelie Palace, I have not once crossed paths with him on one of my many visits.

Horns blared, the students rising as the announcer spoke, "King Markos Shadawn."

The king entered, his son and a few advisors following after. The prince had his circlet on, looking more beautiful in this light. Our eyes locked across the room and everything else faded into the background.

*Mine,* my heart repeated.

The king spoke, ripping my attention from the prince, a slight ache gnawing in my chest. "Be seated."

I could see his resemblance to the prince easily. The king was just as beautiful, but where the prince was graceful, the king was more of a warrior. He had a close shaved beard. His hair was shoulder-length, black with loose waves. The king's clothes were rather bland. Plain black breeches, regular riding boots, and a loose tunic opened to show off his muscled chest and his raven tattoo that rested right over his heart. The raven being the king's emblem. The only thing king about him was his crown, a steel base with onyx spikes.

"Welcome, students." The king waved to us. "I'm glad to see so many of you filling these seats and joining our territory. You are to stay here for the next four years, learning all that you will need to help aid this country." He gestured to the prince. "As you may know Prince Levington, my son, is a part of your class. I hope you will help aid him in becoming a great king for our territory. Females, please feel free to breed with him. He needs an heir."

Everyone then erupted into laughter, but the prince looked directly at me, his face serious. He was looking at me as if to say, *You*.

The king continued on as Jessamine leaned in, whispering in my ear, "He is giving you the look."

"No, it's you," I said too quickly. "You two have already fucked. Maybe he wants you." I knew that was a straight lie. He was looking at me. Every time he looked at me, a sensation crawled all over my body and a tugging in my chest alerted me to his presence.

Jessamine laughed under her breath. "If he wanted me, he would have claimed me. Trust me, he doesn't, nor I him." She ran a finger down my arm, giving me a suggestive look.

I laughed nervously, tucking a curl behind my ear. "You have to stop saying stuff like that or I might get the wrong intentions."

"Maybe I want you to have the wrong intention, bunny." She winked, then turned her focus back to the king.

"As for some ground rules, none of you are allowed in sanctioned court areas without permission. If you are partying outside, bring a guard and do not get your guard drunk. We do not want any fae getting severely frostbitten. Lastly, do not kill anyone on purpose. I shouldn't have to announce that as a rule, but it happens. If you break any of these rules, you'll answer to me. Do you understand?" We all nodded. "Okay, great." He scanned through the students. "The Seelie girl?" All the students turned to me. "Follow me to my office. Everyone else is dismissed. Have a good party. No drowning in the springs, please."

I stood, Jessamine's hand finding my lower back. "I'll wait for you back in your room."

Giving her a smile in reply, I made my way to the dais. Nerves wracked my body. Firstly, because the prince was still looking at me with that 'I want to breed you' face. Secondly, because I had no idea why the king would want to see me.

"The Seelie girl?" the king said as I approached. He gave a charming smile, his eyes holding a glint, and I couldn't help but blush in his presence.

"Her name is Marie," the prince grumbled, stealing my attention. Our eyes clashed. His stare intense, and I might even say possessive. Apparently, I liked possessive because my body grew instantly hot with need at that look.

There was something else that I noticed within his gaze that I more so noticed within myself. When I looked into his eyes, I felt like I knew him, and he knew me. No words ever needed to be exchanged between us; we just knew.

I broke the connection, following the king to his office. I shouldn't feel that way about the prince. He was a stranger. A very pretty stranger, but a stranger who I'd known for three days. I didn't know many males my age, and he was new. My creature was just intrigued by him.

Fae were beasts who caused chaos. Especially if that chaos could be attained by fucking or fighting. It was an urge we all had, and the prince would cause major chaos in my life. That was why I wanted him. He would flip every plan for my future on its head, then make me drown in him. He was the type of male who would consume me, and I would probably—stupidly—love it.

"Please sit," the king said when we entered his office. I sat in one of the seats that faced his desk, the prince going behind me to the couches that sat in front of the fireplace as the king opened a magically chilled cabinet behind his desk. "How about a drink?"

I nodded nervously. King Markos sat in front of me on top of his desk, flashing that charming smile. I could feel the prince studying us, and for a second, I indulged in the urge to glance back at him. He looked relaxed, lying across the couch like he had no care in the world, but his energy was thick and obtrusive. It felt as if at any moment, he'd pounce and attack. Like I—the only fae that cried at the sorting ceremony—would harm his father.

Focusing my attention back on the king, I waited for him to take a drink. It was considered rude to drink before someone of higher respect. As if he was testing me, a sensual smirk played across his face. "A respectable young lady," he flirted. "Marie, is it?"

I nodded, taking a sip of the liquid to calm my nerves.

"Well, Marie, you do know why I called you here today, don't you?"

"Uh, no, sir." I took another sip, my glass slightly trembling as it made its way to my lips.

The action drew his gaze. "No need to be nervous. Just need to see if you are a Seelie spy, and if I need to kill you and send your head to my buddy, Dominick." I nearly choked on my wine, dribbling some down my chin.

The king chuckled and handed me a napkin, cocking his head to one side. "Maybe not."

"N-no, sir, I'm not..." I felt like I might vomit.

The king rested a hand on my arm and gazed into my eyes. His aura was calm like snow, making me instantly relax. The sound of leather shifting brought my awareness back to the prince, the tension radiating from him growing heavier.

I took a breath, regaining myself. "I'm not a spy, sir. Frankly, I would never choose to come here."

He smirked. "Of course, but I have to make sure." He took a drink from his wine. "So, Marie, tell me about you." His eyes roamed down my body.

"Uh, I'm born Seelie. You already know that. Uh, I'm half-human. My mother, fae, Corivina Foxglove. My father, human, Maurice. I don't know his surname. He's dead, died before my birth, killed by my adoptive father, Darius Foxglove. You may know him. He's the commander of the Seelie Army."

The king stared deeply at me for a long moment. His charming demeanor dropped, and his face grave. He rubbed his hand over his chest where his raven laid, and as more time passed in silence, I grew nervous. I finally figured his change of attitude was because of my father. Maybe he thought I was a spy.

It felt like forever until he finally spoke. "Corivina?"

My brain scrambled in confusion at his response. "Yeah, my mother's name is Corivina." Then my brain chimed with understanding. "Oh yes, you may know her. She was born Unseelie. I believe her surname was ice or snowflake or—"

"Snow," the king answered for me, his voice thick and slightly strangled.

"Yes, Snow. Did you know her?"

The king looked down at his wine before answering, "Her family was a part of my father's court. We knew each other before she was sorted." His eyes trailed over me, this time without an ounce of appeal. "I see the resemblance now that you bring it to my attention. The shimmer, which runs in the Snow family. The claws as well, though yours are smaller. But your eyes... You have her eyes."

It seemed the king knew more about my mother's family than my mother herself because the comment about my eyes was completely wrong. My eyes were black, like my mother's, but they came from my father. His eyes were a warm brownish black, whereas my mother's were a straight black, almost cold.

"Yeah, we don't look that much alike. I look more like my birth father."

He took a deep breath before looking out the windows that lined the wall. His face pinched, jaw set tight.

"Look, I don't know if you have a problem with her family, but I don't know them, nor do I want to," I stated, seeing as he said they were a part of his father's court, not his. "I have no intention of spying on you or any Unseelie affairs. I just want to go to school and get good enough grades so that I may get a job in the Seelie Territory where my family is. If you need me to swear on it, I will."

His eyes flared in shock at my words. I did just offer to spill my blood, which fae try to avoid doing, but I wanted no problems while I was here, and spilling blood was a quick way of attaining that.

The king cleared his throat, eyes somber. "I have no intention of sharing blood with you, little raven." His hand gently trailed down my face, and I swore I heard the prince growl. It was so low I really couldn't tell, but the king glanced back, confirming I wasn't the only one who heard it. "It was nice to meet you, Marie. Levi will show you the way back to your room."

# TEN

## Corivina
## 199 years ago.

*I* was covered in dirt. Every fucking day, I left the gardens covered in dirt. I was afraid if I continued like this, I would have dirt permanently in places it should never be. The worst part was the dirt was exported from Un-fucking-Seelie.

This was my life now—thanks to Markos. Because of him, I spent the first three years of my training skimming by. I was under the impression that I would be getting married, and any time I doubted that, he would reassure me. He'd tell me I had nothing to worry about. For three fucking years, I believed every lie from that bastard's mouth. If I thought I was going to be stuck here, I might have put more effort into my studies. I could have attained a scholarship for further training in Seelie magic, or I could have at least gotten a better job than an herbalist apprentice.

The job was an ad in the paper—room and board for forty hours' work. It was in a shitty town near the border, called Lightwood. The herbalist needed someone to tend to the gardens in the burning sun as she stayed in her magically cooled shop, mixing potions and healing tinctures. At least she allowed me to watch the shop after my eight hours in the garden to get extra coin. *Yay!*

Quickly scrubbing off all the dirt and scarfing down some food, I mentally prepared for another night behind the counter, and having to deal with annoying Seelie customers who had to sample everything before they actually bought anything, if that.

I looked at my exhausted face in the mirror. I used to have a beautiful flawless skin that shimmered like ice. Hair, black as night, that effortlessly flowed down my back. Now, my skin was full of healing burns, the burns so bad and so painful, my fae healing couldn't keep up. My coffee-black eyes were rimmed with bags, because it was either I got a full night's rest, or I got money. My hair, tangled and was a muddy brown color, due to too much time in the sun.

If I had the energy, I would cry more. That was how I spent my last year of lessons, crying and trying to fix my grades. I studied my hardest, but it didn't matter. No amount of work I did in my last year would erase the first three.

Thank you, Markos.

I walked downstairs to see the herbalist, Ms. Masel, in the hall. "Corivina, dear, you have a visitor," she said as she walked out the back door. Just like that bitch to leave me with a customer when it wasn't even time for me to start my shift.

Walking out to the front of the shop, I was faced with blue-black shoulder-length hair on pale white skin. "Markos," I breathed.

He turned to me, smiling softly. "My raven."

For a second, I let myself feel the joy of seeing him. *Home.* He was my home. As he walked toward me, arms extended for an embrace, that joy quickly faded into rage.

I dodged his arms. "What are you doing here? How did you find me?"

He faltered, taking a step back, face pinched with the pain from my rejection. "You weren't answering any of my letters."

"Why would I?"

"Cor, I still love you. I still want to be with you."

I folded my arms and gave him a quizzical look. "Are you going to marry me?"

His face contorted slightly. "I can't."

I walked around him, starting my work behind the counter. "Then you are really wasting your time by coming here."

"Corivina, I can't live without you. I've tried and I just can't."

I looked him in his eyes, the desperation simmering in them along with truth, a twisted truth at least. "Markos, have you warmed another's bed since we broke up?"

Guilt painted his features, answering my question without words. "You must really think I'm stupid. I know your scent better than anyone's. You smell like a calm winter's night, not like whore. Multiple, if my nose is correct."

His hand scrubbed against his beard. "I'm the Prince of Unseelie and I have certain duties to my kingdom. I need an heir. Especially with my father stepping down."

Fire burned within my heart at the thought of him being with another, but I buried it down, saving the pain for later when he was long gone, and I could cry myself to sleep. "You make it sound like sex with any female you like is the most torturous thing in the world."

"I can't have sex with any female, or I would have you warming my bed."

I ignored his comment, turning to start gathering the dried herbs. "Did you really think you could just show up and I would take you back?" I turned back to face him. "Markos, I hate you."

He flinched, his body stiffening. "Why?"

I gave a hearty chuckle. "Are you serious? Markos, look at me. I was a lady. Now I'm nothing. I'm stuck in a place I hate. I'm poor and ugly. This"—I gestured at my current state—"is all your fault."

"You are just as beautiful as the day I met you. And if you need money, I'll happily provide—"

"Oh, fuck you! I wouldn't be working my ass off as some herbalist apprentice if you never had lied to me to begin with! I would have tried to make a life here, or I would have perfected my magic so I could find another way to go home. You said you'd marry me. You said you'd love me forever. You said I was your one, yours only. I trusted you and you lied!" Tears cascaded down my cheeks, and I furiously wiped them away.

Markos walked behind the counter and took my face in his hands. "You can come home with me right now. I know it's not what you wanted, but I will make sure you are happy. I will try to give all that I can. Yes, I'll have to sleep with other women, but we can do that together. Who knows, maybe you'll bear my child…"

I snorted, wiping more tears from my face as I pushed away from him. "You disgust me."

Anger flashed through his eyes. "This is fucking insane. I get you are angry, but we are meant to be together!"

"No, we are not!"

He went quiet, his eyes locking on mine. His rage filled the room, suffocating me as it grew. It was the type of rage fae only got when the beast that rest inside was set free from their cage.

Hands roughly wrapped around my arms, pinning them to my side. "What are you doing?" My voice held a bit of a squeak as panic creeped up my spine.

The grip became stronger, fingers burying into my flesh. I tried to fight back, but I was no match against him. He easily took both of my hands in one of his, trapping them between our bodies as he pushed up against me. Fabric ripped, and I looked to see my dress's shoulder was gone. His face inching toward my neck.

"Markos, don't." I struggled to get free.

His mouth opened, all four canines sharp and ready. "No." I thrashed. "Markos, no!"

The sting of pain registered as his teeth pierced my neck. He bit down harder, setting the mark in deep, penetrating my collarbone. A shriek exiting out of my mouth was soon cut off as he released a huge amount of venom into the bite, making it feel toxic instead of pleasurable. Tears poured out of my eyes as my body went numb, the world fading from my grasp.

I awoke in a bed I had never seen before. Lifting the sheets, I found myself naked, covered in bruises. My body sore, my neck hurting the most. Trailing my fingers across the area, I discovered there were at least five bite marks. I shifted, noticing that I was sore in another area of my body.

"No," I whispered to myself, hoping that this was not what it looked like.

*Markos wouldn't do that. He was calm, loving, and caring. He would never hurt me.*

But he already did.

I brought a finger in between my legs, feeling a wetness. I pulled my hand out from under the sheet, revealing Markos's seed mixed with a little bit of blood—my blood.

A hollow feeling stole over me; the world tilting off its axis. Markos, my lover, my friend, *my home*, did this to me.

It was unfortunately common among the fae. Mainly to humans for children, or desire, or just to fuck with them. Markos didn't do this because of that. He wanted to mark me, claim me.

Claims were not something that was taken by force, not anymore. A claim was a beautiful act that fae did when they loved another. Venom was used for pleasure, for love, but Markos violated that.

A creek on the floor had me jumping to cover myself. He stood in the doorway, his back against the wall, his face riddled with guilt. He had been standing there the whole time, watching me figure out the horror of what he'd done.

"Cor," he said gravely.

My face fractured, a flood of tears spilling down my cheeks as sobs poured out of me. I loved him. I was mad that he lied, but I didn't stop loving him. He was my home, my everything. A small part of me knew I would eventually cave to him. All he had to do was wait a little fucking longer, and I would have been his.

Sobs scratched the back of my throat, my body shaking with each one. I cried over the loss of my family. Yes, they disowned me, but that was fae. It didn't make me stop loving them and I hoped I would one day see them again. I cried for the loss of my home, the Unseelie, the cold, the snow. I cried over the love I thought would last forever was fully shattered. I cried because I let this happen. *This was all my fault.*

I should have just given in, and I would still be in love. I should have fought against him harder. I should have broken it off with Markos five years ago. I should have relied on myself.

Why did I trust him? Why did I pose my whole life for him? Did I really want to even be the Queen of Unseelie? *Why did I do this?*

In that moment, I realized I was fully lost. I had nothing, nobody, no future, no love, no home.

"Cor," Markos repeated.

I looked up into his blue-black eyes. Eyes that I used to drown in. Eyes that would calm me. Eyes that I would think of in my room late at night when I was lonely.

He sat on the bed, his hand reaching for my face. I flinched, and he dropped his arm, those eyes filling with sorrow. "I'm sorry."

I looked away from him, hiccuping from a sob that escaped my mouth. I bunched the sheet to hide myself from him as they continued to wrack my body.

"I love you," he whispered.

My hiccups seized, my spine stiffening. I turned toward him, my magic burning through me, drying the tears on my face. "You love me," I said, cold and detached.

"I didn't mean to." His eyes flicked back and forth between mine.

"You did mean to," I repeated.

Tears welled up in his eyes. "I-I never meant to hurt you."

"What the fuck did you mean?"

"I was just going to mark you, then take you with me."

"And the raping just kind of happened."

He flinched at my words. "Cor, I—"

"Where am I?"

He ran his hands through his hair. "An inn, a short walk from the shop."

I got up from the bed. "Where are my clothes?"

"I… uh…" His eyes took in my bruised body for a second before glancing away.

I stared at him, knowing what he couldn't say and grabbed the sheet from the bed to wrap around me.

"What are you doing?" he asked, starting to reach for me.

My magic lit up my veins in warning. "Don't fucking touch me!"

He put his hands up in surrender. "Okay," he said softly. "What are you doing?"

"I'm fucking going home." I shifted about the room, looking for anything else to cover me up.

"You can't leave."

My nostrils flared, and I set my angry eyes on him. "Do you honestly think I would stay here another second? Did raping me not fucking get you off? You want more?"

"No, I know I fucked up, but you can't leave just yet."

"Why the fuck not?"

"We have to make a deal."

My brain stalled for a moment. "What?"

"You can't tell anyone about this. I'm the Unseelie Prince."

"Are you fucking serious?"

"Cor, I can't let this get out. I know you hate me. I know you won't forgive me, but I can't let you leave until you make a deal that you won't tell another being about this."

"Another being, so I can't even tell a fucking plant?" I chided.

He didn't respond. I began to laugh. My chuckles quickly turning into tears.

He walked over to hold me before remembering that he was the reason I was crying. "Anything, Cor. Your silence for anything," he said softly.

I sobbed harder. I just wanted to leave. I didn't want to be in the room with him. A deal! He wanted me to make a deal with him. I wasn't in the right headspace to make a binding deal right now.

I took a deep breath. I knew he wouldn't let me leave until I made it. *What do I need right now?* "Coin, a lot of it. I need you to get me clothes so I can leave. Then I never want to see you again."

"I can't promise you won't see me again. I'm soon to be king."

I gritted my teeth from letting another sob out. He was right; the deal would be void if I saw him in the paper or a poster on the street. "Fine. Coin, clothes, then I want you to leave me alone."

"Okay," he whispered.

"Okay."

He went over to the desk in the corner of the room and grabbed a letter opener. Coming back over to me, he held out his hand. I ignored it, using my claws to cut the inside of my palm instead of letting him inflict more pain on me.

His lips pressed together before he cut his palm, holding it out to me. "I, Markos Shadawn, promise that I will get you the coin you need, a change of clothes, and after you have these items, I promise to leave you alone."

"I, Corivina Snow, promise to never tell another being about any of the events that have happened over the last night." I grasped his hand, mentally recoiling from the contact.

As our hands clasped, black veins started to coil up my arm as gold veins coiled up his, mixing my blood with his forever.

After the magic bound the deal into our veins, the blood receded, Markos peering into my eyes. "It's done," he said, pain dripping from his voice.

I snatched my hand away from him, and he just stared at me, not moving.

"Go!" I yelled at him.

He snapped out of his trance and headed toward the door. "I'll be back soon."

# ELEVEN

## Marie

The prince and I walked quietly through the palace. Unfortunately, the king's office was on the other side of the building, and I had to spend more time with the prince than I'd like. At least this time, he walked at a normal pace which was a huge improvement from the last time he had to escort me to my room, but he was still his brooding self.

I don't understand him. He looked at me like he wanted to devour me, but when we were together, he acted like he hated being near me. Jessamine did say he was a loner; maybe he just liked to look but not touch. That was okay with me because if he ever did touch me the way his looks promised, I would probably be putty in his beautiful hands.

Today his brooding was at an all-time high, which did nothing to my libido—thankfully. I actually found it rather irritating. The prince may act like he didn't want to take up space. He may rarely speak and walk with the grace of a dancer, but he did take up space. His energy field was like a hundred-foot radius around him, warning people to fuck off. Being three feet next to him, I felt like I was drowning in his hatred. Every couple of minutes, he'd make a huffing sound. Each time caused me to tense slightly, afraid he was minutes from bursting into flames.

I paused in the middle of the hall. The prince noticed and turned, his blue-black eyes narrowing on me in question. "I can find the way from here if it really bothers you that much," I stated.

He looked at me like I was an idiot before taking in a breath and rolling his shoulders. "My father told me to walk you, and I will."

"Then stop being a pussy over it and walk like a normal person," I blurted out.

He stared at me for a while. I expected him to get angrier, but instead, his face creased in confusion. "What do you not like about the way I'm walking?"

His question was odd. I studied him to see if he was joking, but he was serious, as if he really wanted to hear my answer. "You're upset. Obviously about walking me. It would be better if you could hide or at least not openly express your distaste with me."

He pondered what I said for a moment, then said, "Okay," turned and continued walking.

I ran to catch up with him because no matter what I said, I would probably get lost in this place by myself.

As we continued, I noticed he was definitely still angry, huffing every couple of minutes. "I thought you said you wouldn't do that."

He stopped and turned to me. "No, I said I wouldn't openly express my distaste with you. You assume I'm upset because I have to walk you to your room. I'm not upset about that." He started moving again.

"Oh," I said.

"Oh."

"What are you upset about, then?"

"Do you actually care?" Even if he wasn't upset about walking me, I knew it had something to do with me.

"Yes."

We approached my hall, and he stopped abruptly, turning to back me into a wall. When he spoke, his voice low but full of disdain. "You don't even want to be here. You are just here to waste everyone's time. So, you can *maybe* get a job in the Seelie Palace. Which is rare; you'll probably have to marry whoever gave you that fucking mark and that male isn't even right for you."

I stared at him for a while. A part of me was scared by the cornering. The beast in me knew that his beast was way more powerful than mine. Another twisted evil part of me was turned on by his show of aggression. I wanted to rip off his clothes and have his beast savage mine. "How would you even know that he isn't?"

He looked at me for a moment, his eyes trying to say something his mouth wouldn't. "He isn't."

"How would you fucking know?" I stood my ground even if my beast wanted to cower in fear.

"If he was, you would have never been able to leave him. You would have just stayed with him and never came here. He wouldn't have given you the weakest, saddest mark one could offer. He would have made sure everyone knew you were his and made sure you were proud of it. If he was the one for you, you wouldn't become aroused from a single look from me. Your heartbeat wouldn't pick up when I come near, and your scent wouldn't change, noting me to your need to be fucked."

It took a moment to let that settle in. Even when it did, I still had no idea what to say.

I pushed away from him, walking toward my room with tears building in the back of my eyes. Embarrassment and guilt filling me. What he said wasn't untrue, but it didn't mean I wanted to face it on my first day of being here.

Before I could reach my door and escape him, the prince walked in front of me, blocking my path.

"What do you want? My room is right there, so consider your job done," I said, not meeting his eyes. I knew if I looked into those midnight colored orbs, I would crumble.

"Don't fuck my father."

Shocked, I looked up at him. "Why would I fuck your father? If you don't remember, I'm marked, and yes, I may be attracted to others, but I love him. I wouldn't have the mark if I didn't."

His jaw clenched before he leaned in, my body tensing for the wrong reasons. "Then don't fucking touch anyone while you're here. Don't let them touch you, and keep your scent to yourself."

I scoffed, enraged, moving away from him, and heading toward my door. "I don't know why the fuck you think you can tell me what to do."

He blocked my path again. "Just don't." His eyes were serious and demanding. His energy warned me to back down, and something inside me demanded I yield.

Jessamine opened my door, but didn't defuse the tension. "Oh hey, Levi," she purred.

Voice flat, he didn't break eye contact to look at her. "Hello, Jess."

"Do you want to help me get Marie into her new swimsuit? It has a lot of straps and could be hard to figure out with just two people." I almost snapped at her to shut up. I got that Jessamine was being the annoying friend who was secretly great because they push you and your crush together, but this was not that. I wanted to cut the prince right now, not fuck him.

His eyes stayed locked with mine. "I'm good, thanks."

"I guess that will just leave me and bunny by ourselves. I hope we don't get all tangled up." Jessamine ran her hand down my arm, which caused the prince to tense. Breaking eye contact, he looked at Jessamine, his eyes speaking murder. She dropped the seductive act and immediately removed her hand.

My anger intensified. He had no right to control who touched me. Jessamine, though new to my life, was my friend. She could touch me all she wanted. "Goodbye, *Your Highness*," I said, hatred spewing from my words.

His eyes met mine, and we stared at each other for a while before his jaw ticked and he stormed off.

Jessamine turned to me. "What the fuck was that?"

I brushed it off. "He's just being an arrogant male who gets pissy anytime someone challenges his word." I entered my room, throwing myself on the bed.

Jessamine laughed. "Oh, you two are going to have amazing sex."

"I'm not having sex with him, or anyone here for that matter." I was slightly annoyed at myself because somehow, I was still following the prince's demands.

She snorted. "Sure, you, a faeling who has raging hormones, is going to not fuck anyone while you're here for the next four years. Fae share lovers, even when they are marked. Life's too long to be monogamous."

"I'm not that type of girl," I said, getting up and fishing out the bathing suit she'd picked out earlier.

"Sure, and I can't tell that your panties are dripping wet from whatever went down with Levi."

I let out a groan because they fucking were. This whole situation had me hot, bothered, and hating myself. I wasn't supposed to feel this way about another guy. I loved Kolvin. *He* was my male. I wanted to spend the rest of my life with him, at least I thought I did. One day here, though, had me questioning everything.

Jessamine came over and rubbed my back. "Look, bunny, we are not creatures who like to be caged."

"I'm not in a cage." The second I uttered those words, they felt like a lie. I rubbed my face. "Kolvin and I are in love. We have been in love since we were children."

"Yeah, but weren't you homeschooled and sheltered your whole life?"

I stared at her, not liking where she was heading with the conversation.

"All I'm saying is that maybe you should test out your options before settling on the first male who shows interest. That's why I don't let Gregor mark me, even if I prefer him."

"I'm not settling," I argued.

Jessamine held up her hands in surrender. "Whatever you say. Let's get this swimsuit on and head down to the springs. I want a drink, and you definitely need one."

The swimsuit Jessamine picked out for me was indeed hard to get into. It had a thousand straps crossing over my body. The black fabric covered my breast and in between my legs, but the rest was just straps connecting the two pieces and accentuating my curves. It was honestly the hottest thing I had ever seen or worn, and I was ever thankful to meet Jessamine as I looked at myself in it.

The hot springs were located in a cave under the palace. All the students I saw during the assembly were already there when we arrived, including the prince. He sat against a wall with a book in hand, wearing a tight pair of swim trunks that showed off that amazing body. He was all lean, tight muscle, and I hated that I wanted to run my hands over every defined line.

The prince sensed my stare and looked up from his book, locking eyes with me. He stared at me the way he did at the assembly. His eyes hungry as they trailed down my body. I swore I could feel them caressing every inch of me. An ache settled between my legs, my body urging me to go to him and demand he relieve it. He settled back on my face, his eyes holding a question.

*Do you want to play?* they seemed to ask.

*Yes.*

I hated that I didn't hate him. Most of our interactions, he had been a prick to me, but Jessamine and him were right—I wanted to fuck him.

She stopped me from drowning in his eyes by handing me a much-needed drink. I took the wine and downed the whole thing.

"Woah, slow down, bunny."

I wiped my mouth. "I really needed that." Humans were often told not to drink fae wine, not because the wine was strong, I mean it was, but it contained human blood which fae drank to help soothe the beast that hid within. The beast that wanted to create chaos by killing or *fucking*.

She chuckled. "I bet you did."

Jessamine finished her drink, and we slid into the main pool. Many fae were already fucking, and some were about to start fucking—which was a common occurrence among fae parties. The whole scene was not helping my ache, and the blood wasn't soothing my creature like it was supposed to; in fact, I think I was hornier than before.

"Damn, Seelie, you look hot," Gregor said as we approached, right before grabbing Jessamine and devouring her mouth. "But you are way hotter."

She moved out of his grasp. "I'm not fucking you tonight."

He grumbled but didn't seem pissed. He just pulled her in for another passionate kiss which she returned.

Finch nodded in hello but wasn't paying much attention to our arrival. He was staring across the pool, making eyes with a female he was probably about to pounce on.

"Finch, just make your move. You've been staring at her for way too long," Gregor said.

"This is how I work, and I get way more pussy than you. Females enjoy the chase. Maybe you should watch and then you'll actually get your dick sucked off every once in a while."

We laughed as Gregor grumbled a "Fuck you, bro," and went to push Finch under, but I stepped in the way.

"Hey, it's true. Don't fuck up the game, *bro*," I said, smiling.

Gregor chuckled and splashed me with water.

"Hey!" I squealed.

"I got to stand up and show my alpha male status by at least splashing someone with water. Unfortunately, you volunteered." He smirked.

"Oh yeah?" I said, splashing him back. It hit Jessamine, who shrieked, and she splashed me back, starting a war between the three of us. When we grew tired, we started seriously drinking and dancing. We got so drunk we were at that point where we would laugh at almost anything.

I looked over to the prince who still sat and read his book. My ache was so bad I thought I might be sore later. The prince had been here for over two hours but hadn't put down that book to swim or have one drink.

"Why is he still here?" I said to Jessamine.

She looked over to him and smirked. "He probably wants to get fucked." Her eyes trailed to me.

"I am not fucking him. He pissed me off. You know he told me not to touch anyone? Like he can tell me what I can and can't do with my body."

"What a dick."

"Yeah!" I agreed.

Jessamine looked directly into my eyes. "You know we could show him who's the boss," she said, her voice full of lust.

"What do you mean?"

Jessamine grabbed my hips, pulling me into her arms. Her eyes held the same question as the prince's earlier.

I nodded my head slightly, wanting to know the taste of her soft plush lips.

She leaned in, pressing a soft kiss to my mouth. Her lips were like clouds, and I moaned at the tastes of fae wine and honey.

Our kiss grew heated, our drunk lust edging each other to keep going. My limbs wrapped around her, grinding my aching core into her.

She pushed me against the edge of the pool, her hand going to the small strip of fabric in between my legs. Moving it to the side, her delicate fingers found my swollen heat. She entered me and began pumping her digits in and out at a glorious rhythm. Her mouth trailing down my neck as my eyes opened to blue-black ones.

The prince was staring at us from across the pool—staring at me. Searing anger swirled in his eyes, and I smiled defiantly before moaning. Jessamine removed the fabric covering one of my breasts before attaching her mouth to my nipple, swirling her tongue as she continued to slowly pump her fingers.

I kept my eyes locked on the prince as she curled her finger, hitting the perfect spot. His angry stare turned me on in the craziest of ways and it didn't take me long before I was coming, staring into those midnight eyes.

Once I settled down, Jessamine covered me back up. She gave me a soft kiss on my lips before looking at the prince and giving him a deviant smirk.

His jaw cocked to the side before he got up and stormed out.

Jessamine and I glanced at each other, smiled, then burst into drunk giggles.

# TWELVE

## MARIE

*I* woke cold, naked, and with my brain pounding in my skull. I guess my drunken self couldn't have bothered to get under the covers last night, and she couldn't get out of the bathing suit either because it was on the floor, ripped into pieces from my claws.

Rolling over, I opened the curtains and immediately regretted it as the waning sun burned my irises. I groaned and sat up; the action too fast for my throbbing head, my stomach suddenly churning and my insides climbing up my throat.

I quickly scrambled to the bathroom, emptying my stomach into the basin. The memories of the last night coming back to me as I laid my head on the cold seat.

I let Jessamine finger me; Kolvin hadn't even done that.

*Fuck.* Kolvin!

I had been here for three days. What the fuck am I going to tell him? Oh, I was trying to make another male jealous, so I let a girl—who I'd known for a day—finger me?

After emptying the contents of my stomach until there was nothing else, I laid on the cold ground, missing my mother. If she were here, she would make my father carry me to bed, then brew me a cup of tea and let me sleep in. My father would rub my back as she cooked me the most delicious breakfast. My body would eventually heal, but she would let me pretend I was sick for the rest of the day.

Tears burned my eyes, and sobs soon followed. Three days in Unseelie and I already felt like a completely different person, living a completely different life. I wanted to go back home where my family was. Where Kolvin was. Where the sun was. Where I was.

It took me a while to calm down and get up off the floor, but it was only to run a hot bath. I soaked in the steaming water, letting myself sink in the warmth. I was safe here in the heat, but when I stepped out and rejoined the cold, I would have to deal with my problems.

When the water grew cold, I exited my small oasis, dressing in my school uniform. The uniform was a black long-sleeved tunic with a silver collar and a pleated skirt that cut off mid-thigh. I wore my new boots and black stockings to keep my legs warm and styled my curls into a half up-half down, leaving out a few curls to frame my face. Topping the uniform with the prince's cloak for added warmth.

As I dressed, I still managed to push the preening thoughts back, but I could feel them trying to come to the forefront. Guilt coated my skin, making me feel dirty even though I just bathed. More tears built behind my eyes, and I couldn't deal with them right now, so I pushed them back.

When I was mentally ready, I made my way down to the cafeteria and was instantly greeted with Jessamine smashing me into an embrace. "I'm so sorry, bunny," she whispered, burying her head into my neck.

I pulled her close, wanting to melt into her soft body. "It's okay, Jess. I'm fine," I lied.

She sniffled. "I didn't mean…"

I pulled her head from my neck, her eyes shining with worry. "Jess, I wanted you to do what you did." I smiled lightly, and she reciprocated before brushing her mouth against mine. I wanted to drown in her soft lips, but I pulled back. "You can't do that anymore though."

"I know; I just wanted to do it one last time." She winked, and we laughed, warmth bubbling in my middle, overshadowing my worries.

Thank the gods for Jessamine. If I didn't have her here, I would be a total wreck instead of just a mess. She felt like a piece of home. She had so much life to her, and she was so loving. I may have only known her a day, but I felt safe when I was around her.

We ate with the boys, Gregor eyeing me every few seconds. His look said *stay away from my girl,* and I gave him a *she's not your girl* look, before putting my arm around her.

I wasn't jealous of him, and I didn't want Jessamine to be mine. She was one of the most beautiful females I had ever seen, and I wished I could take a swim in her eyes, but I liked males more. Jessamine was a free bird, not meant to be caged. Gregor was a typical fae male, beautiful and super sexy, but possessive. He also didn't want to play the game; he just wanted to skip to the end with Jess. Fae played. We were beasts who enjoyed the hunt as much as the feast.

Jessamine, knowing what I was doing, leaned into me. I pulled her closer, my eyes connecting with Gregor's as I pressed a kiss on her cheek.

Gregor growled low, stuffing his food down his throat in annoyance.

Jessamine and I shared a look, then burst into laughter.

We made our way to the main laboratory after breakfast. The room wasn't much different from all the other rooms in the building. Dark with warm fae lights, filled with tables that sat two and faced a chalkboard.

Jessamine and I sat at one of the tables as the professor cleared her throat, her honey-blonde hair refracting the light in the room. "Good evening, students, welcome—"

The prince walked into the room like he owned the place, which I guess he did. "Prince Levington, you're late as usual." The professor tsked at him.

He made his way to the back of class, and with his voice low but loud enough for anyone with fae ears to hear, said, "Maybe don't fuck my father like every other whore here, and I would actually respect you."

The class erupted into laughter. It took a moment for the students to quiet down, but the professor shook it off and continued speaking. "Welcome, students. I'm Professor May. I will be teaching you the fae history as well as the basics of magic. I will be your main professor this year besides Mr. Vandeer who will teach you the basics of combat and battle magic. At the end of the year, you will decide which subject you prefer, and for the remaining three years here, you will study that subject in detail.

"The first and most important lesson for all fae to learn is the importance of unity. The Seelie cannot live without the Unseelie and the Unseelie cannot live without the Seelie. This is a fact every fae must accept. We have tried many times to live separately, but it always fails. We have to come together to create a balanced land for our magic to be stable. To teach you the importance of unity, for the first year, you will work with a partner.

"You will be able to choose your partner, and you will be graded together. There is no switching once you choose. You need to learn to work with anybody to truly understand this lesson. If you choose your best friend and he sucks, sucks for you, learn to adapt. We will first pick our partners, then we will start."

Jessamine and I stared at each other with a knowing grin.

Every single hair on my body rose as a dark gravelly voice spoke, "You are my partner." I turned around to see the prince standing right behind me, his face stone cold, his expression saying he wouldn't take no for an answer.

I opened my mouth to reject him anyways, but Jessamine spoke first, her voice three notches too high. "She would love to be your partner, Levi. She was just talking about how she wanted to get to know our lovely prince."

I raised my eyebrow at her, and she smirked at me devilishly. "I thought *you* wanted to be my partner, though?" I said, hoping she wouldn't see this whole bit through.

"No, me and Gregor are partners." Gregor perked up and immediately ditched Finch to wrap his arms around her.

"Yes, we are." He made eye contact with me before kissing her neck, getting me back for challenging him earlier.

Jessamine pushed him away. "School partners, Gregor. Not sex partners."

Gregor pulled her back and kissed her sweetly. "What do you want me to do, Jess? A male can only wait so long."

She nipped at his lips. "Males chase their prey; females play with it. Learn the rules," she purred before taking his hand and leading him to an empty table.

I was left alone with the prince who looked annoyed by their interaction. I looked up at him. "Fine," I huffed. I had no other choice anyway. No one would challenge a prince for a Seelie girl they didn't know, so I was stuck with him since Jessamine ditched me.

He gave me a sexy smirk of triumph, before grabbing my hand and leading me to the back of the lab. The contact of our skin touching awakened something mystical inside me. Sparks pulsed through my skin, heat pooling at my core. He gripped my hand harder, sending shockwaves through my body that went straight to my clit. My heart pounded in my chest as a thousand little lightning bolts vibrated through me. My nipples, clit, and core were their targets, the sensation overwhelming and exhilarating. I was seconds away from coming, but before I did, the prince let go, breaking the connection, leaving me hollow and empty. It was so sudden and abrupt that I nearly fell to the floor, but he wrapped his arm around my covered waist to steady me.

After a few seconds, I began to feel normal. The prince's panting breaths fawning over my cheeks. "What the fuck was that?" I whispered.

His hold loosened a bit as he glanced down at his pants. There was a huge bulge there. I guessed, he was feeling the same thing I was and let go because he was about to come too.

Everyone had their eyes trained on us. One whiff of the air and you could smell mine and Levi's arousal mixing together, creating the most luscious scent.

"Look somewhere else." His voice was dark and deadly as he commanded others, scaring even me. Everyone found something else to do with their eyes, including the professor. His hand slid from my covered waist to the small of my back and he led me to the back table. We sat down, and he said to the professor, "Begin the lesson."

Ms. May started to talk about the beginning of the fae, a lesson that we all learned when we were babes. Levi, pretending nothing had happened, started taking notes. Which was crazy of him because I could still see that he was hard.

I poked him, and he tensed but ignored me. I did it again, and this time, he looked at me, eyes hard and jaw clenched. "What?"

My brows smashed together. "What the fuck was that?"

"Nothing," he said and went back to taking notes.

I went to grab his pen, and the second our skin was an inch from each other, I felt a spark, causing me to jump and pull my hand away.

His eyes blazed as he looked at me. "Just leave it alone, Marie," he gritted through clenched teeth.

"Leave it alone?"

He gestured to the class. "Not fucking here."

I gave him my most stern stare, which probably did nothing to him, and said, "At lunch."

The lesson was long and boring, and I couldn't sit still. My panties were soaked, my skin irritated, and I needed to know what the hell he did to me.

When we were finally let out for lunch, Levi and I were the first to leave. We walked down the hall, and at the first private corner, I turned on him, arms crossed, eyebrow raised in accusation.

He started to take a deep breath in, then stopped mid-breath, blinking hard and releasing any of the air that he had just previously taken in. "Go bathe and change. I'll have someone bring you food."

"You are not seriously giving me another command right now."

He leaned into me, his proximity making my body go on edge. "Marie, smell me."

I breathed in a shallow breath, and fuck… he smelled good. Really fucking good, causing my core to clench and all my thoughts focusing on scenarios where he pinned me to the wall and fucked me good and hard. I had to ball my hands into fists to stop myself from ripping his clothes off. I hadn't acknowledged his smell earlier in class because my mind was distracted as to how that situation even happened, but now it was overwhelming my senses, suffocating me in the best fucking way.

His eyes burned with lust, and I knew he saw the same reflecting back in mine. We stood there for countless moments, our breaths sharp and shallow, both of us holding back from attacking another. Except I was weaker to the urge than him because I leaned in slightly, and he tensed and took a step back.

"I have been trying not to rip your fucking clothes off for the last two hours so if you don't want that to happen, then go upstairs, bathe and change." His voice was demanding and dominating, making me loose and pliant.

I wanted that to happen. I wanted him to take me right here and show everyone I was his. I wanted him to rip off my clothes and punish me for making him wait those two hours, like I knew he wanted to. I wanted to be his.

The thought scared the shit out of me. I wasn't his. I was Kolvin's. Brushing my hand over the mark for some grip on reality, I saw the lust in Levi's eyes quickly fizzle to hate, and without another word, he left.

I did go to my room to bathe and change, and soon after, a human servant brought me food. It wasn't the normal food they had in the cafeteria, either. This was the top-level shit, reserved for royalty. There was roasted turkey bathed in the finest gravy, mashed potatoes that were probably grown by the best farmers, and the sweetest corn I had ever tasted; the whole meal making my beast roll inside me.

When I headed back to class, I didn't see Levi and figured he was just late again, but after a half an hour, I realized that he probably wasn't going to show.

The lesson that was taught was about how fae went from beast-like to civilized. Fae may look down upon humans, but humans were actually the reason we lived like this. They lived in huts, so we built huts. They bathed, so we bathed. They cooked their food, so we cooked our food.

At first, human civilization made them more advanced, but we quickly surpassed them because we had magic. Living like they did, it didn't get rid of our beastly nature. The savage nature of the fae was to fuck, fight, and feed. We didn't need to feed on humans to survive but since they were emotionally intelligent, it made the hunt more enthralling. They built weapons for their protection against us, but it just goaded us up more, loving the chaotic mess it was to capture them.

Our nature was to fuck things up. We enjoyed the panic they felt, then the lust and confusion our venom caused. We loved to toy with their minds. We didn't just do this to humans; we did it to each other. We played, chased, and taunted another for no other reason other than to fuck with each other. There were too many fae wars to count. We would go to war for the pettiest of reasons, any fight inciting a thrill in us.

The lesson went on for a few more hours, and I tried to write as many notes as I could. Even though this was basic history of the fae, I didn't know what Levi knew, and I really didn't want to have to deal with him making me fail and ruining my plans to go home.

When the lesson finished, I grabbed dinner, finding a seat with Jessamine and the boys.

Gregor spoke first. "What the fuck happened in class earlier? You and Levi smelled so good I had a hard-on."

Jessamine rolled her eyes. "Gregor, anything will get you hard." She turned to me. "But seriously, bunny, what was that?"

I shrugged. "I don't know. Levi was supposed to tell me, but he never came back after we left for lunch."

"You mean you too didn't fuck like animals after that?" Gregor asked.

"No, I'm marked," I said, annoyed.

He snorted. "I almost forgot. I think your mark is even fading."

Subconsciously, my hand felt for it, and I breathed a relieved breath when I realized he was just playing with me.

Gregor laughed. "I would hate to be your male; you make him look weak as shit."

"I do not."

Gregor leaned in, his face serious. At this moment, he looked more like a warrior than an arrogant faeling. "Marie, you've been here two nights and have already been with one fae who isn't your male."

"I know but—" I began.

"But nothing. Even if you were drunk, if you respected your male, you wouldn't have done anything with Jessamine. When she kissed you, you would have pushed her away. You wouldn't have challenged me this morning either because even if you were joking with me, a challenge is a challenge and fae are one to fight for what we want. You know that and should've stayed out of the way because you are a marked female who doesn't want to have others question your loyalty to your male. I don't know what the fuck happened with you and Levi, but you obviously want him. Not your male. You literally cheated on your male to make him jealous. You make your male look weak by how you disrespect him. Yes, fae share lovers but rarely marked pairings. If a marked fae wanted to be with someone else, they would either remove their mark or discuss it with their claimed. I doubt a hormonal faeling would mark a female he would want to share. I know I wouldn't." He looked at Jessamine, then back at me.

He said all the shit I was trying not to think about this morning. All of the stuff I didn't want to face. I cheated on Kolvin, my best friend. I cheated on him to make another male jealous, a male I couldn't deny I secretly yearned for.

My lips quivered and I looked down at my food, trying not to cry. I didn't deserve to cry. I was the bad guy. I was the one who fucked up.

Jessamine put her arms around me, pulling me into her chest. "Fuck you, Gregor."

"I just told her the truth. I doubt her male is okay with any of this, and he'll probably remove his mark when he finds out."

A slight whimper escaped from my mouth, and I hid my face in Jessamine's neck. "Gregor, if you want to keep your dick, shut the fuck up." She raised my face. "Bunny, it's okay. You're fae.

We are terrible creatures. He will understand," she said, trying to comfort me.

It didn't. Kolvin wouldn't understand. When I'd tell him, he will remove his mark. How could I be so fucking reckless? I was only half-fae. I shouldn't be such a fuckup. I should be able to respect my male. If I really loved Kolvin, I wouldn't even entertain thoughts about another male. But did I really love him? I came here a hundred percent in love with him. Blind, heart-jerking love, and now it felt like it was diminishing.

I cried for a while in Jessamine's arms. When I calmed down, I pulled back, wiping my tears. "You okay, bunny?"

I gave a tight smile in reply.

"Do you still want to go to the party with us tonight?"

I shook my head, traumatized by the last party I attended.

When we finished eating, Jessamine and Gregor walked me to my room. When I got inside, I just crawled on the bed. Levi's cloak wrapped around me, it still smelling of him. I hated that it brought me comfort. I hated that I didn't take it off. I hated that I wished he was here to comfort me. I hated that I wanted him.

# THIRTEEN

## Corivina
## 199 years ago.

$\mathcal{M}$arkos did as promised; he brought me enough coin to live a life of luxury for the next five years and a pair of clothes. After he left, I went to the herbalist and asked for a few days off. She didn't ask questions. However, she had worn a new steel necklace, telling me she was probably paid off by Markos like I was.

I rented the room Markos had assaulted me in. That's where I was now, sitting in the corner desk, staring at the bed that had remained unmade and stained with my blood. I sat there for hours, drinking some shit ale from the kitchen downstairs.

I didn't remember it. I kept trying to. The bruises on my body had healed. Now, all that remained was the marks. I counted eight in total. Six along my neck, one on my shoulder, and one on my breast. Of course, the bastard thought to claim that, because seven claims weren't enough.

The ale wasn't doing anything for my memory. It had been days, more days than I told the herbalist I'd be gone. I kept hoping I would remember. I wanted to remember the look on his face while he did it. I wanted to see the moment he realized I would never take him back when I woke. The moment he realized he was hurting someone he loved. I don't know if I would remember anything, or if I really should.

It was driving me crazy. I knew I wasn't fully conscious during it, but I felt like I needed to remember. If I could, I could erase the love I had for him. I could make him the bad guy, and I wouldn't blame myself for being stupid enough to love him.

Tired of trying to regain my memory, I stood from the chair and went to the bathroom. That was the first time I saw myself. I looked hollow, lifeless. My body, haggard, since ale was the only substance I had consumed the past few days. My coffee-black eyes had changed into a cold straight black. My shimmer made me look like a glowing ghost.

Then, I removed the tunic Markos got me.

I tried to cover the sob that bubbled from my throat, but the cry still broke through. I didn't look at the marks when I counted them; I just felt them out with my fingers. The marks weren't supposed to look like this. Red, angry, and unhealed.

I continued to wail into my hand as I stared in the mirror. The boy who used to write me poems twice a week... did this to me.

When he first marked me, it resembled love. It was once the most beautiful thing to have on my neck besides the necklace he gave me. Now, it was the ugliest thing in the world.

I didn't know when it started, but I viscerally clawed at my neck in anger. Severing every bond between us, until the only link left was the one deeply embedded in my shoulder. It was too deep to sever with my claws. I struggled, frustratingly crying to cut it out, but I couldn't sever it.

Frantically, I searched the room for something to cut it out with, not able to bear another second with his marks. I found the letter opener on the floor where Markos left it, covered in his blood. Blood that now ran through my body because I let him pay me off. I made a deal with him to never tell another being.

Markos had time to think about his deal as I laid unconscious. I had a few seconds. Anything! Anything I could've asked for, and I asked for a chest of coin and some clothes. I should have asked for his fucking balls so he could never create an heir.

I grabbed the stupid letter opener and severed the mark. Then I looked down at my bloody body. I thought I would feel better. I felt worse. Empty. Hollow. Lifeless. Alone.

I ran a bath, making the water scorching hot and scrubbed every inch of myself, trying to erase his scent from me, trying to erase the last few days away. I washed my clothes and pulled my wet hair into a braid, then used my magic to dry the garments and put them back on.

With some coin in hand, I headed out to the square. I didn't know what I was hoping I would find, but I just wanted to fill the hole that had ripped open inside me.

I walked around aimlessly for a while, watching others carrying on with their day. The thing about the Seelie was they're always so fucking happy. They embodied the sun and fucking shit rainbows. They all acted like they were so much better than Unseelie, but they were just as sadistic as the rest of us.

I spotted a spell shop and ducked inside to get away from the cheer. I was instantly hit with the potent smells of frankincense and myrrh. The smell too strong for my fae senses, pain starting to shoot through my skull.

"Fucking witches," I muttered under my breath.

The only humans who dared to roam the fae territories freely were the ones who were gifted with magic. Their magic was different from the fae and less powerful, but they could hold their own against a fae.

The shop was mostly lit with candles instead of fae light, giving it a warm, eerie feeling. A pang entered my heart as it reminded me of the Unseelie Palace, and I gritted my teeth, closing my heart off from the reaction.

There were shelves that held herbs, spelled candles and jars, and to my surprise, fae wine! I grabbed two bottles—nothing like a little wine to fill the void. I might even feel a positive emotion, or I might cry all night and tear up the room I was renting. It really was a fifty percent chance of either, which sounded like good odds, so I grabbed a third bottle.

Not bothering to look at anything else since I found what I needed and was now ready to get drunk, I walked over to the table in the back. "You'd think a human wouldn't sell fae wine knowing what is in it," I said.

The witch looked up at me. Her skin was dark brown, her curly hair was long and pulled up into a bun on her head, and she had golden yellow eyes, letting you know she had the gift. "Not many fae need a hex. Have to make a living somehow." I found myself slightly smiling at her comment. "Ah, you haven't done that in a while."

My smile dropped. *Witches*.

"I have the gift of the gods, fae. I know things and you have just had something truly evil happen to you."

I groaned internally. I hated witches, always poking their heads into things, acting all high and mighty. No matter how much magic you have, being human sucked. They got old and died. "Look, witch, I just want my wine. I'll pay you extra to not give me a divine message right now."

She pointed to the chair. "Sit."

*Does she not have ears?* "I really have somewhere to be," I lied. Well, it wasn't a lie. I should be at my job.

"No, you don't. Sit." She pointed at the chair again.

"Can I just—"

"I'll give you the wine for free if you sit," she stated.

Living the last four years poor and scraping by, I couldn't pass up three free bottles of fae wine just for a witch to do a little juju.

I was helping her out; she obviously didn't get enough customers that she had to beg. "Fine."

She picked up her tarot cards and started to shuffle. "What is your name?" she asked.

"Corivina."

"Crow?"

"Raven." I grimaced.

"Ah, and you were meant to soar, but someone cut your wings?" she asked.

My eyes flicking back and forth, my foot tapping on the wood floor, I replied, "Something like that."

She laid out a card. "Two of Cups reversed. A lover did this to you."

*Fucking cunt witches and their fucking cards.* I didn't answer, and she continued to shuffle.

She laid out another card that said *Temperance*. "Don't worry, you'll heal."

I found myself asking, "When?"

"The cards don't work like that, girl."

See what I meant—a cunt.

She laid three more cards. "You'll have three great loves in your life." She pointed at the first card—Three of Swords. "One who will break you." She pointed at the second card—The Star. "One who will heal you." Then she pointed at the last card—The Tower. "One who you'll destroy."

My eyes narrowed. "How do you know that?"

She gave me a look. "Do you really doubt the gods?"

"No, but I doubt humans."

"I am a human with the gifts." She started to pick up the cards. "Anyway, fae, the gods have spoken to me, and they have never lied."

"One who will break me, one who will heal me, and one whom I will destroy?"

"Yes." She blinked her golden eyes.

*One whom I will destroy.* I felt my heart come to life at the thought of crushing Markos. "Do the cards tell you who I will destroy?"

She snorted. "That anger you carry will guide you."

"What?" Humans were always saying how fae talked in riddles, but it was really them who spoke such nonsense.

"Let it go."

Anger swirled within me as I took in what this witch just fucking said to me. The gods must have not clued this cunt in on what the fuck just happened to me. "Fuck you."

She smiled with the grace of an old wise person even though she couldn't be over thirty years old. "I see your pain. It's fresh, but fae are fickle creatures. They are beasts who walk on two legs. It's in your nature to retaliate against those who wronged you, but if you hold on to that hate, it will eat at your soul."

I laughed. I was done with Markos, but it wasn't wrong of me to wish he died for what he did. "Listen, I came here for wine, witch."

"Then off you go." She waved her hand, dismissing me.

I was stunned by her reply. I didn't even want her advice and she was dismissing me? I was pitying her because the poor human looked lonely and sad, and she was dismissing me?

"Don't worry, you'll be back."

I gave her a look that said *like hell I will,* and I picked up my bottles and walked out, ready to drown in my wine and forget that bitch ever existed.

# FOURTEEN

## Marie

*T*here were tears crusted on my face when I woke up. I took another hot bath, contemplating my last two nights here. I tried not to let my emotions unravel, but I failed and ended up crying again. After pulling myself together the best I could, I dressed in my uniform.

While I was dressing, I looked over at my desk to see Kolvin had written to me. I was supposed to write back to him two nights ago, but I forgot during my self-sabotaging spiral.

*Marie? How was your first day?*

*Marie?*

*I woke up early so I could talk to you, but I have to go to my lesson now. I love you.*

*I just got home, write to me when you wake.*

*Marie, you ignoring me is driving me insane.*

*I don't know what's going on with you, but please answer. I'm starting to worry.*

I sighed heavily and scribbled out: *I'm sorry. I was just really busy the last few days.*

The pen began to move. Part of me just wished he wouldn't write. A part of me wished he was a bad male and I could justify my choices the last few nights, but he wasn't, and wasn't that what all females yearned for?

*Okay, I'm just glad you aren't dead. Can you talk now?*

*No, I'm sorry I just have a lot of work to do.* Lie.

*Oh, okay. Love you.*

"Fuck." I grabbed the pad and threw it across the room, sinking to the floor to start sobbing. Why did I fuck this up? Kolvin was my best friend. He didn't deserve this. He deserved a female who was utterly loyal to him. That girl was supposed to be me. I had a plan—four years here, then find a job back home and marry him. There was no way he'd forgive me when he found out. I didn't even know if we would still be friends after this.

I wiped my face furiously, sick of crying. The past week, all I had done was cry. I needed to pull myself together. I fucking did this, but it would be okay. I'd figure it out. I just needed to not fuck anything up for the next three weeks. Even if Kolvin and I decided not to be together anymore, it would be better if I didn't smash his heart into pieces by fucking the whole Unseelie Territory.

I headed down to the cafeteria and didn't see Jessamine. I didn't know Gregor and Finch well enough to sit with them without her, so I sat by myself. Which was great because I couldn't fuck anything up by myself.

After I ate, I felt determined to stay focused the next three weeks. I wouldn't lust for Levi, and I wouldn't make out with other girls to make him jealous. I would just have a good time, but not too good of a time. I'd go home and make it up to Kolvin and everything would be all right. I hoped.

My eyes met Jessamine's when I walked into the laboratory. The air thickened and the false bravado I just cultivated flew right out the window. Something was wrong. Her sky-blue eyes held remorse, indicating that there was something she wanted to tell me, and it wouldn't be pleasant. We didn't have time to talk before the lesson, so I walked to my seat and let it drop for now. Whatever it was, I could worry about it later.

The lesson began and Levi walked in late again. The professor ignored him this time as he made his way to the seat next to me. The second he sat down, I understood Jessamine's look. They fucked. Not only that, but she also marked him.

My heart squeezed painfully, feeling like I'd just been punched in the chest. All the nerves in my body tightened, and my vision colored red. Rage poured through my veins like hot lava, and I clenched my fists to keep from unleashing the volcano.

*They played me.*

They ruined my life. The prince acted like he wanted me. He volunteered to escort me, then dry-humped me while I fucking slept. Jessamine encouraged the whole thing, playing it up, making it seemed like he liked me, wanted me. Then they destroyed my relationship.

I should've been raging over these details, but all I could think in that moment was,

*She marked what is mine.*

It took every bit of my will not to get up and rip her throat out. She marked what was mine. *Mine.* She deserved to die because of that.

*He is not yours.* I tried to calm myself.

It didn't change my feelings. It smelled so fucking vile, wrong. It should be my scent on him, not hers. It should be my mark. Not only did I want to kill her, but I also wanted to rip that mark off his neck and punish him for doing this to me.

The rage in me was so potent that tears started to silently fall down my cheeks as I warred with myself not to lash out.

Levi shifted and another whiff of the scent—their scent—hit me. My claws dug into my palms until they drew blood. I focused on the pain, trying to cover up the anguish that was ripping at my heart.

Tears spilled down my chin and blood dripped from my hands onto the table as the professor continued her stupid lesson about one of the fae wars. I wanted to rip her throat out too for forcing me to sit here and endure this.

"Marie." I flinched at Levi's hushed voice.

I didn't look at him. I couldn't. If I did, I might burst. If I looked into those midnight eyes, eyes that could've been home for my soul, I would shatter. I didn't know if I would break down sobbing or if I would rip everyone in this room to shreds.

"Marie," he whispered again. More tears fell. I let out a slight whimper as I smelled it again. It was absolutely torturous. Wrong, just so wrong. I kept looking straight, my hands covered in my blood. I was surprised that no one was looking back here. There was no way they couldn't scent the blood.

Levi reached for my hands, but I snatched them away, finally looking at him. "Don't fucking touch me," I snapped. Guilt painted in his blue-black eyes. It made me sick to see his pity. He hurt me and now he felt guilty because the weak Seelie girl couldn't handle it. I decided then that I would rather rip everyone's throat out than cry anymore, including his. "Fuck you."

He flinched back like I had just stabbed him. Good. I hated him. I hated Jessamine too. My mother was right about these Unseelie bastards—they couldn't be trusted. I was here two days and these two people managed to fuck me over in that small amount of time. So fucking Unseelie they couldn't even be sly about it and draw out the pain. If they were Seelie, they would have played with me a little longer, maybe even a lot longer, before showing their hand, but now that they did, I would be watching my back.

The second Ms. May finished her lesson, I got up and left the room. I was practically running, not wanting to embarrass myself for the third time in front of the class.

I heard footsteps following me closely, and by the scent, I could tell it was both of the fuckers. I walked faster, but my legs were too short to take me far.

"Marie," Jessamine called out, her traitorous voice making my stomach turn.

I stopped and turned, seeing both of them. What a lovely couple they would make. They would have cute backstabbing little monsters together.

Jessamine had tears streaming down her face. That fucking bitch thought it was her time to cry. "Marie, it isn't—"

"It isn't what it looks like. I'm pretty sure it is what it smells like, though. I thought you were my fucking friend? You made me feel safe here and you pushed me toward him. You made me cheat on my male just to make him jealous and then you go and sleep with him? And you fucking mark him too? But of course, you're too good for his mark? Fuck you, whore, and leave me the fuck alone." I looked at Levi. "Both of you."

I turned, starting to walk up the stairs. "Marie…" Jessamine half sobbed.

I didn't have time for her bullshit, so I flipped her off with my bloody finger.

# FIFTEEN

## MARIE

$\mathcal{S}$kipping the rest of my lessons, I spent the night curled into a ball in my bed. Levi sent food to my room, but I didn't answer the door to receive it. Fuck him. I didn't want his fancy food. In fact, I wished he was here so I could make him choke on it.

My senses were still fucked up, their scent still haunting me. Each time I thought it was gone, I would get a new whiff and a fresh wave of fury rolled through me along with a pristine set of tears. The whole night was excruciating; I didn't want to care about this, but the beast inside me was riled and I couldn't get it to calm down. It wanted to rage, and I wanted to cry, so here I was, on my bed, rage-crying.

I wanted to kill. I had never wanted to kill anyone ever. Honestly, one more second in that room smelling that terrible scent, I would have probably killed her.

*I would have killed Jessamine.* That thought made me cry harder. I knew I didn't really know her, but I had bonded to her. I shouldn't be mad at her for sleeping with Levi. He wasn't mine. I hated that I had to keep reminding myself of that. My stupid heart thought he was; maybe my beast did too, because what? He looked at me like I was the only female in the world? Because when we touched, sparks shot through me?

*It was just lust, Marie. Lust that you got swept up in.*

I wanted to take it all back. To go back to past Marie and slap her for being stupid enough to ruin things with Kolvin. To take back every lustrous look I gave Levi, and to give back his cloak that I stupidly still had wrapped around me.

Around when classes were let out, I heard a soft knock at my door. If it was Jessamine, I'd probably kill her. If it was Levi, I'd probably fuck him and show him he was mine. Two things I didn't want to do. So I chose to ignore it.

Whoever knocked eventually left, and a little while later, more servants came with food from Levi. I took the food this time. If Levi wanted to give me food as an apology, that was fine. I wouldn't forgive him, but I'd take the free, expensive food.

Rising early the next day, I opened the curtains. I missed the sun, the warmth it provided, the feel of it on my skin.

The sun was close to the horizon, about an hour or two before it set. The world was growing darker earlier, meaning the summer was turning to fall outside of the fae territory. I wanted to sit there and see the sun off, but I had something I needed to do, so begrudgingly, I got out of bed.

I cleaned the blood off my hands from last night, as well as the tears that stained my face. I wanted to be done crying, but if I could do what I wanted to do, then I knew there was more to come.

Dressing in my clothes more set for Seelie, I pulled my curly hair into a low bun, grabbing my bag full of coin, leaving my room. Unfortunately, I only had Levi's cloak for warmth, so I had to wear it or suffer from the chill that permeated the palace. I tried not to find comfort in wearing it but failed. I was addicted to his scent, and every time it filled my nose, my creature rolled within.

I stood in front of the king's office, and nervously knocked on the door. I hoped he could help me. If he couldn't, I might start bawling right here in front of him.

The king called for me to come in, and I was met with him relaxed, his feet propped on the desk, reading a book. Half of his midnight black hair was pulled into a bun and the rest laid back on his shoulders. His tunic was fully unbuttoned, showing off his beautifully sculpted body and the raven tattoo that rested over his heart. He continued reading the book, not paying attention to me.

I stood there, back stiff and stomach churning, feeling out of place before clearing my throat to get his attention. He looked up at me and his eyes widened. Immediately, he stood, and used the book to cover his torso. "Marie, sorry, I thought you were someone else."

I turned around to give him a sense of privacy and button up his shirt. "Sorry, I know it's early."

"It's fine. What brings you here?"

I turned back around and found his blue-black eyes, acid filling my throat at the reminder of his son's betrayal. "I know that this is probably out of line, but could I ask a favor from you?"

The king walked around the desk, sitting on the edge. "What do you need, little raven?"

"Do you have a portal mirror?"

"I do."

"Could I use it? I'm willing to pay." I showed him my satchel of coin. "If this isn't enough, then I'm willing to make a deal." Looking down at the bag, I realized how stupid of a plan this was. He was the King of Unseelie, the richest person here by default, and he probably could get anything he ever wanted. What could a faeling like me offer him?

He ran his hand through the stubble on his chin. "I told you earlier I won't share blood with you."

My pulse quickening with desperation, and I moved closer, my hands drawing to my chest. "Please, Your Majesty. I will do anything. I really need to talk to my mother."

"Your mother?" he queried.

"Yes, I need to speak to her. I haven't been this long without her."

The king thought for a moment. "Okay, I will let you use my mirror. No cost, but I have to listen in to make sure you aren't committing treason."

I threw my arms around him, and he tensed. I remembered my place, and quickly backed up. "I'm so sorry. I…"

"It's fine, I just wasn't expecting that." He gestured to one of the couches that rested near the fireplace. "Sit. I'll grab the mirror."

A portal mirror allowed you to talk to anyone who also owned a spelled mirror; you just had to say their name. My father, being the commander of the Seelie Army, owned one to communicate the Seelie King. They were very expensive to own because they had to be crafted by both races of fae, just as a portal did.

The king handed me the mirror. It was oval shaped with a steel rim, decorated with roses and ravens. The mirror required magic to activate it in the form of blood. Since I didn't know how to call upon my magic, the king did it for me. The veins in his hands turned black, with a dagger, he cut his finger, letting his blood fall onto the face of the mirror.

"I'll sit at the desk to give you a sense of privacy."

The mirror reflected my face. I used to embody the sun. Now, my caramel skin was pale, making it more of an ash brown. My shimmer was still there, but it looked wrong against my skin. My eyes were red-rimmed, and I had bags underneath. I was slowly dying, slowly becoming Unseelie.

Taking a deep breath, I said, "Darius Foxglove."

My father should be awake since the sun hadn't even set. It took a while for it to work, but eventually my father's warm blue eyes and toffee brown hair appeared, and a smile painted my lips. "Father."

"Marie." His grin spread warmth through me, and I wished I was wrapped in his embrace, but the reminder that I would only get eight days a year to be draped in his arms sent a chill over that newfound feeling.

My father noticed the change in my expression. "What's wrong, my flower?"

I loved my father, but I always talked to my mother about things. My father was the most loving person in the world. When I was happy, I loved to go to him and share my joy. When I was sad, I would go to him for someone to hold, but my mother was always the person I went to when I needed to talk. She just had this way of listening where you felt heard. She always made me feel strong. My father would hold me while I crumbled, but my mother would pave over any cracks and rebuild me, and that's what I needed right now.

"Can I talk to mother?" My father gave me a light smile, hurt shifting in his eyes when I picked her over him. It had been one of the main stresses in my family. I was attached to my mother as a child, and it took me a while to warm to him. He tried so hard to make me feel like his real daughter, and I did. He was my father, no one would replace him. I loved him but that didn't change how he felt when I always went to her, always wanted her.

"Yeah, honey, I'll go get her."

I sat in silence while he walked into our family room and handed her the mirror. When I saw my mother's face, I couldn't help but burst into tears.

"Marie." Her regal voice made me cry harder. I missed her more than I thought I did, and I couldn't stop the sobs that came from my mouth. I didn't even care that the king was listening to me cry. "Marie, I can't help you if you don't tell me what's wrong."

It took me a moment to catch my breath. "I hate it here, Mother. Please find a way for me to come home."

"Marie, there is nothing more that I want than to have you here, but there isn't anything I can do about it right now."

"Please, I don't want to be here any longer."

"Flower, the only option you have is to finish school. Did something happen?"

I didn't say anything, just sobbed into my hand.

"What happened, Marie?"

Sniffling hard, I whispered, "I cheated on Kolvin."

There was no judgment in her voice when she asked, "Why?"

"I was drunk at a party." I couldn't tell her the whole thing. One, I didn't want to tell her the stupid reason I did what I did. Two, I could barely get those five words out. Three, I really didn't want the king to know how I made out with a girl to make his son jealous.

"Marie, you are young. You will make mistakes."

"You never make mistakes."

"Marie, when I was your age, I made many mistakes. Have you told Kolvin? I'm sure he will forgive you. That boy loves you."

"Mom, I..." It was hard for me to say this. Admitting this was something that I'd been avoiding, but it had crossed my mind more than once over the last three nights. "Mom, I don't know if I do."

"You do what?"

"I don't know if I love him." Saying it out loud hurt my heart, but it was the truth. Ever since I stepped foot in the Unseelie Territory, my feelings for Kolvin started to diminish.

My mother's face broke from her usual calm, stony expression to shock. "Marie, you and Kolvin have been best friends since you've been able to walk."

I bit my lip. "Yeah. Best friends, not lovers."

She took a heavy breath. "It's okay if you don't, but you should tell him sooner than later."

"But if I don't, then what will happen when I get out of school?" Kolvin was one of my fail safes to go home.

"You can't hold on to Kolvin because he will keep you here. That wouldn't be fair to him or you. You deserve a love that burns through you like I have with your father."

I heard the king breathe in sharply, making me turn to look at him. He was pretending to read that book from earlier, his face sculpted into a blank expression. I looked back to my mother. "Yeah, but—"

"Your father and I will do everything in our power to keep you here, but there is nothing we can do right now. You have two weeks till you can visit, so let that fuel you. You should take those two weeks to figure out if you want to keep things going with Kolvin."

I wiped my tears. "Okay," I breathed. "I miss you so much."

"Flower, I physically ache from you being gone. Eight days a year will not be enough."

"Also, the lunar eclipses."

"Honey, those days are for fucking and partying. Two things I will never do with you."

I laughed but it was more of a sob.

"It will be okay, flower." She paused for a moment, her head cocking to the side. "Marie, how are you calling us right now?"

"The king let me borrow his mirror." I glanced at him.

"Is he there?" Her voice had turned stern. The voice she used on me when I was in trouble.

"Yeah, he has to listen in to make sure I'm not trading secrets of the Unseelie."

"Sure he does."

"Did you want to talk to him?"

"No." Her reply was quick and harsh, stunning me. My mother closed her eyes and took a moment to compose herself. "Look, Marie, there is nothing we can do about you being there right now. Tell me about your time while we have each other."

I told her about everything except the stuff with Levi and Jessamine. We spoke till sunset. After a while, the king told me he had a meeting, and I remembered he was expecting someone when I came in. I said goodbye to my parents and then the call was over.

Handing the mirror to the king, I sniffled. "Thank you, Your Majesty."

"Markos," he said lightly.

My brow creased.

"You may call me Markos in private, Marie. If you need something from me, anything, I will happily get it for you."

The king gave me a smile, and I grinned back, my body relaxing while I was around him. He had an energy that just soothed a person. "Thanks, hopefully I'll be okay."

"Yes, but if you need anything, I'm here."

He walked me to the door to leave, where I was faced with Levi, leaning against the wall.

"Levi, I'm sorry. Miss Marie needed to borrow my portal mirror. I wanted to give her some time with her family," the king said.

Levi stared at me intensely. I could feel his demand to connect my eyes to his, but I disregarded it. He didn't have the mark anymore, nor did he smell like Jessamine. He must have taken a five-hour bath to remove the stink. A part of me was relieved that he did, but another part still burned with anger at the sight of him.

I turned to the king. "Thank you again, Your Majesty."

"Markos." He grinned.

"Markos. Have a good night." I smiled.

Giving a slight bow, I turned, ignoring Levi and his glare, and made my way back to the academic wing.

# SIXTEEN

## MARIE

*I* bought a new cloak from the store. Keeping Levi's was stupid. Even if my creature loved his scent, I shouldn't have paraded around the palace in his cloak, but a part of me liked that. It made me feel like I was his, which I wasn't, nor would I be, so I needed to get a new cloak. It wasn't as fine or as warm, but it would have to do for now.

When lessons began, I went to get breakfast, deciding to skip class again tonight. With Mr. I-would-rather-read-at-a-party as my partner, I was sure he wouldn't let us fail. Was it reckless to trust him with my grade, yes, but I wasn't worried, since the last two days we were just going over basic history that everyone should already know.

Heading back to my room after eating, my plan for the day was to cuddle up in my bed and maybe watch the winter night through my window. As I approached my door, I found another tray of food from Levi laid out for me. I grumbled, pushing the tray out of the way with my foot so I could get to my room.

"Is the food not good?" I almost jumped out of my skin, turning to see Levi leaning against the wall.

"Where the fuck did you just come from?"

He disappeared into shadow, then reappeared. *Magic*. Of course, he knew how to do magic. "So, you're going to spy on me now?"

"You weren't eating the food," he said, ignoring my question.

"I ate yesterday." I turned away from him and put my key in the door. All my hairs stood up as the lock clicked, my body growing tight at his nearness. I sighed, turning around to see him inches away from me. "What, Levi?"

"Why were you in my father's office this morning?"

Crossing my arms, I huffed. "Why?"

"Did you fuck him?"

"Do you not have a nose?" He seriously didn't need to ask. He could smell it like I smelled Jessamine on him.

"He can hide his scent with magic." His eyes searched mine frantically for the truth, his face tight and body tense.

"Fuck off. I didn't fuck your father."

"He asked you to call him Markos, and you did."

My brows pulled together. "Yeah, he probably did that to make me feel a sense of comfort. I had just spent an hour in his office bawling over the fact that I hate being here and how it's mostly your fault."

He stared at me, his breath harsh, eyes intense. His silent stare gave me enough time to decide I didn't want to deal with him right now, so I turned around, walked into my room, and slammed the door on his prodding eyes.

I spent the rest of the night in my room. Levi sent food again at lunch, and I decided I would rather starve than take another thing from him. After the class was dismissed, there was a knock on my door. The servants who brought the food always announced their presence, so I assumed it was someone I wanted to ignore. They didn't get the message and continued knocking. I tried to ignore them, but they wouldn't go away. It had been half an hour, and I thought their arm was going to fall off.

I groaned, loud enough for the person on the other side of the door to hear, then I got up. The second I opened the door, I immediately tried to close it, but Levi wedged his foot into the frame to prevent me. He didn't even wince at the pain. Bastard.

"You can't ignore me. We are school partners."

"Yes, *school* partners, as in we don't need to see each other outside of them," I replied.

"You stopped going."

"For one fucking day."

"If you fail, I fail. Then my father will get pissed and make us run around the outside of the castle in only shorts for half the night."

I frowned. "He really made you do that?"

"Yes, it is very unpleasant. So I would really not like to fail."

"It was only one day, Levi."

"Just open the fucking door," he growled.

"It is open," I said, pushing it against his foot.

"Marie." He used his commanding voice that made my insides tingle.

I gritted my teeth, hating what he could do to my body without even touching it. I stared at him. I knew he wasn't going to leave. He just stood out here, knocking on my door for thirty minutes.

I let out an annoyed breath. "Fine." I opened the door, leaving it wide open, so I wouldn't have to be trapped in here with him and his sexy-as-fuck voice.

Levi walked in, carrying a load of books. Going over to the desk, he set them down. He lingered for a moment, his eyes scanning the desk. It took me a second to realize he was reading Kolvin's messages.

I snatched the pad off the desk, hiding it in the desk drawer. "Do you even understand privacy? Or how to mind your own fucking business?" I snapped at him.

His eyes connected with mine. "You are my business."

"For school. That's it."

His jaw clenched as his stare bore into my eyes, trying to get me to yield and get caught in his web. I ripped my eyes from him and pointed to the books, avoiding getting swept up in his poisonous looks. "You brought books?"

"This is all the work we went over in class today and yesterday. I highlighted the important stuff. There's a quiz over all we've learned so far tomorrow. We will go over it, then I'll test you."

"I will just read it and you can leave." I pointed to the door.

"I need to make sure you know it."

"I already know most of whatever she has been teaching this week."

"We started talking about the basic manifestations of magic. Do you even know how to call your magic?" he chided.

"No, but I'll learn. I'm guessing by reading these books. Thanks for bringing them. Have a good night." My voice was anything but nice, and I gave him a *fuck you* smile, to top it off.

He sighed and softened, throwing me off balance. "Look, I'm sorry. I didn't know you'd react that way."

I looked away from him. His apology seemed genuine, but I couldn't trust my gut when it came to him. "I couldn't control it.

You two smell really bad together, and it made my senses go crazy. Sorry about that. Maybe take a bath after you fuck your whores."

I grabbed a book off the desk and started to flip through it, deflecting the conversation. I noticed that not only did he highlight everything, but he also wrote little notes for me in the margins. I wanted to smile at the gesture, but I kept it to myself.

"Marie. Jessamine and I are nothing."

"I don't care what you are," I said, pretending to find something interesting in the book.

He pushed the book away, drawing my eyes to his, a spark flaring to life in my soul. "We are nothing."

"Okay." I swallowed roughly, my body heating. We were so close right now; my brain was short-circuiting. Our hands were almost touching. The air between us charged with tension—thick, heavy, and obtrusive.

I pulled away, setting the book on the desk. Somehow, when I was around him, I managed to be uncomfortable and comfortable at the same time, fucking my brain up even more. "Thanks for the books, I'll read them tonight. I don't want to fail either."

"Marie, I've been studying magic since I could read. I know you hate having me as your partner, but I'm the best choice. Let me help you study tonight. I know those books better than I know my own dick."

I giggled at that, and he smiled. His canines sharp and prominent, accentuating his angular face, his midnight eyes sparkling with stars. I turned, avoiding the way my heart squeezed when I looked at him. If we stayed in this cramped room, I was destined to fall into his web. "Fine, but not here."

He looked around the small room. "Why not here?"

*There is a bed in here.*

I couldn't deny that a deeper, more primal part of me wanted Levi, and I couldn't let myself get swept up in him again. The pain would be too great if he hurt me.

"It's just small. Not really good if we are going to be switching from book to book and writing notes." *Why do I sound like I have no idea how to study?*

He examined the room for a bit before looking back at me. "Okay, I know a place."

We walked far away from the academic wing. The farther we got, the more anxious I grew. I didn't see why we needed to study outside the academic wing. There was the library and the cafeteria, two very public places. Levi didn't seem to notice my inner panic. He walked like he normally does, making me practically run to catch up. I loved that even though right now I was dealing with nice Levi, he still managed to be a dick in minute ways. I almost smiled at the fact, but the burn in my legs kept a slight grimace on my face instead.

He literally took three steps at a time. It was normal for a fae to take two depending on their height, but I was seriously short. I didn't even know why. I asked my mother how tall my father was, and she said he was the same height as her. Meaning they were both tall and I came out a short fucker who could never take three stairs at a time even if I wanted to.

We made it to a room that was sealed with magic. Levi took a knife out, calling his magic as he cut his palm and placed his hand on the door.

"Isn't that going to stain the door?" I asked.

"It's magically preserved. Maybe you would know that if you spent some time in class."

"I don't need to go to class if you already know everything there is to know about magic, *Your Highness*."

He opened the door to a room that was *white*. It shocked me for a second because nothing in this castle was white. Everything was dark and cozy, but this room was light and bright. There were huge windows that lined the walls. If it was daytime, you would be able to see the sun set and rise from inside this room. In the middle of the area, there were two light pink couches with white painted wood and a glass coffee table that had herbs growing under them. By one of the windows, there was a little picnic bench also painted white. The place was astonishingly beautiful, but the most beautiful part was the pink roses. They grew everywhere throughout the room, filling the air with their sweet aroma, the smell relaxing my body, reminding me of my mother—pink roses were her favorite flower.

"Wow," I breathed.

"My father made this greenhouse when he became king two hundred years ago. He doesn't let anyone in here except the botanist who takes care of the plants. I think he used to come in here to think when he was younger, but now, he rarely even comes to this part of the castle."

"Why? It's beautiful."

"This is the queen's quarters, and my father likes to stick his dick into a new female every so often." Levi eyed me accusingly.

"Levi, I haven't fucked your father. I wouldn't."

"Yeah, because of your male who you love so much."

I stared at him, unamused. "I'm here to study, not for you to accuse me of fucking your father. If you're going to do that all night, I'll just leave."

He pointed to the small bench that looked out the windows.

I sat, looking out to the winter wonderland that was illuminated by the moon's glow. Instead of taking the seat across from me like a normal person would, he sat right next to me. He was close enough for our knees to touch. I moved mine away, but he widened his legs, reconnecting us. I wanted to get up and move to the other side, but I didn't want to let him know how much his nearness bothered me.

"The quiz is over fae history, the use of magic, and the basic manifestation of magic. If we can call upon our magic, we will get bonus points because some fae may not be at the age to do it, but I'm confident I can show you."

Smart, nerdy Levi was probably my favorite of the Levis that I had met so far. He went over the basic fae history, though I knew most of it, Levi knew more. I could tell history was his favorite subject. He could talk all day about it. He knew way too many fun facts. He even started debating with himself over the causes of some of the pinnacle fae wars. I let him ramble, just enjoying his enthusiasm. Unfortunately for him, I had to stop him at a point and direct him back to what was going to be on the quiz. He gave me a look like I just took his favorite toy away. The look made my heart squeeze. I wanted to let him talk for days, but I needed to know what would be on the test.

After fae history, we went over basic fae magic. Seelie magic mostly dealt with light. Their magic could heat things, and some Seelie could even create fire with a snap of their fingers. They could cast light beams too.

Unseelie magic was the opposite. They could control shadows and freeze things. I learned that the forever seasons of the separate territories weren't controlled by one person. The collective energies of the same race of fae in one place made the forever seasons. If we weren't separated, the seasons would be normal.

When the fae used their magic together, they were more powerful. No one really had an answer to why our magic, when bound, could create things like portals. It was theorized that since the magic was fully balanced, it could basically do anything because our magic broke down to bending light and manipulating matter, but there wasn't any proper research on it, so it was just a theory. To prove that, it would require Unseelie and Seelie fae to join together without a diamond wall to separate them.

"You know a lot about magic," I remarked, in awe of how much stuff was in that beautiful brain.

"My father had me start studying when I was young. Ms. May was my tutor. She hated it because she was an upper-level teacher who had to teach a bratty six-year-old prince who just wanted to play. She would get so mad at me sometimes and threaten to quit, but my father would just pay her more and bang her every once in a while to keep her happy. I think I was twelve when I walked in on him fucking her. I didn't talk to either of them for a week because like most twelve-year-old boys, I had a crush on her."

I grinned. "No wonder you're so afraid everyone will fuck your father."

"Not everyone." He gave me a look.

I evaded his lingering looks and changed the subject. "Why are you even in our class if you already know how to do magic?"

"My father wants me to make friends." He said that as if the thought pained him.

I covered my mouth to hold in my laugh.

"It's not that I am incapable of having them; I'm just not interested."

I laughed harder. "You are the grumpiest person I know. Does your father force you to go to parties too?"

He didn't answer and his lips thinned. I laughed so hard tears built in the corner of my eyes. "Levi, parties are supposed to be fun. You know you wouldn't be stuck up all the time if you listen to your father and let loose every once in a while."

"I do." He squirmed, his cheeks reddening.

I leaned into his face, getting close enough for our noses to touch but not quite. "When was the last time you weren't in control?"

"I'm always in control." His eyes shone with intimidation, making me smirk.

*How do you like it?* I sat back. "How boring."

"I'm not boring."

"Okay, whatever you say, *Your Highness*." He tried to hold his grumpy act but failed and cracked a grin. That smile was the most amazing part of him. Maybe because he always seemed too serious to smile. My hand reached out to touch it, but I stopped myself, remembering the last time we touched.

Staring into his eyes I wondered, *Why him? Why do I want to ruin my life for him? I don't even know him.*

Midair, I dropped my hand onto my lap. Smiling awkwardly, I tucked a curl behind my ear. "So, calling upon magic? How do we do that?"

He quirked a brow. "Are you hungry?"

My stomach took that time to rumble from hunger. I had skipped lunch and was overdue for a meal. "Uhm, yeah." I blushed.

"Let's take a break and get some food. I can have the kitchen cook you anything you want."

The fact that he kept trying to feed me made me uncomfortable. My creature absolutely loved it, but my brain thought it was kind of weird to just take his fancy food and not expect he'd want something in return. "Why don't we just go to the cafeteria? It already has food prepared."

His expression turned concerning. "Do you not like the food I give you?"

"It's lovely. I just want to eat regular food."

He gave me a tight smile. "Okay." He stood and held out his hand to help me. I refrained from touching him. If he was ticked off by my rejection, he didn't show it. In fact, I think this was the longest Levi had stayed in a good mood around me. The change of pace with him was jarring. I was still hesitant to expect that he wouldn't go back to being the brooding prince I had known him to be.

Everyone stared at us as we entered the cafeteria. I could feel their eyes on me, but I tried to ignore it. We got food and found a seat near the giant windows. Levi, again, sat right next to me.

"Why are they staring at us?" I whispered.

"I never come here." He put a spoonful of soup into his mouth. "The food is shit."

I nodded in agreement. After having one meal made by his royal chefs, I didn't think I would ever be able to look at other food the same.

I shivered while we ate. Sitting by the windows was a terrible decision. We were too far away from the huge fireplaces, and I still hadn't adjusted to the weather. Plus, my new cloak barely kept me warm enough.

Levi pulled the hem of my cloak through his fingers, studying it. "What did you do with mine?"

I tugged the cloak out of his grasp. "It's in my room. We can pick it up if you want it back."

"Is there something wrong with it?" His eyes swirled with an emotion I couldn't read.

"No. I just thought you'd want it back."

"You can keep it." His fingers went back to playing with the cloak.

"No, I don't want to put you out of a cloak," I said, trying not to shiver as I spoke.

His hands found the ties, and he gently unlaced them, removing the cloak. "Levi," I whispered. Then he took his cloak off and wrapped it around me. His scent—burnt pine—filled my senses, and I purred. I fucking *purred*. I didn't mean to, but I did, and I couldn't take it back. Levi took my hair and pulled it out of the cloak, careful not to touch my skin. His eyes lingered for a moment on my mark, but he didn't say anything about it.

He played with my hair until he was satisfied, then he looked at me with a look I can only describe as male satisfaction. "You can't keep this one. My father gave it to me for my birthday last year and he has a thing about presents. You can wear it for now and we will stop by your room and get the other."

I tried to look annoyed, but it was hard to when I knew he fucking heard me purr.

I toyed with the hem of the cloak. It was much finer than the other one. This one was lined with silver thread and had twice as much fur. "This one is nice."

His eyes flared with what I thought was panic, and he took a deep breath in. "I suppose you could keep this one."

I couldn't help but smile. "Levi, the other one is fine."

"You like this one more." He talked to me like it made total sense for him to give me this cloak he got as a gift.

"You don't have to give me your cloak in the first place."

"I do," he said it as if it pained him not to.

"Why?"

He twirled a curl in his fingers. "You know why."

I didn't. I didn't understand why he insisted that I take his cloak. Nor did I understand why he sometimes acted like this with me.

I was about to argue with him, but we were interrupted. "Marie."

Rage filled my body as I slowly turned my head to see Jessamine standing near our table. I gritted my teeth to hold back the urge to jump over the table and rip her throat out. Levi slid his hand over my thigh to hold me back, then he looked at Jessamine, which caused me to growl.

*What the fuck is going on with me?*

"Jess, go away," Levi demanded.

Her face contorted before she opened her mouth to speak, but Levi spoke again.

"Jessamine, I am your prince."

She stared daggers at him, hesitating, then huffed and left.

Levi turned to me, tears building behind my eyes. "Marie."

"It's fine," I said, blinking them back and shaking off his hand. "I don't know why I even forgave you." I started to clean up my food. Unfortunately, I lost my appetite. "Let's just go and finish preparing for the quiz."

We made our way back to the greenhouse and sat on one of the couches placed in the middle of the room. He read to me the basics of calling your magic from the textbook and I ignored him.

Why did I forgive him so easily? Why did I react like that upon seeing Jessamine? I looked down at Levi's cloak. Why am I still wearing this?

"You should forgive her."

"Why? She stabbed me in the back, and you helped." My tone came out flat and harsh.

"I pursued her." His words punched a hole through my heart.

I turned my head and bit my cheek to hold back the tears that were starting to blur my vision. "Great."

He moved closer to me. "She just fucked me because I asked her, and she marked me for the same reason."

"So, you just wanted to get off," I said, my head turned, my throat burning.

"Yes." His voice was clipped.

"Great."

Levi placed his hand on my shoulder and turned me to face him. His face was riddled with guilt. A part of me wanted to forgive him, to pull him close and never let him go. Another part of me was so hurt beyond measure that I wanted to punish him for hurting me. The two sides warred with each other as I stared at him. The latter won out, and I pulled away.

"Levi, I don't know why I'm reacting this way. I can't control it. I feel like I'm going crazy. I shouldn't feel this way. I don't want you."

He closed his eyes for a moment. "I know, just—" He took a breath. "Just know that Jessamine only slept with me because she just wanted to have fun. It meant nothing to her, and she wasn't thinking about you, nor was she trying to hurt you." But he was. He said it earlier, didn't he? He said he didn't know I would react that way. He wanted me to react.

Enraged, I took his cloak off and threw it at him. Then, taking mine, I walked out. I felt stupid. I didn't know why I was getting wrapped around him like this, but I hated it. I hated who I was here, a crying fucking babe who allowed a male affect her every emotion. Not to mention it was a male I'd known for a week. That wasn't who I was. I was a 'go with the flow' girl who was in love with her best friend. I wanted to stop whatever it was that was going on with me and Levi, but that feeling in my chest pulled me toward him. My heart yearned to be near him. I wished I could just rip it out because it was really ruining my life.

# SEVENTEEN

## CORIVINA
### 197 YEARS AGO.

*I* spent the next two years in the darkest parts my conscious could find, absorbed in the shadows my mind created. My routine was quite the same every day—get lost in the garden at work, then go to my room at the inn and drink myself to sleep. Wake up and repeat.

The witch was right; I would see her again. The bitch had good wine. Ginger, the witch, and I developed a bond. Not what one would call friendship, but one where she tolerated me and my terrible moods, and I kept paying her for her wine.

I was sitting at her table drinking her amazing orange infused concoction while she assisted a customer. I only spent an hour here every so often, stocking up on wine and chatting to her about how everyone and everything sucked. She listened, but then she would start lecturing me on the gods and their plans and I knew it was time for me to leave.

As I tipped the wine bottle to my mouth to get another delicious sip, the bottle was wrenched out of my hand. "Hey!" I whined. "Give that back!"

"You're cut off." Ginger's gold eyes bore into mine, offering no room for argument.

"I paid for that!" I growled.

"The gods said you're cut off," she said as she dumped the wine into one of her plants.

"The *gods* can fuck off."

"Corivina, you've had two years to drink yourself into oblivion and annoy the fuck out of me. Granted fae, you needed it after the hell you have gone through, but today is the day. The gods have spoken."

I threw my head back and groaned. "Seriously? Today. Today is the day they have spoken?"

"Yes." She crossed her arms.

I mimicked her position. "What do they have to say?"

"That you need to get your shit together and start living your life."

"I am alive, am I not?" I gestured down at my alive body.

"You know what I mean, fae. Go home, bathe, and then do something."

I rolled my eyes. Fucking *witches*. "What should I do?"

"There is a festival tonight. Maybe you'll meet someone," she supplied.

"Like who?"

"Like a man?"

I wrinkled my nose. "A human? Ew, no thank you."

"A *male*," she corrected, her jaw tightening with her annoyance for me.

"Why would I want to meet a male? They are terrible beings who only use you for their own needs."

"Corivina, it is time to let it go."

Rage bubbled within me. She knew what I had gone through over the last few years. She had listened to it all and was there at my lowest of lows. She knew why I had to drink. She knew the shadows that lurked in my mind. She may not know everything because of the deal, but she knew enough to know I would never be able to just let it fucking go. "I can't."

"You can, and you will." Her eyes flickered slightly with her powers. "Now please get out of my shop. You aren't the best for business."

I grumbled but got up. I hated witches and their connection to the divine, but I wasn't going to ignore it. You didn't fuck with the gods. They were nasty little cunts who would fuck you over if you didn't listen to what they said. They were a lot like humans, acting all high and mighty, but really, they were just as flawed as the rest of us.

So, they wanted me to bathe and go to some festival. A festival that was destined to have wine. Fine, I'd go, but if I still woke up and felt like shit the next morning, I would continue my wallowing.

At the inn, I pulled on a white sundress and some simple sandals. This was one of my only dresses that wasn't covered in dirt from the garden. Honestly, I spent more time in the garden than was probably necessary, but it was the only place I found solace, and I finally mixed the perfect salve to prevent the burns, so I didn't mind spending my days in dirt, nor did I mind messing up my dresses.

Most of the dresses I owned were gifts from Markos anyway or were bought with his money. I still had most of what he had given me, and I rarely spent coin on anything other than wine and this room at the inn.

Ginger told me I should move out of here because this inn was a huge reminder of what had happened to me. Which was exactly the reason I kept it. I never wanted someone to betray my trust. I didn't want to feel the pain I felt ever again. This room was a reminder to always keep myself in check.

Brushing my hair out, I stared at my eyes in the mirror. They used to be a brownish black like coffee, but heartbreak and trauma have left them a cold, lifeless black. I wonder if they will ever return to their original color or if I will always be dead inside.

Finishing up my hair, I parted it down the middle and then left for the festival. The fae were celebrating the Summer Solstice—the longest day of the year. The Seelies' favorite day of the year. Literally every shop had gone all out, flowers decorated everything, fae lights and banners lined the shops. The fountain in the middle of the square even had flowers floating in the water with lights at the bottom to illuminate it. If I wasn't annoyed with all the festivity and cheer, I might even appreciate the beauty of it all.

I stopped at a stall that was selling ale. It wasn't wine, but alcohol was alcohol. It was the first stall I had come across that was selling it, and I wouldn't be able to get through this night without something to aid me.

I paid for the ale and took a drink before almost spitting it out. Swallowing quickly, I gagged at the piss-like aftertaste.

"Alirick's stuff is better." A smooth, rich voice floated through my ears.

I flinched, taking a step away to get a look at the male who violated my personal space. Toffee brown hair, a close shaved beard, and the softest blue eyes. His eyes reminded me of a calm sea, comforting and safe.

The male gave me a warm smile that did things to my insides, and I found myself smiling back.

The action alone shocked me enough to reach up and touch my face to check if the grin was really there.

The male's eyebrows pulled together. "What? Do I have something on my face?"

I snorted. "No."

His warm blue eyes glinted. "I know you." His smile turned sensual and sent shivers down my spine.

"I doubt you do. I've never seen you in my life."

He gasped and covered his heart with his hand. "You wound me. How could you forget our first meeting?"

"I didn't forget something that never happened," I remarked.

"Three years ago, lunar eclipse. You were wearing a pink dress."

Three years ago, Markos and I broke up on a lunar eclipse. It was the worst night of my life at the time, but I did remember meeting a male that made my insides flutter. "You're the male that was going to kidnap me."

"If I recall, you implied I was a kidnapper. Which obviously, I am not."

"You're not a kidnapper but stalking isn't ruled out," I chimed.

He rubbed his face in frustration before grinning. "How so?"

"Well, I haven't seen you since that night, but you somehow ended up in the same small town as me three years later? Seems like you're stalking me."

His laugh rolled through my body in sensual waves. "I've lived here my whole life. In fact, if I'm not mistaken, you are born Unseelie."

"I was. So?"

"*So*, it would be *you* stalking *me*." He smirked.

I laughed, then. "I wish that was why I was stuck in this town."

"So, if not to stalk my beautiful face, then why are you here?"

I studied the ground, unsure what I should say in reply. I didn't want this conversation to end. It was the first time I really laughed or smiled since Markos. This male made me feel good. Though I lived in the forever summer, my insides were as cold and dead. This male was warm, and I wanted to sink into his warmth.

I decided to go with a short truth. "A male."

"Ah, I remember you were marked."

My muscles tightened as the image of my marred body came to mind. "I was."

"And now you're not."

I subconsciously rubbed my neck where Markos's mark used to be and shivered. That was something I would never want on my neck again. "Yeah, I'm not with him anymore."

The male didn't poke; he just bit his lip, his eyes perusing my body for a second before he held his hand out. "Darius Foxglove."

I grasped his hand and the heat of him warming my cold limbs. His palm was tough and calloused, and I wondered how his rough hand would feel on my soft body. I hadn't been with another since Markos. I didn't think I could, but it didn't stop my attraction to this male. "Corivina Snow."

He let go of my hand and wrapped his arm around my shoulder. I flinched and tensed slightly, but his vanilla scent filled my senses, calming and relaxing me a bit.

"Let's get better ale?" he asked.

I smiled again. "Yeah, okay."

# EIGHTEEN

## MARIE

*I* stood outside the cafeteria, waiting for Jessamine. I didn't have to wait long before sky-blue eyes and red lipstick appeared in my vision. She looked wary of me. I was leaning against the wall, arms crossed, my eyes only on her, so I probably looked like I was plotting her murder. I straightened up, giving her a small smile to show I had come in peace.

She took this as a good sign and immediately wrapped herself around me, causing me to stiffen. The beast inside me hadn't forgiven her, but my beast was hellbent on fucking Levi, who one second loved to cause us pain, then the next, dress us up like his doll, so I really didn't think my beast was a trusted ally.

"Marie, I'm so sorry. I didn't mean to hurt you. Levi asked and I didn't really think it through. I was tipsy and horny, and Gregor was getting on my nerves with his jealousy. I just—I'm so sorry." Tears lined her lashes.

I softened and embraced her as she cried into my shoulder. "I never wanted to hurt you," she whimpered, and I pulled her tighter into me. I had grown a space for her in my heart over the past few days and seeing her cry like this made my heart ache.

"Jess, I forgive you. Levi is a dick. He slept with you to hurt me. Also, *I'm sorry*, I shouldn't have called you a whore. You're not one and it was uncalled for me to say."

She pulled back enough for me to see her face and wiped her eyes. "I totally forgive you, bunny. If it makes you feel better, just know it was probably the worst sex I ever had. Normally, Levi's great. He's distant but not a bad time at all. This time, he seemed like he didn't even want to be there. He tried to make me come as fast as he possibly could, then he pulled out of me right after I did and asked me to mark him. He hadn't come and I thought he just wanted a venom boost. You know, when you bite someone so they can get the effects of the venom, but then they remove it. He didn't come as I bit him, instead, he ran to the bathroom and started throwing—Ow! Marie… you're crushing me."

While she was speaking, anger rose within, blinding me from my actions. I realized I was digging my claws into her skin. Snapping out of it, I quickly took a step back from her. "Sorry, I just… I don't need to know the details."

She looped her arm through mine. "Noted. Let's eat, shall we?"

We got breakfast and made our way to the table where Gregor and Finch were already eating.

"Look who's back," Gregor said through his food.

"Can it, Gregor. I like Marie, and if you want to make me happy, you will be nice to her," Jessamine stated.

I smirked at Gregor. "It's okay, Jess. He just thinks I'm trying to steal his girl." I sat in front of him.

"Is that right, bunny?" Jessamine put her arm around my shoulders and whispered in my ear loud enough for him and Finch to hear. "If he was a smart male, he would try to have us both."

I had forgotten how Jessamine can make anyone aroused in seconds. Mine and Gregor's scents changed, and Finch spoke up.

"Jess, if you are going to fuck both of them, can you not do it while I'm eating?"

She removed her arm from me and smirked sensually. "Finch, I was going to let you join, but I guess you'll just have to watch. Shame, I've heard things."

Finch choked on his food.

"Jess, you're going to make everyone in this room go wild," I said.

"It's not my fault all of you secretly want to fuck me."

"I have fucked you plenty of times," Gregor stated, getting his arousal in check. I, on the other hand, had not. Thoughts of me fucking Jessamine and Gregor kept rolling in my brain. They were both hot. Jessamine with her soft curves and Gregor with his warrior's body. No one would pass that up.

"Yeah, well then, that means I need to fuck Marie enough so you'll be tied. Isn't that right, bunny?" Jessamine replied.

Gregor gave me a look of pure hatred. I smiled and let my arousal linger as I stared into his black eyes. "Yeah, but only if he watches."

That caused his scowl to drop.

Finch stood up. "I'm fucking leaving."

Jessamine and I burst into giggles as he stalked away. "I'm going to get some cinnamon rolls, you want some?" she asked.

"No, I'm fine."

"Okay, be right back." She kissed me on the cheek, leaving red lipstick on my face.

I rubbed at it as I realized I was left alone with Gregor. Blowing out a breath, I spoke, "Look, I don't want Jessamine."

"I know. You want the prince, just like everyone else."

"I don't want the prince."

"You do. Jessamine stayed with me the last two nights crying about it. She told me about how she messed things up and how you reacted. Brutal. You can deny it all you want, but you want

Levi, and he wants you. I saw the way he acted with you last night. He has never acted that way with a female, ever. Though, I doubt a female has rejected him. They all think it's an honor to fuck the prince. All he has to do is ask and they will get on their knees and start blowing him right then. Honestly, if you really don't want him, fuck him. He probably is just working this hard because you're something he can't have." Gregor leaned in. "Then when he's done with you, I would love to take you up on your offer, except I won't be just watching." He winked at me.

I shivered, clenching my legs together. "Why is everyone trying to fuck me?"

"We are fae, and you are new."

I nodded. "That makes a lot of sense. You know, you are very smart for someone, who most of the time, acts like a dumb warrior brute."

"Yeah, got to keep them guessing." He grinned.

"Sure, you do."

Jessamine came back with two cinnamon rolls, one for her and one for Gregor. She didn't ask if he wanted one, but he took it and ate it like it was the best thing he'd ever received. Fae were weird with food. If someone fed you, it normally meant they were trying to court you in primal fae terms.

I finished my food and left them to themselves and headed to the classroom early to talk to the professor. She was sitting at her desk, preparing for the quiz this morning. "Ms. May?"

"Yes. Marie, is it?"

"Yeah, I just wanted to ask you if there is any way I could switch partners with someone else?" It was clear to me Levi just picked me so he could fuck me, and if he didn't threaten to ruin everything within me, I could probably stand it for the next year, but Levi had too great of an effect over me. He could make me come from the slightest touch. He made me burn with desire, but he also made me burn with a rage strong enough to kill. He had already cut into my heart great enough to leave a scar. If I got involved with him, he would tear me into a thousand pieces. He would just use me like Jessamine or any of his other females, then throw me away when he got bored. I would get too attached to him and the pain of being used like that would consume me.

"Marie, the whole point of having a partner is that you are supposed to learn to work with them despite your differences."

"I know, but my partner is Prince Levington," I said, hoping she will remember how much of a dick he was to her.

"I am aware. You should be excited he is your partner. His father is grooming him to be a fine king, which means he is the best student I have."

"But he's—"

"I can't change the rule for you. You are partners with the prince whether you like it or not. It's only for a year. Just—" She paused and looked behind me.

I didn't need to turn around to know who was there.

*Seriously, today is the day he decides to be early to class?*

I breathed in before turning to find his midnight eyes glistening with pain. He looked gutted, and it broke something in me to see him like that. My creature wanted to go to him and hold him. I had no idea what to do. While I was warring between my beast and myself, Levi turned and stiffly walked to our table. His features were fixed into his normal void of emotions, but I could tell it was a mask.

I sat down next to him. "Hi."

He ignored me, staring intensely at the chalkboard, like he was trying to drill holes into the wall. His leg bounced up and down impatiently. His whole body taut with tension. Eventually as time seemed to stretch, he started to tap his pen on the desk.

"Levi," I tried again.

His body tensed up even more, but he continued to ignore me. I couldn't imagine what he was thinking. I could see his mask cracking and it was fucking painful to watch. It felt wrong to see someone like him breaking. I didn't want to care that my rejection hurt him, but his pain eviscerated me. I'd rather him be angry or bossy than be an anxious mess. A part of me wished it was me hurting instead.

*Hurt me. Hurt me, Levi. Take your pain out on me.* I wanted to tell him.

I felt a tear slip from my face, and I turned away from him, so he didn't see how I was reacting to him. I wanted to sever whatever was happening to us. I didn't want this connection. Unfortunately, my heart disagreed. My heart didn't realize how much of a bad idea he was. I also barely knew him. No one should have the power over us that Levi had. He just wanted me. He didn't care if it would destroy everything I was, crumble everything I wanted. He was used to people yielding to his wants. This time, though, he wouldn't get what he wanted. I couldn't allow it.

I needed everything to just work out the way I had planned. Get good grades, get a job at the Seelie Palace, go home, marry Kolvin. Though I was sure that the last part wasn't going to happen. Gregor was right; I wanted Levi. I couldn't deny that. It wasn't fair to Kolvin to be my backup. He is my best friend, and I did love him but not the way I was supposed to.

When class began, Ms. May handed out the quizzes. We were supposed to do the quizzes as a pair, but when we received ours, Levi took it and started filling in answers. He finished within minutes, got up, and practically sprinted to the front to turn it in.

By the time I reached the desk, Ms. May was grading the test. It was multiple choice, so it only took her a minute to look over everything. "Good job, guys. Not one question was missed." She looked up from the desk. "Now, for the extra credit. Levi, I already know you can manifest magic, but Marie, did you want to give it a try?"

"Uh, I don't know how to."

She nodded. "That's fine, I'll just give half since Levi does. Next quiz, you'll have the opportunity to try again. You guys are free to leave. Classes are done for the week."

Levi bolted out the room. I thanked Ms. May, then chased after him.

"Levi," I called to him.

He ignored me and kept walking.

"Levi, wait."

He didn't slow, walking at a brutal pace. Eventually, I stopped chasing after him. There was nothing I could really do. He didn't want to talk to me. I couldn't barge into his room and demand that he listen to me, so I turned and made my way back to my room.

# NINETEEN

## MARIE

The weekend was pure fae chaos. Since there was no class, the faelings partied the whole weekend. I went with Jessamine, but only had a few drinks. I didn't want to have more guilt on my conscience by giving in to my nature and fucking everything up. I knew I was going to end things with Kolvin, but I still wore his mark, and I didn't want to disrespect him more than I already had.

Levi didn't attend the party at all. I knew he wouldn't, but it didn't stop me from searching him out and seeking those eyes. I knew I shouldn't take it personally. He only goes to parties if he is forced to, but I wanted to see him. I didn't like how we had left things, and I just needed to make sure we were on a good page. The feeling to do so was so strong within me I almost went to the royal wing in search of him.

This week, we would begin physical training. Every dusk, we would train and every night we would practice magic. This was how it would be for the rest of the year. The first week was to catch us up on basic fae history if we missed that in our prior learnings.

Rising early the night classes resumed was easy for me. Since I was being responsible, I went to bed fairly early. Jessamine teased me the entire time, but today, she looked like she got trampled by a horse.

"Ugh," Jessamine groaned next to me.

I rubbed her back as we sat waiting for training to begin on the gym floor. Her head rested between her legs and her hair was pulled away from her face tugged into a tiny little ponytail, her hair so short the bottom hairs not able to be pulled within. She wore no makeup, and her face was pale from her hangover, but to me, she was still the most beautiful female.

Gregor sat next to her. "Jessamine, come on, we barely got drunk last night."

"Fuck off, Gregor," she snapped. "Not everyone has a perfect fae body that heals in seconds."

He kissed her on the cheek. "Thanks for calling me perfect."

Jessamine grumbled but leaned into him when his arm came around her shoulders.

Adjusting myself in the tights that had been issued for training, I thought about how whoever made these didn't think about how some of us have curves. The only other option was spandex shorts, and I wasn't wearing shorts in this frigid place. I paired the pants with a black tank top in case I got hot during the workouts.

Gregor and most of all the other males wore a black shirt and shorts. The shorts were form-fitting, leaving nothing to the imagination. I couldn't help but stare at Gregor's pants. I didn't see why Jessamine kept him on the hook. The male was packing, he was beautiful and completely devoted to her. I couldn't believe I even challenged him. If I were a male, he would have probably beaten me to a pulp.

Levi entered, stealing my attention away from Gregor.

My eyes went straight to his shorts, and I sucked in a breath. I couldn't help from biting my lip as heat unfurled in me. Our eyes met, and I expected him to give me his sexy smirk, but he looked away, the familiar hollow feeling settling over me whenever he did that.

Our training instructor walked into the room. He was pure fae warrior brute. His hair was shaved. He had muscles on his muscles, and his face had a scowl so deep he had wrinkles, which were very uncommon among the fae.

"Evening," he said. "I am Mr. Vandeer, the Commander of the Unseelie Army. Unfortunately, that somehow means I should be training you halfwits who don't even want to be here. I will be showing you the basics of battle magic for the next year. If you are skilled in the trade or are too dumb to perform skilled magic, you will be with me for the three years that follow. Then I will really teach you. For now, I'm just going to torture you because the king has nothing better for me to do since fae are *the happiest we could be,* making my job useless."

I decided then that I definitely didn't want to learn battle magic. My father always tried to make me his little warrior princess, and I attempted it but I hated every second of it. I would rather fight with my mind than with my fists. Also, I had claws so punching almost always resulted in me accidentally stabbing myself and it 'wasn't correct' for me to use my claws to attack my opponents, which just pissed me off. I was born with them. I should be able to use them.

"First a demonstration," Mr. Vandeer spoke again. "You may know my son, Gregor." I looked over to the said male. The second Mr. Vandeer had entered, he became serious, losing his normal, easy-going mood and becoming the warrior his body was molded to be. His father being the Commander of the Unseelie Army made sense. Gregor would be a great leader. He knew how to laugh, but he also knew how to be serious, and he made others believe he was an idiot, but that was a misdirect.

Gregor raised and stepped up to the mat. "Father." He got into a fighting position, ready for his father to attack.

"Stop that, boy." Mr. Vandeer waved his hand in his face. "I'm not sparring with you. I want you on your back and you know all my moves too fucking well. If I go up against you, you'll embarrass me in front of all your peers and you'll go around for the rest of the week with an overinflated ego. If you're going to be taking over in the next ten years and finally give me the retirement I desperately need, you need to be humbled." He looked through the room, then smiled. "Prince Levington."

Every muscle in Gregor's body tensed, and he slowly closed his eyes. I could tell that was probably the last name he wanted to be called out. I couldn't see why. If you asked me to guess who would win in a brawl between Levi or Gregor, I would guess Gregor. The latter had more muscle and that warrior's body. Levi was slim, his body was still toned and muscular, but he carried the grace of a prince.

Levi stood from where he was sitting on the other side of the gym—which was as far as he possibly could be away from me. He approached Gregor and Mr. Vandeer, then nodded, his face stoic and arms crossed behind his back.

Mr. Vandeer noticed Gregor's annoyance at his choice of opponent. "Come on, son, this is the guy you'll be answering to in a couple years. You should be happy you get to beat him up a little because when he pisses you off by forcing you to teach teenage halfwits how to fight, you can remember a time you got to punch him in his face."

Levi smirked and raised a brow, taunting Gregor. Which prompted Gregor to release a low growl.

Both males took off their shirts, exposing their sculpted bodies and getting into fighting stances.

"First back on the mat," Mr. Vandeer called, stepping out of the way.

The males circled each other for a while. Gregor was hunched, ready to attack. Where Levi was loose, appearing open and fragile, the gleam in his eye said otherwise. In this fight, Gregor was a bull, whereas Levi was a jungle cat.

Gregor looked for openings, but since Levi appeared open, he was lost in the decision of where to strike first. While Gregor was distracted, Levi pounced, striking Gregor in the side, then going for the face. Gregor pivoted, blocking the second strike, and aimed for Levi's stomach but Levi blocked his advance.

The males went like this for several minutes, striking and blocking until Gregor faked a punch to Levi's stomach with his left arm and then actually struck Levi in the face with his right.

I gasped as blood spilled down his face. Every nerve in my body tensed, and that rage that only burned for Levi filled me. My creature prepared to attack Gregor for hurting him.

Levi stepped back, dodging another punch. He struck Gregor in the stomach before making eye contact with me, giving me the slightest nod that he was okay.

I softened, the anger receding but my body still tense.

Gregor caught the look and glanced at me, then back at Levi, a wicked smile growing on his face. "Oh, I forgot to tell you about how me and Jess took her last night while you were away reading your books."

Levi didn't look at me, but he slowed, his muscles tensing.

"I went down on her as she went down on Jess. *Gods*, she tasted divine. You know? Oh wait, you don't know."

I gritted my teeth, wrath consuming me. I was going to kill Gregor after this. I definitely didn't fuck him. He was just saying that to throw Levi off.

Gregor threw another punch and Levi barely dodged it. "The noises she makes while she rode my tongue were fucking divine. Then after I paid her a favor. She got on her knees and—"

Levi struck Gregor hard and fast, straight in the face. Gregor had gotten too caught up in the fantasy he was creating, leaving himself open. Levi didn't give him time to recover, striking Gregor in the face over and over until he fell down on the mat. Levi followed after him, his punches hard and full of fury. Soon, Gregor was unconscious.

Mr. Vandeer called for Levi to stop, but he didn't let up and Mr. Vandeer didn't step in. Levi was blinded with anger. It was clear if anyone did step in, they would be next. Still, Levi was crushing his son's skull. He was the commander of the army; he should know how to get him to calm down. He just stood there and watched as Levi's fists met Gregor's face.

Panic consumed me as I watched. Levi was going to kill Gregor for saying those things, and it was because of me. I couldn't handle him killing someone for me, and a scream bubbled out of my throat, "Levi!"

He stilled, turning his head to make eye contact with me. Standing, he walked over, everyone around me scattering. All of our creatures recognized his was out and ready to wreak havoc. He extended his bloody hand to me. I didn't take it, but I stood, peering into his eyes that showed no emotions within.

"I didn't do what he said." I felt I needed to assure him, to calm him, to comfort him.

He gave a curt nod. "Come," he said, jerking his head toward a doorway that I had no idea where it led to before turning and starting to walk in that direction.

I looked at the class, their eyes wide and mouths agape. So much for not embarrassing myself in front of them again. Mr. Vandeer and a few males were picking up Gregor's unconscious, bruised, and bloodied body, while Jessamine bawled next to them.

"Marie."

I snapped my head toward Levi. He was across the gym, waiting for me. The pull to go to him was strong and demanding. I knew he needed me, and I had to go. It wasn't even a choice as I walked over to him. When I approached, his eyes briefly searched mine before he turned, walking out of the main gym.

# TWENTY

## MARIE

*T*he lights were dimmed low in the small room that held workout equipment. Levi had barged in, going over to the sink, and beginning to scrub his hands and face clean. I had no idea what to do so I sat on one of the benches and watched him take his aggression out on his bloody hands.

When he was done, he leaned against the sink, his back muscles rippling as he blew out a heavy breath.

"I'm sorry," he whispered.

I chuckled nervously. "I'm not the one you beat to a pulp."

He looked to me, his eyes blazing with emotions. Something in his gaze cracked my heart, my soul trying to leave my body to go to him. Before I could give in to the urge, he turned away and grabbed a sweater from one of the cabinets that lined the wall, tugging it on to cover his bloodied torso.

He sat next to me, his elbows rested on his knees, his head hung in his hands. I could hear his shallow breaths and rapidly beating heart. My skin crawling with a need to comfort him.

Getting up, I walked over to the cabinet, grabbing another sweater, and pulling it on. I turned back to see Levi watching me.

I made my way back, sitting close enough so our thighs touched. I took his arm, making sure not to touch any exposed skin, and placed it over my shoulder, then wrapped my arms around his waist.

His other arm came around me, and he buried his head in my hair. His body relaxed into me as he squeezed me tight. When I squeezed back, a sob stole from his mouth and then he just let it all out.

He almost killed someone. He was so blinded by rage; he couldn't stop until I called his name. I was so concerned with what this connection between us was doing to me that I never thought to think about what it was doing to Levi. I bet he was going just as crazy as I was.

He cried in my arms for a while. Eventually, he stopped, but I didn't let go. I needed to make sure he was okay. More than just that, I needed to make sure he was happy.

We moved to the matted floor, Levi lying on his back as I held him, my head resting over his now calmed heart, his hand caressing my spine. Neither of us talked. We understood the need for this serenity. We needed a break from all the crazy.

After some time passed, I finally asked, "Where are we?"

He chuckled as if surprised I asked. "These rooms are used for private training, but most faelings just use them to fuck. This one is mine."

"Have you fucked anyone in here?" The question was out before I had time to realize it. Lying here with him had stripped me bare and I didn't have a filter to hold back my thoughts.

"No," he replied.

I felt myself soften with a tension I didn't know I was holding. I gave a laugh that was half a sob. I hated that it relieved me. The power he held over me... He could cause pain without even trying. What would I have done if he'd said yes?

I needed to cry in his arms. To be held by him. To smell his scent, burnt pine and snow. I needed him. I just needed him.

I didn't cry as much as he did since I had pretty much spent the entire last week crying. I had a feeling Levi was the type of male who was too good to cry. Which resulted in a hurricane when he did. After a few moments, I calmed, and it was silent again, just the sound of our hearts, beating off tempo, filling the room.

Levi kissed my forehead, the contact causing a spark to run through me, but he pulled away within seconds. "Sorry."

"It's fine," I breathed, hugging him tighter.

"Fuck, Marie," Levi wheezed.

I panicked, sitting up to look at him. "What? Are you hurt?"

He smiled that beautiful fucking smile that melted my heart. "Just a few bruised ribs. Nothing to worry about. You should see the other guy."

I laughed, my hands finding the ribs that were bruised. "These ones?" I asked. He nodded, and I pushed down, causing him to hiss.

"Fuck."

I smiled, my thumbs caressing his chest to soothe the ache. "Don't beat people to a pulp, and I won't hurt you."

"Marie, you hurt me more than anyone ever could."

My heart stilled, my smile dropping off my face. "I don't want to."

"I know." He sighed. "Same for me."

"We should talk about…"

He shook his head. "Not now, I just want to pretend for a little longer."

I wanted to argue with him, but I couldn't. I wanted to pretend too. Pretend that this would work out. Pretend that I could have him and my family, and also somehow not hurt my best friend. Everything in this moment felt right, and I wanted to feel this a little longer. So I laid my head back down. "Tell me about your favorite story from history."

He began to talk about the creation of the Seelie Palace. It was built by King Julian Lightfire, fifteen thousand years ago. He created it for his mate. He was one of the only kings to have a mate in history. He wanted to make his mate a palace that represented his love for her. The palace took two thousand years to build because if she so much as disliked a misplaced tile, King Julian would tear the whole thing down and start from the beginning. Eventually, he was able to satisfy her for a few years before she grew bored of it and wanted a smaller home for her and their children. The king kept the palace for his court, and he stepped down from the throne so he could focus on building his mate a new house. His son took over and he spent the next year building his mate a small home for her and their children. They lived in that house for a few years before it grew too small. Mates were extremely fertile, and King Julian birthed fifty children. That was a lot even for mates. Their children would grow old and move out, but they would always have a small faeling or two running around. King Julian started to build her another house that was bigger than the old palace. His mate was so tired of him building homes at this point that she never shared her opinion on the new place. She actually wanted him to stop building and renovating the palace, but since she didn't love the home, he felt like he couldn't stop until she was happy with it. This new palace would become the current Seelie Palace and the king spent the rest of his life renovating it, trying to make his mate happy. Eventually, he couldn't deal with the stress of not satisfying his mate, so he committed suicide to free himself of the torment. His mate felt the bond break, and when she found him, she killed herself too, unable to live without him.

I laughed after hearing that ridiculous but true story. "I can't believe he did that."

"Mates will do anything to make their mate happy even if it drives them mad."

"That's stupid." I scoffed. "They should realize that the other is completely obsessed with them as much as they are."

"It can be hard to tell," Levi said as he played with my hair.

"They are mates! Like they are literally made for each other. How could the other doubt that?"

"We are fae, creatures of chaos. He was probably afraid she would leave him if he didn't make her happy."

"Well, that's ridiculously stupid. I hope I never find my mate." Levi stiffened under me, and I looked up at him, confused. "What? Am I hurting you again?"

"No—"

The door to the training room swung open. "Levi, I heard—"

The king looked down at us cuddled on the floor with wide eyes. "Marie." He wiped his face. "I'm sorry I didn't mean to interrupt."

I quickly sat up. "No, nothing is happening. We were just…" I looked at Levi who glared at his father with annoyance. I touched his shoulder, so he'd look at me, but he continued to stare at his father. "We were just talking," I supplied. "I should go."

That caught Levi's attention, and he turned to me. "You could stay."

"I didn't eat breakfast and you probably should wash the blood off you."

He gave me a tight smile before saying, "Yeah, I'll send something to your room." He brushed a stray curl out of my face. "See you in class later?"

"Yeah." I got up and looked at the king who studied me intensely. "Your Majesty."

He gave me the same tight smile Levi did and nodded. "Marie."

I glanced back at Levi, my heart slightly aching to go back to him, but I ignored it and turned away, making my way back to my room.

# TWENTY-ONE

### Corivina
### 197 years ago.

*I* spent almost every day of the following month with Darius. He was charming and methodical. Everything about him was solid and well kept. He was older than me by eighty years. He, unlike me, had his life together. He had a grand estate here in Lightwood and a job as the Commander of the Seelie Army.

Darius always had a smile on his face. He wore that smile today while he trained with the other soldiers. There was a field just south of the Lightwood Forest where the army did their drills. Almost every day for the last month, I waited for him to finish training after I spent the morning in the garden. I wasn't the only one who watched the soldiers train. Honestly, if I had known that they trained here, I probably would have come out of my wallowing a lot faster. The males never wore shirts; their sweaty chiseled chests on display for all the females to gawk over.

I absolutely loved coming to watch him. Darius was a thousand percent Seelie. His skin never burned from the sun; instead, he bronzed. His toffee brown hair lightened, turning slightly blond. I knew some of the females came here just for him, and I couldn't help feeling a little victorious over the fact that he spent most of his time with me.

As training finished, Darius jogged over to where I was sitting. He bent down and pressed a kiss to my forehead, the scruff on his chin tickling my skin. Every day he did that, and every day my heart swelled at the gesture.

Darius extended out his hand to help me up and greeted me with that warm smile. "Hey, beautiful." He pulled me into his sweaty body, crushing me into him.

I tensed for a second before relaxing. "Darius, you're all sweaty." He also did this every day, and though I pretended to hate it, I secretly loved to breathe in his musky vanilla scent.

"I thought a female loved a sweaty man," he said, squeezing me tighter.

"To look at, not to be smothered by." I squirmed in his hold.

"So, you admit you were looking at my body?" He pulled away and gave me the look, his eyes coated in lust, his mouth arched into a smirk instead of a smile. Darius and I hadn't had sex. We hadn't even kissed, besides the forehead kisses, and I didn't know if I was ready for more. Most males probably wouldn't understand since fae loved to fuck—*fucking often happened before courting*—but Darius didn't seem to mind. I wanted to, badly, but every time things seemed to be moving that way, I would panic and feel out of control.

"You have a nice body. Every female here is obsessed with it."

"But do you like it?" His eyes glinted.

I blushed, compelled by his warm blue orbs. The world started to close around us and then his eyes dipped to my lips, and his face inched closer. Then the closing feeling started to feel more like suffocation instead of a gentle fade. I stilled as panic filled me, then I did the only thing I could think—I faked a coughing spell. Darius rubbed my back, but his face was tight, his eyes holding an edge of disappointment.

We made our way to town in awkward silence. This was probably the tenth time I not so subtly rejected Darius's advances. He seemed to be okay with taking things slow, but he probably wasn't okay with just forehead kisses.

Darius sighed heavily. "Vina, are you even into me?"

I paused, turning to look at him. "Yes."

"Then why do you keep dodging me when I try to kiss you?"

A lump formed in my throat, and I tried to swallow it down before replying, "I just… I'm not ready."

"Why?" he asked with genuine curiosity.

A shuddering breath left me. I didn't know how I should tell him about my past relationship. There was stuff I didn't want to tell anyone, and then there was stuff I just couldn't say because of the deal. "The male I was with before… he… wasn't the best to me. At first, he was, then when I didn't do what he wanted, he wasn't." I couldn't look at Darius as I spoke, tears clouding my vision. "I'm over him, but he messed me up pretty badly and it's hard for me to trust another male."

His hand gently found mine. "I notice you flinch sometimes when I touch you," he said softly.

I covered my face in embarrassment. I had hoped he hadn't noticed that. "I'm sorry."

Gently brushing my hand away, he cupped my face. "You have no reason to be sorry. I don't want to kiss you if you're uncomfortable. Thank you for telling me, and fuck that male for hurting you."

"So, you're okay with waiting?" I asked, voice slightly broken.

"Vina, I've been secretly hoping for the past three years that I would run into that female with skin that shimmered like the clearest sea. I did, and she turned out to be one of the most amazing females I've ever met. I can wait three more years for a kiss, even more, if I have to."

I laughed through my tears. "I don't think it will take that long."

"I don't care how long it takes." He pulled me into his chest, now covered with his tunic. He gave me one of those sweet forehead kisses that melted my heart, and I cried harder in his embrace. This is what I needed over the last two years while darkness had consumed me. I needed someone to hold me while I cried about all the shit Markos had put me through. I needed someone who respected me, someone who was patient and knew how to provide comfort. That was what I needed.

Darius was what I needed.

About a week later, I went to visit the witch, Ginger. I hadn't seen her in over a month since I had been spending every second with Darius. Annoyingly, I found that I missed the snobby bitch, and I also missed her wine. I have no idea how she wasn't rich beyond her measure because her wine was fucking amazing, and every fae should be lining up at her door to buy a bottle.

When I walked into the shop, incense clouded the room, assaulting my nostrils. I didn't miss this. Humans with their lesser senses could never tell when too much was too fucking much. Now, I understood why no one knew about her amazing wine. They would have to fight off the blasted headache you'd get from the overuse of frankincense and myrrh.

My eyes found Ginger's, a knowing smile stretching her lips. The witch probably did this shit on purpose.

"Corivina, the gods said you'd be stopping by."

I made an irritated face. Why was I 'friends' with a witch again? Wine, good fucking wine. "The gods need to mind their own business. I just want some of your amazing wine. Please, *please,* Ginger, if my life is about to implode, do not tell me. I would like to go out on the illusion that my life was getting better."

"I swear, you never listen when I tell you things," she chided.

"I don't because they are never good."

"The one who will heal you has come into play."

"What?"

"The reading I gave you when we first met. Your love prophecy."

It took a moment for me to remember what she was talking about. "One who will break me, one who will heal me, and one whom I will destroy. My three greatest loves." I gave her a fake smile.

She nodded her head. "The one who will heal has arrived."

My annoyed smile turned to one filled with joy. I knew she was talking about Darius. We definitely weren't in love yet, but I could feel my heart yearning for the opportunity. "You know, witch, I'm actually glad for one of your messages. Now, if you can only confirm that the one I will destroy is my ex, then I will be satisfied."

"The gods do not work for us. We work for them."

A low growl left my mouth. *We work for their enjoyment. Why do you think this world is so fucked up?* I didn't mention this to Ginger because she was directly connected to the bastards and would defend their honor or some shit.

"I am here for good wine. I have a date tonight." Tonight, I had a romantic evening prepared for Darius. I was planning on letting tonight be the night I kissed him. It felt ridiculous. I felt like a child anticipating kissing their first boy on the playground, but I couldn't help the fear of being intimate with a new male, even if that male was someone as jovial as Darius.

Ginger, thankfully, shut up about the gods and gave me some of her top shelf wine, and I made my way back to my room at the inn. Now that I was starting to feel good in my life, the need to cling to this room actually became more apparent. I couldn't forget what happened to me, or what I had become in this room. The last two years were darker than the night itself. I don't think I would ever fully recover from what had come about during that time. I knew Ginger said the one who would heal me had entered my life, but I wasn't just going to trust someone because the gods said it was okay. They led me to Markos, so they were distrustful bastards.

Darius had walked me home many times and had asked why I lived here. It was more expensive to pay for a room here than to get an actual cottage, so it didn't make sense to him. I couldn't tell him the real reason, so I just told him that it was nice to have someone clean up after me. He offered to pay for a self-cleaning spell in a new cottage. I refused, especially since we have had only known each other for a month. Still, every time he walked me home, he'd ask me about it. I absolutely hated that he would point it out. Maybe he knew there was a bigger reason for me keeping this room, but I would never tell him. I needed this room, no matter how much it cost. I was using Markos's money to pay for it anyway, so it didn't really hurt me. I should be able to live in this inn for the next ten or so years as long as the innkeeper didn't raise the rate.

As I entered the room, my eyes instantly went to the bed. The sheets had been changed many times, but I could still see the rumpled, blood-stained ones. I could still see Markos's face, guilt-ridden and haunted. I hated that he felt guilt. I hated that he probably hated himself for what he did. It made him, in a way, innocent of his crime. I wanted him to be a monster, but his stupid, shattered face would haunt me. It would make me think about the what-ifs. What if I just had said yes, then I would be happy. I would be his concubine, his whore, not his wife, but I wouldn't have had to go through the pain of the last few years. I wouldn't hate myself when I looked in the mirror. What if he had found a way to marry me? If he loved me so much, then why couldn't he?

The what-ifs made me hate myself. It was stupid to think Markos didn't have a monster lurking under his skin. A monster that, if angered, would retaliate by 'showing who owned me.' I hated myself for letting him break me, for taking two years and a piece of my soul that I would never get back. For what occurred during those two years.

If I got rid of this room, I would forget my hate for myself, and I couldn't forget that. I would never forgive myself if I did.

I walked into the bathroom, splashing my face with water to wash away the dark thoughts. I was trying to move on, but every time I let myself be happy for a moment, guilt plagued me. I didn't deserve to be happy. The gods had proven that with the last three years of my life, but Darius made me want to be happy. He made me want to forget everything that had happened and move on. He had this aura about him that screamed safety, and I wanted to trust it.

But then I would remember Markos was once my home and that house had crumbled.

Punching the mirror in frustration, shards of glass embedded themselves into my skin as blood dripped down my fingers. Markos made me think like this. I used to be a spoiled bitch who thought life would be great for me. When I was sorted Seelie, I learned my lesson, but Markos made it stick. I wished I hadn't made that deal with him because I wanted to see him again, to see his pain. I wanted to make him feel what I had felt, to rip a part of him out like I had to rip a part of me out during the past two years. I wanted him to burn. If the gods would confirm I'd be the one to destroy him, I wouldn't mind being a pawn to play with for their entertainment. Fuck, I would put on a whole costume and dance around like a jester for the opportunity to ruin Markos like he did me. But I had made a stupid deal bound in blood to never see him again, so the joke's on me.

I cleaned my bloody hand, the skin closing up immediately. I would have to pay extra to fix the mirror. It wasn't the first one I had broken, and it wouldn't be the last. Honestly, the innkeepers should really stop fixing it if they didn't want me to break it.

Exiting the bathroom, I pulled on my dress for tonight. It was red lace with a halter top neckline. It was comfortable enough to frolic in but still elegant enough for our date. This was the first dress I had bought in three years, and I marveled at the silky feel of the material and the rich color. It was one of the things I actually loved about the Seelie—color. The Unseelie rarely wore color, and if they did, it was a dark variation. They loved being dramatic with the whole 'we are people of darkness' thing.

I left my hair down in my signature middle part. I wasn't really the type of female to change up her appearance. What I did worked, and I didn't feel the need to change it, but to spice things up a bit, I bought ruby clips to keep my hair out of my face and red lipstick that made my lips scream *kiss me*.

Darius was waiting just outside of the door of the inn when I stepped out. He had a green tunic on with a couple of the buttons undone to show off his beautiful bronzed chest, and simple trousers.

He grinned brightly. "Vina, you look amazing. If you would have told me what we were doing, I would have dressed up more."

"We are going on a picnic, so you actually dressed perfectly." I smiled, his eyes dipping to my lips for a brief second.

He wrapped his arms around me and then pulled me in for a hug that was complemented with one of his forehead kisses. "I still feel underdressed when I see how beautiful you are tonight."

I blushed. Thankfully, my face was hidden in his chest, so he didn't see. I hated when I blushed, but around him, it was something that I couldn't control.

Darius grabbed the basket I packed for our picnic, and we headed to the forest. After finding a place to rest, we sat, and Darius laid everything out. I got him his favorite pie from the town bakery, the finest cured meats and cheeses from the deli, the wine *of course*, and some oranges, just because I loved oranges. Hopefully, they would wash away the meat taste from our mouths. Not that the creature part of me wouldn't mind a little meat. I mean, there was human blood in the wine.

"Vina, you went all out."

"There's something else in there under the blanket."

His eyes gleamed as he reached in to find the present I got him. It wasn't anything too fancy—a simple watch. We didn't know each other well enough for me to think of anything super special, but I needed to get him something to thank him for his patience.

"Vina, I didn't get you anything. I didn't know—"

"Darius, you needed a watch. The present is more for me; I was growing tired of you always asking me the time."

He moved over and kissed my cheek. "Still, thank you. I'll cherish it forever."

I blushed again and then motioned for us to eat. We talked about small things like our jobs. He alluded to me not having to work because he would take care of me, and I would brush it off because the idea of relying on a male again completely scared the shit out of me.

Eventually, the sun set, and we laid down, my head resting on his chest, our food forgotten. "The stars are my favorite part of Seelie," I said.

"How so?"

"Since we lived at night, the stars became a mundane thing. Something that was always there unless it was cloudy. When I moved here, it was something I missed. Only getting to see them for an hour or so before I sleep makes me appreciate them more."

"If you weren't here, you wouldn't have rediscovered your love for them."

"No, I wouldn't have." I snuggled into his chest. "I wouldn't have met you either."

"I'm glad you're Seelie."

I sat up then, Darius coming with me. "There is something I wanted to do tonight."

He hummed in question.

I leaned in and cupped his face with my hand, looking at his lips. He tensed and his breath labored. He was so still as if afraid to ruin the moment, but nothing could ruin this. If the world closed around me, I knew he'd be there keeping me safe.

My lips lightly brushed his and he let out a small sigh. He finally moved, caressing my face, and softly deepening the kiss.

He pulled me into his lap, lightly teasing his tongue with mine, his taste of wine and oranges. He kissed me like I was the air he needed to breathe. His hand moved up and down my sides, and I ground my hips into his, causing him to groan into my mouth.

We didn't move further than some light dry-humping, but we spent hours kissing. We kissed until the night grew cold. We spent another hour kissing against the inn's door. Since then, whenever we were alone, our lips would find their way to each other and we would spend hours connected. I couldn't get enough of his lips on mine, absolutely obsessed with the taste of him.

# TWENTY-TWO

## MARIE

After the events that took place during training, the king gave the students a few days off so those who suffered could recover.

I spent most of that time in my room. Jessamine was busy nursing Gregor, and I didn't really want to go to a 'someone almost got beat to death, so we don't have to go to class' party. I did some schoolwork before I grew bored and then I exchanged messages with Kolvin. I told him about the fight, not my involvement, but just that it occurred. He was ecstatic about males beating each other to the brink of death. There was no question that Kolvin would take my father's position when he retired. Our families were so close, and since I was never interested in fighting, my father took the time to groom Kolvin for the position.

We talked for a while, not much really being said, and the wedge between us grew even wider with each passing day. Eventually, we ran out of stuff to talk about, and I was left to do nothing in my room.

Bored out of my mind, I went to the library to grab a book to read. I wasn't very fond of reading unless it was full of smut.

Fortunately for me, I found a plethora of smutty books in the library and spent the rest of the time off reading.

I was disappointed when I had to leave the comfort of my bed to go back to training. Gregor was there with his nose taped, but he was completely healed besides that.

The training room was filled with unresolved tension from Levi and Gregor. Mr. Vandeer did everything in his power to keep them separated, and as training went on, the tension seemed to dissipate as they focused on the exercises.

I couldn't help but watch Levi as he trained. He moved like a god, flowing through the drills like they were nothing. Unfortunately, my focus was deterred from the ass kicking my body was taking from the drills, and thankfully, Jessamine was there with me to complain about the torture we were going through.

After the lessons, I headed to the dining hall to get breakfast.

"You doing okay, Greg?" I asked when we all sat down. I couldn't help but feel slightly guilty that he almost died. Even though it was entirely his fault for provoking Levi and then losing focus.

"Well, I was out for the whole night, but when I woke up, I was mostly healed. I'm just pissed that I got my ass handed to me by the fucking 'Great at Everything' Prince. And my father and Jess have been on my ass the last few days for almost getting myself killed."

Jessamine, who was sitting on his side of the table, piped in, "You weren't complaining when my lips were wrapped around your cock."

He leaned into her and kissed her head. "No, I fucking wasn't. Thank you for taking care of me, Jess."

"You're welcome, and I was only nagging you because you told lies about my best friend."

I looked at her, shocked. "You mean me?" I pointed to myself.

"Yes, bunny, of course you're my best friend. I mean, I know we haven't gotten off to the best start, but I know you feel the bond that we are going to be friends for life."

I did. Jessamine had this air about her that made you want to be around her. She was funny and never serious, and she oddly felt like home. Maybe it was because she had no shame or acted as if the universe revolved around her, but I was fucking in love with her. I was unfortunately one of many who was caught under her spell, but at the same time, a small part of me was still mad at her for what happened with Levi. I hated that I did, and I was determined to let it go. Levi had used her to piss me off, and though my stupid heart had forgiven him and not her, my brain knew she wasn't in the wrong. There was also the fact that I had no right to get mad about it. Not only was I marked, but we were fae, and fae fucked. Even if I didn't know Levi's intentions, sex was one of our main primal urges, and a lot of the time it meant nothing but finding a way to deal with our beast.

"Yeah, you're right," I replied, then turned to Gregor. "Not cool saying what you did."

"Sorry, Seelie, won't happen again," he said, shoveling more food into his mouth. The male was built like a warrior god and certainly ate like one.

After we were done eating, we headed to lessons. Levi showing up right when Ms. May started to begin the lesson.

"Today, we are going to learn about siphons," she began. "As you already know magic is random and doesn't follow any rules unless we manipulate it to do what we want. One's magical strength is also random, and your strength will depend on how you manipulate the magical reserve you have. Some of you may be full of power, but don't have the ability to direct it with preciseness. You'd be best on the battlefield because you would be able to blast your power without having to worry too much about control. Some of you may have little power, but are great with direction. You'd be great with mining or tinkering, and some of you may have great power and great direction and you will probably go on to work with a Seelie and craft new spells and potions in aid or enjoyment of our people.

"For now, most of you don't know how to call upon that power. Which is why we will start working with siphons. A siphon often comes from the earth in the form of a crystal or gem and can contain magic. In the hands of the gifted, that magic can be harnessed to aid in achieving a goal. Lots of smaller spells, like a preserving spell, can be achieved by using a siphon. Many fae seek to use a siphon because you don't need a fae of opposite race to balance the energy. Though, a siphon doesn't have an endless supply. They need to be returned to the earth every once in a while, so they can cleanse and rejuvenate. The better choice would be to suck up your pride for a day and hang out with a Seelie than having to keep updating your spell every couple of weeks.

"Today we will be using smoky quartz, a gem that has a similar energy to an Unseelie fae. The aim of the day is to match your energy to the stone and then call upon your magic. Some will find this easy, but many of you may not be fully ready. There's no pressure. Our goal is to get your magic to rise this semester, but it is not a requirement until next. Now, we are to learn the basic mechanics of magic, but the lessons are better understood when you have a grasp of it.

"Come and get a crystal, and today we will just see what you and your partner can figure out together. I'll come around and offer pointers, but I want to see what you discover when left to your own devices."

Levi went and got the crystal, then set it in front of me. The crystal was mostly clear with what looked like little tendrils of black smoke flowing through it.

Peering into the stone, seeing if it would magically combust or something interesting, I asked, "What do you think they use for the Seelie?"

"Probably citrine."

I raised a brow, and he just shrugged, leaning in to pick up the crystal in one hand. He closed his eyes for a second, his face taking on a serene expression before he opened his eyes and tendrils of shadow filled his other hand.

He smirked, his eyebrow slightly raising in taunt.

I rolled my eyes. "It's not fair that you already know how to do magic."

He laid the crystal on the table. "Or you're extremely lucky to have me as your partner."

"Or you are extremely unlucky to have me as yours."

He brushed a curl behind my ear, eliciting a jolt to run through me. "No, never."

My heart fluttered at his sincerity. I knew things had gotten more intense with Levi since we last saw each other, but I was hoping we would ignore it. I also knew Levi didn't want that. He wanted me to be his. Everything in my body was screaming that I submit to his desires, and I had to constantly remind myself of the heartbreak and pain he had already caused.

I looked away from him and focused my attention on the task at hand—or at least I tried. I was distracted by the fact that Levi was still playing with my hair. Normally, it bothered me when even Kolvin played with my curls, but I loved it when Levi did. I loved the way he looked so content with playing with one of my curls like it amused him to no end.

I was never going to be able to focus with him around. He stole all of my attention, all the time. Even when I would pretend he didn't, my mind was always on him. I was seriously growing tired of my heart's relentless obsession with him. It wasn't going to happen, and the sooner my heart understood that, the better.

I picked up the stone and tried to focus. After a minute of nothing happening, I huffed and put the stone down in defeat.

Levi snorted at my half-hearted attempt. He leaned forward, abandoning my curl. "It's going to take more effort than that. Actually, it will take less effort."

"What?"

"When you channel, you're opening up instead of narrowing your energy. You are trying to match your energy with the rock, which requires you to adapt by opening yourself up."

I rubbed my forehead, pondering how I was supposed to bond with a rock.

Levi took the opportunity to laugh at me. The sound caressing through me and harmonizing with my heart. "You're so cute when you're confused."

Immediately, I dropped my hand. I didn't want him to think I was cute. Nor did I want him telling me I was. It made my heart flutter, and I definitely didn't want that. Ignoring my body's reaction to him, I picked up the crystal and tried opening myself up to the rock.

Nothing happened... as expected.

I exhaled and put the stupid rock back on the table. "Maybe, I'm not Unseelie."

"We were all there when you bawled your eyes out because your blood ran black," Levi said matter-of-factly.

I growled at him.

He stood from his seat. "Stand."

Cocking my head, I gave him a puzzled look.

"I'm going to help you call your magic. It's easier if we stand."

I looked around to see others standing, trying to call their magic from the crystals, so I obeyed him.

"Some people are able to channel another if they can bond. So instead of channeling the crystal, try me."

"How do you know we will bond?"

He gave me a blank look before he said, "We will."

I waved my hands in exasperation. "Whatever you say, Your Highness. How do we do this? You know we can't touch."

"We don't have to touch, but it's better if we have a physical tether." He gestured for me to come closer, and I did. His scent coating my senses. My body became tight and somehow loose at the same time. He turned me and pulled me into him so my back was flushed with his chest, his arms cinching around my waist.

My whole body came alive at the contact. My heart pounded in my chest, and my nipples pebbled. The fact that Levi's scent was starting to become spicier, and a slight thickness was growing at my back, didn't help with my body's reaction.

Levi didn't seem as bothered by the situation as I was because when he spoke in my ear, his warm breath brushing over my skin, his voice remained normal and focused. "You're going to focus on opening your energy to me and matching it."

Why did I think this was a good idea? There was no way that I was going to be able to focus while his cock—which I was starting to learn the exact size and shape of—was poking me in the back. My panties were growing wet, and I was surprised the class wasn't wondering what the fuck we were up to.

Levi's hands moved across my stomach. "Relax, Marie," he whispered. His voice took on a slight husk and had the opposite effect.

I took a deep breath, breathing in more of his scent, and forced my body to relax. I opened myself to him. A shock cascaded through me when we connected, but then I opened my eyes and focused my energy on my palm. Black veins permeated my skin and a small shadowed tendril flowed out of my hand.

A laugh of surprise bubbled out of me before I turned around and threw myself at him. He groaned slightly; his cock now squished between my stomach and him. I eased back with an apology.

He breathed out a shaky breath. "I'm fine."

A smile formed on my face, so wide the action stung my cheeks. "I did it!"

He grinned back. "I told you."

We stared at each other like lovesick idiots until a voice had me jumping out of Levi's arms. "Good job, Marie!" Ms. May complimented.

The entire class was staring at us. I was definitely tangled in an embrace with the prince, and the entire class witnessed it. I was honestly surprised I hadn't died from embarrassment at this point.

# TWENTY-THREE

## MARIE

*D*espite the awkward situation earlier, it didn't seem to break the bubble Levi and I were starting to create. When we were together, everyone else faded, and we had each other's complete focus.

At this moment, he was going over one of the lessons we would be tested on next. He read to me from a textbook; one that had been read many times. The thing was beaten and battered with lots of writing in the margins. He wasn't even reading it word for word. He would just summarize some topics and then delve deeper than the text on others.

We were in the greenhouse, sitting on one of the couches in the middle of the room. The smell of roses filled my nose as I watched him. He loved this nerdy shit. Normally, Levi talked slowly like he didn't care, but when it was something he did care about like history or magic, he talked like he walked, too fast to keep up. I had a feeling that no one ever really listened to him. Why would they? When people did listen to him, it was probably because they had to, not because they wanted to. I wondered if this was why he was always alone. If he felt like no one would want him for Levi, only ever caring for Prince Levington Shadawn.

"You have to slow down and go back a little. My brain needs time to digest whatever you are saying."

He smiled at me, and it pulled at my chest every single time he did. Levi wasn't the type to smile, but around me, he did it more. It made me feel special that he chose to share something so rare with me. It made me want to stop smiling at others and only smile for him. Unfortunately, I was just the type of person who smiled all the time so I don't think I could actually do that. Deep down though, I knew if he asked, a part of me would try, for him, only for him.

I hated that I felt like that toward him, toward anyone. I wanted to give this male the world and then all the stars and then the sun and moon. I wanted him to be happy beyond life. I wanted every second of his existence to be ecstatic. I didn't know why him. I didn't understand why I felt so much for someone I barely knew. I didn't even know the most basic information about Levi. I knew he liked history, but that was about it. He was a mystery to me—a mystery I wanted to change my whole life for, just so I could unravel it. My feelings for him terrified me, and I wanted to run away from them, but the more time I spent with him, the harder they were to ignore.

"Why don't we stop and do something else?" he suggested.

"Like what?"

He glanced out the giant windows. "Let's go outside."

I crinkled my nose. "It's cold out there, and it's warm in here."

"I'll get you something to keep you warm. Come on, it's stuffy in here. I promise it will be fun." His eyes promising mischief. I've never seen him excited about something. Enthused, yes, but not excited. There were stars in his midnight eyes, and I couldn't be the cloud that covered them up.

"Okay, fine," I grumbled, dreading the forever winter of the Unseelie.

He snapped the book shut and stood from the couch. "Follow me."

Our journey from the greenhouse was a short one as we entered a part of the palace I had never been to before. It seemed that not many were allowed in this area. Only a few servants and guards lined the halls. We stopped at a room, and Levi pulled a key out of his cloak to unlock it.

The second we walked in, I knew exactly where we were—Levi's bedroom. His scent was everywhere, and it flooded my senses. His room was huge compared to my small one. Walls covered in dark wood. Plush rugs. A huge four-poster bed with many, many furs atop it in the center. A fireplace next to the door. A mantel, covered with books. It seemed Levi might have a slight addiction to them. All the free wall space was lined with bookshelves that were filled with books. Even the desk chair had a pile of books on it.

His room was a little messy. I assumed that he would've been a clean freak. It would definitely fit his grumpy persona. I liked a little clutter, it gave a room comfort, which Levi seemed to enjoy as well. There weren't many fae lights, the fire acting as the main light. It was surprising Levi got anything done in here because I would always be cuddled in that bed sleeping.

He went to a room to the right, which I assume was his closet. "You can sit on the bed."

I tentatively walked over and stared at the bed for a moment before plopping down. I had the intense urge to lie back and cuddle up in the mountain of furs. His bed looked like the most comfortable place on earth and his scent was the strongest here. My creature craved to roll in the sheets and breathe him in.

Levi was taking a while rummaging through his closet, so maybe I could? The urge was so strong I couldn't fight it much longer.

*Just for a moment*, I told myself, sneaking a glance at the closet.

I laid back and was pleasantly rewarded with plush softness.

I purred again. I was really going to have to ask my mother if purring was a normal thing fae females did because it weirded me out. I rubbed my face into the furs, breathing in Levi's pine scent. The creature in me was immensely satisfied and wanted to stay here forever. I was seconds away from climbing under the furs and making this place my new home.

"Having fun?"

I froze and looked up to see Levi towering me. He was smirking, probably inwardly laughing.

Thankfully, it was dark enough that he couldn't see the blood filling my cheeks when I sat up. "Sorry, it looked comfortable."

"You can stay if you want," he said, his tone holding a suggestive note.

I quickly stood, not thinking about how he was right in front of me and crashed into his chest. He held me and looked down with a knowing grin.

*This male.*

He bit his lip, and my core tightened, heat stirring inside me. "Take off your cloak."

Incredulous, I just blinked.

"I got the stuff to keep you warm," he said, raising his hand filled with weather-appropriate clothing.

"Oh."

Levi gave me that stupid sexy smirk again that was really starting to annoy me.

I took off my cloak, and he handed me an oversized sweater. I pulled it over my shirt, and I was greeted with more of his scent. If I could rip my stupid beast out of me, I would. That motherfucker needed to learn that we wanted to be at home in Seelie. That this male, while sexy as fuck and probably the most beautiful creature we have had ever seen, would most definitely destroy us if we got involved with him.

I let out a shaky breath, trying my best to control my creature.

Levi wrapped the cloak he was wearing earlier around me. It was the one his father had given him. I guessed he switched this one out with a less, yet still exceptionally, fine one while he was in the closet.

He handed me a pair of gloves next. "Here, I don't want to go all the way back to your room to get the ones I bought you. These should fit; they were mine when I was younger."

The second I put them on, I knew he was lying. The gloves didn't smell like him. They felt brand new. There was a rubber lining at the fingertips as if they were made for someone with claws. Also, they were quite girly—the fabric black with black roses embroidered all over them.

A smile formed on my lips.

Levi gave me a blank look, but I could tell it was forced. "What?"

"Nothing, the gloves are nice."

He ignored my comment. "Come on, let's go."

We left his room and went down the hall to the double doors that led outside. The cold stung my cheeks, but I was quite warm in Levi's clothes. The moon shone through the clouds that were lightly powdering the earth with fresh snow. I might hate the cold, but the snow was something magical.

The doors led out to what I can best describe as an Unseelie garden. Only the strongest plants could survive in this place, mostly shrubs and a few various types of trees. The black rose was the only flower I had seen outside. I knew a lot about plants because of my mother, so I was aware that roses didn't do well in temperatures this cold. Though, the black rose wasn't a common flower in Seelie. I didn't know roses could even be black. It was a part of the Unseelie Royal Crest, so it must be native or magically created.

The rest of the 'garden' was decorated with ice sculptures. There was the king's emblem, the crest, and various other Unseelie figures. The garden seemed to be private. Black steel gates lined the area, which made me assume it was only for royals.

I was lost in the beauty of the place when something hard hit my shoulder, further splashing in my face.

I wiped at my chin and realized it was snow. Levi stood there, holding two balls of snow and that gleam flared in his eye. As he raised one of his hands, my eyes widened, and I ducked behind one of the ice sculptures for cover.

"You know the ice is clear, Marie. I can see you," he teased.

"You are attacking me with snow. What am I supposed to do?"

"It's a snowball fight. You're supposed to throw it at me as well."

"If you would have told me that before attacking me, I would have understood the assault."

"Then I wouldn't have seen that cute little look on your face when you're shocked."

I bent down and gathered snow, packing it in my palms, eager to pay him back. When I looked back up though, he was gone. "Where did you go?" I called.

That's when I felt a pelt of snow hit my back. Again.

I groaned, turning to see him smiling in victory. "I've got you two times now."

My eyes narrowed. "Not fair, I wasn't ready."

"I don't play fair."

"Don't I fucking know it."

"Huh?" Levi smirked.

I threw my snowball at his face. He dodged and threw one back. I squealed, moving out of the way, barely dodging the ball, and scrambled to the ground to make another. Levi threw one very close to my face. He was taunting me because he definitely could have hit me if he wanted to. I wasn't even trying to hide behind anything as I formed my ball.

I got to my feet and ran behind a shrub for cover as I made a second ball for backup. I slowed my breaths and used my fae hearing to listen for Levi. It was deathly quiet, but the snow wouldn't provide any stealth to Levi's approach. Hearing a crunch from my left, I popped up out of my cover and threw a ball. It hit him square in the face.

He dramatically wiped the snow on his face and gave me a death glare. That caused a giggle to bubble out of my throat.

Then he pounced, rushing for me.

Shrieking, I turned to run from him with no real direction. Levi was hot on my heels, his stupid long legs providing an unfair advantage to me. I threw my other snowball and tried to pick up my pace.

It didn't help because seconds later, he grabbed me around the waist. I twisted, trying to escape his hold, but it just made us tumble to the ground.

The hysterical sounds of my laughter filled the air as we struggled in the snow. It was about a foot deep where we fell. Snow seeped its way into our clothes. Levi finally got a hold of me and pinned me on my back. "You are a squirmy little thing."

I smiled as I looked up at him. He looked so fucking beautiful with his cheeks reddened and hair frazzled.

"I won this round."

"You cheated using your long legs," I pointed out.

"I said I don't play fair."

"Fine, but it will be you on your back next time."

"Marie, you could have me on my back anytime you want. All you have to do is ask," he purred.

While Levi was busy heating my insides, I took the opportunity to flip us. He probably let me, but I wasn't going to let the small victory go to waste. I got up and sprinted. Levi soon followed, trying to catch me again.

We played in the snow for a while, throwing snowballs and tackling each other. I had never laughed so much in my life.

We called it quits when our faces were numb, and our fingers were frozen. After, Levi walked me to my room. His pace was so slow, as if he wasn't in any rush for the night to end. He held my hand, still covered with my glove. I probably shouldn't have let him, but it made my heart squeeze and my creature satisfied.

When we reached my door, Levi pulled me to a stop. He took my other hand and stroked his thumbs over my outer palms.

Our eyes connected, my soul trying to escape out of my body to make home in his midnight eyes. "I had fun with you tonight," he whispered.

"Me too."

His thumbs continued to rub back and forth on my palms as his eyes dipped to my lips. He leaned down, our faces inches away from each other. I sucked in a breath as his lips neared, then his eyes dropped to my neck where Kolvin's mark lied, and he stilled.

Anger seeped into his features, and he stepped back, letting go of my hands. He tried not to let his anger show but he was so tense, I thought he was going to explode. Giving a curt nod and a tight smile, he turned abruptly and walked away.

Watching until his back disappeared from view, the hollow feeling settled over me again. My creature was utterly disappointed that we didn't get to taste his lips, and I was kind of disappointed too.

Exhaling in frustration, I banged my head on the door a couple times—contemplating the idea of abruptly severing the bond to Kolvin and rushing to Levi—before opening the door and going in.

# TWENTY-FOUR

## MARIE

*L*evi avoided me the next few days. Even during the weekend, he avoided me. He evaded everyone, which meant I shouldn't take it personally, but my heart still ached to see those eyes.

I tried to point out to myself that this was exactly the reason why we didn't want to be involved with him. My heart didn't care—it wanted Levi; my creature wanted Levi. And I wanted all of this to end.

My brain was fried. I was so tired of the last few weeks here in Unseelie. I was going home in two days, if only for a day, and I was excited to be with my family. I was excited to be wrapped in my parents' embrace, to breathe in my father's roasted vanilla scent, and my mother's sweet rose. Even to see Kolvin, though, I knew that wouldn't end well. He was still my best friend. I hoped I could grovel enough that he would forgive me for my past actions.

In the greenhouse again, Levi and I sat at the bench by the huge windows that looked out toward the winter scape. We hadn't studied since we almost kissed, but there was a test tomorrow, so we had to.

He sat next to me, going over what would be on the test. We recently learned about the science of magic. Since no one really knew why we had magic, where it came from or what the true properties besides light and matter were, all of the teachings were just theory. There were just about a thousand theories that we had to know by tomorrow.

He was obviously getting frustrated with me because I hadn't spent my childhood studying magic, and I didn't know everything by heart. "It's not like you need to know. Our test is together, so I can just take it," he grumbled.

"No, we won't be partners forever and I need to learn this," I snapped.

The tension between us was tight and on the verge of a combustion. It was like we were in the carriage again—Levi brooding for no good reason, me wanting to slap him in the face.

Levi's fist clenched around his pen, and his hard eyes met mine. "If you had spent time studying instead of partying this weekend, then you would know it and I wouldn't have to waste time repeating myself."

"If you would have studied with me once this week, then I would probably know them."

"It's not my fucking job to make sure you know it."

"As my partner, which you forced me to be, yes, it fucking is!"

"No, it's my fucking job to pick up when you slack."

"You know what, fuck you." I stood and started grabbing my books. "I'll figure it out on my own."

Levi grabbed my arm. He stood, towering over me. "We have other stuff to go over."

"We can go over it separately." I tugged on my arm, but his grip was tight. He wasn't hurting me, but I couldn't get loose. "Let go!"

"No," he growled.

We stared at each other for a long moment; our breaths short and fast. My heart pumping violently in my chest. I was so fed up with Levi's shit right now. I dropped the books on the table. Levi, thinking I had submitted, let go of my arm. Then I pounded my fist into his chest.

The action hurt me more than it hurt him. My soft fist hit strong taut muscle. My hand would probably bruise while he didn't even move from impact.

I didn't care—I hurt. He was ripping my fucking soul and it hurt. I just wanted payback, for him to feel this pain. To feel crazy like I did, and flip his life over and question everything. I mostly just wanted him to stop. Stop ruining me, stop making me feel for him and then taking himself away. I swung again and again. Tears streamed down my face and a sob tore from my throat.

When I swung again, he grabbed my hand. The vibrations traveled through my body violently, but I ignored them and the heated lust that came with, and swung my other hand. He caught that one too.

I tried to pull away, but my attempt was useless. He was trained in battle, body built like a god, and I was powerless compared to him. "Let go!" I cried.

"No."

"Let go!" I struggled.

"Marie, look at me," he commanded.

I ignored him, continuing to stare at his chest as I struggled to get out of his hold.

"Marie."

I wanted to be free of him as the vibrations ripped through me. It felt like they were trying to change me, trying to urge me to yield to them and fall into him, but I couldn't do that.

"Marie! Look at me!" Levi yelled.

I stopped struggling, his voice evoking something within me to still. He let go of my hands and cupped my face, pulling it up to meet his blue-black eyes. Eyes that felt like home for my soul. Wiping my tears, he said, "I'm sorry."

He said it like he knew why I was mad at him. I don't know why, but I just knew he understood me on a different level. He knew me, and I knew him.

I bore into those midnight eyes for a long moment before doing the thing I wanted him to do days ago, weeks ago. I pressed my lips against his.

The kiss felt like fitting the last piece in a puzzle. It felt like finally finding something you've spent hours looking for. It was something so small, just the brush of his lips to mine, but it felt huge.

It took Levi a minute to catch up before his lips moved, deepening the kiss. A moan escaped my mouth. Finally, I let the vibrations of our touch affect me, pulsing through my body, focusing on my nipples and clit, making me want more than just a kiss. I wanted everything, all of him. Mind, body, heart, and soul. I wanted to consume him as he consumed me.

My hands moved around his neck, pulling him closer, needing him closer. His hands moved down from my face to my throat. His fingers creating shockwaves that sparked throughout my body. He moved down further, stopping right after he brushed the mark.

Abruptly, Levi pushed me away, breaking the kiss as he took a step back.

"Levi, I—" I tried to reason.

"It doesn't matter." He wiped his mouth like I was filth and moved to the table to pick up his stuff.

"Levi—"

"Stop, Marie." He collected all his things and then looked at me. His eyes were cold and distant. No anger, no sadness, no lust, no love. Like what had just happened didn't affect him like it did me. "Figure out the theories yourself, or don't. I don't care." He turned, bolting out of the room.

Gutted, my hand covered my heart, trying to shield it from the pain. My whole world disorientated for a moment as I was lost outside myself. It was like I was trying to escape the impending hurt, but I lost, and it was like a tornado wrecking me into a thousand pieces.

A sob tore through me as I crumpled to the floor in agony and wept. Everything hurt. I have never cried like this in my life. I thought leaving my family was the worst pain I had ever felt but that was nothing compared to the pain of Levi leaving me. When we kissed, it felt like I had everything and then within moments, it was taken away, extracting out my heart in the process.

*Why did I feel this way?*

I laid on the floor, crying for what felt like hours until I finally calmed down. I stared at the white cold floor, the smell of roses—reminding me of my mother—filling my nose. She was the female I loved most in the world. The person I wanted to get back to. The reason I couldn't fall for Levi. I couldn't be without her.

I was weak without her.

Getting up off the floor, I went back to my room.

I was done with this place. I'd be home at the end of my four years here and nothing would hold me back.

The next night in class, I walked in late. I could feel Levi's stare boring into me. I bet he thought I wouldn't show. That's what I would have done if I wasn't done with this. I would have hidden from what scared me, but you can't be scared if you no longer cared. I only cared about one fucking thing—going home.

I didn't so much as glance at him as I sat down. When the paper for the test was passed out, I snatched it and started filling in the answers. I finished, not letting Levi check it before I just got up and handed it in.

Being the first pair to finish again, Ms. May graded the paper right in front of us. I could feel him behind me, his energy tense and sporadic. He probably thought I fucked up his perfect grades and was seconds away from throwing a fit.

"Good job, guys! Not one question missed!" Ms. May shifted her attention directly to me. "Marie, did you want to try calling your magic for extra credit?"

I lifted my palm and concentrated, opening my senses and feeling the blood pump through my body. The faded blue veins under my caramel skin turned a dark vivid black as swirls of shadow formed in my palm, and if I wasn't in a piss mood, I'd have smiled.

"That makes you guys the first to be able to call your magic!" Ms. May grinned. "Merry Mabon. You are free to go, classes are over for the day."

Turning, I walked out. I spent the whole day studying those fucking theories and calling my magic. I didn't need Levi. Even if I felt like I was about to collapse from exhaustion.

A hand on my shoulder stopped my steps. "Marie."

I didn't turn to face him, instead, I just stood there waging a war within myself. My stupid heart wouldn't give up. It wanted Levi. My creature wanted Levi. I wanted to not get crushed. I kept trying to call up the feeling I'd felt when he left me after we kissed—how I felt utterly shattered, but I couldn't.

Turning, I looked up into those eyes that had enraptured me since I first saw them.

Levi cupped my chin, leaning in and kissing me. It was a soft sensual kiss, lasting seconds, but it still made my toes curl. I knew in that moment this male had me, no matter what. I would never win against his pull. It wasn't even a choice. I would never be able to deny him, because my fucking soul would always be his. It didn't make any sense to me. I've known him for three weeks, but the pull toward him was too great. I could fight it day and night, but I would never win. Honestly, I was tired of denying how right he felt.

He rested his forehead against mine. "Sleep, then come to my room later. Okay?"

I nodded, and he kissed me again. Another quick kiss that pulled at my heart. Then he was gone, and I was walking toward my room, realizing that all my plans to go home were probably fucked.

# TWENTY-FIVE

## CORIVINA
## 194 YEARS AGO.

*I* had been with Darius for the last three years and we still hadn't had sex. We had done almost everything except sex. At first, it was me stopping us before things got too far, afraid of what might happen if we took another step closer to that edge. Eventually it was Darius who would stop us. He would spend hours lashing me with his wicked tongue, but when I would pull his head up and grind my core into his cock, he would halt us.

I speculated that maybe Darius might have another female. A female who would please him and wasn't afraid to let him get too close to her, but he couldn't have had another partner. It would be impossible for him to keep that a secret. He spent almost every second that he wasn't working with me. The only time he would be able to was when the king required his presence in the palace. He could be with another then, but when Darius returned home, he never smelled of someone else.

Lying in his bed, I stared at his back as he slept. I spent every night here. I practically lived here, but I didn't let my room at the inn go. Darius knew I still had it. He didn't ask me to get rid of it, knowing it was a sore subject, or maybe he never wanted me to in the first place.

He had his fingers inside me a couple of hours ago, hitting the perfect spots to make me sing, but he hadn't let me do anything to him after. He had been doing that all week. When he first did it, I thought it was odd but chalked it up to him being exhausted. Then the week went on and it was the same thing. I felt incomplete to not return the favor. I had his cock buried in my throat many times, but not tonight or the last several. As if he had no need for me and was only entertaining me to keep me satisfied.

Over the past year, I was developing deeper feelings for him, deeper than just a silly fling. I was starting to trust him fully. Starting to tell him of my past, but just snippets. I thought we were working toward something bigger. It felt like he wanted something bigger between us, but in bed, it seemed maybe he was losing interest.

It was driving me crazy that we weren't fucking. I needed his cock deep inside me, scraping at my inner walls. I hadn't had sex in six years. The last male to be within me was the male who hurt me. I wanted to wash him away, and I wanted Darius to be the male to do it.

Maybe I scared him with my dark and tattered soul. Maybe he didn't want someone who was broken and shattered. Maybe he wanted someone who was whole and happy. Maybe this was it for us. Ginger said that the one who would heal me had come but she didn't specify who. I assumed it was Darius, but maybe it wasn't.

I got out of bed. It was still dark out, but I didn't care. I found my dress on the floor and slipped it on. Over to the dresser, I pulled out the top drawer. I had been reluctant to leave anything here at first, but it would happen from time to time, and Darius would put it in the drawer if I did. I liked that I had a small part of his home, but I should have had never let this happen. I shouldn't have gotten so close.

Grabbing the items, I put them in a bag and left Darius's manor.

Coming back to the room at the inn was like going back to war. A part of me was excited but another part was dreading. That dread grounded me, making me feel safe even if in chaos.

I put my things away—where they belonged—and laid down on the bed. I breathed in the freshly laundered sheets. A little stale since I hadn't requested they clean in a long while.

I had forgotten this place when I was wrapped in Darius's comforting aura, but I kept this place for a reason, and I needed to remember that reason.

Reaching under the pillow, I pulled out the steel letter opener Markos had used when we had made our deal. It was the only thing of him I had left besides the memories. Our blood still tainted the blade. A part deep within me missed him. Missed his voice, soft and comforting. His scent of roasted chestnut that reminded me of home. I missed his love. It was fierce and overwhelming. He loved me so much, he couldn't be without me. He loved me so much it turned him into a monster when he lost me.

Markos was to be crowned within a year as the Unseelie King. His father had been king for the last nine hundred years and wanted to be done. It was announced that Markos's emblem for his reign would be the raven. When I heard the news from Darius who was discussing his recent time at the palace, it took everything within me not to get up and come here.

I was Markos's raven. He was still following the deal and leaving me alone, but he could never truly let me go. I knew he still loved me and wanted me. Even if he knew he had broken us.

I wished I could talk to him right now. I wanted to go back to when I was nineteen—that was our best year together. We knew each other deeply enough to not fear the judgment of the other. When we hadn't been sorted and ripped apart. When we weren't communicating in letters and fucking under the lunar eclipse. When we weren't broken and shattered. When we were teenagers with dreams to marry and have children. When we decided we would name our first child Kinder.

*Kinder.*

It was a stupid name we came up with when we talked about our future.

Tears built behind my eyes, and I slipped the letter opener back under the pillow.

The past was the past and it was gone. I could never go back. I could never change it. I was dealt these cards, and this was how I chose to play them.

The one thing I missed most about Markos was how in sync we were. We wanted the same things. We like the same things. Everything was easy at the time.

I couldn't help but compare Darius to Markos in this one manner. I tried not to. Me and Darius were at different points in our lives. He had it, for the most part, figured out. I wasn't even able to stay above water.

I hadn't progressed within the last three years besides moving five dresses to a male's top dresser drawer and now those dresses were back here. I couldn't help but think I was holding the male back. That he would be better if I just stayed here.

The inn room was filthy—dirty dishes laid about and bottles of wine scattered the floor.

I took a few days off of work. Ms. Masel didn't mind since I hadn't taken a day off in five years. I usually found solace in the garden. I enjoyed caring for the seeds and seeing them bloom into strong healthy plants. The garden would clear my mind, pushing away my shadows. Cooking gave me a similar feeling, but it also made me feel light and warm inside when I saw someone enjoying my meal.

I didn't want that right now. Now, I wanted to be in the dark, cold space. The part of my mind that was full of thoughts. I craved the poisons they spoke of. The deep smoky depths to drown in.

I had been here for four days, crying, screaming, tearing things apart. It felt like the past three years hadn't happened. Like I was back in that place that Markos had left me in five years ago and I couldn't get out and I didn't want to get out. This is where I was supposed to be, this is where I deserved to be.

Last night, Darius came by. He knocked on the door asking if I was in here. I laid still in the bed. The door muffled the sound of my breath, and when I didn't come, he assumed no one was in here and left.

He returned tonight.

Heavy pounding sounded against the wood. "Corivina, I know you're in here. I went to see the witch and she told me you're here. Please, Vina, please, just open the door." Panic coated each word he spoke.

I laid in bed, not responding, not moving.

"Vina, please. I'm worried. Just let me see your face. Please."

I sat up. I didn't care about Darius seeing me like this. Maybe he'd see me and he'd leave. See that I was a lost cause and he had wasted his time for the past three years and would move on.

Walking over, weaving myself through the trash, I opened the door. His face was exhausted and haggard. His warm blue eyes were rimmed with red. His beard was a couple millimeters longer than he normally kept it and his hair disheveled like he had ran his hands through it many times.

Darius and I stared at each other for a moment before he uttered my name.

I didn't really want to see his disappointment in me, so I turned and walked back into the room.

I was a few paces in before I felt his warm fingers wrap around my wrist and I was tugged into his chest. His body enveloped mine, trying to comfort me, but I didn't sink into him. My walls were up, and it was going to take a lot more than a little warmth to break through them. Those walls were made of steel.

Pulling out of his embrace, I gave a broken laugh. Making my way to sit on the bed. Knees in my chest more laughter erupted from me. Each laugh shuddering closer to a sob until I was bawling.

"Steel," I whimpered.

*Steel. Unseelie. Markos. Home.*

I cried into my knees. I should have been Unseelie. I should be there now. I should be with Markos as he prepared to be the king. I should be crowned with him as his queen. I should be his wife. I should be in his bed. I should have his child. Our child. *Kinder.*

Darius sat on the bed in front of me while I wept. I sobbed for a while, mourning the life I should have had. Wishing things were different. Wanting not to be broken. Not wanting Darius to have to deal with this version of me. Wishing I was whole. Wishing I could erase the past before Darius and I came together. Wishing I could be the person he needed instead of him being the person I needed.

My thoughts spiraled and fused, mushed, and separated. I followed them as I cried, letting them slowly drive me to madness, breaking me further than before.

Eventually, my sobs calmed to slight whimpers. Darius moved in closer and lifted my head so my eyes met his. "Vina, what is wrong?"

*Me. I am wrong. My existence is wrong. My life is just entertainment for the gods, and I am their favorite fucking toy.*

I stared at Darius. My heart yearned for him. My feelings for him were different than my feeling for Markos. With Markos, it was easy, seamless... until it was not. Darius was hard because it felt like I had to fight for him. Every day I had to wake up and choose to be there for him. Though it was hard, it was more rewarding than any moment with Markos. He felt like my one. Deep in my heart, he felt like forever, but what if our forever was painted in tragedy as was my life? That was why it was so hard—the fear that I would fall for him, only to be ripped apart because of it later.

I knew Darius didn't have the same thoughts. He was whole. I was broken. And I hated it.

I hated that when I woke in his bed from a nightmare, he was the one to hold me. I hated that when he went too far and triggered me, he comforted me. I hated that he wanted to take care of me and make me feel whole when I was a broken, shattered thing.

I wasn't worthy of him, but I wanted to be, badly.

"Why don't you want me?" I whimpered. "Is it because I'm this? Is it because you found another? Do you think I don't want you? Because I do. The last person I was with... he... he was the last person I was with. I want you to be the last person I am with. I want you, but you don't want me." I started to cry again, my cries making my body shudder.

Darius scooted closer and pulled me into his lap, so I straddled his hips. "Vina, I want you. How could you not see that?"

"You keep halting us." I cringed at how weak my voice sounded; how pathetic I must look.

He rested his forehead against mine and blew out a breath. "I... I'm scared, Vina. Nervous. I want it to be special. I want our first time together to be perfect. I keep halting us because I'm afraid that the moment isn't right and that it won't be good for you, or I'll mess up and hurt you. It scares me to hurt you. I... I love you, and I never want to see you in pain."

I replayed those words in my head.

*I love you and I never want to see you in pain.*

"I do too. I... I..." I stammered, terror coating my lungs as I trembled out a breath.

"You don't have to say it. Not until you're ready," he whispered, kissing my forehead gently.

Shuddered cries escaped me, I hated myself so much in that moment. I wanted to say it, but I couldn't. I couldn't say that I loved him out loud. If I said it out loud, then the gods would know, and they would take him away. They loved to give me pain, and the pain I would feel if that happened to me would be exponential.

I needed to say it. He needed something from me. I couldn't just take and take from him. I needed to give. I needed to give him this.

I sniffled, gaining some type of bearing. "I love you," I whispered so quietly that only he could hear it, hoping that the gods couldn't.

That prophecy weighed on me more in this moment.

*One who will break me, one who will heal me, and one whom I will destroy.*

I didn't want to destroy him. I didn't want him to ever experience pain. Right now, he was in pain because of me. He was worried about me. He had demons haunting him because my demons haunted me.

"I love you," I whispered again. "I love you, and I never want to see you in pain. Not even when it's because you are worried for me."

He intertwined our fingers. "I will always worry about you."

"I don't want to be broken anymore, Darius. I want to be whole for you."

"No one is whole."

"You are. You are whole and pure and bright. You're so fucking Seelie it hurts."

"Vina, I have demons just like you. I had a brother."

"What?"

"He died when I was thirty and it gutted me. My mother died after my childbirth and my father retired and left me to him, so he was all I had. But he died after managing a trade that took him across the human lands. It left me alone, and terrified. It took me *years*, Vina, to just be okay." He kissed my temple. "I understand what it is like to hurt. When I see your pain, I remember what it was like to be alone with that pain. I don't want you to be alone."

He took a shuddering breath, tears starting to stream down his face. "I was in so much pain when I woke up with you not in my bed and all your stuff gone. I thought you were done with me. That you didn't love me, and you were ready to move on, leaving me alone again. I wanted to give you your space, so I waited a couple days to stop by the shop. I was going to beg you to reconsider. When Ms. Masel told me you took a few days off, I knew something was wrong and came here, but when you didn't answer and I went crazy. I begged the manager to open the door, but she said she would never in a million years break your trust, not even for a few thousand coin. Then I went to the witch and pleaded with her to help me find you. She did a spell and told me you were here. If you didn't answer that door, I probably would have broken it down."

He closed his eyes for a moment, gathering himself before he spoke again. "I was so scared, Vina, scared that you were dead in here. That your pain finally caught up to you and took you from me before I even got to tell you I loved you. That I loved how beautiful you were inside and out. How I loved that you were trying to be okay even if you think you aren't doing enough for me. That I loved how you smiled for me even when you feel like death inside. That even though you felt down, you would make sure to uplift me. Vina, I love how you see beauty in the smallest things like plants, food, and stars. How you are never in a rush and you want to enjoy things because you're afraid they will end. But they won't end. I won't let that happen. I want you to be my female, Vina. I know it scares you to rely on me, but you can. I'm not going anywhere. I will always be here for you."

I never thought he paid so much attention to me. I knew he was observant, but I didn't know he noticed all of that.

I was even lying to myself, trying to convince myself that I was okay. It made sense why I ended up consumed again in the darkness. The darkness didn't just go away because Darius was here to light me up. He may be the one to heal me, but his presence wasn't just going to make me okay. I would have to do the work. He was nudging me in the right direction, but I would have to be the one to take the first step.

"I am yours, Darius. The gods have said it so."

He moved his head to kiss me. I loved the feel of his lips on mine, even if we both tasted of salt from our tears. He trailed kisses down my throat and lingered where my neck met my shoulder.

Tensing, I pulled back, panic creeping its way up my spine. "I'm not ready, not for that. I'm going to need time for that, but I'm yours, Darius. I am, believe that."

He kissed me gently. "I can wait. I will wait a thousand years if I have to."

I smiled at him. "But I am ready for us to do more." I couldn't say the exact words. I was vulnerable right now, and I felt too shy to say it. "You don't have to worry about it being special or perfect. It will be perfect because it is with you."

"Okay." He pressed his lips to mine. The kiss carrying a different tone that had a wave of heat pooling between my legs.

I broke the kiss. "I want to but…" I looked around my room. This room was a place of pain and darkness. I didn't want to taint our first time with that darkness. "Not here."

"Yeah, okay. We can just sleep and…"

"No, let's go home. I've been wanting you for a while and I don't want to wait any longer."

"Home?" He kissed me. "I don't think I heard you correctly. Can you repeat yourself?"

I rolled my eyes. "Do you want to get fucked or not, Darius?" I felt less scared to speak my mind as my core throbbed for him.

He growled, thrusting his growing erection up into me.

I laughed, then stood. "Come on."

# TWENTY-SIX

## MARIE

*I* slept restlessly. Anticipation racked my whole body as to why Levi wanted to see me. I tossed and turned in bed for a few hours. When I finally went to sleep, I ended up waking myself a few moments later, from the fear that I would oversleep and miss the opportunity. I was exhausted, but I couldn't wait any longer, so I got out of bed and went directly to his room.

The dark-stained wood of his door faced me. I had rushed over here without thinking about what would happen when I stepped over the threshold. I knew when I walked in, I would walk out Levi's. Even if he didn't claim me as his. There was just a part of me that knew that I belonged to him—not fully, not yet. I could go back to my room and continue to avoid what my heart and soul wanted. I could be logical about this, but I was fae and we weren't logical.

"Creatures of chaos," I whispered as I raised my hand to knock. It was stupid to try to argue with one's heart. The heart didn't care if he would destroy us. It didn't care if being with him would ruin our brain's plans. It wanted to be on the other side of that door with him, and I was tired of denying my heart, so my knuckles met hardwood.

Levi opened the door a moment later. His face blank, not allowing me to gauge what he was thinking, which made me more nervous. I wanted to always know what thoughts swirled through his beautiful head. It was painfully frustrating that I couldn't read the emotions through his face.

"Come." He jerked his head toward the room.

I walked in, my movements slow, my whole body buzzing. The urge to play with my claws acute.

Hands came around my shoulders, making me tense slightly then instantly relax. Levi stepped closer to me, his front inches away from my back. His hands slid from my shoulders to the ties of the cloak, and he began to unravel them. He moved closer, his breath brushing my neck as he pressed a gentle kiss to my ear. A slight vibration zinging through my body straight to my clit.

He took my cloak—his cloak—off me and laid it at the end of the bed. His hand found mine and he led me to the side. "Sit."

My bottom met the bed and I looked up at him. It was dark in the room. The fireplace the only lighting. His black hair reflected the red-orange glow and shadows lined his face, making his sharp feature look even more crisp. He lowered to his knees, staring up at me, and I could finally see emotion on his face—admiration.

Stars shimmered in his midnight eyes as he took me in. He looked at me like I was the center of the universe. His stare always made me feel gutted and vulnerable. I felt it penetrate straight through my heart and then deeper into my soul. It was something I hated, but secretly, I craved to have it always.

His hands rested on my outer thighs, his thumbs making little circles on my stockings. "I'm not supposed to kneel for anyone," Levi spoke. "Only my father, but no one else."

"Why are you for me?"

"Because I want to give you a gift."

I raised a brow. "A gift?"

"For Mabon."

I smiled. "Mabon is a harvest sabbat. You're supposed to feast and spend time with loved ones."

"We won't be together tomorrow." My heart squeezed painfully at the notion that he thought of me as one of his loved ones.

"Okay, where is it?"

"You have to agree to accept the gift before I give it to you."

"Why?" My smile widened, cheeks tingling from the action.

He smiled, then brought his nose to mine and nudged it. "Because I said."

"And I have to do everything you say, Your Highness?" I rested my forehead on his, enjoying the sensations that passed through me from his touch.

"Do you want your gift?" he questioned.

"Okay, fine. I accept."

He kissed me, and I fell into his lips. My body alive and heady. I deepened the kiss, pulling his face closer to me before he broke the embrace, leaving me whimpering at the loss.

He chuckled lightly. "That's not your gift."

I looked at him, confused.

"Lie back."

I raised a brow.

"I promise you'll like it."

A grumble left me, wanting his lips back on mine, but I did as he asked and lied back.

His hands moved up my thighs and he tugged me to the edge of the bed. I almost yelled at him to ask what he was doing until his hands lifted my skirt and he unhooked the garter holding up my stockings.

He kissed my naked inner thigh. The vibrations making me arch my back. He trailed kisses up my leg, right to my black lace panties, then he stopped and did the same to the other. When he reached my panties this time, he breathed in my scent and groaned before planting a kiss right over my clit, my body jerking at the contact.

Levi bit into my panties. His teeth scraped against my flesh, making me moan. With his teeth, he pulled my panties down my legs until they reached his fingers that were still drawing light circles on my outer thighs.

I propped myself up on my elbows to see him pocketing my panties.

He smiled at me, his grin wicked and full of mischief. "Lie back," he demanded.

"I want to watch."

"Marie, I've imagined eating your pussy since the first moment I saw you. I don't think I can resist tasting you. But if you don't do as I say, that's all I'll do, just a taste." His voice was assertive and made my already dripping core wetter. I wanted his mouth on me. I had never had anyone do this to me and I wanted the full experience, so I obeyed him.

"Good," he whispered.

His hands trailed up my inner thighs, and he pushed them wider as he moved closer. I could feel his breath on my exposed lips, my blood pounding through my veins. My breath short and shallow as I anticipated the feel of his mouth on me. He hooked my legs over his shoulders and his hands found mine as he laced our fingers.

Then his tongue trailed through my slit.

My back arched, and I cried out. The vibrations from his hands in mine, sensually flowing through me. The contact from his tongue like lightning through my core, breaking me right down the center. His touch so close to my clit made the sensations more dramatic and overwhelming. My toes curled in my boots as the feeling racked through my body violently. My cry turned into a scream as the wave of pleasure crested and my come gushed out of me.

I came from one taste, one brush of his tongue.

Levi chuckled as I settled my breathing. "Mabon is a sabbat for feasting."

He delved back into my flesh, lapping at my juices like a starved animal. The whole experience was profound and intoxicating. He played with my slit, his tongue slightly stretching and prodding at my entrance. His nose lightly teased my clit, driving me insane to the brink of madness.

I made noises that I had never made before. I didn't even know if they came from me, but I was the only female in the room. I knew I would be embarrassed of them later, but at the moment, I didn't care. The feeling was too good, otherworldly. The vibrations attacked me in the most delicious way, flowing up from my clit to my nipples then back. My heart was beating so fast I thought it might explode. At some point, I let go of Levi's hand and found purchase in his silky strands, pulling him closer, needing more of the exquisite pleasure he brought me.

I felt myself building unlike the first time. The vibrations pulsating higher and higher. It felt like I was floating off the bed as Levi feasted on me. I ground my hips into his mouth, and he growled. The action adding to the vibrations. My moans became pleas, whimpers, and cries. I was begging Levi to take me over, but I wasn't able to properly form any words.

Then finally, finally, his tongue lapped my clit.

A scream ripped through me as I fell from the clouds. Every muscle in my body tightened as pleasure flowed blissfully through my veins. I quivered and twitched, having no control over myself. I was lost in ecstasy, unable to even grasp the concept of life. Until I finally relaxed enough to remember where I was.

My breath came in shallow pants. I opened my eyes to the dimly lit room, taking in the environment I had just abandoned moments before. I realized that my claws were digging into Levi's scalp. Sitting up way too fast for someone who just had their mind shattered, I examined his head.

"Did I hurt you?" My voice alarmed. I don't know why, but the idea that I had even caused him a microscopic amount of pain sent me reeling. I couldn't see much through his dark loose curls, but I smelled blood. "I did. Fuck. I'm so sorry." I bent down and pressed a kiss on his head.

Levi grabbed my hands and laughed. "I'll heal. In fact, I think the wound has already sealed, nothing to worry about." He gave me that smile. That fucking beautiful, perfect, crafted by the gods, smile.

I pulled his face to mine and brought my body back to the bed. I loved the feeling of Levi's body over mine and my taste on his lips.

I just had the best orgasm of my life, but I felt unfinished. There was a need set within me. A need that has been within me since I first found those blue-black irises. I wanted him within me. I wanted his cock scraping and scratching inside my walls. I wanted him fully, right fucking now.

Our kisses were hungry and animalistic. We completely abandoned our human etiquette and went full fae, attacking each other's lips like starved beasts. Our canines scraped and grazed but didn't bite. I wrapped my legs around him, caging him in. I never wanted to let him go. He was mine.

I needed his cock. I needed to touch it, to feel it. I needed it pumping through me. I just needed it.

My hand traveled down to his pants and found his hard length. He groaned into my mouth, his teeth almost biting my lips. Then, abruptly, he pulled away.

He sat back on the ground, catching his breath, running his hands through his hair. "Levi?"

He looked up at me, leaning his forehead on mine. "I want to, Marie. I really fucking want to," he breathed. "But I will not have you, I cannot have you, when you are another's."

I deflated slightly and nodded.

A part of me wanted to argue that the mark meant nothing to me. That I was his, even though I wore Kolvin's mark. I wanted to tell him that the mark would be gone soon, but it didn't matter, it wouldn't be fair to Levi. He deserved to have me when I was free of another's claim.

"Thank you for my gift," I whispered.

He snorted and bit his lip before saying, "Did you like it?"

"I loved it."

"Good."

"Did you enjoy your feast?" I questioned.

"It was the best thing I ever tasted. I couldn't get enough."

"Good." I grinned.

Chuckling, he stood. "Move over."

I moved back, delving deeper into the nest of furs. Levi laid down, pulling me into his chest. A purr left me as I burrowed my face into him. I didn't care that my creature was a whack job who purred. I was too busy enjoying his scent.

He covered us with one of his furs. It was slightly weird that I was wearing boots in bed, but I couldn't be bothered to move from this position. The bed was soft and warm, and Levi was Levi. My heart throbbed, content and happy that we had stopped fighting it, and I was happy as well.

Levi played with my curls, the twiddling motion massaging my scalp. The sensation, the fact that I was running on no sleep, and had two life-altering orgasms, making me sleepy. My eyes kept drifting shut, and I jerked myself awake every few seconds.

"Sleep, Marie. I'll wake you an hour before you have to leave."

I hummed in response, let my lids close, and oblivion steal me away.

# TWENTY-SEVEN

## MARIE

$\mathcal{L}$evi woke me about two hours before sunrise. I only had twenty-four hours with my family from sunrise to sunrise on Mabon. It was a shit deal because I only got eight days to see them out of the year. No matter how well the fae were doing at the current moment, Seelie and Unseelie could never fully trust each other. I didn't see that changing anytime soon. In fact, I think all would collapse and crumble within the next hundred or so years.

With our hands intertwined, Levi walked me to my room. The vibrations had calmed down since I orgasmed. It wasn't gone, just a light buzz instead of an intense chasm of energy. The hum reminded me of how unfinished I felt. It was strange to feel satisfied but also incomplete.

We didn't talk while we walked, but no words needed to be said. I felt comfortable with Levi, more than I ever have with any person, even my mother. I didn't feel like I had to pretend with him, I could just be. I didn't have to be anyone or anything. I didn't even have to be Marie.

When we got to my room, Levi came in and leaned against the bookshelf as I packed a few things for my day at home; a pair of clothes, and a rose from the greenhouse for my mother. I knew she would love it. The king paid a lot of coin for those flowers, and they were probably the most beautiful roses I had ever seen.

Looking over at Levi, I saw him reading the messages.

*I love you and I miss you. Can't wait to see you in a few days.*

That was what Kolvin had last written. I saw it and didn't reply. I couldn't bring myself to lie to him. I didn't miss him; not like I was supposed to. I still loved him as my best friend and the idea of breaking his heart was terrible. I wished I hadn't made any promises to him before I had left, but I didn't know I'd meet Levi, and everything would change.

Walking over to the desk, I stepped in front of Levi to grab the pen. My eyes met his as I put it in my pocket. The message was clear; I wasn't going to be someone else's when I got back.

I let out a huff as I put the pad of paper away, guilt blanketing me.

Levi rubbed my shoulders and leaned down to kiss my cheek. His arms wrapping around me in a comforting embrace. I turned, stepping up on my toes, and gave him a quick kiss in gratitude.

A half-smile painted my lips when I pulled back. I enjoyed his comfort, but it didn't make me feel any less of a shitty person.

Levi walked over to my dresser. He opened a few drawers, searching through the contents for something before pulling out a pair of panties and handing them to me. "I love that you aren't wearing any right now, but I want you to wear them while you're gone."

A smile formed on my face. Levi was a fae male. The bastards were controlling and possessive. I would argue that he couldn't tell me what to do even if we were whatever we were. It would be pointless though. I was going to wear them while I was gone. I would probably struggle with keeping a pair if he kept stealing them, but I wasn't the type of female to walk around without, even for my male's enjoyment.

I pulled the pair on and secured my stockings to my garter.

Levi kissed my head; I think to reward me for listening. I wanted to laugh at how much of a male he was being right now, but I just snorted.

He pulled back and quirked a brow. I covered my mouth trying not to laugh at him.

"What is it, Marie?"

"Nothing. You're just cute when you're demanding." I grinned.

"Cute?" He grimaced.

My grin widened. "Yes."

He rolled his eyes, a muscle in his jaw flexing. "I'm being serious."

"You're being a male."

He grumbled, then picked me up. My legs instinctively wrapped around him. It was surprising that he could pick me up like I was nothing, because I was not nothing. Though, he was probably only muscle. His fingers possessively dug into my ass as he pinned me against the bookshelf and kissed me. His kiss was demanding and dominating, and I couldn't help but submit. His hand moved, trailing to my inner thighs, finding the panties I had just put on and he moved them aside. I was soaking wet, and he hissed into my mouth when he realized. He lightly played with my clit for a few strokes, his touch featherlight and teasing before he slipped two fingers into me.

He broke the kiss as his digits scraped that perfect spot, my eyes rolling in the back of my head. "Look at me, Marie."

I did, biting my lip and whimpering as he did it again.

"You are going to be good and wear underwear while you're gone. Okay?" He added the *okay* to make it seem like a question, but his tone offered no argument.

I nodded, moaning slightly as he continued teasing that spot.

"Good." He pumped his fingers into me a few more times, then stopped and set me down, causing me to whine in annoyance.

"Come back to me," he said. His eyes boring into me with an intensity that said things wouldn't be good if I didn't come back.

I watched this male almost kill a guy because he said he touched me. I wouldn't doubt Levi would tear down the diamond wall to find me if I didn't come back.

"I will." A promise.

He gave me a brutal kiss that reminded me that he left me unfinished and wanting. He pulled back and stuck the two fingers that were in me a couple moments ago into his mouth, then groaned and sucked them clean before he gave me that smirk that twisted me up inside. "Thanks for the snack," he said before winking.

I rolled my eyes and pushed him out of the way so I could pack.

When I finished, Levi walked me out to the front of the castle. The cold air whipped through my hair. I was excited to go home to the warmth. I missed the sun and the heat, and I couldn't wait to feel it on my skin. A part of me was sad to leave Levi, but I was only going to be gone a day. I wasn't going to die. At least that was what I was telling myself.

Levi stopped me a few paces before the carriage that was set up to take the Seelie students home—which would be just me because I was the only one born Seelie. He kissed me. The kiss intense and making my heart ache. My fingers grasped his cloak, and I pulled him closer.

We stayed there for a while, letting our lips do all the talking. Levi had caged me in his arms, his grip possessive but caring. I felt so safe within his grasp, it made leaving even harder, but I had to go.

I pulled back, and Levi rested his forehead on mine. I studied his face. His eyes were closed, his jaw locked, and nostrils flared.

He was angry. A sense of dread stole over me as I watched him battle with his emotions. Was he angry at me?

I stared at him while he composed himself. I was terrified of what he'd do when he finally did open his eyes. Would he shatter what we just created? Would he break me before I even got to truly have him?

We stood there frozen for what felt like forever. When his eyes opened, I could see I had misread his emotions. What shimmered through his eyes was not anger but fear.

He kissed my forehead, breathing me in before he pulled back and looked at me with pleading eyes. "Come back." Before I could reply, he turned and walked stiffly toward the palace doors.

This time, the carriage ride was only an hour. The portals were free to use because most didn't work on sabbats.

The sabbats were sacred days to the fae—eight days of power celebrating the sun. The sun was our life. If the fae lived in harmony, then the sabbats would be a celebration of the seasons as well, but since the fae didn't live in harmony, the seasons were split and out of balance.

The fae had to work around the unbalanced seasons. The Unseelie would provide a rich and fertile soil from their lands and Seelie grew the food. It was working, but it was a flawed system.

Each sabbat marked a certain high in the magical properties. During this time of the year, the power was mostly held by the Unseelie since the nights grew longer and the days shorter. Yule, the winter solstice, was the first sabbat of the year. It was the longest night of the year and the Unseelie would be more powerful during that night. Yule was also the rebirth of the sun; it signified for the Seelie that the sun was soon to return, and light would make its way to power again.

Mabon was the second to last sabbat in the year. It celebrated the beginning of fall and was the second harvest festival. The day was often spent feasting with family and friends. It was a relaxed sabbat if you weren't the one who cooked the feast.

Our Mabon was often spent with my father's soldiers and their families. My mother normally made dinner and I would help. Kolvin's family would be there...

I dreaded that I had to break Kolvin's heart in front of his family, especially his two older brothers because males were quite cruel to each other, but I had to do this in person and had no other time.

I arrived at the wall a few seconds before sunrise. They were lifting the gate when I stepped out. I showed my papers to the guards, and they waved me forward.

The feeling of coming home was like a butterfly coming out of a cocoon. I knew I was Unseelie, and I belonged in the forever winter, but this was where I grew up, this was my home. There were some good things about Unseelie that I liked. One of them being a tall, grumpy male with midnight eyes. The snow was beautiful and there was this sense of peace and comfort among the Unseelie, but I would always hold Seelie near to my heart.

The heat begin to defrost my frozen face as I scanned through the crowd of people for my parents. I caught sight of a blue ice-like shimmer, then I was running.

Her eyes locked with mine. When I was a few paces away from her, I dropped my bag and flung my arms around her slim frame. Her rose scent filled my senses, and I relaxed into it.

"My flower," my mother whispered in my ear.

"Mother," I cried, tears running down my face. I had never spent this long without my mother. She was my anchor and I felt unbalanced without her.

After a few moments, I pulled back and turned to my father, wrapping my arms around him. I loved my father's hugs. I loved my mother, but she wasn't a hugger. When my father wrapped me in his arms, I felt safe, secure. I snuggled into his embrace, letting his warmth wash away the leftover Unseelie chill.

I gazed up into his warm sea-blue eyes. "Father," I breathed.

He smiled brightly. "Flower, we have missed you so much."

I hugged him again, and then my mother, father, and I were walking home arm in arm.

It was warming up, but since it was so early in the day, I didn't feel the need to remove Levi's cloak, and a small part of me didn't want to. My mother inspected the garment as we walked. She was subtly picking at the fur and running her fingers through the hem. If I didn't know my mother's prodding well, I would think she was just appreciating the fine cloak. I knew she and my father could smell the male all over me. I knew she would question me about it later. She always demanded that I tell her everything and I always did; I felt safe telling her things, but I didn't want to tell her about Levi for some reason.

Deep in my gut, I knew she would disapprove. She wasn't very fond of Kolvin as just my best friend, and he was Seelie. My mother hated the Unseelie; it was like one of her personality traits. She loved gardening, cooking, and hating Unseelie bastards. If I told her that I was courting the Unseelie Prince, she would flip. I hoped we didn't have much time to talk about it because I didn't want her to ruin what had barely begun to bloom.

When we got home, I set my bag down and pulled out my mother's rose, the gift I brought back for her. It was in a box so it would stay plump. Handing it to her, I grinned wide. "The king has a greenhouse full of these in the queen's quarters. I don't know why he has a greenhouse for a queen he doesn't have, but they are the most beautiful roses I have ever seen, and they reminded me of you."

The look on her face was cold and disconnected. My mother often put off a detached and cold expression but never toward me. My grin faltered and I pulled the rose back. "Do you not like it?"

She plastered a smile on her face. I could tell something about the rose bothered her, but she wouldn't hurt me by not accepting it. "No, flower. I was just stunned that you brought me something." She examined the rose, still not taking it. "Why were you in the queen's quarters?"

I decided not to lie but withhold most of the truth. "The king's son is my partner in school. I didn't have much of a choice in the matter before you ask. We study there."

Her eyes almost popped out of her head and her smile grew tighter. "Why didn't you tell me his son was your partner in any of your letters or when we talked over the portal mirror?"

I shrugged, looking away so she couldn't see the lie in my eyes. "It's nothing. Levi is a big grump who hates everyone."

"It's a pretty big deal, he is *the prince*." Her words were coated in disdain, affirming my worries.

"Mother, do we need to talk about this right now? I missed you and I brought you this flower because it reminded me of you. I thought you would like it."

She took the flower from me, holding it out slightly, as if it might burn her. "Marie, I love it. I'm sorry for interrogating you. I just feel lost, not being in every part of your life anymore." Her body was still stiff, but her hard black eyes had softened slightly.

"Me too." It hurt that this was our first interaction. We had been apart for so long and it had driven a wedge between us. It would only get worse. We would never have time for me to sit in her shop while she messed with her herbs. Or for us to talk for hours about stupid things that didn't matter. Or for her to read to me on late nights in the library. I didn't really think of it before, but I would possibly lose that deep connection with my mother over time. My lip started to tremble, and I could feel tears trying to escape my eyes at the thought.

She laid a hand on my shoulder. "Do not cry, my flower. I know this is hard, but everything will work out in the end."

I didn't believe her for one sole reason, Levi. If things got serious with me and Levi, I would probably stay in Unseelie. I couldn't deny that Levi had a hold over me that no other had. I would give up my relationship with my mother for him. That part of me that was afraid of our connection built up within me but was quickly overshadowed by the deep-seated desire I had for him. I felt like a terrible person. Who gives up their relationship with their mother for a male they've known for three weeks?

"Well, I have a feast to prepare." My mother lightly smiled. "Why don't you rest? We got you some blackout curtains so you can sleep while you're here."

I nodded and hugged my parents before climbing the stairs to my room.

# TWENTY-EIGHT

## CORIVINA
## 192 YEARS AGO.

$\mathcal{T}$he rough stone of the Seelie Palace scraped my back as Darius pumped into me. I moaned into his mouth as his cock brushed that perfect spot. He thrust harder, letting me know he was almost there. I wrapped my legs around him, cutting myself on the bush we were hiding behind, as my body threatened to explode.

"Darius," I gasped as I tightened around him. I had to bite my lip to hold back the scream that built in my throat as I began to shatter.

Darius pumped harder, making my pleasure extend to new heights. I dug my claws into his neck, and he hissed. He gave one last powerful thrust, then emptied himself inside me.

I held him close as we both took time to catch our breaths. Since Darius and I started having sex two years back, we could hardly be apart. We fucked at every opportunity, our bodies needing to be tangled together.

Darius kissed me. We could go again, but we were late. The king was throwing a party for something important, and it required Darius's presence. We were already running late because he needed to take me in the carriage, and now, we were super late because I needed him to take me against the palace walls too.

Darius set me down and began pulling up his trousers from his ankles. Before he could, I wrapped my hands around his firm ass and dug my claws in.

He hissed. "Vina, the king is going to fucking kill me for being late."

"We are here," I purred.

He smirked at me and pushed me against the wall, then brutally kissed me. "I fucking love you in red. It reminds me of the first time I kissed you."

I pulled him closer, wanting him again. I was so fucking in love with this male I needed him always. I would never not want him. His warmth was intoxicating. His kiss was ecstasy, but his cock was fucking euphoria. I craved it deep within my bones. I would never get enough.

He pulled away, causing me to growl.

He chuckled lightly, then said, "We have to go."

I pouted with pleading eyes.

"Look, we will go in, dance, drink. I'll see the king and we will leave. I haven't been to his last few parties, and he said my presence was mandatory tonight. If I don't show up, he'd cut off my balls. I know you are very fond of them and probably want them to stay where they are."

I frowned. "Fine."

He tied the laces on his trousers. He wore his commander's uniform, white with gold stitching. He looked so hot in it, he looked hot in everything, but I loved when he had to be a diplomat and dress up.

I fixed my red dress; it was silk and flowed with my body, curling around my hips but giving my legs space to move. It was great for dancing or fucking. The neckline was low, the straps just string and my back left exposed. It was just a scrap of a fabric, easily rip-able. I hoped that later Darius would tear the thing off me.

We walked into the ballroom. The walls painted white with gold accents. The tablecloths gold and the floor a dark mahogany. Sunflowers and yellow lilies spewed about. Everything in the room screaming Seelie.

Darius immediately pulled me to the dance floor. A squeal of excitement leaving as he twirled me, I smiled at him.

He tugged me close and kissed me sweetly before his sea-blue eyes met mine. "I love you, Vina."

"I love you too." I kissed him back. Tonight, I wanted us to get drunk on fae wine and then fuck like wild animals.

"Commander Foxglove, is it?" The voice was soft and comforting but made every hair on my body stand.

I turned to the voice and met blue-black eyes. My whole body frozen in place.

*Markos.* Markos was here. He wore his crown, signifying his recent ascension to the throne, and he was here staring at me.

Darius turned, his arm coming to rest on my lower back, and gave Markos a nod. Seelie didn't bow to the Unseelie, but a nod was a sign of respect.

I never told Darius who my ex was. I was still telling him bits and pieces, but I never told him a name. He didn't know that he was nodding in respect to the male who broke me.

"King Markos," Darius said. He shifted his attention to the male behind Markos. "King Dominick. Sorry we are late, sir." The Seelie King stepped into my view. His long blond hair brushed his naked shoulders. He never wore a shirt, choosing to showcase his bronzed chiseled chest. He was godly beautiful, but he wore gold trousers, which made him look ridiculous.

"If we weren't close friends, Dare, your dick would be missing for being absent from my last few parties. But you brought your gorgeous female again, so all is forgiven. What was your name again, miss?"

I ripped my eyes from Markos's to look at the green eyes of the king. "Corivina." My voice was surprisingly even, given that I felt like the earth was falling out from under me.

"*Corivina*," he purred. "You sure you wouldn't rather be with a king than a silly commander?"

I couldn't help but glance at Markos. I was already with a king and that ended terribly. "No, I'm fine."

He chuckled, then turned serious, looking at Darius. "I need to speak with you."

Darius looked at me, his eyes communicating he would be back soon.

"I can take her off your hands while you're away," Markos offered.

I squeezed Darius's arm. That was the last thing I wanted. My eyes pleaded with him not to leave. He looked at the king and then pulled me close. "I have to go, but I'll be back as soon as possible."

Darius handed me off to Markos, whose hand slid around my waist possessively, and I watched Darius leave without a second thought. I was too stunned to do anything. Markos's chestnut scent wafting around me, reminding me of home.

He took my hand and started to move us along the dance floor. I just stared at his chest. His black tunic splayed open enough for me to see the raven that laid across his heart. To everyone else, the tattoo would seem to symbolize his love for his people, holding them close to his heart. Really, it symbolized his love for me. I was his raven.

"Cor."

I looked at his face, noticing not much had changed about him, his hair was still shoulder length, and his beard was still close to his face. The onyx pointed crown was new, but he was still the same male I had fallen in love with, the same male who broke me.

I finally unglued my tongue from the top of my mouth and said, "How are you talking to me right now? Our deal was that you were to leave me alone."

"I did, but you didn't specify how long. The second I left you, I had fulfilled the deal."

A wave of emotion stole over me, and I blinked harshly, trying to hold it back.

"Cor, I'm sorry. You know I'm sorry. I know what I did was terrible and awful, and I never meant it to go that far."

His fingers drew circles on my back, and I found it comforting. I let out a slight sob, and Markos pulled me into his chest to not have us cause a scene. He walked me off the dance floor to an abandoned hallway. When we were alone, I crumbled, sobbing into his chest as he held me.

I was disgusted with myself because I felt safe in his arms. I still felt like he would fix everything, like he could somehow erase my pain and make it okay. That he would take care of me like he promised. I hated that I liked his arms around me. The realization did nothing but make me cry harder.

"Cor, I'm sorry. I'm so fucking sorry." He pulled my face from his chest so I could find his eyes. "I would do anything to take it back. I would do anything to get you back."

The words made me step away from him. "Markos, we can never get back together. Never."

He took my hands. I hated my body for not flinching away from his touch. I spent years avoiding males because of him. Afraid they'd hurt me as he did but now that he was here, my body didn't seem to care.

"Cor, marry me."

I felt that small foundation I had spent the last few years building shatter within that moment. I snatched my hands from his, rage crawling up my neck. "Are you fucking serious?" I snapped.

"Yes," he said, eyes pleading. "Corivina, you are my fucking world. I can't be without you. I knew that then and I really fucking know that now. It's you… It will always be you."

"You realize that if you had just married me in the first place, I would've been yours." Anger swirled deeply within me, and my magic heated my body, making the tears that fell from my eyes burn.

"Yes, I know. *I know.* I should have. I should have told my parents to screw themselves. I should have chosen you over them. I should have married you and made you my queen. If anyone had a problem with you being Seelie, I should have told them to fuck off. I should have done that, but my raven, I didn't, and it is my second biggest regret."

"You should have!" I yelled. "But you didn't. Instead, you… did what you did and now there is no going back. I have moved on."

"With that commander? The male whose scent is all over you? Who you told you fucking love? Who calls you *Vina?*" He seethed.

"Yes," I growled.

"You don't even wear his mark."

"I can't! I can't let anyone put their teeth near me because of you! Because you ruined it! You took something beautiful, and you turned it into a horrid wretched thing. I love him and you broke me so fucking badly that I can't give him what he deserves. I can't show him how much I fucking love him because of you. It makes me hate myself but above all, it makes me hate you and I do. I fucking hate you!"

Markos took a step back, his anger rising within him. He was trying to calm it. This was his problem. Markos would always be calm, cool, and collected. It was all an act. It's what made what he did so shocking because I would have never expected it.

He spent all his time trying to be civil. Trying to be calm and gentle. Trying to not be fae. He would push down his anger and his creature's urges, until it was too much, and he exploded. I never realized it before, but this was how he always was.

He took a deep breath, pushing his shoulders back to shake off his rage. "Corivina, please. Marry me. I will spend my life trying to make it up to you and atone for my mistakes. I will do anything you ask of me, and I will love you till the end of my days."

I looked at those blue-black eyes. I saw how desperate he was for me to say yes. I could… I could go back to this monster and hope he'd change. I could be the Queen of Unseelie. I could have everything I wanted before all of this. I could let him try to make up for all his wrongs, but would I ever forgive him? Could I ever forget the years I spent in darkness, what the darkness did to me? What it had me do while I was consumed by it? Or the fact that he violated my body when he didn't get his way? The answer to that was simple. "No."

I turned and walked back into the great hall. I found Darius drinking wine and talking to one of his army buddies. My claws ripped into his uniform as I grabbed his arm and stared daggers at him.

His eyes widened. "Vina—"

"Take me fucking home. Now!"

# TWENTY-NINE

## MARIE

$S$omeone gently shaking me woke me from my slumber. "Flower, the Denmors are here, and dinner is starting in a few hours. It's time to get up." My father's voice filtered through my groggy mind.

I pushed myself up and yawned.

"Kolvin has been antsy to see you. He arrived a few hours ago and has been pestering your mother and I about you all day." My father brushed a few curls from my face, the simple watch he wore glinting from that light the streamed from my bathroom.

I grimaced. "Did mother tell you what I did?"

"Your mother would never betray your trust like that. Though, I can guess by your scent that you found another?"

"No… well, maybe, I don't know. I just got there and things just…"

"Do you want to bathe? I can stall the kid a little longer if you'd like."

I wiped the tiredness from my eyes. Even if I did bathe, it wouldn't get rid of Levi's scent, and a deep part of me didn't want to. Scents were weird; if you spent an intimate thirty minutes with someone, you'd smell like them for days even if you bathed.

"No, I just want to get this over with. He'll know the second he comes near me."

My father sighed. "Flower, you're about to ruin one of my brightest pupils. You know I'm training him to take my place when I retire one day."

I smiled. "We both know you are never going to. You'll have to be forced out of the position because you're too old."

"That's true, but the king wants a backup in case I die in the upcoming battles."

My eyes widened, tiredness fully slipping away from me as worry and panic filled my veins. "Upcoming battles?"

He rubbed my shoulder. "Nothing to worry about; the king is just paranoid as always. He is practically best friends with the Unseelie King, but he always fears a betrayal and wants to be prepared. We haven't had a war in a while, and one is bound to happen sooner or later."

I let out a breath. "Good."

My father embraced me and kissed my forehead. "I really missed you, flower."

"I missed you too. Were you and mother okay without me?"

"Your mother went to the inn when you left."

My mother had a room she continuously rented at an inn in town. It was the room I spent the first five years of my life in. I knew my mother kept the room. I figured because she wanted to have the place that I grew up in, but I had never been back there since we moved in with my father. I had forgotten about it until a few years ago when my mother and father got into a huge fight—about me—and she left. She stayed there for a couple days. I tried to visit, but the innkeeper told me Mother had requested not to allow me in. She returned a few days later and we continued on like nothing happened.

"Has she been there the whole time?" I asked.

"No, she left for a day before I went to get her."

"Why didn't you get her immediately?"

My father stiffened. "Me and your mother have a unique relationship, flower."

"Because of me."

He shook his head. "No, because of me, your mother as well." He exhaled. "I knew that after I killed your birth father, it would ruin our relationship."

"But you still love each other," I interjected.

He gave me a half smile. "Flower, we should go downstairs. Kolvin will probably bust down that door if you don't come down soon."

"Father—"

"Marie, I shouldn't talk to you about what goes on between me and your mother."

I grumbled and climbed off the bed. When my father used my real name, he was not to be argued with.

We walked downstairs, my father in front of me, distancing himself. I had about five steps left when I heard Kolvin's voice.

"Marie." My father had reached the end of the stairs and stepped out of the way. Blond hair and honey-green eyes met mine. One second, Kolvin was at the bottom of the stairs; and the next, he was one step below me bringing his mouth to mine.

The kiss was a second long but so much happened in that one second. My whole body recoiled as Kolvin kissed me with a passion that would have probably left me with a burning lust before I had left. Then he stopped moving, breathed in through his nose, stiffened and pulled away.

His hand cupped my cheek, eyes searching mine. It hurt my heart to see his face after he smelled Levi on me, and shame filled me.

I removed his hand from my face. "Can we go outside?"

I looked to see his family, my mother and father, and a few others staring at us. I could see the disapproving looks on his parents' faces, the hidden smiles behind his brothers'. They didn't have to be near enough to smell me to know what was wrong.

"Yeah." Kolvin turned and walked down the steps, then directly went out the front door. I followed, feeling everyone's eyes on me.

Kolvin walked to the treehouse, stopping when he reached the pond that we had made love in three weeks ago.

When he heard me approach, he turned, his eyes already lining with tears. "What the fuck, Marie?"

"Kol, I—"

"You fucking cheated on me. Anyone with a fucking nose could tell that. You smell freshly fucked," he snapped.

"I didn't fuck anyone," I whispered, feeling cowardly in that moment. I thought I would be able to do this, but instead, my shame had me shrinking into myself.

"Then what did you do?"

I opened my mouth, but nothing came out. I couldn't say it. I couldn't break my best friend's heart. I was already doing that, but I didn't want to make it worse than it already was.

Kolvin started to pace, his hand covering his mouth. I just stood there, not knowing what to say.

Eventually he stopped and looked at me with the most broken expression I've seen worn on his face. "Why?"

Tears clouded my eyes.

*Why? Because I met a male who just felt right.*

I couldn't say that, so I pulled out the pen from my pocket. The gold-plated accents glinting against the fading sun. Then held it out to him.

"I'm sorry," I said, my voice cracking and just above a whisper.

"Marie," he said without taking the pen. "I love you. You're my best fucking friend. I have known you, I have loved you, since we were kids."

"I know," I said, pushing the pen out as my lip trembled.

"Do you love me?" he asked, the tears in his eyes threatening to fall.

I tried to hold back the sob that came out my throat, but I couldn't. "No," I cried. "No, I don't. I did. At least I thought I did."

The dam of tears broke, traveling down his cheeks. He looked away from me, hiding them. "You wear my mark, Marie."

"I didn't want to remove it before I could…" I hiccuped.

"Before you could break up with me."

"Yeah." I sniffled. "Kol, you're still my best friend. I still want to be that. I know I fucked up. I know I betrayed your trust, but I will do anything to earn your forgiveness."

Kolvin looked down at the ground and shook his head. "No."

"Kol—"

He looked up at me, his green eyes swirling with hurt. "No, Marie. I can't forgive you. What you did is just unforgivable. You wore my mark and were with another. It doesn't matter if you didn't fuck them. It's not even the fact that you're marked. It's the fact that we have been best friends since we were fucking babes and you disrespected me like that. It's the fact that you barely wrote me back and made me go insane over the past few weeks wondering if you were okay. It's the fact that you didn't even bathe after you were with the male to at least give me the decency of not having his scent suffocating me while you trampled all over my heart. It's the fact that you let me look like a fool in front of my whole fucking family. Now I have to go back in there and tell them that the female that I have spent my whole life pining over cheated on me while she wore my mark. It's the fact that I will have to see you every sabbat because our families spend all of them together and be reminded of how you humiliated me. So no, when we go inside, we are nothing, not lovers, not best friends, nothing."

The look he gave me was pure hatred and I deserved his hatred. I was a fucked-up person. I hadn't even told him about Jess. I didn't want to rub salt in the wound, but also, I was just too fucking cowardly to own up to what I had done.

"I am sorry," I replied.

"You can go fuck yourself, Marie," Kolvin spat as he walked away, wiping his face.

# THIRTY

### Corivina
### 192 years ago.

*I* didn't speak to Darius during the carriage ride home. When we entered the manor, I immediately went upstairs, him following close behind. The second I got to the room, I pulled open my dresser.

I had pretty much had fully moved in over the last two years. It happened gradually and then Darius got rid of his old dresser and bought his and hers dressers for us. It was cute at the time, and I fucked him against it, but I should have demanded he got rid of them.

I started to pull my clothes out, piling them on the bed. Darius grasped my arm, turning me to him. "Vina, what are you doing?"

I ignored him and broke from his hold to continue packing my things.

"Vina," he pleaded.

"Did you know the Unseelie King would be at the party?"

He nodded.

"Why didn't you tell me?" I snapped.

"It slipped my mind, Vina."

"How could something like that slip your mind?"

"I don't know, maybe because all I think about is a female that I can't get enough of, and I spend every second wanting to be with her."

"If that were true, you wouldn't have left me with him."

"Vina—"

"I hate the Unseelie, and you fucking handed me over to him like it was nothing. You're the fucking Seelie Commander. You'd think that you wouldn't just hand your female off to just anyone, let alone the Unseelie fucking King."

"I didn't think it through, Vina. I have been so distracted with you lately that I started to slack off at my job. I knew I had pissed off the king and he literally threatened to take my position away tonight. I'm sorry I just handed you off. My mind has just been all over the place. Did he do anything to you?"

*Everything.* "No." I continued to gather my things. I felt the walls of darkness threatening to close me in, and I needed to get out of here now.

"I said I'm sorry, Vina. You said he didn't do anything so what is the big deal?"

"What is the big deal? The big deal is that I was stupid to ever think that I would ever be happy. That I could ever get over my past and be happy with you. That I could ever let go of my darkness and fully trust you enough."

"Vina, what are you saying?"

"I'm leaving. I'm going to my room at the inn, and we are over."

I needed to leave, and I needed to be alone while I went into the smoky depths of my darkness and drown within them. I had escaped this darkness before, but now, I was unsure if I'd succeed again. Seeing Markos had reopened the wounds of my past and I felt it all over again, the emptiness, the pain, the sorrow, all mixing together creating chaos within.

I was losing my grasp on reality, losing my hold on life. I needed to be in my room in the dark, staring at that tattered ceiling as everything shattered within me. I couldn't bring Darius with me as I went, not this time. The demons I had battled before just rose from the dead and were stronger than ever. It would consume me and anyone who got in the way.

Darius grabbed me by the shoulders. I saw the recognition in his eyes as he realized what was lurking right behind the small wall I had built to get me through the carriage ride here and this.

"No," he said. "No, Vina. I'm not losing you to your darkness. I'm not letting you go. I'm not."

"It's not your choice or your problem. We are done," I said, my voice cold and void of emotion. I knew that later I would fracture from the loss of him, but he had to stay, and I had to go.

"It is my problem, Vina. I love you. I share your pain. Feel it. Live it. I'm not going to let you leave and go back to that room and let the darkness swallow you whole. I'm not going to let you fight the demons by yourself because I can see it in your eyes, Vina. I can see that you aren't going to put up much of a fight. I will not lose you to them. You are staying here in your home because *this is* your home. I don't care what you do—fight with me, scream at me, cry with me, but do not leave me. You are everything to me and I will do anything to not lose you. Even if I have to fight every single one of those demons by myself."

His words broke that small wall I had erected to hold the darkness back, and tears streamed down my face. "I'm sorry, Darius, but I can't be fixed."

He brushed a lock of my hair behind my ear. "I don't want to fix you, Vina. I want you to see that there is nothing broken within."

"But there is! Don't you see I'm just a magnet for darkness? Don't you see that *he* broke me, and I cannot be fixed? I can't even show you how much I love you because of him. He has ruined me and tainted me forever. Every time your teeth come near my neck, I think of how he destroyed me. How I trusted him, how I loved him, how he was everything to me, my light, my life, my world, and then he mangled that. I think about how you are everything to me now. How you are my life, how you are my light, my fucking universe, and how you could do worse to me. How you could ruin me within minutes, break me as he did. It is fucking terrifying to love you, Darius. It is terrifying to trust you.

"I know it's not fair of me to compare you to him. You are perfect. You're everything I need and could ever ask for, but I can't trust it. It feels like a trap set by the gods. I feel like a terrible person for being with you, for loving you but never being able to give you enough. For never being able to be your light, for never being able to wear your mark. It pains me deeply that I can't get over what happened enough just to let you—the person I love most in this world—bite me for *five seconds* so that he can show the world who is his.

"Being with him… the king, just reminded me of all the love I had felt for him… my male before. It reminded me of the way he ripped me open. It cut me up inside and now everything I had built over the past few years has crumbled, Darius. I can't keep doing this, *it's killing me.* It's killing me to keep falling into darkness, only to have you pull me out. I know I haven't told you much, but those two years after he broke me, I did things, things I can't even get the courage to whisper to myself. I can't, Darius, I can't keep reliving those years, I can't keep falling. I'm done. The darkness wants me and I'm tired of fighting it and I'm sorry that I brought you with me."

Darius pulled me into his arms, his warmth soothing the cold that the darkness brought along. "No, Corivina. No," he breathed. "I'm sorry, I'm sorry that you keep experiencing that pain. I'm sorry that the darkness is calling for you again, but I can't let it swallow you. You *are* my light, Vina. You may think you give me nothing, but you anchor me. You may think you're broken, but you are a rock, an impenetrable fortress, a diamond. You are stronger than anyone I know. You get up every day and fight. You may think you're not winning but you are." He pulled back, a sad smile painting his lips as he looked into my eyes. "*You are* giving me what I need. You are. I want a female who is strong but knows when to be gentle. I want a female who is graceful but an animal in bed. I want you, Vina. I don't care if I can't mark you. I don't need that for you to show me your love and if you need something that represents your love for me, then mark me."

My heart stilled. "What?"

"Mark me, Vina. If you want, make me yours. If you really want something between us that represents our love, you can mark me. Or we could find something else. If you need something physical to prove that you are worthy of my love, then we will find it because there is no one more worthy."

I stared at his face for a while. Others would think him weak if I did that, but Darius didn't care. He didn't need others' validation to be secure within himself. He didn't need to prove that he was a male. He would allow me to mark him with nothing in return because he loved me and wanted me to feel worthy of it.

I searched his blue eyes and what reflected back was worry and love. "You're serious."

"Of course."

In that moment, the darkness that was threatening to take me alive dissipated. It was still there, but it was lurking in the corners of my sanity, instead of drowning me. I looked at Darius. I was never deserving of him. His love. His patience.

Darius was my light, my sun, and I was his moon. He illuminated me through my darkness, keeping me safe when the dark swallowed me whole. When I was lost, he slowly brought me back until I was bright enough to illuminate on my own. A deep part of me knew he would never let the darkness fully overtake me. I knew he would always try to bring me back so I could shine fully. It made my heart swell with the deepest love I had ever felt for another person.

"Yes," I whispered. I reached up and caressed his face. I looked into those sea-blue eyes... eyes that were always full of love. "Yes, I will mark you as mine."

I pressed a gentle kiss to his mouth, thanking him for this. Thanking him for being alive. Thanking him for being my sun. For being the thing that gave me hope for a brighter future. I needed to thank him for loving my broken mess of a heart.

He kissed me back just as gently. He cupped the back of my head and moved us closer to the bed.

There was a fire between us, but it burned slowly. There was no rush at this moment as he lowered me to the bed, pushing away the clothes I had piled.

I was grateful that the gods had given me Darius. They were bastards, but they couldn't break something that was already broken. They needed me to hope, to see happiness before they wrecked me again. At the moment, I didn't care what the gods had planned for me. I was happy to be in this male's arms. I was happy for this moment, the only moment that mattered.

Darius's hands were on my thighs as we continued our light, gentle, sensual kisses. He hiked my dress higher.

"Rip it," I whispered.

He gave a curious grin. "What?" He bent down to kiss my lips before pulling back to meet my eyes again.

"The dress, rip it, tear it off me."

He chuckled. "I told you—*an animal.*" He stood at the edge of the bed, grabbing the hem of the dress. He made a small rip and then slowly pulled the edges apart. The dress gradually tore, starting at my legs and traveling all the way up to my neckline, the frayed edges tickling my skin.

When my breasts were revealed, nipples hard and aching, Darius leaned down and sucked one into his mouth. A moan exited me as my core grew wet with need, aching for his cock.

I sat up and pulled him closer. Unbuttoned his commander's coat and pushed it off his shoulders. Splaying my fingers across his chest, I moved my hand up his tunic, where my claws were at the neckline. Then I sank my claws in. Not by much, just a graze.

He hissed, thrusting his hips out slightly.

I moved my hand down his chest, cutting the tunic off him. When I reached the bottom, I pushed the fabric away and explored his sculpted chest with my mouth, cleaning his blood off with my tongue.

Darius undid the ties to his pants and kicked off his boots. He pushed his pants down, revealing his hard length. I took him in my hand, giving him a gentle squeeze, a light groan coming from his mouth.

He pulled back and dropped to his knees. His hands splayed on my thighs, ready to open them so he could devour me whole, but I stopped him.

His eyes met mine, questioning.

Right now, I didn't need foreplay. I was soaking, and I wanted him inside me. "I want your cock."

He leaned up and kissed me, pushing my back against the bed. My hand found his cock, and I guided him where I wanted him.

He slowly sank into me, both of us moaning at the connection. When he was fully sheathed inside, he kissed me. His kisses gentle and loving as he began to slowly move his hips.

He broke the kiss to stare into my eyes. The look full of pure love and admiration as he fucked me like I was a goddess.

I realized he wasn't actually fucking me. This was different—it felt like he was worshipping me. His thrusts were slow and calculated, like he wanted me to feel absolute pleasure.

My brows pulled together. "We're making love?" I whispered.

"Yes." He leaned down and gently kissed my lips.

Tears built in my eyes. "I've never. Not even with him."

He wiped my tears as he continued to make love to me. "I'm glad to be the first, but I hope to be the last."

He kissed me once again, then went back to gazing into my eyes. His hips kept their slow pace, mine meeting his with each stroke. I could feel myself building within as I got lost in the sea of his eyes. My heart trying to rip out of my chest so it could join his. My body knew that even if we didn't have his claim, we were still owned by him. We were still his and he wanted to be ours.

I kissed his lips before trailing kisses down his jaw to his throat. He tensed in anticipation as I lingered in one spot. My mark would be prominent on his neck. I wanted people to see he was mine. I wanted the gods to know that he was mine. If they did anything to take him from me, I would burn this world and them with it.

I sank my canines in, releasing my venom into his blood. His body went rigid as the sensation of my venom trailed through his body. His thrusts grew faster and harder, until he was pounding into me and breaking me apart.

Darius let out a roar as I bit down harder, moaning around his neck as I tightened around his cock. His fingers dug into my sides as he let his seed paint my walls.

I removed my mouth from his neck, seeing him frozen in pleasure. His orgasm extended as my venom let him reach an extensive high. I brought his mouth to mine and kissed him gently as he crested.

His body relaxed, and I pulled back to meet his glazed eyes. "Thank you, Darius. Thank you for everything."

# THIRTY-ONE

## MARIE

*M*y mother always cooked the most delicious dinners. What Levi fed me from his royal chefs was heavenly, but nothing would beat her cooking. She cooked with love that just couldn't be replicated.

I sat at our dining table with twenty of my family's closest friends. I was at the end by my father, who sat at the head of the table, and my mother to his right, across from me. Kolvin would normally sit next to me, but he was sitting a few seats down from me. I could still see him though; his head down as he ate his food.

My parents were asking me about my time in Unseelie and everyone was pretending not to listen, but I knew they were hanging on to every word.

"They treated you well?" Father asked.

"Yes, everyone was nice. Well, as nice as a fae can be."

"And the king?"

"He's a nice guy. He let me use his portal mirror when I was crying from missing you guys so much. I offered him coin which he refused, probably because he is rich beyond his means. But I offered him a deal—"

My mother's fork scraped across her plate. "You offered him a deal?" Her tone was harsh and full of menace.

"Yes, but he refused. He said he would never share blood with me. Probably because I'm your daughter," I said to her.

"Why would that matter?" my father queried.

"They know each other."

My father looked to my mother. "You know the Unseelie King?"

My mother's face turned distant and expressionless. "We are the same age. We went to primary school together."

"He said that your family was on his father's court," I remarked.

My mother gave me an annoyed look before answering. "Yes, my family was on his father's court."

"So, you grew up together?" my father questioned.

"Yes, I supposed we did."

"Why did you never tell me you knew the king?"

"I thought I did?" She evaded.

"No, you didn't."

"I don't see why it would matter. Yes, I knew him when we were faelings, but I sorted Seelie and then I was shunned by my family and had to make a life here."

My father studied her quizzically.

She blew out a breath and turned to me. "And his son is your partner in school."

"Yeah, Levi. He is my partner." The second I said Levi's name, I knew I had fucked up. I felt Kolvin's eyes on me instantly, his gaze burning into my side.

*Who is Levi?*

*He was my escort to the palace.*

"The prince escorted you to the palace?" Kolvin asked from down the table.

My mother's eyes pierced into me. "He did?"

Nervously, I played with the ties on Levi's cloak. "Uh yeah, he did."

"You didn't tell me that."

My face grew heated. "It was nothing. He wanted to get out for a few days, so he volunteered to escort me. He spent most of the time reading his book, ignoring my presence."

"He's your partner in school. Does he ignore you now?" my father asked.

"No, he... he's nice. He knows a lot about magic. His father made him study it as a child. He doesn't really need to be in school, but his father wants him to make allies now so when he is king, he will have a trusted circle. What the king doesn't understand is that Levi hates people and would rather spend his time with his nose in a book than at a party."

"So, you got to know the prince quite well?" Kolvin asked, voice harsh.

I gripped my fork in a death grip before answering. "Not really."

"But you two spend a lot of time together, don't you? He is your partner after all."

I opened my mouth, but nothing came out. I was caught in a trap, and I didn't know how to get out.

Thankfully, my mother interrupted, "Kolvin, I understand you are angry with my daughter for what she did, but you had time to interrogate her in private. You will not accuse her of anything at my table. Do you understand?" My mother's voice was gentle, but in the most menacing way. She was scary as fuck. No one would ever get on her bad side if they knew better. I'd never seen her hurt another soul, but she carried an aura that warned she was dangerous if provoked.

Kolvin gulped. "Yes, ma'am."

I knew she was trying to help me, but her interjection made me look more guilty. I knew what everyone was probably thinking. *The prince was the male I cheated on Kolvin with. The prince was the male that I smelled of. The prince was the male I was leaving Kolvin for.* They were all true, but I didn't want anyone to know. It was none of their business, not even Kolvin's.

The rest of the dinner was awkward with me and my parents talking about the weather in Unseelie. *The weather*, like they didn't know it was cold there and it snowed.

After dinner, my mother took me to her room while my father said the goodbyes. She sat me down in front of her vanity and went in search of something.

"Speak, Marie," she said as she rummaged through a drawer.

"About?"

"Whatever you are not telling me." She pulled out a dagger and went to the bathroom to rinse it off.

I rubbed my forehead. "Mother…"

She came up behind me and grasped my shoulders, her eyes meeting mine in the mirror. "Marie, we tell each other everything."

"No, we don't," I said.

Her expression turned confused, an argument about to bubble off her lips.

"*You* tell me nothing. Father told me that you went to the inn when I left. You didn't tell me that. You also didn't tell me that you knew the king or that your family was on the old king's court and that there would be a possibility I could run into them. You don't tell me anything."

"Flower, I am your mother. I don't need to tell you everything."

"But I do?"

"No, but I hope that you trust me enough to."

"But you don't trust me?" I pushed.

"I do, but there are just things a parent can't tell their child. A parent wants to be the hero in their child's eyes, and if I told you that sometimes I'm actually the villain, you wouldn't look at me the same."

"Mother, you will always be my hero. I love no one more than I love you."

"I love no one more than I love you, my flower." She pressed a kiss on my head.

"Mother, do you love Father?"

She paused for a moment, playing with my hair, and fixing my curls. "Yes."

"He didn't answer when I asked him. Why?"

"If I answer that, Marie, I will be the villain."

"Does he not love you?"

"He does; that is why he wears my mark."

"But you don't."

"Yes." She moved my hair and started to untie Levi's cloak. A small part of me panicked, and I grabbed the cloak so it would not fall from my shoulders.

"What are you doing?" I asked.

"Relax, flower. I assume you don't want to keep Kolvin's mark? It will hurt when you remove it. It would be better if I did it."

My shoulders relaxed. I took the cloak off and folded it in my lap. My mother eyed the action, her eyes questioning.

She grabbed the dagger, angling my head to the side before she placed a wet cloth just below the mark. "Hold this while I cut." I did as she asked.

One of her hands came to the back of my neck as she held the dagger against my skin with the other. "This will cause him pain too. He will know when it is broken. Are you sure about this?"

*More than anything.*

I nodded.

She pushed the dagger into my skin. The pain of the knife making me hiss. I held still as she cut through all four points where

Kolvin's canines had penetrated. Internally, it felt like there was a slight tether that was connected to my soul that was cut. I assumed that the cut was supposed to hurt, but it felt like a release. Kolvin was wrong for me and removing his mark was right.

When my mother finished, she wiped my blood from my neck, my skin closing up but not fully healing. My human blood slowed down my ability to heal quickly.

My mother's black eyes met mine. "Marie, I hope you realized the value of the mark. It is an act of love and a claim of one's soul. It is not something to be played with."

I nodded. "I know, and at the time, I thought I loved Kolvin."

"I thought you loved him too."

My mother cleaned me up, then. "Mother…"

"Yes, my flower."

"You don't wear father's mark."

"I did," she said, continuing to clean.

"Why did you stop?"

"I can tell you when you are a little bit older, Marie. When you've lived long enough to see some demons, know how they can consume you and hold you back from fully being able to live."

# THIRTY-TWO

## CORIVINA
## 189 YEARS AGO.

*I* stared at the most beautiful pink roses I have ever seen in my entire life. They were full, luscious, and perfect in color, smelling sweet and delightful.

Pink was my favorite color; roses my favorite flower and Markos knew that.

This wasn't the first time Markos sent me flowers or other gifts. He started sending me things soon after the king's party three years ago. Sometimes the gifts would have notes begging me to take him back. Sometimes it was just a gift that would remind me of him. Snowflake earrings, our favorite books, paintings of the most beautiful ravens.

The flowers were the most constant. He'd send them on days that meant something to us. The day we first kissed, the day we first had sex, the day he claimed me as his, my birthday.

Every time one of these items arrived at the shop, I would close down, go to the inn, and just stare at the item. I knew Markos thought what he was doing was an act of love, but in reality, it was fucked up. Every time I received something, I would feel the darkness threaten to take hold of me and I would have to come here and try to collect myself.

I only had a few hours to sit here because I kept the gifts a secret from Darius. If I told him, I would have to tell him who they were from and why he couldn't go over the border and kill the Unseelie male who mentally tormented me.

I really fucking hated Markos. I wished he would get that I would never take him back. We had only been together for six years. It's been eleven years since we broke up and ten since he broke me. You would think he would get the fucking hint I wasn't going back to him. I told him—I fucking *told* him I hated him.

I got up and threw the flowers in the fireplace. I never understood why Seelies keep them in their homes. It was always hot here. There was no need for a fire unless to cook or burn shit.

Honestly, I wished I could burn Markos.

When I arrived home, I went upstairs, seeking Darius's warmth. After I spent a day fighting the darkness Markos erected, all I wanted was to be wrapped in his arms.

He wasn't in our room, so I called out for him.

"Just got out of the shower, my love," he hollered from the opened bathroom door. "Could you get me a shirt? I'm planning to go for a drink tonight with some of the males if you want to come."

He knew the answer to that. I wasn't very fond of his male time. They got drunk and did stupid shit that would either result in them being banned from whatever bar they visited, or they were littered with fees from the damage they caused. Also, when he meant 'some', he meant pretty much the entire top tier of soldiers.

I pulled open the first drawer of his dresser, and my heart stilled.

There, in his underwear drawer, was a blue velvet box. A blue velvet box that was only big enough for one thing.

With trembling fingers, I grabbed the box and carefully opened it to reveal a diamond ring. The ring was simple, just one diamond on a silver band. Something so me, classic and elegant.

A sob broke from my throat, and I covered my mouth as tears started to spill down my cheeks.

The fae didn't marry; it was rare. Marriage was something humans did in place of mating or marking. Fae only married when it was for political gain, their loved one's blood ran a different color, or when they loved someone so much, they couldn't live without them. They didn't care that they weren't fated mates—they would live and die with this person no matter what.

"Vina?" Darius popped his head out of the bathroom.

I turned to him with the ring in my hand and a snot-covered face.

"Fuck," he cursed.

He walked over to me and took my face in hands, wiping my tears.

"I don't know why I thought my underwear drawer would be a good hiding place. I've had that thing for two days."

I laughed through my tears, then looked back to the box in my hand, my lips quivering and small whimpers escaping my mouth.

Darius kissed my forehead. "Here, let me have this." He took the ring from my hand, got on one knee, his hair wet, his chest glistening with water. My eyes met his, and it was as if nothing else in the world existed. It was just me and him—no Markos, no darkness, nothing. I swore there was a halo of light surrounding him. My sun.

"Corivina, I love you. You are the strongest, smartest, most beautiful female I have ever met. I never want a day where I wake up and you're not by my side. I never want a day when I don't hear your voice or see your smile. It would be an honor to me, the highest of honors, if you would call me your husband and let me be yours for the rest of my days." He paused for a breath. "Corivina Snow, will you marry me?"

A sob released from me as I nodded vigorously. I dropped to the ground and kissed him with all the love I could ever muster. I had never been more grateful in my life for another being. I didn't deserve him, but he loved me anyway.

He pulled away to take the ring out of the box. His fingers wrapped around mine and he slid the silver band on my left finger. I never knew a piece of jewelry would ever feel so right. I held up my palm, taking in my hand of light skin that shimmered blue, black claws, and a simple silver ring with a diamond.

A pain stung my heart at the moment. Darius gave me so much and I would never be able to repay his generosity. All I had ever done in our eight years together was mark him. He created a safe space for me. He made me laugh like no one else. He was always sharing that smile that melted my frozen heart. He took care of me like a male was expected to, even if I feared letting a male care for me that way. He'd never step over, but he'd push. His pushes always gentle.

I looked into his warm sea-blue eyes and said, "Mark me."

He stilled, taking in a sharp breath. "Corivina, I don't want you to feel pressured. I didn't ask you to marry me because I wanted to mark you."

I brushed a strand of wet toffee brown hair from his face. "Darius, you give me everything and more. You love me and make me feel safe. You are patient and caring. You are the male I need but will never deserve. I want to wear your mark. I want you to claim me as yours. I want to be yours for all to see. I love you and I want to give you this."

He kissed me gently. "You are sure?"

"Yes."

He picked me up and laid me on the bed. I placed a hand on his chest to stop him from lying atop me. He backed up, his face worried. "I don't want to have sex, not the first time," I said, sitting up. "I'm still scared of this, still afraid. I don't want to be vulnerable as you do it. I trust you, but my body might not agree with me. I want to feel safe while we do. Just the first time."

"Vina, we never have to have sex while we do this. It's an honor to have you ever allow my teeth near your neck."

"I want to, at least I want to work up to that. I don't want there to be any walls between us, Darius, and there are. I know they are all from me, but I don't want there to be. I want to break them down so I can be completely free with you. I know you are okay with me just sharing little bits, but I'm not. I want to give my whole self to you."

"There are walls from me as well, Vina." He rested his forehead against mine. "Sometimes I hide behind your darkness, making you the focus so I don't have to deal with my own shit. I'm the Commander and the king is a relaxed male but a rigid boss. I'm often so stressed that I get these fucking attacks where I leave my body and I never tell you about them." He let out a deep breath. "There is the trauma I don't ever want to face from losing my brother. I would rather take care of you than focus on my own pain. I could open up to you, Vina. I know you would understand. I know you would hold me while I cried. You honestly don't know how much you do for me when you're not trying. When I'm lost in my stress, you're the one who anchors me. You never let me get too far before you bring me back."

"When does this happen?" I hated that I never noticed. To me, Darius was perfection, always happy and whole.

"Often after work, I'll come home stressed, then you'll come from the garden and demand I sit in the kitchen as you cook. It's probably my favorite time of the day. Sitting at the island as you chop and get lost in the food. I love that you ask me about my day and just listen to me ramble as you prepare the meal. Before I talk to you, I'm all jumbled up, but when I start, I can somehow figure out my problems. It's always been that way with you even before you started to play around in the kitchen, even before we ever kissed. I would talk to you, and you just made me feel grounded."

"Why didn't you ever tell me this before?"

"I'm a male. Males aren't supposed to be seen as weak. I don't care if anyone outside of us thinks I'm weak. Many do; they think I'm too soft for a commander because I care about my soldiers. They think I'm weak because I wear your mark and you don't wear mine. I don't care what they think, but I do care about what you think. I just couldn't tell you before because I didn't want you to think I couldn't continue to take care of you."

My lips pressed to his, love and support from me pushing into him. "You are the strongest male I have ever met. I respect no one as much as I respect you."

"Thank you."

"Thank *you*." I rested my forehead back on his. "I'm ready for this, for us."

"I love you," he said before moving his head to trail kisses down my neck. I tensed up, but his hand rubbed my back to soothe me. He kissed up and down my neck until I was fully relaxed, then he settled in one spot. He licked and kissed that area long enough to let me know this was the place he picked for his mark. He opened his mouth and rested his canines against my throat. He didn't bite, though. Just lingered.

I threaded my hand through his hair, pushing his head down slightly. I wanted this. I wanted to finally be free of the darkness Markos had put between us. I wanted to finally have his teeth pierce my flesh.

He bit down lightly, and euphoria poured through my veins.

My breath shallowed, and I felt my core tighten as the venom coursed through me. It felt like receiving a thousand kisses on every single blood cell within me.

I gripped the back of Darius's head as I let out a moan that bordered on being a scream. My muscles tensed to the point of pain until my pleasure crested and everything released.

I had never had an orgasm from just a mark alone, but I think my love for Darius was just that deep, that all it took was his bite.

I floated in bliss as Darius removed his teeth to look at me. Blood flowed from the corners of his mouth, and I gave him a blissful smile. I probably looked like a whack job smiling at him like this as the high from his venom faded.

He leaned in and pressed a gentle kiss to my forehead.

"I love it when you do that," I whispered. "I always have."

Eventually the pleasurable bliss washed away and then it was just me and Darius in each other's arms.

"My males are probably going to barge down the door and drag me out for drinks if I don't leave soon," Darius whispered.

I sat up. "Let me change."

He raised a brow. "You're coming?"

I smiled wide and bright. "I want to celebrate." I flashed him the ring. "I just got engaged after all."

We went out that night and partied like we were faelings, trashing the bar. I normally never let loose like that, but I felt safe. The mark on my neck made me feel protected. I had a piece of Darius with me at all times. The darkness from Markos would always linger, but when I was reminded of my sun, my light, the darkness would drift away.

# THIRTY-THREE

## Marie

*I*t was a little past sunrise when I got back to the Unseelie Palace. The ride felt like it was five hours long when it was just an hour. The second I got back, I went to my room to put my bag away, then I was half running, half walking to Levi's room.

I probably looked like a lunatic, but I couldn't help it. I had to see him.

When I got to his door, I knocked, stood there for a few moments and knocked again. There was a frenzy building within me, and I didn't care if he was asleep—which he probably was—I needed to see him now.

When I was about to knock a third time, the door opened. He wasn't wearing a shirt; his face sunken and hollow, his eyes red, lined with tiredness. When he saw me though, all his tiredness melted away.

His midnight gaze trailed over my neck and then locked onto my eyes.

"Thank the fucking gods," he muttered before he pulled my face into his.

The vibrations were once again violent, pulsing and pushing me toward him. It was like they knew what was going to happen between us and they were ramping us up.

Levi pulled me into the room and closed the door. He was practically dragging me to the bed. Though I was pushing him, needing to finish what we had started a day before.

His hands found his cloak that was wrapped around me, and he ripped the ties off.

"Levi!" I gasped.

"I'll buy you a thousand more," he said before pulling his mouth back to mine, devouring me hungrily. That primal feeling that had come upon us before was back but it was more powerful than ever.

I pulled off my shirt while he unlaced my boots. It was cute to see him struggle with the ties. He was too excited to actually make any progress with the laces, so I cut them with my claws, adopting the same philosophy that I'll buy new ones later.

I kicked off the boots, then my hands were at Levi's waist, trailing down to his pants. They were baggy and hung low on his hips. I loved the way he looked in them, but I really wanted them off.

Before I could get my wish, Levi picked me up and threw me on the bed. He crawled on after, looking beast-like. He ripped my stockings off, then pulled off my skirt and panties. His actions rough and violent, exciting the creature inside me. We were ready for him to take us. Consume us.

I thought he was going to devour me after he got my clothes off, but he just sat back on his heels, the firelight illuminating him like a god, and looked down at my naked body. "You're so fucking perfect," he whispered.

I didn't know what to say to that, so I kissed him, slower than our previous kisses but still as hungry. I let my hands drift to the ties at his pants. His hands took over and I sat back, waiting for him to reveal himself to me.

He untied his trouser ties, then let his hands rest at his sides. A frustrated growl left my mouth and a smirk adorned his—that sexy as fuck smirk that made my core clench. I knew he was teasing me, making me wait for what I wanted, like he had to wait for me.

"Levi, if you don't take those off now. I will rip them off with my claws, and I won't be sorry if I accidentally nick some sensitive areas."

He wasn't wearing any underwear, so I watched as the hem of his pants slid down his hard length and his cock bobbed free.

"Fuck," I breathed. His cock was fucking beautiful. I never thought I would ever say that in my life. I liked cocks, but I would never describe them as beautiful, but Levi's was that, fucking beautiful. I reached for him, but he grabbed my wrist.

"Not yet," he purred. "Lie back."

I grumbled but obeyed as he shrugged his pants off, then went back to staring at me.

I dug my claws into his bed. So ready for him, I was dripping on the sheets. "Levi," I whined.

"You want this?"

"More than anything."

His eyes bore into mine and then he pounced, his lips finding mine. Our kisses were carnal and possessive. My claws dug into his back and his fingers into my hips. Our teeth scraped and our tongues wrestled.

I wrapped my legs around him, locking him in and grinding against him. I wanted him to enter me and make me his, but he was still holding back. One of my hands slipped down his back and found his firm ass, squeezing before my claws broke skin.

"Stop torturing me," I said between kisses.

He smirked over my lips, then his hand left my hip and he guided himself into me.

Time stopped as his cock slowly scraped against my walls, fitting so perfectly within me, stretching me just right.

*Right*. That was the best way to describe it. It just felt fucking right.

We both groaned when he was fully sheathed in me, his cock lightly hitting my most inner wall. Levi held my face, and when he looked into me, I knew he was looking into my fucking soul.

Then he pulled his hips back and slammed them back into me.

I cried out, the pleasure from his cock and the vibrations ripping through my entire body.

I pulled his face to mine, needing his lips as he pounded into me, and I meant *pounded* into me. We were not making love or playing any games right now; we were fucking hard and brutal, our desire for each other overpowering other emotions. I needed him and he needed me, and we were too impatient to take our time.

Levi growled and grunted as I screamed and cried. There was a frenzy between us. Primal, carnal, and animalistic. We had let our beasts out and they were ready to rip each other apart.

Nothing… nothing had ever felt this good. Calling it good was actually an insult. There wasn't even an exact word to describe the visceral feeling of him inside me.

It was like we both knew exactly what the other needed.

His cock perfectly scraped that right spot, spreading violent bolts of pleasure through my body. I had no idea how long we had been fucking. It could have had been minutes or hours, but I honestly couldn't understand how my body could endure this type of pleasure. He was torturing me in the most blissful way, and I was riding on the edge the entire time, but something was keeping me from falling. I couldn't explain what it was, but it reminded me of that incomplete feeling that I had felt after Levi had lashed me with his tongue.

Not that I ever wanted it to end. I would be content to fuck Levi for the rest of my life. After having a taste of this pleasure, I knew I would always want it. I would always crave it.

Levi pulled away from our hungry kisses, his hips still savagely thrusting into me. His eyes held a question that he didn't speak out loud, but I knew in my bones what he was asking.

It was crazy for me to say yes to this, but it felt right, so I nodded.

He kissed me, quick and harsh, before attacking me with kisses down my chin and neck. He opened his mouth and paused, waiting.

My hand came around his head, fingers threading through his silky strands. I lifted slightly, my mouth covering his throat.

We stayed like that for a moment. Both of us knowing that what would happen in the next second would change us forever.

Then, simultaneously, our canines pierced flesh.

Pleasure racked through my body violently, and I bit down harder, causing Levi to do the same to me.

Everything was surreal and godly. My muscles tensed as I felt my soul attach to Levi's. Stars exploded behind my lids, and my heart squeezed so painfully I thought it would burst. Everything became so overwhelming that I was lost for a moment as we connected in every way possible. Heart, body, and soul.

I was brought to a place of pure peace.

The same word repeating itself over and over in my mind.

When I rejoined reality, Levi and I removed our teeth from each other. His blue-black midnight eyes met mine and he said that word to me.

"Mate."

# THIRTY-FOUR

## Marie

*I* woke up feeling warm, comfortable, safe, and loved. Lying in Levi's bed, wrapped in his arms, my head resting on his naked chest, us buried under the mountain of furs, I had never been so happy in my life.

Purring, I burrowed further into his chest, breathing in his scent that was now mixed with mine.

The action caused Levi to stir, the fire light lining his face as his sleepy eyes took me in.

I smiled, bringing my nose to nuzzle his before pressing a soft kiss to his lips. "Mate," I whispered.

His nose nudged mine back. "Mate."

That had been the only word we had uttered the whole day. We spent the past hours fucking like savages. We finally went to sleep, but I could tell it was only for a few hours because I could see a sliver of sunlight streaming through the curtains Levi didn't close all the way.

Moving over him, I straddled his hips, finding him hard and ready before I guided him into me. I was sore, unbelievably sore, my human body not having enough time to heal from our previous sessions. The soreness created a new sensation, though. The pain adding to the pleasure that his cock caused as I slowly rode him.

Levi watched me. He had a look of pure male satisfaction on his face as his hands found my breast and his fingers played with my nipples.

I knew I was going too slow for our carnal need for each other, but I was exhausted. My pace slowed even more as my body tired out, but my mind never wanted to stop. Never.

Levi's hands left my breast to come around my hips. He raised me a bit, holding me in place, then he started pounding his cock into me.

All I could do was hold his forearms as he continued his assault. He was full fae so he had the stamina to finish for us. Soon he was emptying his seed into me, and I was clenching around him.

I fell onto his chest when he let go of my hips, my body feeling like jelly.

"Gods," I breathed my first real word since we mated.

Levi chuckled and kissed my head.

I sat up enough so I could see his face. He was propped up on a few pillows looking down at me, his arms cradling my body. I let my fingers run over his face, over his brows, then his cheekbones. My fingers trailed to his mouth, and he nipped at them, causing me to squeal in surprise before he pressed a gentle kiss to them. I continued my perusal, traveling down his jaw and to his neck, lingering on my mark.

It was small but it was everything. Levi had marked me three more times during our mating. He was a male and the need to possess his mate was probably stronger than it was for me. I wanted to possess him, but to me, he felt like a gift. Something to be cherished. The fact that he wore my mark at all meant the world to me and made my heart squeeze.

Mate.

Prince Levington Shadawn was my mate.

I felt stupid for not realizing it earlier. It explained why I felt like he was mine before he ever even uttered a word to me. It explained why I would do stupid shit to make him jealous or went crazy when he did the same to me. All of the chaos that had occurred during the last three weeks made fucking sense. He was my mate, and I was his, and there was an obstacle in our way that kept us apart. It drove our creatures crazy, making them act out in the most vicious ways.

My hand trailed down his chest to rest over his heart, feeling its beats hit my palm.

I studied my hand. "The vibrations are gone."

Levi brought his lips to mine before answering. "We were trying to sync."

"What?" My brows furrowed.

"Mates' hearts are synced. The vibrations are the result of our hearts trying to sync to each other. Though, we needed to mate for our hearts to actually beat at the same rhythm."

Using my fae hearing, I tuned everything out and focused on our hearts. The pumping of blood within our bodies flowed in unison. My heart beating exactly when his did. I could barely tell our beats apart, only for the fact that mine was slightly louder.

Tears pooled in the back of my eyes at the beauty of it, and they would have fallen if my brain didn't ping with a question. "How do you know this?"

Levi shifted slightly, his body growing tight. "I read everything I could find about mates after we first met."

"You knew?"

He sighed. "Yes."

"Why didn't you tell me?" I said, my voice accusing.

"Why would I tell you when you told me that you never wanted to find your mate?"

I did say that. At the time, I did mean it.

"What would you have done when I told you?" he asked.

I slid off his lap. "Levi…"

I probably would have run away. Mates weren't a good thing in our society. Yeah, it was your soul's other half, but the cons really outweighed the pros. At least I thought that way before I had mated. Now, I would never not want to be with Levi, but that doesn't change the facts.

Fae were creatures of chaos and mates were the worst of them all. Mates have been the cause of most of the fae wars, were highly destructive, and would burn down the world to make their mate happy. They only lived for one reason—one person—and if anyone got in between that, they were as good as dead.

Exhaling heavily, I tried to think of the right thing to say in response to Levi. I opened my mouth to speak, but nothing came out.

A flash of panic flared through Levi's eyes at my silence. "Turn over," he demanded.

"What?"

"Turn the fuck over," he growled.

Not wanting to anger my mate, I turned over. Levi's hand came over my shoulder as he bit into the center of my back between my shoulder blades.

His bite was awkward. This spot wasn't exactly the best place for someone to mark without it being uncomfortable, even with the pleasure of his venom coursing through my veins.

The mark was a message—no one but Levi would ever see it, so the message was for me. I could never reach the mark by myself; it was physically impossible for my hand to touch, so I couldn't remove it.

Levi was telling me I was his. Nothing would keep us apart, not even me.

It was slightly scary because of the intensity, but I also knew Levi, as my mate, would never hurt me. He'd kill himself before he let any harm come my way as I him.

Levi removed his teeth and licked the wound. "Mine," he whispered.

I turned over to meet his eyes. They were so fearful it hurt my heart. I brought his face to mine, giving him a gentle kiss before pulling away. "Turn over."

Levi's fear washed away with those two words. He smirked before giving me a quick kiss, then turned over to lie on his stomach. I kissed up and down his spine, then I settled between his shoulder blades, biting into his flesh. He released a groan as my venom flooded his veins, and I pulled back and whispered, "Mine."

He flipped over and kissed me brutally, his body blanketing mine. My hand found his hard cock, and I guided him in. We fucked like animals, hard, fast, and harsh, until we climaxed together. I knew we would always come together. We were mates, so we were in sync.

Levi slid out of me and tucked me into his chest before uttering that word we just couldn't get enough of. "Mate."

I purred, nuzzling into him. "Mate."

Satisfied, we slept. It was one of the deepest sleeps I had ever had. I felt safe and cared for. But soon, our safe bubble was broken by a booming voice.

"What the fuck is this?"

# THIRTY-FIVE

## Corivina
### 21 YEARS AGO.

*P*lush pink roses.

*Markos.*

He kept sending them. I despised him, but I did love that flower.

I hated that for the past one hundred and seventy years, he continued to send them. I hated that he still loved me.

He was the *Slut King*. You would think one of the many females he fucked would have stuck, but no. Markos had a reputation for fucking anything that walked. Females, males, humans, he didn't care, but no one ever stuck. No one could replace me. It would be a sweet sentiment if he wasn't a dick.

His torment of gifts had slowed, though. In the beginning, he would send me different things... things that I loved. Eventually, it just became these roses. He stopped sending them on specific days. It would be months, maybe even a year or so until I would get a gift. The longest being three years. It seemed now he would only send them whenever he felt like it.

The mail delivered these to my shop five minutes ago. The herbal shop I had started at when I had nothing had become mine.

Darius bought it for me for our fiftieth wedding anniversary. He was slightly annoyed that I still worked. He was a male. I understood that males felt like they needed to provide for their females, but I liked to work. It was one of the few things that brought me peace. He thought that I didn't fully trust his love for me and felt like I needed to work so I still had something to fall back on.

After a few arguments about it, he finally got it through his thick male brain that I actually liked it here, so he bought me the whole place. At first, I was pissed because he just ended up giving me more work to do. I didn't know how to run a business. Ms. Masel and her male did that shit. I just played in the garden and handled a few customers. As time went on though, it got easier, and I actually enjoyed running the place.

Grabbing the flowers, I threw them into the compost. I was relatively healthy in mind at this point of my life. My darkness only came out to play with me every so often. It had been years since I visited the inn. If my darkness crowded my mind, it only took a few minutes for it to pass, but I knew that if I wanted to drown in its smoky depths, I could. The temptation was always there.

I walked the cobblestone path from my shop to the square. I hated that Darius's estate was practically in the woods. The walk wasn't that far, but I still dreaded it. I could run and be there in moments using my fae speed, but using that energy was taxing so I just walked.

On my journey, I noticed a male taking down the boards over Ginger's shop.

Ginger died about eighty years ago. Her witch blood allowed her to live longer than a normal human but not anywhere close to a fae. Her loss pained me even today. After I married Darius and found a way to maintain the darkness, we became true friends. I still hated witches and I definitely hated when the gods would send her messages about me, but we were close. Well, as close as a human and a fae could be. Humans were quite annoying, holier-than-thou motherfuckers who could really only be taken in short burst.

I smiled at the thought of her, remembering going to her shop after hours, the incense frying my senses, her waiting at the back table for me. Her gold eyes illuminating unnaturally against her dark skin. I never had to tell her when I was coming because she knew. She'd open a bottle of wine, lay a deck of playing cards down and start shuffling. We'd play for hours talking about all types of shit. She'd talk about the gods and their many plans for random people who visited the shop that day. I'd tell her about my relationship with Darius and the annoying customers that had visited my shop. We'd get drunk off fae wine and I would be slightly disturbed that she would drink it because of the human blood swirling within.

I had grown fond of her, and when she died, it wrecked me. I cried for days, slightly annoyed at the witch for making me care about her and then leaving me in this terrible world without her.

I stomped up to the male uncovering Ginger's shop, rage filling me. "Excuse me, what the fuck to you think you're doing?" That was my witch's shop, and I wasn't going to let this male take this shop and turn it into some club or tavern and ruin her essence.

*Essence?* The witch had me caring about her fucking essence. That bitch.

The male turned to me. He had dark skin, a shaved head, and wore commoner clothes. I realized that he wasn't a male—he was a man, a human. The man was quite handsome for a human, but when I looked into his eyes, something caught me off guard. His eyes weren't gold like a witch's. They were normal, but they looked exactly how my eyes had once looked before I had ever experienced any true pain. Coffee-black.

The man smiled, his grin filled with joy and kindness. It was off-putting because humans usually feared the fae, and for good reason. Fae were vile beasts. "I'm removing the boards," the man chimed.

I rolled my eyes. *Humans.* "I can see that. Why are you removing the boards?"

His grin grew wider. "So that I can get in."

I crossed my arms, annoyed with his act. "Did you buy this shop?"

A gleam of mischief flared in his eyes. "No."

"Then why do you think you have the right to remove the boards?" I snapped.

"Because the shop is owned by my family."

I growled at him, "When did they buy it? I didn't hear of anyone purchasing this shop nor did I hear it was even for sale."

"It's never been for sale. My great grandmother owned it; she was a witch."

I stared at him, stunned. Ginger never really ever talked about herself. She was always going on about the gods. I thought it was because she had nothing better going on in her life. She never told me she had a child that she left behind or even a family.

"Your great grandmother was Ginger?"

"Yes." He went back to tearing off the boards. I could smell his musky scent from here. It enticed me. The creature in me wanted to fuck him or eat him. Or fuck him, then eat him. One of the two. Fae didn't eat humans anymore, but it wasn't like we stopped craving the kill.

"So, what are you planning to do after you take down the boards?"

"Go—" he began.

I held up a hand. "Human, if you say, 'go inside', I will throw you across the square."

The man chuckled, the deep rasp enticing a tingle down between my thighs. "Do you not like to have fun, fae?"

"I just want to get answers as to why you are opening my friend's shop and what you plan to do with it."

"My great grandmother was your friend?"

"Yes. I buried her. I mourned her. I even had my husband put up these boards. Now tell me what you are doing."

"I'm opening it up."

I growled again.

He smiled a pure smile that my creature liked even more than his scent then said, "My sister's a witch. I don't know what you know about the human lands, but it isn't the best place for them. It's why my great grandmother fled here and that's why we are here."

I cocked my head. "She never told me she had a family. How can I believe you?"

"Maurice," a female voice called. "Hope you are done so you can help me with the supplies."

I looked behind me to see a short woman caring way too many boxes. She couldn't even see over her head.

The man, Maurice, put down his hammer to aid the female. When her hands were free, her eyes, gold and illuminated, jumped immediately to me. "What is your name?" she asked.

She had that witch tone. The tone of someone who knew more than you and was wise beyond their years. The holier-than-thou tone.

I wrinkled my nose. "Corivina."

"The raven," she breathed, and I tried not to flinch at the reminder of Markos's pet name.

The woman dug into her pocket, retrieved a piece of parchment, and handed it out to me. "Before she died, she sent a box to my grandmother, her daughter. There was a note for the next gifted—me. This note is for you."

I took it from the woman.

*Fae,*
*Be nice to my own; they know the recipe to my wine.*
*And remember the prophecy of your loves.*
*—Ginger*

I put my hand over my mouth to cover the sob that escaped. That fucking witch. Of course, she couldn't write a note longer than two sentences.

I wiped my tears and tucked the note in my dress pocket. I took in Ginger's kin. The woman looked so much like her it was slightly surreal. "What is your name?" I asked her.

"Melinda. This is my twin, Maurice." She nodded to the man.

"It's good to meet you two." I smiled.

"Yeah, the gods tell me you're important to us, but they block why you are from me," she said, annoyed.

My smile grew wider. "They must have gotten my message to fuck off."

Her eyes lit up and then she laughed. It was so joyful. I wasn't the type of fae to feel out one's energy, but these two had an aura about them that I was drawn to. It seemed even the gods wanted me to know they were important to me.

"Yes, the gods are quite fickle beings." She giggled.

I studied the shop. "I have an herb shop. I used to supply her. I'll give you them for free, if you give me free wine."

"Yes, the wine." She opened one of the boxes and handed me a bottle. "For the raven as well."

"Don't call me that." I took the wine. "It's Corivina or fae from you, little witch."

# THIRTY-SIX

## MARIE

Bringing the furs to cover my chest, Levi and I took in the king staring down at us. Shocked didn't even begin to describe his reaction as he stood there gaping.

"Get the fuck out!" Levi shouted, seething in anger, his body rigid and ready to pounce.

The king blinked, his face straightening into the regal grace of a royal as he looked at Levi. "What did you just say to me?"

"I said. Get. The. Fuck. Out," Levi gritted through his teeth.

I knew Levi would hurt him; maybe even try to kill the king for sneaking up on him and his mate.

Quickly, to stop the violence, I wrapped my arms around his torso and pulled him into my chest. His skin burning hot against my flesh.

I cupped Levi's face with one of my hands. "Levi, look at me."

His blue-black eyes met mine, burning with anger. His need to please his mate overshadowed his need to protect his mate at this moment, which was a good sign. It meant deep down, he knew his father wasn't actually a threat.

"Breathe."

"He needs to leave," he whispered.

I looked to the king who was staring at us with curiosity. "You need to leave. If you don't leave, he will hurt you." I had to keep moving my eyes back to Levi's to make sure he wouldn't do just that.

"Excuse me?" He sounded offended.

"I am his mate." The king's eyes went wide with the information. "You have invaded our space, unannounced and uninvited. You are a *male,* and he feels threatened by your presence so close to his *naked* mate. If you do not leave, he *will* attack you. Please, go."

The king took a step back. Levi snapped his head toward the movement, letting out a low growl.

The king wiped his face before saying, "I'm going. Get dressed and meet me in the dining room for lunch."

Levi growled louder.

"I wasn't trying to fuck with you or your mate, so calm down. You missed training and the first half of lessons. I was checking on you. I had no idea she was your mate."

When he reached the door, he didn't turn his back to open it, knowing Levi would probably take the opportunity to attack him when he was vulnerable. "Dining room," the king stated again before exiting.

The second the king left, Levi took my face in his hands. "Are you okay?"

I grabbed his hands and took them in mine. "I'm fine, Levi."

He rested his forehead on mine. "I'm sorry, I have already failed as a mate."

"Levi, you are a perfect, amazing mate."

"He came in while you were vulnerable, and I didn't protect you," he countered.

"You did. You were going to kill him for offending me. Not that I would ever want you to do that, but you did protect me. I am not harmed in any way, nor do I hold any ill toward your father. He was checking on you. He didn't know that I was here."

"I should have spelled the door. I should have protected you—"

"Levi, I am safe." I brushed my thumbs across the back of his. "We need to go and talk to him."

He kissed me lightly. "I'm so sorry, Marie."

I kissed him back. "There is nothing to be sorry about."

He kissed me again, his body leaning toward me. He deepened his kiss and started to move over me. I pulled away. "Levi, we have to go."

"Just let me make it up to you, mate." His lips met mine. "I promised it will feel good." He smirked over my mouth.

I giggled through the kisses. "It will always feel good."

"Exactly." He pushed me to lie on the bed, then kissed me gently.

My body was alive and ready for him. Even though the vibrations were gone, his touch still ignited something within me. I craved to feel his fingers brush my skin, his lips on mine, his cock inside me. The feel of him was perfect; it was the only way to describe it.

His fingers brushed over my nipples, sending little bolts of pleasure through me. I moaned, pulling him closer. His hand trailed down my stomach and then lower to find my clit. He groaned to find me soaking wet, like it was a surprise to him that I, his mate, would be dripping for him.

He circled my clit a few times before positioning his cock over my entrance. There was never much foreplay within the last few sessions of our fucking. We had been rough and ferocious, needing to be connected. Since we were mates, I would always be ready for him and so would he.

He thrust into me slowly. I cried out as slivers of pleasure cascaded through me, his cock stretching me perfectly.

He moved slowly within me, his hands roaming over my curves, his touch loving, kisses sweet.

I realized we weren't fucking like we were before. The need to ramp up this session was prevalent within my body. My need to fuck my mate was brutal, but I knew Levi wanted it to be like this. He wanted me to feel absolute pleasure as he slowly scraped his cock across my walls. I could feel every inch of him, every vein that pumped blood into our matching hearts as he made love to me.

I wrapped my legs and arms around him, deepening our kisses. Threading my fingers through his hair, I pressed him closer to me. Moans vibrated from our connected mouths at the new sensation.

I was on fire, my body alight with embers as we continued to make love. Tears slipped from my closed eyes as everything became overwhelming and I felt myself open up to him.

I felt Levi's soul tangled with mine, our hearts beating together, our bodies trying desperately to become one. I never thought it could be like this. It just felt so fucking right. Without him, it was wrong.

Levi broke our kisses, and I opened my eyes to meet his. "You're crying," he whispered.

I sobbed slightly and smiled. "This is… this…"

He pressed a loving kiss to my lips. "I know. I feel it too."

I sobbed again, covering my mouth.

It felt better than any substance—better than wine, better than venom, better than blood.

Better than any feeling—better than joy, better than bliss, better than euphoria.

"I'm sorry," I moaned.

He nudged my nose. "Are you happy?"

"Yes," I whispered. "More than ever."

"Then you have nothing to be sorry about."

I sniffled. "This can't be sexy."

He chuckled softly. "You are the sexiest." He kissed under one of my eyes. "Beautiful." Then the other. "Magnificent creature I have ever laid eyes upon." He kissed my lips, the taste of salt filling my tongue. "Nothing you do will ever change that, mate."

"Mate," I whispered back.

His lips found mine again. The fire I felt through my body licked every inch of my skin and pumped through my veins, circulating to my heart. I *never* wanted this to end. I wanted to live like this and die like this. Before was great; Levi and I fucked like animals. This, however, was something I knew we would only do a few times. For us to do this, we needed to slow down our urge to mate. *This...* this was what every girl fucking dreamed about. This was love on the deepest personal level. I was so lost within him I wasn't even Marie anymore. I was just a soul connecting with his.

My body tightened, the pleasure becoming too much for me. Levi thrusted harder, and our breaths grew shorter. I pulled him closer to me and he did the same. Our mouths were pressed so close I could feel his teeth clashing with mine.

With one last push, he stilled as my walls tightened around him. I dug my claws in his back as we crested, and our climaxes crashed through us. The most intense orgasm besides when we had first mated.

When we relaxed, Levi's lips left mine and his head buried into the crook of my neck. We held each other, never wanting to let go.

I couldn't believe the range of emotions I felt for him. I didn't think it was possible to feel this way for another person. He had become my source, my air, my life. I couldn't mentally process living a day without him. I would betray for him, hurt for him, even kill for him. I would do whatever he asked because his joy was mine. The emotions I felt were dangerous, but I couldn't even talk myself out of it. He was my everything. I would do anything to keep him here in my arms. *Anything.*

Eventually, the dam of emotions that had broken within me closed enough for me to function, and I pulled Levi's face back so I could see him.

I smiled, loving his ruffled black hair, sharp features, and midnight eyes. He smiled back, and I felt that dam threaten to open back up. I didn't want that to happen so soon. It was overwhelming and made me feel ungrounded, so I asked the first random question that came to my mind. "Are you taking the contraceptive brew?"

His smile dropped, and I felt my heart crack slightly. "Do you not want my children?"

"I do, just not now. I am on the brew, but I don't know if it will be strong enough for us if I just take it."

He rested his head on mine and sighed. "Yeah, I'm taking it, but I want you to carry my babes."

"I will, just not now, Levi. We are nineteen."

"When?"

I chuckled. "You are being such a male right now."

He kissed me. "It would be the greatest gift for you to carry my babes. Literally, I couldn't think of a better gift. Well, besides your soul. Which you have already given me. Thank you for that by the way."

The urge to please him and have his babes right this second was raging through me. I had to breathe through the urge for a second before I replied, "Thank you, and I will. You will be the father of my children. I promise." A vow.

He smiled. "How many?"

I laughed at his giddiness. "Not fifty."

His eyes gleamed, stars entering them. "So forty-nine?"

"Levi, I have a human body. I doubt I could carry that many."

"Yeah well, not at once." A pause. "You are half-fae. You heal, just not as fast. Which of course terrifies me because there is a bruise on your hip from last night and it would kill me to think I have hurt you."

I moved, lightly pushing him off me, to look at my hip. There was a bruise, several actually, from him gripping my hips as we fucked. I didn't even notice.

"You're going to freak out about this, aren't you?"

"I'm trying not to. You haven't brought it up, so I have been trying to ignore it. But then I thought that you probably weren't mentioning it because you didn't want to worry me."

I cupped his face. "I didn't know they were even there. If anything, I like them, they will probably heal in a couple hours, but I like to have your marks on my body."

A light arrogant smile ghosted his lips before he pulled my body close to him to nip at my neck. I giggled, seeking his lips to kiss him. "We have a lunch to go to."

He groaned, burying his face into my neck. "I do not want to leave this bed."

"Levi, we need to talk to your father. Not only because he is the king but because as your father, he needs to know. We are mates and it's kind of a big deal."

"Kind of a big deal?" he mocked.

I pushed his shoulder. "Move."

"Only because you ask so nicely," he said, sitting up.

I rolled my eyes as I followed him off the bed. His hand found mine and he started to walk us toward the closet. I stopped, tugging him back. "Levi, the bathroom is that way." I motioned with my hand.

"It is."

"We need to bathe before we go to lunch with your father."

He cupped my face and kissed my forehead. "If you think that I'm going to let you wash my scent off you after what he did, then you are greatly mistaken, mate."

"Levi, I have to bathe."

"Not now." His voice held an authority not to be argued with.

"Lev—"

"I said no, Marie." His eyes bore into me, and I swallowed. This was the problem with mates. This was why someone would want to run away from this. He owned me. Not in the cute, hot, and sexy way. He fucking owned my soul, and I would do anything to please him, like not fucking bathing after having sex with him twenty times.

He brushed my curls behind my ears. "After, mate." He pressed a kiss to my lips. "Okay?"

"Okay."

"Good, come."

When we walked into his closet, I noticed there were female clothes taking up half of it. I almost tore the room apart before I noticed they were all my size. There were some uniforms for school though they were nicer than the ones I had; some dresses, mostly black, but some dark colored ones were thrown into the mix. There were two matching dressers in the closet, one on both sides. I opened a random drawer to the one on the side of the female clothing.

The drawer was just gloves—made for someone with claws, all black, varying in designs and fabrics. There was also a pair missing. I looked at Levi, who didn't even seem to think twice about how his closet was half full of clothes fit for me, as he pulled a pair of sweatpants on.

"Levi?"

"What?" he replied, looking for a shirt.

"Why do you have all these clothes?"

"They are for you."

"I can see that, but why do you have them?"

He looked at me then, holding a plain black shirt in his hand. "Because you are my mate."

"I wasn't your mate until a couple hours ago. Where did all this come from? And how did you even know my size?"

"I got your size from the guy at the store after you bought clothes from there. I commissioned these for you."

"That's a bit presumptuous, don't you think?"

He cocked a brow. "How?"

"I was marked by another male. How did you know I would—"

"Marie, I'm going to stop you right there." His eyes lit with rage. "Don't bring that male up again. You are mine. You have been mine even before we carnated on this world. You will always be mine. I got you the fucking clothes because you are mine, and I want you to have the best. If you kept that mark any longer, I probably would have ripped it off your neck; it was driving me fucking crazy. It's why I slept with Jessamine. It's why I asked her to mark me. It was fucking vile to have her mark on my skin, and I hated wearing it for even a minute, but I wanted you to feel the pain I was feeling. It's why I didn't kiss you, or fuck you, or make love to you. It was the reason we weren't together the second I saw you in that carriage. It kept us apart and if that male was Unseelie, he would be fucking dead. You are *my* mate, *mine*, and no one else's." He pulled his shirt over his head. "It fucking hurt to see that on you and I was constantly in pain about it so don't fucking bring it up again."

Tears lined my eyes, my lip trembling at his omission. "I'm sorry."

He pulled me into his chest. "It's fine."

It wasn't. He was still tense as he held me. I could feel him trying to hide his anger from me. I needed to soothe him. The urge to make my mate happy surging through my body. I rubbed my hands over his arms, then I leaned up to bring his mouth to mine, trying to make him feel loved.

The guilt I felt was intense. Three weeks, I wore that mark. And three weeks, Levi had to endure the pain of me wearing it. It had to be miserable. He had worn Jessamine's for a few hours, and I had to hurt myself just to be able to deal with it.

"I'm so sorry, Levi," I said against his lips.

"It's fine, Marie. We are together now. There's nothing that could come between us, and if anyone tried, they would die by my hand."

I stilled and looked into his eyes. "Levi, we can't let the bond affect us like that."

His expression brooked no argument.

"Levi," I breathed.

He kissed my head. "Get dressed, mate. We're late."

I narrowed my eyes, and he nipped at my nose before going back to dressing.

☾

Levi and I walked down the hallway hand in hand. "Are you sure your father will be okay with me dressed like this?" I wore black sweatpants, a sweater, and slippers, which seemed too casual to dine with the king in.

"My father will not care what you wear, and if he does, I will cut him," he casually said.

"You cannot cut your father; he is the king."

"I will cut him during sword training. He will think it was an accident."

I chuckled. "You are crazy."

"For you." He let go of my hand, putting his arm around my shoulder to kiss my forehead. His hand trailed up and he squeezed the bundle of curls on my head. My hair was a mess from all the sex, so I had put it in a bun to look somewhat presentable.

"I love this." He squeezed it again.

I knocked his hand away. He chuckled and did it again. I growled at him in annoyance, and he growled back, doing it again. Grabbing his hand, I laced our fingers to prevent any further bun scrunching. Levi narrowed his eyes at me, and I batted mine innocently.

The dining room entrance was guarded by guards wearing black Unseelie army uniforms. They looked at me, then looked immediately away and bowed to Levi.

We walked into a room of dark wood, lit with fae light and candles. One side of the room had windows lining the wall, looking out to the beautiful winter, and the other side had a huge fireplace.

The king was scrubbing his chin as he paced by the windows. He looked up when he heard us enter and looked directly at me, then my neck, then to Levi, then his neck. He gestured to the small intimate dining table that could only fit about eight and said, "Sit." Then went back to pacing.

Levi didn't seem to care about his father's worry and guided me to the side of the table closest to the fireplace. He pulled out a chair for me to sit and pushed me in. He sat down and immediately started to pile food on my plate.

I felt like an idiot for not realizing what Levi was doing when he had first fed me. He was my mate and food for fae was an act of love. To feed someone was to take care of them, to provide for them. Levi, being my mate, felt obligated to make sure I ate well.

I took a bite of the food and purred, showing my appreciation for his efforts and because the food was fucking good. It wasn't my mother's, but it was exquisite.

The king's head shot up and he looked at me with intense eyes.

I put my hand over my mouth and finished chewing my food before I spoke, "Is that not normal?" I had forgotten to ask my mother about it.

"No, well, the fae don't purr unless deeply satisfied. Often only females do it, but rarely. Well, unless you have a mate." He looked at his son. "So, you have a mate?"

"Yeah." Levi continued to eat his food like it wasn't anything.

"Did you know she was your mate before you mated?"

Levi let out an annoyed breath. "Yes."

The king's stress over the situation showed in the rapidly pulsing vein in his temple. "Why didn't you tell me?"

"I wanted to see if you try and fuck her. Which I would have definitely killed you for if you did," Levi remarked.

The king blinked, frowning. "Why would I fuck her?"

Levi shrugged. "You acted all weird when you interviewed her. I thought you wanted to fuck her."

"No, I would never fuck her."

"Yeah, I would never let that happen."

The king shook his head and took a seat across from us. He slouched, looking exhausted. "Did you know?" The question was directed toward me.

I opened my mouth to speak, but Levi answered for me, "She did, but she denied it."

"Levi, don't be a dick to your mate. Let her speak."

Levi growled, "I'm not a dick to my mate."

I rubbed his neck, soothing him. "You are a dick, Levi, but I still like you." I smiled.

He turned to me, panic flashing in his eyes, and I chuckled with pity. "Levi, I'm not going to lie to you and tell you, you aren't a dick. Not even to comfort you."

"I'm sorry," he said. "I'll try not to be one."

"I like your dick," I said to him.

He smirked before kissing me harshly. Heat pooled in my core as I kissed him back with equal fervor.

The king cleared his throat, and I pulled away, shocked. I had forgotten he was even there. *I had just said I liked Levi's dick in front of his father.*

Levi went back to eating. "Don't interrupt me and my mate again."

"Levington, I am your father and your king. Just because you have a mate doesn't change that fact. You still answer to me, and you will still respect me. Do we understand?"

"Fine," Levi grumbled.

The king looked at me. "Your mother is Corivina Snow?"

"Corivina Foxglove now, but yeah."

He flinched slightly at the name change. It was so subtle that I barely caught it. "And you are mated to my son."

"Yes," Levi answered.

He looked at my mate, cocking a warning brow, then he looked at me for an answer.

"Yes, Levi is my mate."

The king let out a sigh. "Great." He rubbed his face. "And do you two remember why your souls chose these bodies to carnate in?"

Levi stilled and slowly turned his head toward his father, rage starting to burn under his skin. He finished chewing his food, swallowed, and then said, "Do you not approve of my mate?" His voice was even but held a deadly edge.

The king rolled his eyes. "Levington, you have to get *that* under control. I'm not trying to offend your mate. I'm just asking a fucking question. You need to realize that this isn't just some small feat. You are mated. *Mated, Levi.* You are the Unseelie Prince, and you are mated. The people will be in a fucking uproar. We will have to do the crowning as soon as possible and I will have to convince them that you will not cause a war."

Levi groaned, rolling his eyes.

I was confused. "The crowning?"

The king looked at me. "You are the Unseelie Princess."

My brows raised, almost touching my hairline. "What?"

Levi looked at me. "We are mates, Marie."

"I know that."

"Mating is a higher affair than marriage. In fact, by fae law, it makes us married."

I blinked. "So, I'm the princess?" I felt my heart start to beat faster, and my palms start to sweat.

"Not officially," the king chimed in. "We will have a crowning, slash mating announcement, slash me promising that you two aren't going to destroy the fae ball tomorrow night."

"Tomorrow night!" I said, my voice a little too high.

Levi took my face in his hand and studied me. "Are you not happy?"

"I am but…" I looked to the king. "You're not planning on leaving the throne anytime soon, right?"

The king chuckled lightly. "No Marie. Not for a hundred or so years, maybe longer if you two cause trouble. I will make sure that you two are prepared. You have nothing to worry about. If something happens to me though, Levi has been training to take the throne his whole life, and my councilors will also aid you."

I relaxed at that. "Good." I took a bite of my food. "Really good."

Levi kissed my forehead, then looked to his father. "Tomorrow, we will have the crowning?"

The king nodded. "Yes, and I canceled classes for the rest of the night and tomorrow. You will have until then to get your mating frenzy under control."

Levi raised a brow. "We are mates. You think we are just going to not mate?"

"No, I expect that you will mate anytime you get the chance, but you will still go to class and maintain your grades. I have three rules for you two and hopefully they will be easy for you to follow. One, go to lessons. That includes trainings. I don't fucking care if you fucked all day and didn't sleep, you are going. Two, do not fuck in my greenhouse. I know you have been sneaking in there, Levington. I am the one who put the spell on the door. I was fine with it when you were just studying in there. That room is important to me, so do not fuck in there. Three, don't cause a war. I shouldn't have to put that in there, but you are mates, so…" He shrugged.

"We aren't going to cause a war," I reassured the king. "And we will go to lessons and not fuck in the greenhouse, sir."

The king smiled at me. "Thank you, Marie, for not being a crazy mated psycho like my son."

My nostrils flared slightly at the insult to my mate, and I gripped my fork in a death hold. Levi leaned in and kissed my cheek. "You are so cute when angered."

I grumbled and looked back at the king. "Can my parents come to the crowning?"

The king pursed his lips. "Your father is the Seelie Commander. It would take a lot of communicating and arrangements with King Dominick and that could take weeks. We need to announce this as soon as possible."

"Could just my mother come?" I asked.

The king chewed on his lip. "I'm sorry, Marie. You can use my portal mirror to talk to them whenever you like. I would tell them before we announce it because word will get back to Seelie soon after."

I nodded, disappointed.

Levi kissed my neck where one of his marks lied for comfort. "Will you be okay with that, mate?"

"I'm sad they won't be there, but I understand why they can't come. We will talk to them and that will be enough."

"Marie, if you aren't happy, we can wait."

"I am happy." I brushed my hand across his cheek.

"But you are also sad."

"As long as I have you, I will always be happy."

He kissed me. "Mate."

I kissed him back. "Mate."

He pulled back and continued eating. The king was staring at us. I had again forgotten that me and Levi weren't the only two in the room. The king's expression was a mix of wonderment, fear, and confusion. When he realized he was staring, he snapped out of it and began to eat.

# THIRTY-SEVEN

## MARIE

"Levi, I'm extremely sore," I said as I laid on his chest in the claw-foot tub.

He kissed my ear. "I know, mate. That's why I got the salts," he said, rubbing my arms to soothe my aches.

We were in his bathroom, which was the size of my room. It was dark and cozy like the rest of his room, and since there was a tub in here, I think this was probably my favorite room in the whole palace. The tub was solid black, made of onyx. There was also a glass shower across from it. Showers were rare; only those who could afford it had one. My parents had one in their room, and I had used it a couple of times, but I preferred the bath. There was a fireplace on the wall and windows on the ceiling. I had never seen something like that. You could see the stars and I assume the windows were magically protected from snow because there wasn't a single flake on them, and I loved the room more wrapped in my mate's arms.

After lunch, we went back to his room and fucked all night, and I was extremely sore and tired from it. We hadn't slept yet because I wanted to call my parents in the morning before the crowning later tonight.

Levi was of course fine. He was still hard against my back. I really hated that I was half-human and took time to heal. We weren't going easy on each other's bodies either.

"I love you," he whispered, playing with my curls.

I stilled, then turned to look up at him. "Don't you think we should wait to say that?" I asked.

His brow furrowed. "You're my mate."

"But we barely know each other."

He blinked in shock. "Our souls know each other."

"I know but I don't know you, not you in this life."

His eyes bore into mine. "Marie, there is no one else for me and no one else for you. We don't have to spend our lives trying to figure out if we love another because we already know. It doesn't really matter if we don't know who we are in this life. We have our whole lives to figure each other out. I love you and I don't see a reason to wait to tell you that."

What he said was right. I loved him; he was my mate. It didn't really matter if we didn't know each other because we are already perfect together. Our souls had decided to love each other forever and this life was just us spending time together. We had our whole lives to explore our minds and who we had decided to become in this life.

"I love you too, but I don't even know your favorite color."

He kissed my cheek, and I turned back to lie on his chest. "Black," he said in my ear.

I laughed. "Black?" How Unseelie of him.

He thought for a moment. "No, red. The color of the dress I first saw you in. That's my favorite color."

I smiled. "Can I ask you a question?"

He brushed a kiss to my head. "Always."

"Why did you seem mad that your blood ran black? Didn't you already know?"

"I had called upon Unseelie magic, yes, but I didn't know for sure..." He sighed. "I knew. I just hoped I was Seelie or maybe I was like Prince Karnelian."

Prince Karnelian was the first heir to the Seelie throne, but he was also a hybrid. Hybrids were rarer than mates and were also seen as an abomination in fae culture. Because of this, the Seelie King birthed a new heir, Prince Fredrick, to take the throne. "Why?"

"You, I didn't know you were Unseelie. I knew you were my mate, but it's common that mates are of the same blood. I wanted to be with you. I hoped that there was somehow a mistake, or I was a hybrid. Then you sorted Unseelie, and you were crying. I knew you didn't know we were mates because if you knew, then you wouldn't have cried. At least, I hope you'd be excited to at least be with me if you did know."

"I probably would have still cried. I cry a lot," I said, turning to press a reassuring kiss to his lips.

"It pains me when you do," he whispered.

"I was excited to be with you; it's just I didn't really understand why my mind thought you were mine. I thought I just wanted you because you're hot."

He chuckled. "You think I'm hot."

"Yes, beautiful actually. Annoyingly beautiful. The most beautiful creature I have ever laid eyes upon. You were quite hard to resist."

"I love you." He kissed my forehead.

"I love you."

"So, what is yours?" he asked.

"My what?"

"Your favorite color."

"Yellow."

He nudged my nose. "I'll buy you a thousand dresses." He grinned.

"No, no, no, no." I shook my head. "I do not want to stand out like a sore thumb here. You can get me one. A sundress for when I go to Seelie to visit my parents."

Levi stiffened.

"No, fuck no, Levi. You are not about to tell me I can't visit them. They are my parents. They are the only other people besides you that I love in this world. I *will* visit them *every* sabbat. If you have a problem with that, you can fucking deal with it. I love you, but I love them too and I need to see them."

Levi stared at me for a while. With the mating bond, I didn't think there was something that I wouldn't let Levi sway me against. My family was my world before he was my world so it made sense why they were where I would put my foot down.

He nodded but his nostrils were flared, and his jaw was set. "Okay." He looked like that was the last thing he wanted to say.

I kissed his lips. "It's only eight days a year. I will spend the other three hundred and fifty-seven days with you and the rest of my life and eternal life."

"Not when you are pregnant," he stated. "When you are pregnant, you will stay here."

"Levi, I hope to not be pregnant for *years*."

"Then it won't be a problem." His expression offered no argument.

I sighed. "Fine."

He smiled and kissed me. "Mate."

I rolled my eyes and turned around to snuggle back into his chest. "Mate."

It was about an hour before sunrise. Levi and I were sitting on the couch in his father's office. With my back against the armrest and my legs in his lap, I held the portal mirror between us.

Levi kissed my forehead, then grabbed one of my hands and used my claw to cut his palm as he called upon his magic. The action was cute but also extremely weird even for my fogged mated mind but then I found myself licking the blood from my thumb.

When his blood dropped on the mirror, I called for my father. He and my mother should be awake now. My mother always cooked my father breakfast and my father had to rise early to train his soldiers because the fae had the idea that you needed to be sleep-deprived to be a well-trained soldier.

My leg bounced nervously as I waited for him to answer. Levi rested his hand on my leg and gave me a gentle squeeze in comfort.

When my father answered, he smiled his smile. "Flower."

"Father." I smiled back. The way I was holding the mirror, my father couldn't see Levi. I wanted to speak to my parents before I introduced them.

"Is everything all right?"

"Yes, could you get Mother? I need to speak to you guys together."

"Of course, my dear."

My father walked from his study to the kitchen, where my mother was preparing breakfast. "Vina, Marie has called."

"Is she okay?" I heard her ask, worry filling her voice.

"She said she needs to talk to both of us," my father replied.

They sat at the kitchen table, my mother holding the mirror as my father held her so he could get a good view of me. He never did that around me; they rarely touched ever.

"Marie? Are you okay, my flower?"

"Yes, Mother, I'm okay. More than, actually."

My mother's eyes turned to slits. "You are marked. Marie, we just talked about not letting someone mark you unless you were a hundred percent sure of your love."

My father looked at her then, his eyes swirling with emotion before he pushed it back and looked to me.

"I am, Mother," I stated.

"You thought that—"

"Can I tell you something before you start pestering me with questions?" I pleaded.

She sighed. "Sorry, my flower. I just miss you."

"I miss you too."

"There is no one I love more than I love you, Marie."

"There is no one I love more than—" I looked at Levi. He studied my face. That saying is what me and my mother always said to each other, and it was true, but now it wasn't. I looked at my mother, her face painted in confusion.

"Is someone there?" she asked.

"Yeah," I breathed.

"The king?"

"No."

"Then who, flower?"

I took a deep breath before saying it. "My mate."

My parents' eyes grew wide. "What did you just say?" she questioned.

"I have a mate." I bit my lip. "You could probably guess who it is."

My mother closed her eyes for a moment, seeming to gather herself. "The prince, Markos's son," she breathed.

"Yes, King Markos's son, Levi. He is my mate."

A half-sob broke from my mother. She put her hand over her mouth, my father grabbing the mirror, so she didn't drop it.

"Mother." I pulled the mirror close, anxiety filling my veins.

My father spoke then, "Just give us a moment, Marie, it's big news."

He laid the mirror on the table. I could see shadows and hear them talking.

"She is never going to come back," she cried to my father.

"You will still see her," he whispered.

"You promised you would keep her here."

"Vina, she is mated. It's not like I can go around that."

My mother's cries were muffled. I assumed that they were because she was being held in my father's arms.

Her pain hurt me, and tears started to fall from my eyes. I loved her. Being away from her for three weeks was painful and now we would only have eight days a year for the rest of our lives.

"Mother," I sniffled. Levi brought me into his chest, his head resting on mine as I waited for her to reply. All I could hear were her sobs. "Mother," I repeated.

"Vina," my father spoke. "Marie is still on the call."

There was movement and sniffling. She picked up the mirror. Her eyes red, her face puffy, so unlike her hard put togetherness that I was used to.

"Mother, I will still visit every sabbat. The king said I could use the mirror whenever so we can talk every day. I love you more than life. Nothing, not even my mate will change that. I still need you; I will always need you."

"I love you, my flower," she whispered.

"Do you want to meet him?"

"Of course, my flower. I need to see the male who I may have to kill if he hurts you." Her voice was flat but deadly serious.

"I would never hurt her," Levi said, coming into the frame.

My mother looked at Levi and studied his face. She gave a half smile, and I could tell it was forced. "You look like your father." It was a statement with no emotion behind it.

"He is my father," Levi replied, and I elbowed him. "What?" He raised a brow.

"She is my mother," I snapped in a hushed voice.

He looked at my mother. "Sorry, ma'am, I've been told I'm a bit of a dick."

She gave another smile that seemed forced and then looked to me. "Flower, I have to go. I have work in the garden and your father has training."

"Vina—" My mother gave my father a look that shut him right up.

"I love you and I will write to you so we can set up times to talk."

"Okay, I love you too." The image dissolved, and it was just me and Levi looking at ourselves.

The interaction had me feeling off. My body was taut with tension, making me want to cry or scream.

"Your mother doesn't like me," Levi chimed.

"She is just protective of me and doesn't like that you have stolen her flower away from her," I said without emotion.

Levi tipped my chin, so I was looking at him. "You are upset."

"She is my mother, Levi. She always supports me and builds me up. She was everything to me," I said, irritated.

"Are you mad that we mated?"

"No, I just wish it could all work out. I wish they were of the same blood so there wasn't a distance between us."

"Your mother is just in shock, Marie. You told her you were mated to the Unseelie Prince. It's just a lot to take in all at once. She obviously loves you. She loves you enough that I feel threatened by her love for you."

I kissed him. "Thank you."

"Always, mate."

"Nothing will get between us, not even my mother. I promise."

# THIRTY-EIGHT

## MARIE

*L*evi and I hid in an alcove behind the dais in the ballroom. We looked out to the room waiting for the king to call upon us. The dark walls were decorated with steel snowflakes that reflected the blue fae lights. The floor was white and so were the tables. Little snowflakes hung from the ceiling and huge windows looked out to the winter gardens that were displayed in the front of the palace. The whole room resembling a winter wonderland.

The king entered wearing his usual black open tunic and black trousers. As he entered, everyone halted and bowed. He stepped onto the dais in front of his throne.

"Hello everyone," the king boomed. "I'm glad you could make it to my impromptu ball. I have a few announcements and then I will let everyone go on to dance, feast, and fuck as they please.

"It might come as a shock. Everything about this subject matter will be under control. I will personally make sure nothing gets out of hand and that everyone remains safe and secure. You are my people and I want the best for you." He laid a hand over his chest right on his raven tattoo.

"I do want to warn you that if anyone speaks out against this matter, they will lose their tongue. Spreading propaganda around, especially about this, will only cause harm among our people and will not be tolerated. It's non-negotiable. If you have something to say, keep it private and away from prying ears. This is not a subject to get rebellious about. I will not tolerate any disobedience about this."

The king nodded when he felt his words had fully pierced through the audience. He gestured to the alcove. "Levi."

I felt my body tense and my throat closing up as we were called. Levi bent down and kissed my head. "Nothing will happen, mate. I will not allow it." He laced his fingers with mine. I tried to relax, but I was still terrified. What if they tried to kill us for just being mated?

Together, we walked out, the ruffling of my dress swaying the only sound in the room. Levi had given me a dress for this event, and it was perfectly made for me. It was black with gold glitters shimmering like my skin, but brighter and more dramatic. It was off the shoulder, but the sleeves were long, so I wasn't too cold, and the garment flowed perfectly with my curves, cinching at the waist and flaring out with a bottom made of layers of tulle.

All eyes were on my neck at the four marks. Levi only had one, which he wore proudly. He pulled off his father's signature look of a black tunic, unbuttoned at the top to show his mark.

When we reached the king, Levi put his arm around my waist, looking out to the crowd with a look that one could only best describe as a 'don't fuck with my mate' look. He looked like his normal brooding self just this time with a deadly gleam in his eyes.

"Fae of Unseelie, I am pleased to announce that my son, Prince Levington, has found himself a mate."

There was a collective gasp that had Levi's hand tightening around my waist.

"Now," the king spoke. "I promise there is nothing to be afraid of. Levington and his mate are not a danger to our people, but they are mates, so it is best to advise everyone to not fuck with them. I will not speak for his mate, but Levington almost killed a male a week ago for speaking against her, and this was before they were mated.

"Prince Levington and his mate have promised not to start a war, but I don't care if he kills a few of you for disrespecting his mate. In fact, if anyone disrespects our new princess and I hear of it before him, I will kill you. I hope that is understood." The king looked at me and smiled. "I am pleased to introduce you to Marie, Prince Levington's mate."

Fae cheered, which I definitely didn't expect, but then again, the idea of true love makes them hope for themselves. I smiled and waved slightly and Levi kissed my forehead.

They awed at the kiss; I knew that would probably happen a lot. They couldn't be against us so they would do extra to be for us.

The king went to grab a wooden box from a guard. "Marie, it is an honor to have you as my son's mate, our new princess and future queen. I had to fight Levington to give you this gift. He had one of these already picked out for you, but when he saw the one I had, he relented."

He opened the box to reveal a tiara, one that looked actually a lot like Levi's circlet, steel, formed into branches and had little onyx gems embedded in the crown.

Levi released my waist to grab the tiara, then turned back to me. "Marie, it is the greatest gift to call you mine. To have you as my female, my wife, my mate, my everything. I am proud to have you stand by my side and be my princess and one day my queen. I know you will be a great one." He placed the tiara on my head and brushed a curl behind my ear. His hand found mine and he turned us to face the people. "Your new princess and future queen, my mate, Marie Shadawn." All the people bowed to me, then burst into cheers and hollers.

Levi kissed me possessively, pulling me into him. He went a step further and moved the hair covering my marks to show everyone I was his, which had the crowd cheering louder.

The crowd quieted down after we separated, and the king addressed his people. "Now that it's out of the way and everyone has been warned, let us dance, feast, and fuck." He waved his hand and music began to play.

# THIRTY-NINE

## MARIE

*I* sat on the training gym floor doing nothing. Levi was across the room with his shirt off, training with the others. I loved watching him go through the motions of the exercise, his pale skin glistening with sweat. He would look over at me from time to time, catching me staring at him. His lips would twitch slightly, and he would give me a look that promised he would do all types of bad things to me later.

The reason I was on the ground was because no one would come near me. They all kept a distance, afraid Levi would kill them for disrespecting his mate. Mr. Vandeer wouldn't even yell in my direction when he was giving orders. After I realized that I was being ignored and making everyone uncomfortable, I decided to sit down and saw everyone visibly relax.

Thank the gods for Jessamine. She saw me sit and came to join me. Since she was the only person who would come near me, she got the privilege of not having to train as well.

"So, Levi is your mate?" she asked.

I picked at the laces on my shoes. "Yes."

"Did you know?"

"Yes and no."

Her face scrunched up in confusion. "What do you mean?"

"Well, I wanted to be with him, and I felt like he was mine, but I didn't know he was my mate until we actually mated," I replied.

"Do you think that's why you reacted that way when…" she trailed off.

"When you slept with my mate, yes." I tried not to sound bitter about it but failed.

"If I had known, I wouldn't have. You know that, right?"

"Yes, it's not like you owed me anything at the time. You had only known me for two days," I murmured.

"No, I totally did. I'm surprised you didn't kill me."

"I wanted to, badly."

She swallowed audibly, probably thinking about how I still could if I wanted to. "I knew when we met, we were going to be best friends, and I also knew you have a thing for him—"

"I didn't have a *thing* for him; he is my mate," I snapped. I blinked at my sudden burst of anger and brushed a curl behind my ear. "And I don't want to talk about this. I already forgave you." I pulled my legs into my chest. I hated remembering what it was like to have him wear her mark. Even if she didn't want to actually claim him. I knew the only male she actually cared for was Gregor, but I still got the urge to rip her face off when it was mentioned.

"Okay." She looked around for a moment, then turned to give me her seductive smile. "So, what's it like?"

My brows pulled together. "What's what like?"

She rolled her eyes. "Having a mate, duh."

I was at a loss for words, unwilling to share our intimate details with her.

"Come on, bunny. It's everyone's dream. We can all pretend that we don't want it because it often ends in war, but we *all* want it. If we didn't, we wouldn't all travel to the Neutral Territory on the eclipses to party with the Seelie. They may have the party king, but they are boring and snobby."

I snorted. "I didn't dream about having a mate."

"We both know that's a lie. Come on, Marie, spill."

I pulled my knees closer to my chest. I didn't want to tell her or anyone about my mate. He was mine. I wanted him to stay mine.

When I didn't answer, Jessamine prodded more. The female was a heck of a good time, but she had no boundaries. "You guys have to have amazing sex, right? They call you mates for a reason; you guys fuck like a lot. I mean, you reek of Levi so you must have."

I scoffed. "I do not *reek* of him."

"Marie, you smell more like him than yourself."

"I know but his scent is good," I whispered.

"Aww, you are so cute. You and your mate." She scrunched her nose up, mocking me. "Tell me about the sex! You made me dish on the Gregor stuff last week. You owe me."

"I didn't. You just told me," I argued, giving her the eyes to drop it.

"And as my *best friend*, you should tell me."

I squirmed and started playing with my laces again.

"Marie, it's just sex. It's not like I'm—" Jessamine abruptly stopped.

I looked at her. She was ghostly pale, her face painted in utter terror. I looked to what she was staring at. Levi was standing there with his 'don't fuck with my mate' face. He glanced at me, softening slightly, and held out his hand. When I took it, he pulled me up, but his eyes stayed on Jessamine with that face. I felt bad for her, but I really didn't like that she kept trying to ask me about my mate.

Levi turned around, giving her his back. I put my arms around his middle as we walked toward the private training rooms. I didn't care that people were probably staring at us. I wanted to find comfort in my mate after Jessamine's prodding.

When we got into the room, I wrapped myself completely in him. He was mine. All mine.

"Don't kill her," I whispered into his chest.

"She made you uncomfortable," he grumbled.

"So you think she deserves to die?"

"Anyone who fucks with my mate deserves to die."

"Levi, do not kill her," I demanded.

He sighed in submission.

"Thank you." I smiled. "I love you."

"I love you too." He kissed me sweetly before pulling away and saying, "Let's fuck."

I let out a surprised laugh. "What?"

"Let's fuck. I told you I haven't fucked anyone in here, and I would like to break the room in." He looked around the room, examining it, then nodded as if he had approved of that decision. His eyes met mine again. "Take off your pants."

I gave him a sexy smirk and slowly started to remove my pants, teasing him. He watched me as I turned and unhurriedly revealed myself to him. I left my panties on, knowing he wanted me to take those off as well. I liked when he grew frustrated with me. He would start to get more demanding, and he'd fuck me harder.

Levi growled, the sound traveling through my body and straight to my clit. He got on his knees, roughly pulling my pants down and off me. My arousal soaked my panties, and when he breathed in my scent, he groaned.

Levi grabbed my panties from the front and ripped them off. The force stinging my skin and making me yelp. He stood and pulled my shirt off, then picked me up, my legs wrapping around his waist—I loved it when he picked me up like I weighed nothing.

He pushed me against the wall and pulled his shorts down enough to let his cock out then entered me brutally.

"Levi," I moaned.

He started to pound into me roughly, my back scraping across the wood as he did. He bent his head down and sucked one of my nipples into his mouth, slightly kneading it with his teeth, causing my head to roll back.

His mouth found mine, and I wrapped my arms around his neck as he continued forcefully hammering into me. I cried into his mouth, his cock scraping that spot perfectly at this angle. I knew we wouldn't last much longer.

"Levi," I whimpered.

He groaned as I began to tighten around him. I was about to be thrown over the cliff when he pulled out. The loss of his cock made me feel hollow, and I growled in frustration, ready to scream at Levi for stopping.

"I'm sorry, mate, but I don't want it to end yet." He rested his head on mine, catching his breath. He gave me another sweet kiss before putting me down.

"Get on your hands and knees," he demanded as he pushed his shorts completely off.

I did as he asked, and he followed, lining his cock up with my entrance. When he entered me, I cried out. Our mating frenzy before was just us fucking. We weren't playing with positions. We just needed to be connected, so we had never done it like this. In this position, his cock stretched me in the most blissful way, pleasure shooting through me in small rippling waves. His hands gripped my hips, and he began to pound into me.

I screamed in exhilaration. I knew the people in the gym could hear me. I was being super loud, but I couldn't help it. Levi's cock was driving into me perfectly, *beyond perfectly*, and I couldn't contain myself. He knew that they could hear me as well because he started to fuck me harder, causing me to be louder, wanting them to know how well he treated his mate.

He grabbed my arms and pulled me up. The angle had my screams becoming shouts as his cock hit that inner most wall that causes a little pain coated with intense pleasure.

"Levi, don't stop," I moaned. "Don't you dare fucking stop."

He thrust harder in reply, moving his hands so one of his arms came around my breast while the other was on my shoulder, allowing him to move deeper into me.

I began to tighten around him, screaming his name over and over as he continued his brutal pace. As I started to crumble, Levi thrust into me one last time before he stilled.

We almost fell, but he moved the hand on my shoulder to catch us. I put both of my hands down too, because if he let go of me, I would smack my face into the floor.

He held me as we both shuddered through our orgasms. His come filled me fully and was already spilling down my legs. I knew that if we weren't both on the brew, then I would be pregnant from this encounter. There was no way we wouldn't have created life if it was just one of us on the brew.

Levi breathed heavily in my ear, the sensation tingling through me. That and the continued spurts of his come inside me had my walls tightening around him again.

"Fuck," Levi moaned.

My fingers dug into the matted floor, and I cried as another orgasm started to rip through me.

"Marie," Levi groaned as the same was happening to him. I doubt that he would be having another if he wasn't mated to me. Our bodies were linked. I didn't feel when others touched him, but I felt when I touched him.

The force of his first orgasm set my second off and now I was gripping him like a bear-trap as the pleasure racked through me.

"The fucking gods, Marie. You're fucking—" he grunted as his come started to fill me again, and I cried out as my second orgasm finally threw me over the edge.

This time, we did fall. Neither of us could hold ourselves up. I was thankful the floor was matted because my face was fully smashed into it. I liked the feel of Levi on top of me, but I wanted air, so I wiggled my hips which caused him to groan and twitch before he pulled out of me.

He rolled over to my side. "Fuck, mate. That was…" He closed his eyes, basking in his post-orgasmic high. He pulled me into his chest, still not opening his eyes as he let the pleasure wash over him.

I just laid and watched him. I loved seeing him pleased liked this. As his mate, this is what I literally lived to do.

I brushed the strands of hair that had fallen in his eyes. "You need a haircut," I whispered.

He smirked, eyes still closed. "That's what you say after we fucked like that."

I chuckled. "I mean it was amazing. You need to fuck me like that more often."

"Did it feel different to you?" he asked.

I thought for a moment. "Yeah, it did. It felt more…"

"More us, less beastly."

"Yes, more us, less beastly." I smiled. "Maybe we are evolving."

He snorted before saying, "I liked it."

"Only liked?" I questioned, drawing circles on his chest.

He opened his eyes and met mine. "I loved it. I always love it with you." His brows squished together. "Just that time was top three."

"What are the other two?"

"One, the first time. Two, making love. Three, tasting you."

I gave him a confused look. "I thought this was three."

"I remembered how good you taste, and I changed my mind. This is number four."

I laughed. "You think the mating frenzy is over?"

"For the most part, yeah, but I know if we want to fuck like that again, we can. I like this more though. I like being there with you. I like hearing you scream my name." He kissed my head.

"I liked this more as well and I agree with your list."

He chuckled. "You like my tongue lapping at you?"

"No, I fucking love it. You haven't done it since." I pouted.

"I will later."

"Why not now, we have time." My claws lightly tickled him as my eyes became hooded.

He chuckled again. "You are filled with my come right now, and I want it to stay there. Plus, I want to finish my training. This body you love to tear up with those sexy little claws of yours doesn't come naturally."

I giggled and began to sit up. "Fine, only because I like watching you."

He tugged my hair gently. "Wait."

"What?"

"Mark me," he whispered.

My brows pulled together.

"I want another."

I smiled, then kissed him, willing to do anything for him. "Where?"

"Where people can see."

"So... not your dick?" I joked.

"You can mark my dick all you fucking want, but I want another where others will see."

I laughed hard, surprised by his comment. "Really, you'd let me mark your dick?"

"It's yours, and I bet it would feel really fucking good." He smirked, his eyebrows rising in taunt.

"I don't think any other male would allow a female's teeth near his dick."

"Well, you don't need to worry about other males. *And what's between us, stays between us.*" He kissed me. I was glad that he understood why I was uncomfortable with Jessamine without even having to tell him.

I moved my kisses down his chin to his neck, resting just below the chin close to the center, circling my tongue on the area.

A slight moan escaped from Levi's lips as I bit down, tasting his blood. I could drink him dry; he tasted that good, and I bit down harder, letting my venom spread throughout his veins, getting a better taste. Levi groaned as the venom spread pleasure through him and positioned his cock at my entrance.

He slipped inside me as I released his neck and kissed him with his blood on my tongue. He was on the edge of coming, and a few brutal thrusts and we were falling together.

When we exited the training room, Levi was kissing me all over and being extra loving as he walked me back to Jessamine who still sat on the floor.

He pulled me into an embrace, his fingers squeezing my ass, then he said, "I love you," before kissing my forehead and letting me go.

When I looked up to reply, he was looking at Jessamine with a warning glare. He kissed me again quickly, then he turned to continue his training.

I realized everyone was staring at us. Some of the females were giving me glares, some were looking at my mate with awe or me with envy. All the males were smiling at us with cocky grins, confirming they definitely had heard what had just went down.

# FORTY

## MARIE

*W*hen training was over, all the students headed to breakfast, but Levi tried to walk me toward the royal wing.

"I want to eat with my friends," I said, tugging him toward the cafeteria.

He groaned, throwing his head back. "I hate people."

"I know, but you are going to be the king one day, so you have to at least like them."

"I'm not their king now." He refuted, a lazy smile forming on his lips.

"Didn't you say your father wanted you to make allies now. Gregor is a great ally to have."

His smile dropped and his eyes turned hard. "You mean the male who told me about how he tasted you before me?"

"He was lying to throw you off. He apologized to me about the lying, and I bet he would apologize to you too. He's a cool male, super laidback and easy to please."

"How would you know how easy he is to please?"

I rolled my eyes. "Levi."

He blew out a breath. "Fine."

I smiled and leaned up to kiss him. "Thank you."

We grabbed some breakfast. Levi made a look of displeasure at the shitty cafeteria food as I guided him to the table where Gregor and Finch were already sitting.

"So, he's sitting with us now?" Gregor asked.

"Wherever my mate goes, I go," Levi snarled as we sat down.

Gregor smiled widely, his canines poking out.

I giggled and Levi shot me a look. "He's fucking with you."

"Dude, you are too easy." Gregor smirked.

"Shut up, Gregor. I could go on all day about how you pine for a female who only gives you scraps. I could also go on all day about how you fuck that female, what she likes and dislikes."

Gregor rolled his eyes. "I know she likes what I do for her, that's why she keeps coming back even if she doesn't want to."

"Gregor," Jessamine said as she sat right next to me. "It's not that I don't want to come back. It's that stupid shit comes out of your mouth that makes me leave."

Levi glanced at her; his eyes sharp. She was sitting very close to me, like Levi close. I didn't realize it before, but we had always sat this close together.

The problem that had occurred while we ate was Jessamine kept touching me. She had always been touchy and seductive, and I had always been responsive, growing in arousal when she did. Now, it just made me more uncomfortable. She didn't get the cue and I didn't want to ask her to stop in front of Levi because he would flip out. I tried to remain cool, but I couldn't help but shift slightly every time she did it.

It was stupid of me to think my mate, who lived to please me and was super protective and possessive of me, wouldn't notice when another person was touching me. The next time Jessamine's hand grazed my arm sensually, Levi snapped and grabbed her wrist. "Stop fucking touching my mate."

Everyone in the cafeteria quieted. My eyes grew wide, and I pulled their hands apart, quickly examining her wrist to see if there was any bruising. She was half-human too, so if he hurt her, I would be able to tell. Thankfully, his grip on her was light and her hand wasn't even red. Blowing out a breath, I stood, pulling Levi with me to the cafeteria doors.

Before I was fully there, I turned back to Jessamine, who was aghast. That was the second time she angered him, and I would be scared too. We all know that the third time's a charm. She probably thought she only had one shot left.

My eyes silently told her that I would do everything I could to make sure she didn't die by my mate's hand, smiling tightly, before walking out into the hall.

"What the fuck, Levi! You can't just fucking grab her like that," I whisper-shouted.

Levi turned that deadly stare to me. Fuck, it was scary when he looked at me like that. "*What the fuck?* She was fucking touching what's mine. *Mine*, Marie. Not only was she touching what was mine, *again*. She was making you uncomfortable, *again*. You're asking me what the fuck? What the fuck to you? You just sat there and let her touch you. You let her touch what is mine. How would you feel if I just let anyone touch me?" he snapped back in a hushed voice.

"Levi, we had a close relationship before—" I began.

"I fucking know. I watched as you came on her fucking fingers."

My nostrils flared. "You fucked her!"

"Because you did *that* first."

"You knew we were mates and you fucked her. I didn't fucking know."

He just stared at me, his breath fast and fuming.

"You can't expect she will know that the relationship she and I shared has changed because we mated. We were on the road to being best friends and now we can't be that because of you."

Levi blinked, taking a step back. His mouth parted as if lost for words.

I sighed and rubbed my face. "Levi, I didn't mean it like that."

"No, you fucking meant it. You said it before, you didn't ever want to meet your mate. You never wanted this. You fucking said it to her *today*. You think I wasn't listening? You don't want me, and you don't want a mate. You never have, and now that you do, you can never have what you want. You want to be with your mother, who you loved most in the world before me and you want to be best fucking friends with Jessamine, who you also wanted to fuck, but you can't do that either because of me. I'm supposed to make you fucking happy. I'm supposed to please your every fucking need, but you don't want me. When we first mated, that's what you were going to tell me. If I had told you we were mates before, you wouldn't have mated with me. If I had told you that my fucking soul loved your soul, that I was your perfect fucking match, that I would let everything I had go for you, my crown, my seat on the throne, my fucking life… The thing I have spent the last nineteen years training for, that was immediately in jeopardy the second we mated. If I would have told you that before we mated, you would have laughed in my fucking face."

Tears burned in my eyes, and I wiped my face furiously. I hated fucking crying all the gods-damned time. "Fuck you," I breathed. "Fuck you. Of course I was scared. This is fucking scary, Levi. I'm fucking terrified to be your mate. I'm terrified that you will cause a war because you love me so fucking much. I'm terrified to lose you. If we go to war, Levi, I could lose you and it would rip me to shreds. Yes, before we mated, I loved my mother more than anyone and I was excited to be friends with Jessamine and I did want to fuck her, but no one, no one, will ever compare to you. *No one.* I didn't want a mate because this type of love is a lot. You are all I think about, all I dream about. You are the air I fucking breathe, Levi. I can't be without you. I didn't want to be so infatuated by you that I can't function without you. I don't give a fuck about anything *but you.* For you to fucking think that I don't is a dick move. I let her touch me because I didn't want to bring it to your attention and have you react badly. I just want us to remain us. I just want to be with you. I don't want to cause a war or an uprising or anything. I don't want there to be even a chance that we can't be together. I'm sorry that I don't want to ruin us. I'm sorry that I'm trying to protect this and make sure we are never apart." I turned and started walking to my room.

"Shit," Levi muttered under his breath before he turned me and pulled me into his arms. "I'm sorry, Marie." He kissed my head. "I just can't fucking handle the way I feel about you. The need to have you, to possess you, is so fucking prevalent within me. It drives me crazy. Second to that is my need to protect you, to comfort you, and she just set that off. I don't want to ruin us, but I can't help my feelings when it comes to you. You are everything to me, and if someone hurts you…" He took a breath. "I'm sorry for what I said; I just feel…"

Cupping his face in my hands, I kissed him. "I feel the same way about you. Okay?"

He nodded, kissing me back. "Okay."

"Want to go fuck in my room really quickly before class?" I asked.

He chuckled. "Your room is all the way on the other side of the palace. Why don't we fuck in your old room here?"

I shook my head, mock annoyed, and took his hand and started running up the stairs.

Levi pulled out my chair for me to sit. Scooting his chair right next to mine, he put his arm around my shoulder as Ms. May started to shuffle through her papers for today's lesson.

"Today, we are going to take a break from magic theory to learn a bit more history." Ms. May spoke slowly as if she was afraid to speak. "Today's topic of interest is mates."

Levi stiffened, his jaw ticking.

"The first recording of—"

"What the fuck would you know about having a mate?" Levi spoke.

She flinched. "Nothing." She smoothed her blond hair back and looked around nervously before speaking again. "Your father requested I make a lesson about them so that we can inform the other students and show them that mates are not harmful creatures that only cause wars."

"Is that so?" he replied. I placed my hand on his thigh as a warning because he was causing another scene.

"Yes," Ms. May replied timidly. Ms. May was a graceful fae but she never appeared fragile. She always seemed to be able to hold her own. Now, she looked like she might crumble if someone so much as poked her.

"All I and my mate want to do is fuck each other. We are not going to cause a war, and no one will die as long as no one harms or distresses my mate."

Everyone in the room tensed. The part where he would kill anyone for hurting my feelings, probably making them sit on the edge of their seats.

"Levi," I whispered, but the room was so quiet they could all hear. "We just went over this."

"Marie, if someone so much as messes up one little curl on your pretty little head, I will kill them," he deadpanned.

I squeezed his leg harder. "I do not want you to kill anyone."

He leaned in and kissed my forehead. "And I won't as long as no one fucks with my mate."

I knew that everyone had just received a crucial piece of information about Levi and I. It wasn't that he would kill anyone who harms me; they probably already knew that. They learned who was the top and who was the bottom in our mateship. Even though I rode his cock plenty of times, Levi was the one in control.

I hate to admit it, and my mother would probably kill me if I did out loud. She tried to raise me to be a strong independent female like herself, but I was, in nature, submissive. Levi was dominant and it turned me on that he was. I liked that he wanted to possess me, to have me, to even at times control me. It was typical for fae males to be dominant, but Levi took it to another level. I could pretend that I wasn't the one who got the short end of the stick because he held most of the power in the relationship, but that would be a lie. Levi would do anything to please me and I had power over him. I knew that he listened when I had told him what I wanted for us, but my power over him was nowhere as near as much power as he held over me.

Mates were not equals. Mates balanced another out. We were more like puzzle pieces that were different but fit together perfectly. Whatever I lacked, he had, and Levi, annoyingly enough, was good at everything but people and not being a dick.

Levi turned to Ms. May. "Continue to finish your stupid pointless lesson. You will never understand what having a mate is like until you meet them. But continue to read accounts about how when something is in the way of a mateship, what one will do to be with their mate. You are all lucky Marie is Unseelie because if her blood ran gold, I would have done *anything* to get her."

Ms. May's throat bobbed, and she gave a tight smile. "Thank you, Prince Levington."

# FORTY-ONE

## MARIE

We fucked a lot. Anytime we could, we fucked. It also seemed that we kept getting better at it, which was crazy. How could the best sex of your life get better?

We had acquired a routine. Wake up, fuck. Go to training, fuck in the middle of it. No one, not even Levi's father tried to stop us. Go to breakfast with my friends, Jessamine would sit on the other side of the table and didn't prod into our relationship but still remained her flirty, funny, heck of a good time self, which I was thankful for, fuck. Go to class. Go to lunch, fuck. Go back to class. Get out of class and fuck for several hours, then study for a few. Go to dinner, then fuck until we grew tired and went to bed.

The month went by in a blur. Levi and I would have small hiccups of him trying to kill someone for offending me but since everyone except Jessamine, Gregor, and Finch kept a ten-foot distance away from me, not much happened. It was slightly annoying that everyone did that, but I didn't really need any more friends.

Even though we fucked a lot, we also talked a lot too—in between the fucking.

I was breathing heavily, lying on Levi's chest as I regained myself from the mind-blowing orgasm he just gave me. Rolling off him, I hissed, "You know it's not fair that you have a full fae body that heals within seconds." I was sore constantly, my body never getting the time to fully heal between sessions.

Levi kissed my head. "If you were full fae, you wouldn't have that beautiful curvy body I love so much."

I rolled my eyes. "You would love me in any body."

"Yeah, but you chose this body for a reason."

"Well, me and my soul need to have a talk about the next time we carnate. I need to have longer legs if you are going to be a cunt who takes three stairs at a time."

"I like that you're short too."

"I like that you're tall, but you can be tall and not take three stairs at a time."

He laughed and I sat up so I could see his smile. He did it all the time now, always only for me, but I still wanted to see it.

"You know you're my best friend," I said to him.

"I thought Jessamine was your best friend?"

Exhaling, I smoothed the crease in his brow with my thumb. "Are you ever going to not hate her?"

"I don't hate her. I just find her incredibly annoying, and it annoys me that you like her."

"I like her because she is annoying. She is fun."

"But she's not your best friend, I am," he chimed, grinning.

"Yes, you are. I can tell you anything. The only other person I can do that with is my mother, but she…" My smile weakened.

"She hasn't written to you."

Blinking profusely to keep the tears back, I said, "She said she would, but my father did. He never does that. My mother does the writing telling me how my father is, not the other way around."

Levi nudged my nose with his. "She will come around; you are going to see her in a few days anyway. Maybe she was just too busy to write."

"She has never been too busy for me."

He kissed me tenderly, the hand on my back caressing me and adding comfort. "You know my father was my best friend before you. I mean he technically still is, at least he's my only other friend. I haven't talked to him more than what we do at dinner as of late, but I used to tell him everything. Not because he is the king either, just because he's always been there for me. That's why he was surprised I didn't tell him about you because I always do."

My nose wrinkled. "I thought you hated your father for fucking Ms. May when you were seven."

"I was twelve," he corrected.

"Sorry, when you were twelve."

He smiled. "Yeah, he often doesn't fuck females I—" He stopped abruptly.

I patted his chest. "Good male, you know when you are about to set yourself up for failure."

He snorted. "No one mattered. No one was you."

I wish I could say the same back to him. At the time, Kolvin did matter. He still did. He was my best friend, not like my mother or Levi, but he was just the boy who used to make mud pies with me and would play in the imaginary worlds we created. I missed that. I fucked it up and it still hurt.

Levi tipped my chin up. "What are you thinking about?"

"Nothing." I sighed.

He kissed my cheek. "You lie."

I nipped at his nose, then kissed him before changing the subject. "Are you excited to be king?"

He took a heavy breath. "Before you, I couldn't wait. Now, it scares me."

My brows pulled together. "Why?"

"I'm afraid I won't be a good king because I will have to be a good mate."

I looked into his midnight eyes. "There's nothing that will make you a bad mate."

"I haven't fucked it up yet. I almost have."

My brows were almost touching now. "When?"

"*I hate being here and it's mostly your fault.* That's what you said to me after you called your parents. That's when you took my cloak off. I thought what I did ruined us before we even started but when I did it, I wasn't thinking. I was just pissed that you had that mark and that you let her touch you like that. I just wanted to punish you like you were punishing me. Then you hurt yourself just to fucking deal with what I had done, and you were crying. I fucking wanted to kill myself then and I felt like more of an asshole because you said Jessamine had made you feel at home, and I ruined that for you."

"Levi, I forgave you. I forgave Jessamine too. I don't like talking about this."

He pulled me in to kiss my forehead. "I know, but I just needed you to know I was sorry."

"I do, so we can never ever talk about it again ever?"

"Yeah."

"So, you're scared to be a bad king?" I prodded.

He growled low. "You weren't going to let that one slip through the cracks, huh?"

"It's important, it's our future. You and your father haven't taught me how to be queen yet, either."

"Well, we kind of would have to fuck less for us to squeeze that in right now."

"We already don't fuck enough," I joked.

"I know," he said seriously, causing me to chuckle. "I'm hoping that I will figure out a way to be a good mate and a good king, but I will always put your wants over others' needs, always."

"Levi, I haven't asked you for anything but not to kill people."

"And that's fucking hard," he said, exasperated.

I rolled my eyes at him. "Okay, something easy. Tell me what kind of king you want to be."

"What do you mean?"

"Well, your father is the Slut King, King Dominick is the Party King."

Levi snorted. "My father is complex, yet he gets stuck with *Slut King*."

I giggled. "What do you want to be?"

"The Mated King, or The King Who Loves Marie, or The King Who Will Kill Anyone Who Fucks With His Queen." He pressed his lips to mine lightly.

"You are annoying."

"You like annoying people."

I pinched his nipple and his eyes gleamed with chaos, then he was moving, and I was moving, squealing, trying to get away from him. He caught me and then was on top of me, pinning my arms with one of his hands on my stomach. "Your tits look amazing when your arms are like this, remind me to fuck you like this."

"You aren't going to fuck me right now?"

"No, right now, I'm going to pay you back for assaulting my nipple."

"I'll probably like it."

"If you like it, then I'll have to do it again harder," he purred. "If you like that, then I'll have to bite them."

"And if I like that?" I questioned.

"I'll bite another little nub that's more sensitive."

My smile grew wider. "Oh, I definitely will hate that. You should probably do that if you really want to pay me back."

"Really?" he chimed.

"Yeah, I'd absolutely hate it," I said, sarcastically.

"Well then, that would probably be the best punishment, wouldn't it?"

He started to move to where his face was in between my legs, his hand still holding both of mine. "Yes." I nodded in excitement. "That would probably be the fairest punishment."

Levi stilled and smiled wickedly. "Fair?"

"Yeah, fair."

"Oh, Marie, but I don't play fair, remember?" Then he was biting my clit. *Hard.*

I screamed, the pleasure and pain mixing together. He bit down even harder, and I screamed louder. He pushed his fingers into me and then found that spot that created waves of pleasure within me, pinching it with his index and middle finger.

My hips bucked off the bed as an orgasm rammed through me. It was violent and visceral. I screamed so hard I lost my voice midway through. Tears streamed down my eyes because though it was pleasurable, it was also fucking painful at the same time, making my brain and body overtly confused.

Levi let go of the hold he had on my clit and that pleasure spot inside my core and started lapping my clit as my orgasm started to subside. The feeling of his wet tongue on my sore clit felt like a whole new sensation, causing me to fucking cry in ecstasy.

His fingers slowly pumped through me, confusing my body even more and making me feel tangled up. I never stopped coming. It just kept happening over and over again. My cries sounded like I was being murdered. I was surprised that no one tried to make sure he wasn't. Eventually, I was too oversensitive, and I had to beg Levi to stop.

He finished and kissed me, making me taste my come before lying back beside me and tugging me into his arms.

"I want to be the Wolf King."

I blinked hard; my brain too fogged up to understand whatever the fuck he was talking about. "What?" I whispered.

"My emblem, our emblem, I want it to be the wolf."

It took me a minute to process what he was saying. "The wolf."

"Yes, do you like them?"

"They are fine creatures. Why them?" I was surprised I could make a coherent sentence.

He pondered for a moment. "I just always liked the wolf."

"You kind of look like one." My fogged brain spat out.

He blurted out a laugh. "Yeah, I guess I do."

"You're still a hot wolf."

"Thanks, mate."

"So, the wolf? That's going to be your emblem."

"Yeah, unless you—"

I stopped him, knowing what he would say. "I love it, Levi."

"I love you, Marie."

"I'm sleepy," I grumbled, burrowing my head deeper into his chest.

"I would be too if a hot wolf guy ate me out like that."

"You want a wolf boy to eat you out?"

He kissed my temple, smiling. "Go to sleep, mate."

"Mate."

# FORTY-TWO

## Marie

*I* spent the night before Samhain wrapped in Levi's arms. We had been that way for hours. Earlier, we had a test in class. We attained a perfect score and were the first to finish as usual. Ms. May seemed impressed that we managed to fuck all the time and still maintain our grades.

After, we went to our room and made love. It was the second time we had. The mating bond made us want to mate, the sex aggressive and mind-blowing, and I would never get enough of that, but making love to Levi was the best feeling in the world. We made love for as long as we could, both of us trying to hold our bodies back from falling off the edge so we could remain in that state of bliss and pure unconditional love. When our climaxes did approach, they ripped through our bodies in a harsh and brutal way that had us both shuddering in pleasure for several moments.

We held each other after our love-making, lying on our sides, my head buried into Levi's chest. Our legs tangled together, my fingers caressing Levi's back, his twirling my curls. We didn't speak or sleep; we just held each other. As time passed, Levi pulled me closer and closer, his long arms almost wrapping around me twice. He held me like he never wanted to let me go. I didn't want him to but eventually he would have to. I was due to visit my family in a few hours.

"Please don't leave me," Levi whispered.

I pulled him tighter into my embrace. "I'm not leaving you."

"You are."

"I'm visiting my family for a day."

"The definition of leaving someone is going somewhere without them. That's what you are doing."

"I'm coming back."

"I don't want to do this again. Last time you left, I went crazy. I hardly slept or ate, and it was Mabon, the day to feast."

"You did feast, though," I chimed.

"I'm not joking right now." He burrowed his head deeper into my neck. "Please don't leave."

"We have talked about this." We have. Over, and over, and over again. As the day got closer, we argued about it more.

"Let me go with you," he demanded.

"No," I replied.

"Please."

I looked up and cupped his face. "Levi, I want to have a day with my parents. Just one day. I want to talk to them and to see how they feel about you. I don't want to leave you. I don't ever want to spend a day without you, but I need to be alone with them."

"You keep saying them, but you mean your mother," he muttered.

"Yes, my mother. Levi, she owns a part of my heart. Our hearts are mates, so she owns a part of yours as well.

"My mother is a good mother. She always wants the best for me, but she is also a person, and it hurts her that the best for me isn't with her. It has always been me and her. I am my mother's flower, and she is my soil, my rock, my anchor. She built a safe place for me to grow and flourish and she kept my roots, my secrets, my fears, my truths, safe within her. Before you, I loved no one more than I loved her. She did the same for me. I need to talk to her to show her that nothing between me and her will change. So no, you can't come. Plus, it's too late for us to make the change in the decision. The Seelie King has approved for me to come, just me."

Levi didn't respond verbally but moved his head into the crest of my neck and breathed me in. It hurt me painfully that I was doing this to him. I was his mate, I lived to please him, to love him, to take care of his needs. He held most of the power in our relationship, he could sway me to agree with whatever he wanted—except this.

My family, my mother, was the only other thing I cared about. With the mating bond, it was hard to not let my care for Levi completely overshadow my care for them. In those moments I felt myself slipping, I would remember the times I spent with them, how my mother and father loved me so unconditionally that I always felt loved. Even when I got in trouble for going over the border to play with humans and stole my father's favorite horse to do it. They were so furious with me but even then, I still felt their love.

Levi was different from me in this situation; he didn't care if his father rejected me. If his father rejected me, Levi would have cut his father off or attempted to kill him—no matter how crazy of an idea that was. If my mother rejected Levi, it would gut me and tear me apart. I wanted her to like him and approve of him. I needed it. I needed her and him. If she didn't approve of my mate, I couldn't see her anymore because if it was her or him, I would always pick him. I didn't think my mother would make me choose. I knew she wanted to still be in my life, but she just didn't know how to deal with the news.

"I need to get ready soon," I whispered, and Levi tensed, clutching me closer. I took a deep breath and pushed him away, my heart aching at the action. A growl sounded from his throat, and he pulled me closer. "Levi, you have to let me go."

"No," he snarled.

"Levi." I sighed. It was taking everything within me to not give in, to not let him take this away from me. I pulled away again and he didn't want to, but he let me go.

Getting out of bed, I went to our closet. He picked out what he wanted me to wear while I was gone. It was a black sundress that had off-the-shoulder sleeves. It would show all of my marks and would remind people I was Unseelie.

After pulling it on, along with black lace panties, I looked for some stocking when he came into the closet and wrapped his arms around me from behind. Kissing my neck, he said, "I need to do some stuff before you leave."

"What stuff?"

He took my hand and brought me back into the bedroom. "Levi, we have already decided every detail of my trip, every nook and cranny. Everything you can control has been planned for." It really was. He planned everything with my guards, the Seelie King, and my father. Everything he could control, he did.

He brought me over to the side of the bed. "I need to update my marks." He didn't need to, none of them were even close to fading but I knew he wanted to update them so he could make sure everyone got the message I was his.

I softened. "Okay, but I don't want to be late."

He gave me a cocky smile that didn't reach his eyes. "I'm always on time, mate."

"No, you are always late."

"I am the prince and soon-to-be king. Nothing starts till I arrive."

"You are an arrogant prick, and if you make me late, I will cut you."

He gave another half-grin. "Is my violence rubbing off on you, mate?"

"No, I always want to cut you. To dig my claws into your body so deep it leaves a scar. I want to mark you with wounds that will never heal so you will always be mine."

He growled before spinning me around to where my back was flushed with his chest. He bit into my neck where one of his marks lay, and I moaned as his venom entered my veins. He bit another mark and another. He updated all of the ones on my neck, then bent me over the bed to bite the one on my back. I was shuddering, ready to come when he pulled up the hem of my dress and tugged my panties down past my ass.

He slowly pushed into me, both of us groaning as we connected. When he was fully within me, he paused. I tensed with anticipation for the brutal fucking he was about to give me, but he didn't move. When he started to pull out, he was slow, scraping every vein of his cock across my inner walls before slowly thrusting back in.

He teased me languidly, and I wiggled my hips to urge him to go fast, but his hands held my sides to still me. He continued to torture me with slow thrusts, giving me little sprouts of pleasure but not fully giving me what I wanted.

"Levi," I breathed. "Please."

He didn't reply; he just continued to slowly tease me with his cock.

One of his hands came around me and lightly tapped my clit. I tried to push myself into it, but he slapped my ass and said, "No."

"Levi," I whined, and he slapped my ass harder in reply.

His finger tapped my clit again making me cry out in frustration as he kept his slow pace. I could feel my beast clawing under my skin, his edging making my body taut with tension. She wanted to come, *I wanted* to come, but he wouldn't let us.

If I tried to buck my hips or squeeze my walls, he would spank me, the pain adding to the pleasure but still getting us nowhere. I needed to leave soon, and I was afraid he would leave me unfinished, having to spend the whole day craving him.

He didn't stop and finally gave me what I wanted with a hard thrust into me. His cock hit my innermost wall, causing me to scream. He applied more pressure shoving himself deeper, causing another form of pleasure to course through me as he stretched my entrance. I gripped the sheets as I started to coast over that edge; the process slow and frustrating. My orgasm took its sweet time to spread through my body. Then Levi leaned down, triggering another moan to escape me as his cock prodded my entrance more and dug into that inner wall. He kissed my neck before he sank his canines into my shoulder, creating a new mark.

My perusing orgasm violently crashed through me then, my teeth gritting and my claws digging further within the sheets. I screamed into the bed as Levi's seed filled me and he bit down harder. I was sure I was about to black out from the pleasure before he removed his teeth. He remained inside me, letting his seed cover my walls as I coasted through my climax.

My body was jelly after it faded, and I fully sank into the mattress. Levi pulled out then and immediately pulled my panties up. "Do not remove these until you come back," he ordered.

I didn't reply; my mind too fogged and my body too tired to function.

"Marie, answer me," he growled.

"Okay," I softly whispered. It was so low I didn't even know if he heard me.

"If you take these off, I will punish you when you get back."

"Okay." My eyes drifted shut and I heard Levi moving around as I rested. He needed no time to rest after, his full fae body making him godlike.

I felt fabric come around my foot, and I flinched before realizing it was a stocking. Levi pulled them on me, then a garter belt to hold them up and then shoes. He did this while I laid face down in our bed recovering.

Levi flipped me on my back and pulled me to sit up, me groaning at the movement.

"I have a gift for you," Levi said, kneeling on the ground.

I wiped my face with my hand. "The orgasm wasn't the gift?"

"No, that was so you will have my scent while you're gone."

I rolled my eyes; it's not like I already wasn't covered in his scent. "You know Samhain is for honoring the dead, right? Not really a day for gifts."

"I can give my mate a gift whenever I want to," he stated. I realized he had put on pants and had his cloak in his hand. Reaching into his pocket, he pulled out a jewelry box and handed it to me.

Inside was a stainless steel necklace with a ruby pendant.

I smiled, meeting his eyes. "It's beautiful, thank you."

"It's a family heirloom. It's been passed down to the females in my family for years. It's also a siphon so you are always safe. I want you to be able to protect yourself just in case your guards fail." He took the necklace and stood, gesturing for me to stand. I did and held my hair while he clasped it around my neck.

I turned, looking up at him. "I don't really know how to do magic, Levi."

"You can call upon the shadows. Call upon them, channel the necklace, then blast if you are in danger." The look in his eyes was serious, boring deeply into me with gravity.

"I'm going to be fine, mate."

He didn't answer, grabbing his cloak and tying it around me. His body tense as he did. It looked like it was taking every ounce of his willpower to control himself.

My hands cupped his face, but he didn't look at me. "Levington." That was probably the first time I had said his real name to him, which caused his midnight eyes to meet mine. "I love you."

He rested his forehead on mine. "I love you too, Marie."

"I will come back," I promised.

"I will tear this world apart if you don't."

# FORTY-THREE

## CORIVINA
## 20 YEARS AGO.

*I* spent the last couple of months getting to know Melinda and Maurice. They were two pure souls, and at times, I found my darkness couldn't handle being around them, but every time I left them, I craved to see them again.

Darius knew of them, but he hadn't met them because I hadn't introduced them. I would say I didn't know them well enough and wanted to still get to know them better before I did, but the real reason was Maurice.

I felt an attraction to both of the twins, but my pull toward Maurice was greater. He was a simple man who loved simple things, but the beast inside me thought of him as the most precious being to have ever lived. He was aggravating and annoying, but I still never wished for him to not stop talking. I wished to never see those coffee-black eyes lose the purity within and turn cold like mine.

It was probably one of the reasons it pained me to leave them every night. I feared what could happen to him. He was human, left with his shitty human senses to keep himself alive. I spent my nights worried, and I hated the attachment I was growing for him.

He was human and he would die. It would be stupid to be in pain when the inevitable happened.

All the while, Darius and I were having the most amazing sex. Guilt plagued me after each orgasm because often it was imaginations of coffee-black eyes that got me there.

I still loved Darius with all my being, but I was growing infatuated with Maurice. I tried to stop it, but it wouldn't go away no matter what I did.

Maurice and I were mixing herbs for Melinda to make healing kits with. We sat shoulder to shoulder, thigh to thigh, the thin layer of my dress and his trousers separating us. His musky human scent filled my nose, making me salivate. My body tight and my nipples aching.

I wanted to take him and possess him. I wanted to mark him as mine. It wouldn't mean the same thing as a fae marking a fae. It would mean he was mine and under my protection. He would be like a sex toy for me. One bite of my canines into his human flesh and he would be mine forever, the mark never healing. The thought had my already soaked panties dripping.

It was dangerous for me to have these thoughts because one bite could kill him. Venom paralyzed humans and if there was too much of it, he could die. I would have to be careful when I did it.

*When I did it?*

I wasn't going to do that. I wouldn't make him my pet. Though my creature craved it badly, I wouldn't. I understood now why the fae loved humans so much. We were possessive, dominating creatures and humans were weak and defenseless. Beautiful and flawed. Aware in mind but ignorant with ego. The perfect prey.

Shifting, I grimaced as the thick wet fabric of my panties glided across my clit. I was immensely uncomfortable but in the most blissful way. I wished Maurice would go under the table and taste me. I dreamed of his tongue on me and his cock filling me. I dreamed of tasting him, his cock, his mouth, his blood, his flesh. I was glad human senses weren't as great as a fae's or I would never be able to be around him without him knowing his effects over me.

Melinda entered the room, her eyes turning into slits as they settled onto me. She would always try to get a reading off me, but the gods blocked her from seeing my future and theirs as well when it involved me. About a month ago, I had become so entangled into their lives that she couldn't see the future of her and her brother at all. Her reaction was to yell at the gods, which made me love her. Finally, a witch who understood how much of a bastard the gods actually were.

"Corivina, I really hate you," she stated.

I smirked. "Why this time?"

"I can't even see five minutes into my future if you're here."

"Us ungifted don't ever get that advantage, sis," Maurice replied.

She gave him an annoyed face. "Shut it, Maurice."

The immediate urge to attack her for talking to him that way bubbled within me. I wanted to rip her to shreds and offer her heart to Maurice as a gift. Then shove his cock down my throat to ease his stresses, but I couldn't do that.

Rolling my shoulders, I brushed the urge off, trying not to show my reaction. Luckily, they were human, so they were unaware of sensing a threat, especially with the gods blocking Melinda.

Maurice gave a mischievous smile in reply to his twin and then went back to working.

Melinda's gold eyes met mine, glinting with the candlelight. "I would tell you to fuck off if the gods didn't say you were important to me and my brother."

I grinned. "You could tell me to fuck off, but doesn't mean I would listen. I enjoy your frustration with me. It brings me a sadistic joy to torture you, little witch. It feels like I'm paying back your great grandmother for being a cunt all the time."

She pursed her lips, huffing as she went upstairs, leaving me and Maurice alone. My arousal peeked with the realization. It was a visceral feeling how much my creature wanted to possess this man. I had to grind my molars together to keep myself in check.

"Would you?" Maurice asked.

His voice pulled me from my savage thoughts, my body relaxing a hair. "Would I what?"

"Leave if she asked?"

I shook my head slightly.

"And it would be just to annoy her?"

"No," I replied, meeting his eyes. It felt like I could see his pure soul within, and it made mine ache to drown in it.

"Why else then?"

I looked away; I could not say that I always wanted to be near him. I could not say that I wanted to capture him and lock him in my basement, keep him there so no one could harm him. I couldn't say I wanted him to be mine.

His fingers brushed a strand of hair behind my pointed ear. His touch traveling through me sensually, my core clenching as his digits traveled down my face to my neck, caressing my mark. My bottom lip trapped under my teeth to stop a moan from escaping.

"What is it like to be claimed and owned as such?"

I pushed his fingers away, not liking him touching my connection to Darius. It wasn't because I felt like he shouldn't touch it, it's that I felt guilty because I wanted him to.

"It is love," I said. "Not always but this one is that, love."

"Why haven't we met him?"

"He is busy," I lied.

He gave me a smirk, knowing I was. He could always read me. I felt like I could never hide from him, like somehow on a deeper level, he knew me. "Corivina." I absolutely loved when he said my name. "You are the most beautiful creature I have ever seen. I don't know why I needed to tell you that, but I did."

I purred—something I have never done. My eyes widened, the action scaring the shit out of me. When I met his eyes, they were full of wonderment. "I didn't know you purred."

I smiled slightly, uncomfortable with the range of emotions I felt for this man I barely knew. "Sometimes." I stood. "I have to go."

He grabbed my wrist to stop me. "Did I offend you?"

I caressed his beautiful face. "No, I just have to go. I'll be back tomorrow, and the day after that, and the day after that. You two won't get rid of me that easily." I looked down at his perfectly plush lips, wanting to press mine to them.

"I can't wait." He smiled, my heart squeezing as I turned abruptly and practically ran home.

When I arrived, Darius was in the study. I didn't want him to know that I was soaking with an arousal for another male, a man for that fact. So, I ran upstairs and showered. When I got out, he was sitting on the bed waiting for me, *naked*. Tight with tension, I basically attacked him, needing to release my pent-up sexual frustration.

We fucked like wild animals, but when we finished, I still ached for the human. A sigh of disappointment escaping my lips.

"What is it, Vina?" Darius asked as we laid wrapped in each other's arms, my head lying on his bronze chest.

"I have feelings for another," I whispered.

He kissed my forehead. "I know."

My brows furrowed as I looked up at him. "How?"

"I can smell you all the way in the study when you get home. I know it's not for me. Who is it for?"

"A human." I sighed.

"The human and the witch?" I hadn't even told him their names.

"Yes, that human."

"Have you done anything with him?" he asked cautiously.

"*No, never.* I love you. I hate myself for feeling the way I do toward him, but my beast within wants to possess him, to fuck him or eat him, or fuck him then eat him. It doesn't matter as long as he is ours."

Darius brushed my hair back from my head. "Vina, we are predators. We can pretend that we aren't, but it doesn't change our urge to hunt, capture, and kill. We are also sexual in nature; our venom literally confuses our prey by delivering them an intense form of pleasure."

"I don't just want to kill him; I want to know him. I'm sorry, I wish I could stop it, but I feel a pull toward him."

"Vina, we are fae. We tend to have multiple partners." What he said was true. Fae took multiple partners when they weren't marked, but when they were, there was a respect between the pair, and one who was claimed wouldn't take another unless their partner was comfortable with it.

"We are married, Darius. We are ours forever."

He kissed my forehead, and I burrowed into his chest more, breathing in his warm vanilla scent. "We are ours forever, but we aren't mates. We don't satisfy all our needs. I want you to be happy, Vina. The idea of you loving another doesn't scare me; it makes me happy you feel that love."

"I don't think I love him. I just want him as my pet."

He chuckled. "Then I want you to have that pet, if he is willing of course."

I looked up into his warm blue eyes. "Really, Darius?"

He kissed me. "He is human, and he will die eventually. If you were to have another affair with anyone, I'm glad it will be with someone I wouldn't have to truly compete with."

"Darius, you are my one. My heart belongs to you and no one else. I won't let things get too serious between me and the human.

I don't want to take his life from him. I just want to enjoy him a little, then set him free." The 'set him free' part felt like a lie. I wanted to tie him to the bed and use him for my pleasure for the rest of his days. Which would be short if I did because I would definitely end up eating him.

"Maybe we will enjoy him together," Darius suggested.

My body stiffened, a growl sounding in my throat. "He is mine." I seethed.

He laughed hard, tears starting to form in his eyes. "Okay, okay. I get it he is your prey, and you don't want to share." He kissed my head. "Just promise me something."

"What?"

"Not in our bed, not in our home."

"Of course," I promised.

"Then I have no problem with you exploring this man."

I smiled. "You know I probably would never let another touch you, right?"

He chuckled. "Not even if I found myself a prey I couldn't resist?"

"I'd kill them before you could sink your teeth into them."

"You are truly wretched, Vina, and not fair. Not fair at all," he whined.

"I love you." I said.

"I love you too."

# FORTY-FOUR

## Marie

Walking toward my father and his top soldiers with come-filled panties ranks top ten on most embarrassing things I have done. I knew Levi just wanted to make sure he had thoroughly marked me, but it was still embarrassing. To make things worse, two out of six of the soldiers that were standing with my father were Kolvin and his father. It made sense why my father had chosen them to be a part of the guard to protect me, but it didn't make matters better.

When I looked at Kolvin, his eyes were on my throat. I knew he wasn't staring at my necklace; he was staring at the five marks that adorned my neck. Five was a bit overkill; most fae didn't mark their partners with more than one or two marks. Most fae weren't mated so they didn't feel the need to possess their partners at the extreme level Levi did.

I was ordered to take my cloak off the second I walked into Seelie by one of the six Unseelie guards. When I asked him why, he said Levi had ordered him to take my cloak from me and wasn't allowed to give it back until we crossed back over into Unseelie. I didn't argue because it was warm enough in Seelie to not wear the cloak and I knew Levi didn't want me to hide my marks.

When I was a few paces from my father, I went to hug him but was stopped by two twin blades. My head snapped to the Unseelie guards. "He is my father."

"We know," one of them replied. "We have been ordered to not allow anyone to touch you."

"By who?" I asked, knowing the answer.

"Prince Levington, Your Highness." I brushed my hair behind my ear, slightly adjusting the tiara I was also forced to wear.

"He is my father; I am going to hug him. You can tell my mate that I ordered you to let me." I said, using the most regal voice I could muster.

"We are under blood oath, Your Highness. If we disobey Prince Levington's orders, he will know and he will kill us and our entire family. We have been told not to go against them for any matter even if you ordered us," the soldier replied.

I rubbed my forehead, embarrassment coloring my cheeks as I looked to my father. "Sorry."

He gave his warm comforting smile. "It's okay, flower. I… I couldn't if I wanted to."

I frowned in question.

"You scent… it uhh… it warns me not to come near you if I want to remain alive."

"What?" I knew I probably smelled like Levi more than myself, but scents didn't warn people.

"It's the essence," he supplied.

I quirked my mouth to the side, still not understanding.

"It's the way he fucks you," Kolvin blurted out. "He fucks you to possess you; the essence of that is carried through his scent."

I met those honey-green eyes, a mask of no emotion showing back. He was in full soldier mode, his face set into a tone of boredom, his body standing tall and at attention. I could still tell he carried pain behind the facade. Kolvin was once my best friend; he couldn't fool me.

My father looked at Kolvin with a stern face before returning his eyes back to me. "I'm glad to see you, flower."

I looked to the two guards positioned in front of me. "You can put down the swords." They did as I asked.

This was not what I envisioned visiting my family again would be like. What I wanted was what I had before. I wanted it to just be me, my mother, and my father, hugging and walking home arm in arm. Not me, my father—who was in his commander's uniform—six Unseelie soldiers, and six Seelie soldiers.

The Seelie soldiers were insisted upon by King Dominick. He didn't want to risk anyone hurting me, knowing that the outcome could turn deadly. He appointed my father to pick six of his best, which included Kolvin.

"Where is Mother?" I asked.

My father's smile grew tight. "She thought it would be best if she stayed and prepared the meal for tonight while I received you." I tried not to look hurt that my mother was ignoring me and failed. "She wants to see you, flower. She just doesn't want it to be in front of all these people, staring at the new mated Unseelie Princess."

I glanced at the crowd of people gathered around us. They kept their distance knowing that coming too close would probably result in their death, but they were still trying to get a glimpse of me. They couldn't because the guards blocked them from view which I realized was probably another order Levi demanded.

My stomach turned as I realized Levi was sending me another message. This is how it would always be. He wouldn't let me leave unless he knew that everything was going to be safe. The only way for me to be safe was to be suffocated with guards and rules. It made sense why he had asked me to ask my parents to come to Unseelie for Solstice when I got into the carriage to leave.

I hadn't thought of that, but it would be easier for them to come there than for me to come here, even with Levi.

Levi was trying to sway me from coming here ever again and I hated that it was working.

As we walked, I couldn't even see what was in front of me. Two guards flanked my sides, one in the back and one in the front, all the Seelie guards around them. It was ridiculous, but it was planned to be ridiculous because I was that important now.

When I entered my home, I was greeted by my mother. She smiled and seeing her smile made my heart ache. I desperately wanted to run into her arms and breathe in her rose scent, to feel her love wrap around me, and let me know everything was okay.

Her eyes dropped to my neck and her smile dropped, and so did my hopes.

Why did everyone have to look at my neck? Yes, I had five marks there. Yes, it was abnormal to have more than one visible. I was in an abnormal relationship. I loved my marks. I loved that they tied me to my mate. I didn't care that he had the intent to possess me when he bit me. *I was his.* I hated that everyone, even my father, was looking down at me. Like I wasn't a person anymore. Now, everyone only saw me as the Unseelie Prince's mate.

"Marie." My mother's voice was stern and held a bit of an edge. "Where did you get that necklace?"

I blinked, confusion filling me. "The necklace? Levi gave it to me."

"Where did he get it?" my mother asked, voice getting slightly harsher.

"I don't know."

Her black eyes bore into me. "Give it to me."

My fingers went to the clasp as a reflex, but I hesitated. Levi gave me this necklace to protect me. The necklace was his family heirloom passed down from generation to generation. It meant something to his family, so it probably meant something to him, but it also looked like it meant something to my mother. I could see in her eyes that it was more than just a family heirloom to her.

"Marie, give me the necklace *now*." The air in the room chilled, and my guards stiffened but didn't attack, everyone looking at my mother with wide eyes.

"Mother—"

"MARIE, GIVE ME THE NECKLACE RIGHT FUCKING NOW!"

The guards unsheathed their swords and aimed them at my mother who didn't even flinch. Her eyes were set on the necklace. I had never seen her like this. She looked like she was about to unleash a hurricane of emotions. I could see tears building behind her lids, but her eyes were alight with rage.

"Put the swords down," I said to the guards, keeping calm as everyone else in the room was on edge.

"Your Highness, she—"

"She is my mother; you will not attack her, or I will tell my mate of how you disobeyed me." I hated using the 'my mate' card, but if they hurt my mother, I would lose it.

They lowered their swords but didn't sheath them.

"Can I take the necklace off?" I asked one of the guards.

"He didn't say anything about a necklace." Levi was going to hate himself for forgetting that, but I would deal with it later. The only good thing about having a mate is that they can never truly be mad at you—at least I hope they can't.

I unclasped the necklace and handed it to one of the guards. "Give it to her."

When my mother had the necklace in hand, she stared at it for a moment, her eyes guarded but churning with emotion, a tear starting to make its way down her cheek. She was gone for those moments, deep inside herself, as if she was lost in a memory.

She snapped out of it as the tears hit her chin and she wiped them away furiously. Her cold eyes met mine, her face returning to stone indifference. "Go to your room," she whispered.

I stood there shocked; my heart burning with pain as if she just had stabbed it with a knife. Tears welled in my eyes, and I pushed them back. Why was she acting like this? Why did she hate that I was mated? Why did she take the necklace?

I swallowed the lump in my throat, along with the unspoken questions and nodded. "Okay." My voice came out low and weak. "I'll see you later for dinner?"

She didn't reply and turned toward the kitchen, walking away from me.

# FORTY-FIVE

## CORIVINA
## 205 YEARS AGO.

My fingers brushed through the lovely plump petals of red roses in the Royal Unseelie Greenhouse. I loved flowers; it wasn't very Unseelie of me to, but I did.

"You smell of them," Markos said into my ear.

He had been courting me for a year now. I had no idea why he liked me. He was the prince, and my family was on his father's court, but they ranked low. I certainly wasn't his parents' first pick, but I was Markos's.

I had known him my whole life. We went to school together, but I never really talked to him before. Until one day, a year ago, I was in one of the royal libraries looking for a book to pass my time when he interrupted my search.

*"Why are you so beautiful?" he asked.*

*I blushed. "What?"*

*"You are so beautiful, Corivina. I have always thought that."*

*"Why are you just telling me now?" I asked, nervously playing with my claws.*

*"Because I finally grew the courage to."*

"Oh okay, thank you." I turned to look at the shelf, hoping he couldn't see how red my face was getting. I hated when I blushed—the pink of my cheeks did not go well with the blue of my shimmer.

"Do you not like me?" he asked.

"Huh?" I raised a brow, turning back to meet his face. His eyes were half-lidded in admiration which caused my cheeks to grow even more heated.

"You never talk to me or seem remotely interested in me. It sucks to be infatuated with someone who never looks your way."

I blinked, unsure what to say. "Uhh, you are nice."

He leaned against the bookshelf. His eyes closed briefly, then met mine as he gave a slight smile. "I guess someone as beautiful and smart as you wouldn't spend her time looking at someone as bland as me."

"You are the prince."

"That's the only thing that makes me interesting. That is the only reason any female ever wants me. You don't even care about me."

"I… uh… My family is low in your father's court. I never thought you would ever look my way."

"Have you seen you? I could never not look your way." Markos trailed a finger down my cheek, smiling at me with the softest smile. "Let me court you."

I stilled, lost for words. I studied his eyes for a moment before blurting out, "What?"

"I like you, Corivina, let me court you."

"You want to court me?"

He smiled, my heart squeezing at its beauty. How could this male ever think he was bland? "Yes."

That was a year ago. Today was our anniversary. Markos brought me to this greenhouse to celebrate, knowing of my love for flowers.

My hands drifted down the stem of the rose, accidentally nicking my finger on the thorn, drawing a fresh swell of red blood.

It would be two years until we were sorted, and we knew what color our blood would change to when our magic manifested.

Markos took my finger and sucked the blood clean, my core clenching as his plump lips sealed around my digit. His eyes rolled back, and he groaned slightly. "You taste so sweet, Cor."

I removed my hand and brushed a strand of hair behind my ear, trying to hide my blush in the darkened room. Markos took my face in his hands and pressed a soft kiss on my lips. "Happy anniversary, my raven."

I smiled, "Happy anniversary, Markos."

"I have a gift for you." He pulled out a velvet jewelry box from his pocket. My fingers ran over the soft edges as he handed it to me. I opened it, revealing a beautiful necklace made of Unseelie stainless steel with a ruby pendant.

My heart paused for a beat, and I covered my mouth in disbelief. "Markos, this is…"

"The queen's ruby. I know." This was the necklace his mother wore, the necklace all the queens wore.

"Why are you giving it to me?"

"The ruby is passed down to all the queens in my family."

"I know but I'm not a queen."

He smiled, wrapping his arms around me. "I hope one day you will be."

"What?"

"Cor, I love you, I always have. I fell for you when we were babes and I spent years pining for you to look my way. I will always love you and I hope to one day make you my queen."

"You love me?" I asked.

He kissed me, smiling over my mouth as he did. "Yes, I do, and I will forever."

"But we haven't even had sex yet."

"We have done things." He kissed my neck. "I don't need to make love to you to know that I love you."

His tongue swirled across my skin, and I shuddered at the contact. "I want to make you mine," he whispered. "Let me."

I pushed his head back. "Are you asking to mark me?"

He nodded with a blinding smile.

"No."

Markos stilled and took a step back, his arms falling to his sides. "Do you not want to be with me?"

"I do but we are eighteen, Markos."

"Do you want to explore other males before you decide or something?" Hurt echoing through his voice.

"No, I just want to wait."

He nodded. "Can I ask how long?"

"We aren't even sorted yet. I don't want to commit to you if we can't even be together."

He gave a small smile that didn't reach his eyes. "So will you not wear my necklace?"

I looked down at the beautiful ruby pendant, then back into Markos's blue-black eyes that were swirling with devoted love. "I love you too." I smiled.

He grinned wide and pulled me in for a deep, soul-rattling kiss. His hands traveled down my body and sent waves of pleasure through me. Next thing I knew, we were on the floor of the greenhouse, the smell of roses filling our noses as we explored our bodies for the first time.

# FORTY-SIX

## MARIE

*D*inner was quiet. My father and I the only ones seated at the table. Seelie and Unseelie guards filled the room, their faces set in stone and their energy tense and obtrusive.

My father asked me a few questions about my life in Unseelie to fill the silence, but I gave him simple one-word answers as I stared at my mother's empty chair.

This was not how this was supposed to be. It was supposed to be a feast for my family and our closest friends. We were supposed to eat and talk about our past loves who had died, then go to the cemetery and party on their graves. It was supposed to be a day to celebrate death but also a day of debauchery and lunacy. We would leave treats for our loved ones and tricks for unwelcomed souls. The soldiers who were staring at me were supposed to be sitting with me, laughing loudly, causing a ruckus, but none of that was happening. None of it would happen, this room would remain silent, and the joys at the cemetery would not include me.

"I'm done," I said to my father, my plate barely touched.

He looked at my food and then to me, giving a half smile. "We can go to the cemetery now."

"Will she be there?" I asked, my voice cracked with desperation. I hated that all these soldiers had to witness my heartbreak over my mother. They all had those emotionless faces, but I could see the pity in their eyes.

My father shook his head.

"Where is she?"

"The inn."

"We should go get her," I demanded.

"You aren't allowed to go anywhere that isn't on the list."

My lip wobbled slightly, tears lining my eyes. I took a deep breath, reining it all in. Turning to my guards, I asked, "What are you to report to him?"

"In short, Your Highness, everything."

"Everything," I breathed heavily.

He nodded. "Yes, Your Highness."

"Are you to tell him word for word what I say to someone?" I asked.

"No, but we are supposed to tell what the conversation is about and who you talked to, Your Highness."

"Stop calling me that." I took my crown off, not wanting the weight it carried. "My name is Marie."

"Your Hig—Princess Marie, you aren't supposed to remove the tiara."

"And what the fuck will you do about it?" I snapped.

The soldier's throat bobbed, worry clouding his eyes. Not in fear of me, but in fear of Prince Levington Shadawn. "I'm sorry, Your H—Princess Marie."

I covered my eyes with my hands. "I can't cry," I whispered to my father. My voice barely louder than a breath.

"Why, flower?" He whispered back.

"Because he will know, and it doesn't matter that she is my mother; he will retaliate if someone hurts me."

"Are you happy?" he questioned.

"When I'm with him, yes."

"And when you're not?"

I hated his question, but I couldn't deny the truth. I knew being mated would have its drawbacks, but it's not like I had a choice. Levi was my mate, my soul's other half, and I loved him deeply. He brought me otherworldly joy, but when I'm not with him... "I feel suffocated, Father. I didn't want it to be like this. I wanted it to be how it always is. I want them to be sitting, not staring at me. I want it to be loud, not quiet." I could feel tears building in my eyes as the next words came out. "I want Mother. I want her to talk to me, to write me back. I want to wrap my arms around her and breathe in her scent. Even though he lives to please me, he could never allow me to come here and do those things. He is..." My throat became dry.

"He is dominant," my father supplied.

I nodded. "I have to do what he asks. The only thing I can deny him is this, and it's not even how I wanted it. I love him and I can barely even stand being apart from him right now, but I just wanted to spend time alone with you and Mother. I don't want the bond to completely encapsulate my life."

"We will figure it out, flower. We don't want to never see you again."

"Really? She will barely even talk to me. She hates me."

"Marie, she doesn't think that. She loves you more than anything. It hurts her that you are mated but only because she has to share you with another. She doesn't want to lose you and she fears she will. Your mother is the type of person to push you away before she can get hurt. She will come around if you just wait. Don't think I'm not working on it, flower. I have been spending my days trying to get her to talk to you, trying to get her to even talk to me. She will come around. She just needs time."

I wiped my eyes. "I'm not crying," I told the guards. "Could you come to Unseelie?"

My father gave another tight smile, lacking that warmth that I haven't seen since I arrived.

"Please, Father. It would be easier for you and her to go there than for me and my mate to come here. I need you. Just because I'm mated doesn't mean I just stopped needing you. Please, just think about coming. If it has to do with safety because you are the commander, I will do everything in my power to make sure you are safe. *Please!*"

"It's not me, flower, it's her. Your mother hates Unseelie. She always has and I doubt she will go to the palace where all of her old friends and family are."

"Convince her, please. I can't do this again. I can't sit at this table with twelve men staring at me like I'm a sick puppy, six of which I have known my whole life and should be at this table with me. Yeah, it won't be the same in Unseelie, but we will make it work. We will create new traditions. I want us to be a family. I want you to love him as I. I know you will, he is perfect."

"We will love him, flower." He rolled his neck in hesitation. "I will try to convince her, but I can't promise."

"Okay." I started to pick at the uneaten food on my plate.

"Do you want to go to the cemetery tonight?"

I shook my head. "No, I don't know any of the dead people I am supposed to care about."—My great-great grandmother, my birth father, my aunt—"I don't want to ruin it for others, either. No one is allowed to be fifty feet near me if they aren't on the list."

He sighed. "Okay."

"But if you want to visit your brother, we can go. I'll just stay in the back, away from people." I didn't want to ruin it for him either. I already kind of was. He should be laughing with his buddies right now, not on duty. Technically, he wasn't, but he sat with an alertness that told me he was awaiting an attack and he still wore his commander's uniform.

"No, he's been dead for a while. Missing one Samhain won't do anything. Plus, we never spend time like this together anymore, just me and you. You want to play cards?"

"Yeah, that would be nice."

My father smiled warmly. It brushed away the chill of today's events and made me mirror one back.

# FORTY-SEVEN

## MARIE

$\mathcal{M}$y knee bounced in the carriage as we pulled into the gates of the Unseelie Palace. My teeth ground in frustration because it seemed the driver wanted to take his sweet time returning home.

Finally, the carriage stopped, and I was out before anyone could open the door for me.

I saw him there, sitting on the frozen steps of the palace. His eyes connected with mine and then I was running and jumping into his arms.

His hands gripped my ass harshly, his mouth possessing mine as I purred contently. I never wanted to spend a day without kissing these lips again.

"I missed you so fucking much," I spoke into his mouth.

Levi kissed me harder and dug his fingers into my ass deeper as a reply. He started to move, not removing his mouth from mine as he walked up the stairs into the palace.

Fae were probably staring at us as Levi took us to our room, but we didn't care. We only wanted each other at this moment and no one else mattered.

Things started to become primal, our lust taking over and stripping us of any formalities. I was practically biting Levi's lips off, wanting to consume his mouth. My panties were soaked with my arousal and Levi's seed, and I ached with the need for more. I knew this time we would be fucking hard and brutal, there would be no slow and torturous. I might be so sore after, I wouldn't be able to walk.

When we made it to our room, he set me down and took a break to study me for injuries. I let him look for a millisecond before I started trying to undo the ties of his cloak. His hands grasped mine, pulling them away. "I need to make sure you aren't wounded."

"Levi, no one touched me, I am fine. I am aching and I need you right now."

Levi's eyes bore into mine, his face turning serious. "Marie."

I huffed. "Fine but make it fast."

He quickly kissed me, the kiss sweet and tender. I growled, wanting it hard and consuming like moments before. Pulling back, he smirked at me before he started to undo the ties of my cloak. His brow creased when he pushed it off my shoulders. "Where is my necklace?"

I tried not to make a face, but at the moment, I wanted to slap myself. How could I have forgotten about that?

I looked down at my neck, playing dumb. "Oh, I took it off and accidentally left it at home." I decided lying would be the best option at the moment. I really didn't want Levi to get pissed right now. I just want to fuck him for hours and then deal with all of this later.

His eyes bulged and a vein in his neck pulsed. "Where did you leave it?"

My brow furrowed. "At home."

"At home," he repeated back to me.

I brushed a curl behind my ear. "Yeah, back in Seelie. I'll have my mother send it back or something."

Levi was eerily calm when he spoke next. "You left the necklace back *at home, in Seelie.*"

"Yeah, I left the necklace back at home, in Seelie."

He inhaled sharply, jaw ticking, eyes burrowing into my soul. "Take off your clothes."

I didn't move; I didn't know why. I just didn't.

My throat bobbed. Last time he asked me to do this, his tone was husky and full of lust. Now, he sounded angry.

"Take off your fucking clothes right now, Marie," he gritted through his teeth.

I snapped out of it and started to hurriedly take off my clothes. I took off my shoes, my dress, then my garter and stockings. When I got to my panties, he stopped me. "Leave those on."

"Levi, I will get it back."

He took his cloak off but nothing else. "Get on the bed and lie on your back."

I did as he asked and he followed, kneeling between my opened legs. He looked down at me. His expression the same as when he asked me what I would have done if he had told me we were mates and I didn't reply—a look of utter panic hidden behind stone-cold calmness.

He grabbed my leg, raised it up, and kissed my ankle. The contact sent shivers up my leg, straight to my clit that was still throbbing for him.

Then he bit into my flesh, then again, then again, then again.

He kept going, marking my leg, traveling from my foot to my upper thigh and then repeating the same on the other. The sensation of his venom tore through me, inciting an intense pleasure, but I didn't indulge.

Levi was gentle in his progression, affectionate and considerate, but he forgot one crucial part of me while he was lost in his panic; I was half-human.

Venom didn't kill fae, but it stopped their healing, creating the mark. Venom did kill humans, but first, it paralyzed them. It could paralyze a fae, but the fae doing the biting would need to be precise with the amount of venom used because too much would just knock them out. I, being half-fae, wouldn't die from the venom, but I was still weak enough to be paralyzed.

I couldn't tell him to stop because I couldn't move my tongue or any part of my body but my eyes. I could blink and see Levi when he came into view, but I couldn't move my head.

He wasn't using enough to make me black out. He was being careful and loving but he wasn't factoring in my human side as he continued to mark me all over. He was so lost in his panic that he didn't notice I was paralyzed. He couldn't feel it through our bond either. He probably thought my increase in heart rate was from pleasure, not from fear.

When he was done with my legs, he moved to my stomach and my breast, my arms, and finally my neck. He didn't bother trying to update my current marks; he just created new ones on top of them. When he reached the top of my neck, under my earlobe, he took his final bite before whispering in my ear, "You are mine."

I couldn't reply, I just blinked, hoping he would realize that I was stuck. I don't know what he would do when he figured it out. It was not like he could stop the venom after it took its effect, but I didn't want to be alone, trapped in my own body. To make matters worse, he got out of the bed while I laid there unmoving, stuck, and trapped. I wanted to scream for him to come back, but I couldn't.

He did come back, and I felt something wet on my calf slipping up my leg. I realized he was cleaning up the blood. There was probably a lot of it—there were probably a lot of marks.

When he was done, he took off his shirt and climbed into bed next to me, pulling me into him where he was spooning my back. His hold possessive, more than ever, his arms wrapped around my waist, his hands gripping my sides, and his head buried into my neck, breathing me in.

Levi shifted, burrowing deeper into my neck before saying, "Mate."

But I couldn't reply; I was still trapped and helpless and he didn't even seem to notice.

Soon, the venom had its full hold of me, the pleasure coursing through me violently and exhausting my body that couldn't move. The world began to fog, and after a few moments—or eons, I couldn't really tell—the world faded to black.

# FORTY-EIGHT

## MARIE

*I* woke up before Levi. His hold on me had loosened during sleep, and I had gained the ability to move again.

Slipping out of bed, slightly woozy from the venom that was coursing through my veins, I carefully tried not to wake Levi as I walked to the mirror.

My hand covered my mouth to hold in the gasp that tried to escape. The fire light was the only light in the room, but I could still see well. I was marked all over, my skin irritated and red. Blood streaked down my flesh that Levi missed when he cleaned me up.

*Why did he do this?*

The mark was a claim, and one was enough for most males. Levi was mated so it made sense why he had marked me six times, but this was too much. He owned my soul already, making it very unnecessary for him to do this. I was his no matter what, in this life and the next. It wasn't even a choice.

This was another reason one would want to run away from their mate. The bond drove mates crazy. I thought the bond would make them crazy because they needed to please another, not to possess another.

From the beginning, Levi needed to possess me in every way possible. Kolvin even said it—he fucks me to possess me. I want to possess him too, but not like this. I would never want to mark his body like this. One was enough for me. I only marked him more for him, to please him. All I wanted to do was please him, but Levi never believed my devotion, even though I did everything he asked.

Looking at my body, I realized Levi's need to possess me overshadowed his need to please me. Nothing, not even me would get in the way of us being together. That was his message when we mated, and I didn't realize how deep that really went.

I looked back at Levi—still sleeping. He probably was exhausted from not having slept while I was gone. He wouldn't notice my absence, or he'd just think I went to the bathroom, if he did.

Tiptoeing to his desk, I searched the contents as quietly as possible. Levi was a prince, skilled in combat; he had to have a knife or a dagger lying around here somewhere.

I wasn't going to keep these. Marks were a symbol of love, not possession, and I wasn't okay with being marked like this. I loved Levi and I loved when he marked me but that didn't give him the right to mark my whole body because he felt panicked about me leaving a necklace at home. I understood the necklace was important to his family, but I knew Levi and he didn't care about things like that. If I had told him I didn't like the necklace, he would have gotten me a different one I did like, which is why none of this made sense.

I found one and moved back to the mirror. I had no idea where to start, so I decided to start where he did—on my leg. I positioned the knife on my upper thigh, trying to decipher each mark from another, but it was hard to tell. I would have to just cut and figure it out.

This would hurt to remove, spiritually and physically. It only hurt slightly when Kolvin removed my mark, but I figured that since Levi was my mate, it would hurt him exceptionally. I never wanted to see him in pain, but I also didn't want these on my body. I figured if I cut fast and he was asleep, he wouldn't feel most of the pain before he woke up.

The second the knife touched my skin, Levi's hand came out of nowhere. He wrapped his fingers around the blade, drawing blood, and yanked it from my grasp. He threw the knife across the room away from me and it impaled itself into the wall. "What the fuck do you think you're doing?"

"Removing them," I replied.

"No, you're not."

"Levi, there are too many. I want them gone."

"You are not removing one of my marks."

"I don't want—"

"Marie, you are not removing my mark." His tone held finality in it, triggering me to obey.

I looked into his midnight eyes. He wasn't going to let me do this and our bond demanded that I yield to him. I didn't want to, but I lived to please him, so I would have to. "Levi, please. Just some, there are too many."

"No."

"Levi—"

"Fuck no."

Tears gathered in my eyes. Levi cupped my face and wiped them, accidentally smearing his blood on my cheeks in the process. "I will not change my mind."

"Why not? Because I left the necklace at home? I will get it back."

He let go of my face and stepped back. His body was fuming with rage, but his eyes reflected that fear from before. "This is your home. I am your home. Not there! Here with me!"

I blinked and stared at him in disbelief. Blazing rage seeped into my pores to match his but there wasn't fear to accompany it. "Are you fucking serious? You did this to me because I called the place I spent the first nineteen years of my life home? The place that has always been filled with love and joy, the place that has always felt safe to me, the place where my family is. You marked me, *you paralyzed me,* because I called that place home?"

He didn't answer, and I saw that gut-wrenching guilt that we felt when we hurt another shift in his eyes, but I didn't let it sway my feelings because I knew he still wasn't going to let me remove the marks, and my anger was too palpable now to be in a forgiving mood anyway.

"Levi, I am your mate! Your fucking mate! How many fucking times do I have to tell you that I love you, that you are the only thing I care about, that I never want to spend a day without you, till you get it through your thick fucking skull that I will *never* leave you?"

"But you fucking did! You left me and you plan on doing it again, and again, and again. I am not the only thing you care about, and you will spend days without me. You fucking lie every time you say that, so how could I ever believe that you actually love me?"

"Levi, I am mated to you! My soul loves your soul! I am yours! You fucking own me!"

"If that was true, you wouldn't leave me. If you love me as much as I do you, then you'd never leave my side," he replied, arms folded.

I took a breath to calm myself; yelling at him to change his feelings wasn't going to get me anywhere. "Levi, let me remove the marks."

"No." His jaw ticked. "Let them fade."

"You are not going to let them fade. You will start to fucking panic the second they do and then you are going to beg me to update them and I'll have to let you because I can't deny you. I want them gone. *Now*."

Levi looked away for a moment, his hand coming up to rub his face before he looked back to me. "I will."

"Put blood on it."

He stared at me, his nostrils flared out slightly, and I could tell by the look in his eyes that he wouldn't let them fade. He wouldn't let me remove them, and I couldn't physically deny him, not when he was this adamant about it. "You said you would put my wants before others' needs. Shouldn't that mean yours as well?"

He just shook his head. "I will let them fade," he lied.

I was so angry with him I didn't know what to do so I smashed my mouth on his. I was taking my anger out on him the only way I could think of, and the bastard was perfectly okay with me fucking him as long as he got his way.

I pushed him back on the bed, pulled his pants off, then my come-filled panties—I can't believe I let him do that. I spent the whole day with my parents in creamed panties to please him and he wouldn't even let me remove one fucking mark.

I straddled his waist. His cock was hard and ready for me. His eyes hooded with lust, mine reflecting with anger. I slid on his hard length, loving the feel of him and started to move, using him for my pleasure.

That was what I was going to do: use him to make me happy. Use him for my needs, not caring about whether or not he wanted it or liked it. Though I knew he did. The fact angered me more and I moved faster, taking my rage out on his body.

Mates were connected in three ways: body, heart, and soul—not mind. It was the chaotic twist of the fae, the thing that made the dominos fall. It was the reason mates were known for being crazy. It was why Levi panicked anytime I said something that could allude to me leaving him or not wanting him. Mates couldn't tell what the other was thinking or emotionally feeling, and to be connected to someone in all ways but one was maddening. He couldn't read my mind to know how much I loved him, so he was constantly insecure that I secretly didn't want him. It was ridiculous, but mates were ridiculous.

As I rode his cock, I focused on the pleasure. He had made me come before without him coming with me. The disconnection in our minds made it possible for him to do so. I was going to take and leave him with nothing. All I had to do was the reverse of what he did to me before.

I closed my eyes and threw my head back. Focusing as his cock hit that right spot, I let the pleasure spread through my body, filling my limbs, and coaxing me toward the edge. Soon, I was tightening around him, and I could tell he wasn't even close.

I moaned loudly as I climaxed, exaggerating what I was feeling, making it sound like the best climax I had ever had when it was in reality mediocre. I didn't care because when I opened my eyes and met his, there was confusion and panic swirling within those inky depths. The look filled me with enough satisfaction to make up for the shitty orgasm. He was utterly confused on how I was able to come without him and it panicked him to think I didn't need him. I knew it was wrong to use his insecurities against him, but they were what made him do stupid shit.

The high was short-lived when I looked at my marks. I would never be able to punish him enough to equal out what he did—another reminder that our relationship wasn't equal. He was in control, and I wasn't.

Letting out a frustrated growl, I climbed off him, walking to the bathroom and slamming the door shut.

# FORTY-NINE

## CORIVINA
20 YEARS AGO.

$\mathcal{M}$y first time with Maurice was amazing. It took time to convince him that our subtle touches and stolen kisses weren't wrong, that my husband was okay with it, but eventually he relented, and we spent a night together.

I had to be gentle with him because I was afraid I would break his fragile human body. I stayed on top, riding him slowly. The slow movements and my constant gaze into his coffee-black eyes morphed our fucking into lovemaking. I wasn't supposed to be falling in love with this human, but I could feel the pull too.

When I stared into those pure eyes, I felt myself tearing. A dam of emotions broke within me, opening up a part of me that I didn't know existed.

Maurice was mine. I didn't care if he found himself a human girl to bear his babes, he was mine. I wanted to stake a claim not only on his body but on his soul. There was just something about him that just felt right. That just felt perfect.

We made love for hours, slow and lazy thrusts between the two of us. My cold black eyes staring into his. Gratitude filled within mine because Maurice felt like a gift from the gods, and it was about fucking time that they gave me something that wasn't tainted with darkness.

It saddened me that I would only get a few years with him—if that. He was in his late twenties, and it was time for him to find a woman. That woman couldn't be me for the obvious reason that I wasn't even a woman. I was a beast who had a sick thing for him. Being with him felt like playing with my food. My beast wanted to ravish him until he was nothing, but the sane part of me knew that it would hurt if I killed him.

I did spend the night tasting him though, not his blood but his flesh. I tasted his neck where I secretly hoped my mark one day would be. I tasted his chest and his nipples, and I even tasted his cock. I loved the salty taste of him, and I just wanted to taste him all day long.

He finished inside me, and I purred again, loving that his seed was planted deep within. It was improbable we would bear a child. Fae females often only had one child in their lifetime, so it was unlikely that we would create life even if his sperm was fertile.

We spent the rest of the night together, lying in each other's arms, talking about Maurice's hopes and dreams. He loved to paint and wanted to be an artist one day and that made me love his eyes more. I knew he saw the world differently from me. He saw light, color, and life; whereas I saw darkness, death, and despair.

I kissed him all over as he talked about his favorite painters and the things he wished to paint. He told me he wanted to paint me. That he probably would never be able to capture my beauty, but he would want to try. I told him I'd let him.

That was a week ago.

At the moment, I was wrapped in Darius's arms. It was early in the morning, about a couple hours before sunrise. He was due to wake up soon. I often woke him. Even a week ago, I left Maurice, bathed in one of our unused guest rooms and then made sure he was up. It was awkward because I couldn't completely wash all of Maurice's scent in one bath—not that I wanted to. Darius noticed. He wasn't threatened by it, but we hadn't slept together since. I knew my times with Maurice would have to be every few weeks or months because I didn't want to make Darius uncomfortable. Nor did I want it to inhibit our sex life. I might feel an allure to the human, but Darius was my one. I would remain with him for life, no matter what. I wasn't going to neglect him for a human, even if my beast craved him.

I pressed my lips against Darius's. I loved to wake him like that. He would tell me morning sex served for a great warm up before the drills that he performed with his soldiers.

I missed the feel of him inside me. A week was a long time for us not to have sex and I needed him now.

Pressing further into his lips to deepen the kiss, I felt him stir slightly. His lips moved and he kissed me back, breathing me in before his body stilled.

He took another breath, then pulled back to look into my eyes, staring at me for a moment, not speaking. His jaw flexed, and there was something in his eyes that I had never seen reflected in those warm blue irises—rage.

He got out of bed and pulled his pants on. I didn't know what was going through his head. I didn't understand how one kiss could inspire a look like that within him.

He walked over to our closet and grabbed his sword, alarming me that whatever this was, it was serious. Then he sprinted out the door without saying a word.

Scrambling out of bed, I hurriedly pulled a robe and shoes on. I ran down the stairs to catch him, but he was already out the door. When I got outside, there was no sign of him.

Fae were predators; hunting was a part of our nature, so I used my senses to follow his scent. He had run to wherever he went because I could barely catch it.

I followed him to the town square, losing his scent in the combination of others. I stood there for a moment, fear churning in my stomach. I didn't know why but my gut told me where he had gone and then I was running.

When I got to the spell shop, there he was with Maurice's lifeless body on the ground. His sister was also dead, decapitated. She must have tried to interfere.

I dropped to my knees and screamed in horror. I stared at Maurice's body and his dead eyes. Eyes that had once captured a pure soul. My soul—he was mine and now he was dead. Gone. We were supposed to have more time. I was supposed to let him go. He was supposed to find a human woman and love her and give her babes.

*One who you will destroy.*

Ginger had warned me, and I had ignored it. I didn't think I was going to love another besides Darius.

I didn't even love Maurice yet. I didn't even get to love him.

Fuck that cunt of a witch. Who the hell lets her great grandchild get murdered for the gods' entertainment?

When I looked up into Darius's eyes, they reflected back cold. My heart fractured at the sight of it. To see the male that was my warmth, my light, my sun, suddenly cold and filled with menace.

"Why?" I cried. "You said it was okay. You said I could have him."

"You're carrying his child," he replied, voice clipped and harsh.

My heart paused for a beat. "What?"

"You have a babe growing in your womb. It smells of him, not me."

I shuddered, tears spilling down my cheeks as I felt lost for air.

I was pregnant with Maurice's child. I was going to be a mother. I had a babe within me.

A slight trickle of hope filled me at the fact but was dispelled as I looked down at Maurice, then back at Darius and his cold blue eyes.

He looked like a different person, a person I didn't know, didn't trust. A stranger. Those eyes threatened to break me again. To bring me back to that place where Markos had put me, and I couldn't go back there. I was to be a mother, and I wouldn't let this child be shadowed in darkness.

Wiping my tears, I froze over everything within me, turning it to stone so it could never break again. I wasn't going to let any of my darkness touch my child. Which meant I needed to be strong and unable to feel, unable to be swept up in the shadows.

I mirrored Darius's stare. My eyes were always cold, they had been turned cold by Markos, but I knew now my eyes were colder than the Unseelie winter because when I turned to Darius, he softened.

Snapping out of his rage, his warmth returned to his eyes revealing my sun—my love, but it was too late. He had already done what he did. He had shown me a different person who lurked in the depth of his eyes, and it changed us.

I turned, walking home, and he followed. When I got to the room, I grabbed a suitcase and started packing as he stood in the doorway, watching.

"Corivina," he said, his voice barely above a whisper.

"We are over, Darius," I said, voice flat and hard.

He moved over to me, placing his hand on my shoulder, and I flinched.

My eyes found his as guilt and sorrow painted within him. Everything we had built had collapsed within one act, and one child. I knew he could see that within my stare as I moved away from him and went to gather more clothes.

"Vina, I wasn't thinking. I just smelled you and it set me off."

Markos had said something similar.

I looked at him and I felt my broken heart trying to beat for his, but it couldn't because I couldn't trust that there wasn't a monster lurking under his skin, trying to be set free. I couldn't trust that he wasn't just pretending to be calm and patient, like Markos. I couldn't trust that he was really who he said he was.

If I didn't have a babe growing within me, I probably would have stayed. We would have moved past this. Deep down, I knew Darius was nothing like Markos, but the babe stole all my focus. I had to protect my child, and I couldn't allow a male I didn't fully trust around them.

Closing up my suitcase, I started to walk out the door, but before I did, I set the suitcase down and pulled off my ring, the ring that was perfect for me. I set it on the vanity by the door, and I left without turning back, going back to the only place that I knew—the inn.

# FIFTY

## MARIE

*L*evi sat outside the locked bathroom door, knocking and calling out my name periodically for hours as I sat in the bath, ignoring him.

When he couldn't handle my ignoring him anymore, he ripped the doorknob off the door and barged in, but I still ignored him as he kneeled next to the tub.

"Marie," he breathed, sorrow laced in his tone.

I didn't answer or look at him.

"Mate." He gently touched my shoulder.

Brushing his hand away, I continued to ignore him. It was hard; every cell in my body demanded I look at him and soothe his panic, but my anger at him helped me fight against it.

"Can I join you?"

"No," I said, with my head still turned away from him.

"Can I get you anything or do anything for you?"

I looked at him then, my eyes meeting his. I channeled my mother's glare as I said, "You can leave me alone."

Pain etched into his face as I said it. It hurt to hurt him, but I wasn't going to cave. He deserved a little time out. It wouldn't kill him.

"Okay." He got up and kissed my temple. I didn't push him away, but I didn't encourage him either. He closed the door as he left.

When I was done bathing, I walked to the closet. Levi had bought me many slips and nightgowns that I never wore. I slept naked because with all the mating we did, it was easier to be naked, but there would be no fucking tonight or for the foreseeable future. When I walked out in the nightgown, Levi got that message.

I climbed into bed. Normally I would snuggle up with him, but I stayed on the edge. I even slept turned away from him to further the point.

When I woke the next evening, Levi was wrapped around me. Either he waited for me to fall asleep so he could, or he gravitated to me in his sleep. Unlike the first time we slept together, I had remained on the edge of the bed. It was nice to know that even my subconscious was on my side this time.

I detangled myself from him, not bothering to try not to wake him up as I got out of bed. I went to the closet to dress. I couldn't wear the school uniform. It would show my neck and I didn't want anyone to see my marks. I wasn't proud of them. Nor did I want to show them off for Levi. I found a turtleneck that went all the way to my chin and a long skirt that went to my toes.

I went back into the room to see Levi lying on his back, staring at the ceiling. "If you're not ready when I am, I will leave without you," I said before I went to the bathroom to do my hair. I pulled it back into a braid, not feeling like having it out for Levi to play with. It was another small punishment, but it was the best I could do with what little power I had in our relationship.

When I walked out of the bathroom, he was ready. I could tell he had hurried because his loose waves were in a tumble on his head, a look I loved on him, but today I didn't indulge in my love of it. I left the room without saying anything. He tried to hold my hand as we walked because we always walked together hand in hand, but I detangled my fingers from his and crossed my arms.

Everyone could tell there was something wrong with us. Probably by how tense Levi was during training. He broke someone's nose and knocked out another. They could also probably tell by the way I sat alone, unbothered and glaring at him. Jessamine did come to sit by me at the beginning of training. She stiffened, probably sensing the marks, but she started talking, pretending they didn't bother her, but I wasn't in the mood for her today. So, I asked her to go away. Levi immediately looked at her with his 'don't fuck with my mate' face when I did, and she turned sheet-white.

"If he hurts you, he'll pay for it," I said to her, and it caused Levi's glare to drop and him to look at me with worry.

After training, we went to eat breakfast. I didn't let him decide what I ate. He would always pick the best food for me. He didn't like me to eat anything that was overly sugary or fatty, so that's what I grabbed. Today, I was going to have cake for breakfast, and he could see what would happen if he tried to stop me.

We took our seats at the table. He put his hand on my leg, something he always did as we sat here, and I picked his hand up and moved it to his lap.

Jessamine and Finch were tense, but Gregor didn't seem to care at all. So, me and him conversed while the other two ate in silence and Levi brooded. I told Gregor about my visit to Seelie, how it was terrible, and how it was basically Levi's fault that it was. I didn't explicitly say it was Levi's fault, but I alluded to it. Gregor was a skilled talker and avoided saying anything that would get him punched in the face by my mate while still carrying the conversation.

When I was done eating, I got up without warning Levi, dumped my tray, and walked out of the cafeteria.

Lessons were the same, though, I paid no attention to them. When we did partner work, I only participated when absolutely necessary. Levi knew everything, so he could do all the work.

After lessons, I went to my room in the academic wing without telling him where I was going. He, of course, followed. I got the library books from the room that were overdue. I doubted it mattered that they were because *I was the prince's mate.*

I read my smutty book back in our room for the rest of the night while Levi stared at me. He was pretending to read as well, but he was just staring at me, and it was getting annoying.

Letting out an irritated breath, I got out of bed and went into the hall to find the first servant.

"Excuse me," I asked the servant girl.

She turned, looked at me, then looked behind me and paled.

"Ignore him, look at me," I said. Surprisingly, I actually sounded regal.

She did as asked. "Yes, Your Highness?"

I ignored the royal endearment. I was going to be queen one day. I better get used to it. "Do you know where I can find a male who repairs things?"

She glanced at Levi before speaking, "Do you want me to find you a female?"

My brows creased. "A female?"

Her throat bobbed. "No male is supposed to service you or your rooms."

I gave a tight smile. "Is that so?" I let out an annoyed breath through my nose. "I want a male. Go find me one." Today, I was really filling that princess role that was expected of me.

She bowed, then scurried off.

Levi paced back and forth in our room as I sat on the bed waiting for the male. When there was a knock at the door, he let out a low growl. I ignored him and opened the door to let the male in.

Levi glared at him the whole time he was there. He didn't like another male in our space. *Of course*, females were allowed to clean our room and our sheets and leave their scents for me to find, but one male couldn't fix a doorknob.

I told the male what I wanted done and he worked as quickly as he possibly could and was out within minutes. When he was gone, Levi sat down on the bed and stared at me, enraged.

Giving him a bitter smile, I went to bathe with the bathroom door opened.

The next night was similar. I woke up with Levi tangled around me, dressed in clothes that covered me neck to toe, and went to training. He knocked out two more men and I had what I wanted for breakfast. He kept trying to touch me or talk to me. I would brush his touches away—I wouldn't even be discreet about it. I couldn't care less if others saw my rejection of him, he deserved it. Then after class, we went back to our room.

When we entered the room, Levi spoke, "Do you want to study, mate?" He hadn't called me by my name in over a day. I think he thought reminding me of who I was to him would make me stop ignoring him.

I looked at him with a cold stare and spoke in a flat tone. "There is no reason for me to know how to do any of that shit. I am just a doll that serves to amuse you. I only need to know wife and mate duties. I know how to fuck, cook, and the servants clean, so there really is no reason for me to even go to class. It was cute of you to humor me into thinking that I could one day be a *master magician,* but we both know you would rather have me weak and powerless, so I am easier to control."

He stared at me, pain lining his face. I rolled my eyes, grabbing my book, and headed to the bath.

I bathed for hours at a time for three reasons. One, to get away from Levi. Two, to wash some of his scent off from the marks since it was overpowering and it made people visibly uncomfortable to be in the same room as me. Three, because they itched like a motherfucker and the baths soothed them.

After I bathed, I dressed in a nightgown and went to sleep.

The third night was the same. Levi wrapped his arms around me in sleep. I had to detangle him from me. Training, where he severely injured more people, lessons, then my bath.

I was super horny by then. Mates were meant to mate, and me and Levi hadn't had sex in days. My last orgasm wasn't satisfying in any way, so I was pretty much bursting at the seams. I wouldn't seek out Levi, though. If I let him fuck me, he would try to control the situation and I didn't want that, but I was still going to get off.

Setting my book down, I let my fingers trail down to my clit.

I closed my eyes and conjured images of Levi when he had pleased me exponentially. I had to imagine him, there wasn't anyone else for me besides him, there never would be. I bit my lip to suppress any moans and tried not to move too much to alert him. I had left the door open, and I didn't feel like getting up to close it so I could please myself.

My fingers teased me in the most splendid ways as I imagined they were Levi's fingers. I breathed heavily through my nose as I felt my body starting to tense. I opened my eyes briefly and that was a stupid mistake because Levi was standing there staring at me.

My eyes bulged out of their sockets, and I pulled my knees to my chest. "Get out!"

Levi kneeled next to the tub. "Mate, let me please you."

"No, I don't want you to *please me*."

He rubbed his face. "Is there anything you want?"

I let out a frustrated growl. "I want you to leave me alone! I want you to stop trying to touch me, stop trying to talk to me. I want you to stop cuddling up with me while I sleep. I want you to stay in the room as I bathe and not walk in on me while *I please myself*. And right now, I want you to get the fuck out!"

He looked like I had just stabbed him in the heart. His face contorted slightly, then he reeled it back in and nodded. "Okay." He leaned up to kiss my head, but I moved away this time. He looked at me for a moment, emotion swirling in his eyes, then he got up and went into the room.

I woke up with my heart thundering in my chest. It felt like it was trying to escape the confines of my ribs. My throat closed up; my lungs unable to fully take a breath. I sat up and looked over to Levi. He was sitting with his arms propped up by his knees, staring at the fire. His body was tense, his jaw set, but he didn't look angry; he looked frightened. I realized it was *his heart* pounding out of his chest.

I touched his arm, his skin burning. "Levi," I whispered.

He took a harsh breath in through his nose and gritted his teeth harder, but his eyes remained on the fire. He looked like he was desperately trying to hold himself together.

I moved his arms and climbed into his lap, taking his face in my hands and made his midnight eyes meet mine. "Mate," I whispered.

He shuddered and then buried his face into my chest to let out a sob. He wrapped his arms tightly around me and continued to break down.

I had seen Levi cry one other time and it was nothing compared to this. He cried like a newborn babe, my heart breaking at the sight.

I lifted his head so he would look at me again. "Levi."

"Anything," he breathed. "I will do anything you want. We can remove every single mark... I... I don't care. I will never... mark you again." He stopped to sob, more tears furiously streaming down his face. "Anything, Marie. Anything. I will do anything, just make it stop. Please, make it stop." He cried harder. "I can't handle it anymore, I can't. I'm sorry, Marie. We can remove them, and I won't do it again ever. Just stop, please, stop ignoring me. Stop not needing me. I need you, Marie." He shuddered again and buried his head into me.

I held him as he cried. It broke me apart that I did this to him. He was in so much pain I could physically feel it when we touched. I didn't want him to break down, I just wanted to punish him.

Levi cried for a while. He incoherently kept repeating the same three words: anything, please, and sorry. I rubbed his back and shushed him, trying to calm him, but he was crying out three nights of built-up tension. It was painful to endure but eventually he calmed to slight whimpers, and I pulled back, moving out of his lap.

"Where are you going?" he whimpered.

I cupped his cheek and kissed his forehead. "I'll be right back, I promise."

He nodded, and I went to the bathroom. I took off my slip that was soaked with his tears and grabbed a washcloth, wet it, and cleaned my chest before heading back into the room. I climbed back into his lap and cleaned his snot-covered face. This was probably the ugliest I have ever seen him, and somehow, he still was the most beautiful creature in the world. I had broken him, I knew mates could, but I thought it would be him who broke me and not the other way around. The only good thing about this was that I also could put him back together.

When his face was cleaned, I kissed his lips that still tasted of tears. Levi tensed before he relaxed fully into the kiss.

"I'm sorry, Marie," he breathed. "We can remove them. I panicked and I didn't think. I let the bond take over, and I'm so sorry."

"I forgive you."

"Can we do it now?" he asked.

"Do what now?"

"Remove them."

"It will hurt you if we do. I don't want to cause you more pain," I whispered.

He nudged my nose. "Then we can just do some tonight and then keep doing a little till they are all gone."

"It will still hurt you and just draw out your pain."

"Marie, I have to do something. I can't… I can't live knowing that you hate them."

"Levi, I don't hate them. I love when you mark me, but this was a lot and how I got them wasn't pleasant. We can let them fade and you will only update a few when necessary."

"Please, Marie, let me make it up to you. I'll do anything, I just need to do something." There was an urgency in his eyes. I could ask him for anything, and he would deliver it. I could ask him to kill his father and he would. He would do anything for me and it scared me that I had that type of power over him.

"Let me do it to you," I breathed.

His brows furrowed. "What?"

"Let me mark you like you did me. That's what I want."

He nodded. "Okay, yeah, anything."

I pushed him back and kissed him gently. "I love you, *always*."

He kissed me back. "I love you always, as well."

I bit into his neck. I didn't want to hurt him or cause him to pass out. I also wanted the marks to fade, and they should fade in a couple days with how little I was using. I didn't want him covered in my marks. Even if each mark I gave him was an act of love, I was only marking him so he could feel forgiven.

I worked my way down his neck and then his arms and torso. I pulled off his pants. He wasn't wearing underwear, his cock hard and standing straight up as I bit into his leg, starting from the ankle, and working my way up. When I finished with one, I moved to the other, repeating my process.

When I was done, my face was inches away from his cock. So, I took him into my mouth.

He groaned loudly at the unexpected action, his hips bucking up slightly. I sucked him, bobbing my mouth up and down on his shaft. I had never done this, but I knew enough from seeing it done by people at parties and hearing Jessamine talk about it. I kind of hated that Levi never asked me to do this before because it was absolutely wonderful. I loved the feeling of his cock in my mouth and seeing him writhe in pleasure.

I found his hands and threaded them with mine, something he always did when he went down on me and continued working my mouth over his length.

The taste of his pre-cum filled my tongue. He was perfectly made for my core but not my mouth. When I was finally able to fully swallow him, he groaned in pleasure, his fingers tightening around mine.

Then I lightly bit down.

He said I could mark his cock and I took full advantage of that as I dragged my teeth back, leaving four vertical lines dripping of blood across his shaft.

"Fuck!" Levi moaned.

I removed my teeth and bobbed my head down again, causing him to whimper. I could feel that he was close. I slid my tongue across the bottom of his shaft, sucking in his delicious blood as I felt him still. I dragged my mouth back across the marks, and he grunted, thrusting his hips up as he released into my mouth.

He came so much that it started to spill out of my lips, down my chin. Every shot of his come was accompanied by a whimper from him until he shot his last string and his body relaxed.

I pulled back off his cock and it slapped onto his stomach, causing him to shudder and release a pained moan. I sat there with his come in my mouth for a while before I tapped him so he would look at me.

When his blue-black eyes met mine, I opened my mouth to show him his mess. Levi gave a lazy smile, and laid back, closing his eyes, reveling in his pleasure.

I bent down and licked his shaft, cleaning his cock of blood and come. He whimpered, then halted my progress with his hand.

"I... Fuck. I need a moment!" More come shot out of his cock and onto his stomach.

I giggled, loving to see him pleasured as such.

It took several moments of heavy breathing until Levi removed his hand from my head, letting me clean his cock. He moaned and writhed as I did. I would lightly lick over my mark, causing him to twitch and put his hand on my head to stop me as he shuddered in pleasure.

When I was done, I climbed onto the bed and laid next to him, burrowing my head into his chest. I released a purr, loving being back here. "I'm sorry," I whispered.

"I'm sorry too," he whispered back.

"I love you, Levi," I said, burrowing deeper into him.

"I love you too, Marie." He kissed my forehead and hugged me tighter.

# FIFTY-ONE

## MARIE

Levi and I spent the next night making love. Mainly because we wanted to apologize for how we treated the other but also because he couldn't fuck me harder if he wanted to. Every thrust into me looked like it caused him pain, but I could feel how much pleasure he felt from the mark I gave him. The pleasure was so overpowering for him. Seeing him struggle not to come and hearing his moans and whimpers as we made love brought me immense satisfaction.

Things were normal the next night. Levi showed everyone my marks while training with his shirt off. He didn't care that I had marked him all over or that his scent was mostly mine. He wore them with pride. I, on the other hand, didn't show mine off. I wasn't ashamed of them, but I didn't feel proud of them. It bothered Levi and he asked repeatedly if I wanted to remove them, but I wanted to let them fade. I didn't want to cause my mate harm and I still loved wearing his marks.

To compensate, Levi got me better clothes to hide them without completely covering my body. A lot of the stuff he bought me was sheer but still covered my arms and neck. They had patterns stitched into them so you wouldn't see the marks unless you were really staring at me which no one would ever do if they wanted to keep their head.

The next two months were normal. When the mark on his cock faded, he asked me to do it again. I told him I would only do it on special occasions because I liked getting fucked hard, but I did start to take him in my mouth every chance I got. I loved having him that way and seeing the pleasure on his face as I made him come. I also liked that when I fully swallowed him, he would tense in anticipation of me biting down, but I never did.

I sent about a hundred letters to my father during that first month, pleading with him to come here for solstice. I even suggested that he come without my mother if she really didn't want to come. After that letter, he replied telling me they would be coming. A part of me knew that the last letter was probably what convinced her, that I was willing to move on from her if she truly didn't want to be in my life again, had scared her into coming.

I started to write to her directly, hoping that I could rebuild a rapport with her. I told her about my life and how much I missed her. I mostly begged her to send me back the necklace. Levi never got the time to have the guards to report to him about what had happened over Samhain because of our fight and then all the sex we had after. He didn't know that my mother took the necklace, and I knew eventually he would find out if I didn't get it back soon. My mother never replied to a single letter. It saddened me to a point where I would wake up way before training to shower so I could cry without Levi knowing.

Eventually the sunrise on solstice came and my parents were arriving at the Unseelie Palace.

The preparations for my parents' arrival were way easier than me leaving. The Seelie King insisted that my father bring a few guards with him for his safety, but besides that, they just needed someone to pick them up from the wall. There weren't any step-by-step plans on their arrival or any rules besides the obvious: don't do any disturbances that would drive a wedge between the kings, which I knew my father would never do.

When my parents got to the palace, they were received in a meeting room where they were checked for weapons. After they were cleared, Levi and I were allowed to enter.

I was so excited. I was practically dragging Levi to get to my parents. I saw my father with his warm smile and my mother who looked like she would rather be anywhere but here. When she saw me though, she smiled, and I was walking faster toward her.

I was a few feet from them when Levi stopped, pulling me back.

I met his eyes. "Introduce me first." He smiled.

I looked back to my parents and stiffened. I was so caught up in seeing them that I didn't notice the guards they brought— Kolvin and his father.

Kolvin and Levi being in the same room wasn't a good idea. I don't think my father thought that out while picking his guards.

I gestured toward my father. "This is my father, Commander Darius Foxglove. His wife, my mother, Corivina Foxglove. Then First Lieutenant Jacoby Denmor, and Private Kolvin Denmor." I gestured to Levi. "Everyone this is my mate, Prince Levington Shadawn, also known as Levi."

My parents smiled but Levi's brows furrowed at Kolvin. "Why would they bring a private?"

"Well, Private Denmor is training to be the next commander and the Denmors are like family to me."

Then Kolvin muttered, "Yeah, if you fuck your family."

The world stopped for a few seconds. Why the fuck would he say that? Was he dumb as shit? Levi was a mate, super territorial, and possessive, willing to kill anyone for fucking with or just straight up fucking his mate.

Levi looked at Kolvin then, his face utterly calm. I watched in horror as the recognition of who Kolvin was flashed through his eyes. Levi had only seen Kolvin from far away once and he had just discovered who his mate was. It made sense Levi didn't instantly recognize him, but since Kolvin had stupidly spoke up, it didn't take long for Levi's memory to connect the dots.

Then he was moving and so was I. I stood between Levi and Kolvin with my hands raised. "Levi, rule number three."

He looked at Kolvin with eyes that promised murder.

"Levi, look at me." His eyes met mine, but his body was still set to pounce. I cupped his face. "Rule number three."

"What's rule number three?" my mother asked.

I didn't look at her when I answered. "The king gave us three rules. One, go to lessons. Two, don't fuck in the greenhouse." My eyes deeply bore into Levi's. "Three, *don't start a war.*" If he killed Kolvin, he would definitely start a disturbance among the fae. Kolvin was here as a guest, and he was unarmed. The fae who want a war would use that as fuel to start one.

"Yes, Levington. Do not start a fucking war," the king spoke.

I didn't hear him enter and he didn't have himself announced so his voice slightly spooked me.

I brushed my thumbs across Levi's cheeks. "Mate," I whispered before bringing his mouth to mine. He softened and brought me into his arms, kissing me back. His hands trailed down my back to my ass where he possessively squeezed. I knew he was doing it to piss off Kolvin, so I purred. Kolvin deserved it for being stupid enough to say that, and I wanted my mate to feel secure with our relationship. I didn't care that he was grabbing my ass in front of my parents or that my face was glued to his; Levi would always come first.

I pulled back and he nudged my nose. "Mate."

I smiled and nudged him back. "Mate."

"They will do that from time to time," the king chimed from right behind us. Levi brought me back to stand beside his father, creating two lines—the king, me and Levi staring at; my father and mother, and Kolvin and his father. "They forget you are in the room with them and try to fuck each other before remembering that there are other people in the world besides them."

The king looked at Levi, silently telling him not to fuck anything up before looking back at my father. "Commander Foxglove." He looked at my mother, his eyes flashing with something as he did. "Corivina."

My mother glared back at the king. "Markos."

He gave a tight smile. "It's a pleasure to have you here again."

"It's not, but your son is mated to my daughter, so here I am," she snapped. It seemed they were doing what the king just accused Levi and I of, forgetting that there were other people in the room. "Those were the rules you gave them?"

The king's jaw tightened before he spoke, "Yes, Cor, those are the rules I gave them. It's not like I have much control over them as mates so I picked the most important things I could think of."

A brow raised on her forehead. "*Most important?*"

The king took a breath in. "Yes, they need to go to lessons. If I didn't enforce that, then they would just fuck all day. Levington needs to be skilled at magic if he's to ascend to the throne, and it's a good time for him to make allies that will follow him throughout life. Marie will be queen so the same should be said for her. They used to sneak into my greenhouse, which is important to me, and I don't want them fucking in there. I think 'don't start a war' explains itself."

My mother snorted. "You got it all figured out, don't you."

The king wiped his face. "Do you think I am happy that *my son* is mated to *your daughter?*"

Levi growled then, pulling me closer into him.

The king raised his hand to Levi. "Levington, we have gone over this. I don't disapprove of your mate. Marie is actually a great pairing for you as the future queen. She is kind, level-headed, and knows how to make friends." He looked at my mother. "In fact, she is good friends with the future commander, a noble's daughter and an exceptionally high-ranking lord's son."

My brows furrowed. I forgot that my friends were actually nobility. To me, they were just my friends. Out of all of them, I thought Gregor was the only one who had any power. I had no idea that Finch was a lord's son. It seems that he was actually the one I should have been pushing Levi toward. They were actually quite similar loner types, so they would probably get along well.

"Well, Markos, I'm quite proud that my daughter will be a good queen as long as your son is a good king to her," my mother remarked.

"Corivina, they are mates. Levi will not hurt her."

"He is your son," she replied.

There was a thick heaviness in the room. I realized then that my mother wasn't mad at me for being mated. She didn't hate me or my mate. She hated my mate's father. It was evident in the way she was staring daggers at him.

I looked at my father, who looked very confused about what was going on. Apparently, he didn't know my mother hated the king personally.

The king cleared his throat. "It is late. One of the servants will show you to your room and you can get some rest before the festivities tomorrow. Thank you for coming, have a good day." The king nodded before turning and exiting the room.

His exit was abrupt and left everyone tense and uncomfortable, everyone except my mother who looked like she was plotting a murder.

"Mother," I breathed.

Her face softened and she looked at me with love. "My flower."

I ran to her then, wrapping my arms around her. She stiffened then sniffed me. I had forgotten that I was covered in marks, and it made people uncomfortable to be near me, but she still wrapped her arms around me before whispering in my ear, "Why do you smell like that?"

"Marie," Levi called. "Come here."

I looked into my mother's eyes, alarm showing through them. I detangled myself from her grasp and moved back to Levi who wrapped his arm around me and nodded to my parents. "We will be going to bed. I look forward to getting to know you in the evening." He turned us, and we exited the room.

"Why did you do that?" I asked Levi as we walked down the hall.

"I don't like it when others touch you."

"She is my mother."

"I know." He kissed my head. "She threatens me like no other, Marie."

She was protective of me. She just wanted to make sure I was always safe and happy. Levi's weariness of her was valid. He didn't have to worry about another male taking me away from him. If anyone would try to get between us, it would be her. She loved no one more in the world than she loved me.

"You will get used to her," I said to Levi, but it was more of a demand. I needed them to get along for this to run smoothly.

"Yes, mate," he replied.

Reaching our door, Levi opened it, and I was greeted with a mountain of presents.

"Levi?" I looked up at him.

He smiled. "Merry Solstice, Marie."

I looked at all the gifts. "These can't all be for me."

He smirked. "You're right, they're not all for you. Some are for my enjoyment." His eyes trailed down my body. "And some we can both play with."

"Play with?" My brows furrowed.

He grinned wider. "Open them."

It probably took an hour to open all the presents. Levi got me multitudes of things: clothes, jewelry, and tons of smutty books. I was definitely going to give him an extra good blow job for that. There were other things as well that had me turning bright red as I opened them. There were chains and whips and other trinkets used to cause pain or pleasure. It seemed he wanted to turn our sex life up some. There was a lot of lingerie, all of which Levi said wouldn't last more than one wear because he planned to tear them off me.

"What are you going to get me next year? You should have gotten one really great gift so that you could outdo yourself next year and the year after that. If you start off too big, then you'll set yourself up for failure," I teased as we sat on the bed, opening the last present.

He grabbed me and pulled me to straddle his lap. "Mate, I will never fail you, and I am an excellent gift giver." He kissed me sweetly. "If anything, I will feast on you for a whole day if you ever find my gifts lacking."

I laughed, then. "You would do that for no reason."

"True, you taste magnificent, and I can't get enough." He nipped at my nose. "I have one last gift for you."

"Is it a real gift or a sexual gift?"

He smirked and kissed my jaw. "Real, but I'll give you tons of sexual gifts after."

I moved back from his kisses that were starting to trail down my neck. "I have a gift for you."

"Is it sexual? Specifically involving your teeth in a very sensitive place?" He bit his lip, eyes gleaming.

I blushed. "No, it's real." He pouted, and I rolled my eyes as I got out of the bed. "I'll be right back."

Getting Levi one gift was hard. Honestly, I didn't know how he got the time to get me any gifts. We were always together. We even bathed together most days. I had to leave a note with one of the servants at dinner to give to Levi's father, just to acquire this one gift. It took me a whole week to orchestrate it.

I went into the closet, grabbing one of my boots and dug my hand in to retrieve the gift.

"You know I'm going to be checking your boots for presents now," Levi said from the closet door.

I looked up at him. "Don't. I don't have a whole palace to hide things in and I don't have a lot of hiding spots."

He chuckled. "This palace is as much of yours as it is mine."

"You know this place like the back of your hand. I would still get lost trying to find my way back to the academic wing if I didn't have you to guide me. So, don't check my boots for presents."

"I make no promises."

"Here." I held out a small black box.

He took it from me, and opened it, a smile painting his lips. The smile raw and genuine, none of his normal cockiness to it. "This is amazing, mate. Thank you."

"Do you want to put it on?"

"Of course."

I took the box from him and pulled out the stainless steel necklace with a small steel wolf. I wanted to get Levi a gift that meant something to him. It was hard to pick just what because he can have anything he wants. He wanted the wolf to be his emblem, but he didn't own one thing that represented a wolf, so I thought this would be perfect. The necklace was small. I definitely didn't see Levi getting a wolf tattooed on his chest so I thought this would be a good supplement.

After I clasped the necklace at the nape of his neck, he turned back around and smiled. "I love you."

I smiled. "I know."

He snorted, then shook his head at me. "Come."

We walked a few paces into the main room before Levi dropped to one knee in front of me, my face coloring with confusion as I stared at him on the ground.

He pulled out a small velvet jewelry box from his pocket. "I didn't get to do this because us being mates makes us automatically married."

My eyes widened as I realized what was happening.

"It's slightly annoying that they take away our chance to marry each other on an altar in front of our family and friends. Though my family and friends consist of one person outside of you, and if you want a wedding, we can have one, of course. I just wanted to do this part." As he looked at me, stars started to enter his eyes.

Tears began to sting my eyes as he opened the box to a ring. The most perfect ring. "You said I couldn't buy you a dress, so I thought I'd buy you a ring." The ring had a rose gold band with a design I couldn't quite see through my tears. Three stones adorned it, two diamonds and a large yellow stone in the middle.

I covered my mouth as I let out a sob.

"Marie Shadawn—I am saying your current last name to remind you we are already married." He smiled that perfect smile. "Will you marry me?"

I let out another sob as I nodded and grabbed his face, smashing my lips to his. "I love you," I whispered.

"I love you." He pulled me to sit on his outstretched knee. "Let me put it on."

He took my hand and put on the ring. I studied it, then I pulled it off to get a better look at the band. It was a wolf chasing a rabbit.

"Bunny," Levi said in a high-pitched voice, mocking Jessamine.

I laughed, and Levi turned my face to look at him. "It is really a good representation of you. You are cute and cuddly, and you love to fuck." He smirked that sexy as fuck smirk. "Mostly it's a great representation of us. You think that I hold all the power in our relationship because I am demanding and possessive, but really, it's you. You are the rabbit, my prey." He nipped at my nose, and I squealed, pulling back. "I need you to survive. Your source of life is abundant, but *I need you*. You are the one with the real power." He sighed looking away for a moment. "When you ignored me, it was the most torturous days of my life and even before we mated, there was this intense need for you. Even before I met you. You don't realize how much I needed you, how alone I was before you. The second I found you, my whole world revolved around you. You were all *I thought* about, all *I dreamed* about, you were the air *I breathed,* and you didn't even seem to notice how much I wanted you, *needed you*. You just kept living like our bond didn't even exist for you and it drove me crazy. I thought I was going crazy." He took the ring from my hands and placed it back on my finger. "I am the wolf not only because I need you to survive but because I will chase you until the end of my days. I will always feel like you are slipping out of my grasp. Yeah, you are mine, my soul technically owns yours but in reality, it's *your soul* who owns mine. *Your heart* that owns mine, *your body* that owns mine. You own me forever, *for eternity*."

He stared into me, and I felt the truth of each word as he spoke it.

Levi reached up to wipe my tears. "I love you, Marie, *for eternity*."

I smiled so wide my cheeks ached. "I love you, Levington, *for eternity*." I pressed my lips to his and then pushed him to the ground.

We made love there, Levi's emotions being spread thoroughly through me with each thrust and mine being spread right back. The drive to speed things up was so prevalent in that moment but we both fought it. We made love for as long as we could before the need to mate was too deep, and we started to ravage each other savagely. Levi thrust into me so hard and so brutally that I was screaming in pleasure. I was pretty sure that my parents could hear my cries from wherever they were in the royal wing. I wouldn't be surprised if the whole palace didn't hear us.

When we came, I felt my soul leave my body to play with his, just for a moment, like when we first mated. Then we both came back, crashing back into reality. A reality where we had each other for this life and *eternity*.

# FIFTY-TWO

## MARIE

Levi and I spent the evening visiting with my parents. We were sitting on a couch across from them. The conversation was mostly just me and my father. Levi only spoke when spoken to and my mother stared at him intensely.

Levi was tense the entire time. My mother was pretty much constantly challenging him with her stares, and it took everything within him not to react. I tried to comfort him in minute ways, but it did little help. My mother's glare was just as threatening as Levi's, if not deadlier.

I tried to talk to her and get her to take her attention off Levi, but anything I asked her was met with a one-word answer and after she answered, she would go back to staring daggers at him.

I couldn't tell if she just hated Levi or if she was just being overly protective. Fae were possessive and I was my mother's before I was Levi's but then there was the stuff with the king that she wasn't explaining. It was clear she hated the king, and that hatred made her weary of my mate. I hoped my mother's love for me would at least give Levi a small pass, but she seemed to have no interest in getting to know him or inviting him into our family.

I knew that if this night didn't go well, I would probably be back in the shower crying tomorrow.

To make matters worse, the situation aggravated my marks. I was shifting constantly in my dress which was also not helping. It was one of the sheer ones Levi bought me. It had black roses stitched into the fabric that covered my neck and arms. The dress had a slip underneath with a sweetheart neckline that cinched at the waist and then flowed out. It was beautiful, but the dress and the tension in the air irritated my skin. Every few seconds I would scratch myself or adjust the sheer. And it wasn't easy to scratch yourself with claws. I didn't want to cut my dress or myself, so I had to pretty much rub the areas so I wouldn't. It looked like I was rubbing out a soreness and every time I tried to scratch myself, I would catch my mother's eye. She would tilt her head slightly as if she wanted to ask a question, then she would return to scowling at my mate.

After an evening of glaring and mindless chatter from me and my father, it was dinner time. We sat in the private dining room where Levi, the king, and I ate dinner every night. The room tonight was decorated for solstice. There were colored lights everywhere, evergreen wreaths and garlands scattered about, and a solstice tree that had presents underneath. The plan was to eat, then open the gifts after. Hopefully food and gifts would lighten the mood.

The table was arranged where Levi and I sat on one side, my mother and father across from us, the king at the head next to Levi and my father. Kolvin and his father stood in the corners behind my parents, keeping guard.

"So how are your studies, flower?" my father asked, trying again to cut the awkward tension. I was surprised he still had stuff to talk about because we spent the hour before this going over every one of his new recruits—in detail.

"Uhh, well, Levi knows everything, so I don't have to do much if I don't want to," I said as I played with my food.

"You shouldn't do that. You should be learning too," my mother interjected.

I looked at her, my spine straightening. "I am. I'm just saying it's easier because Levi knows most of it and he can teach me."

"You should make sure you aren't putting all your eggs in one basket, sweetie." She has never called me sweetie in my life. I could've argued that he is my mate and by divine rights, all 'my eggs' are his, but I could tell that would just start an argument about how I need to be more independent and not rely on my mate. Which would be nonsensical of her, but she didn't seem to be in a sensical mood tonight.

I took a deep breath. I wanted things to turn around and not get more tense and heated, so instead I said, "Yes, Mother."

"So, you're going to be queen now?" My father was definitely running out of shit to say if he thought this was a good topic to bring up.

I shrugged. "I guess so."

The king spoke then. "She is, unless Levi and her birth an heir and decide not to take it."

"Marie doesn't have to be queen if she doesn't want to be," my mother snapped at him, causing everyone to stiffen slightly at her blatant disrespect of the Unseelie King in the Unseelie Palace.

"It is my son, her mate's responsibility, therefore her responsibility. If she doesn't want it, they can have an heir, which I'm surprised they don't already have one growing." The king took a sip of his wine.

She looked at me, eyes hard and demanding my attention. "You don't, right?"

I rubbed my arm to soothe another itch for the hundredth time. "No, we are both on the brew."

"But if we wanted to, we would. You have no say in the matter," Levi added, glaring at her.

She narrowed her eyes. "*Levington*, you shall learn something about females. When you marry them, you are marrying their mother. I don't give a fuck if you are mated to her and if you have a claim to her soul. Her soul chose me as a mother, knowing fully that I would always protect her and be there for her."

"You haven't been there for her for the past three months," Levi muttered.

"Levi!" I whispered.

"It's fine, Marie. He's right; I haven't been there. Finding out that you were mated"—she glanced at the king—"and who you were mated to, was a shock. I apologize for not being there for you, my flower."

"It's okay mother, you are here now."

She gave a half smile, and dinner continued in awkward silence for a while until Levi asked a question, "Why do you two hate each other?"

"I do not hate her," the king replied instantly.

"I do," my mother muttered.

Levi looked to my mother; his brow raised. "Why?"

My mother opened her mouth to speak but the king answered for her. "We were lovers once," he said nonchalantly.

I froze, wanting the king to repeat what he had just said. I had to replay his words over again until they fully registered in my brain. Then I looked to my mother, her nostrils were flared, and her cheeks tinted red from the blood that was probably boiling in her veins as she glared at the king. "*Markos*." She seethed.

The king lazily blinked and took another sip of his wine. "What, my raven?"

My mother's eyes widened, but then everyone paused and turned from her to the king again. It was like a magnet pulling all of our eyes to look at his opened tunic and the raven that rested over his chest.

"Corivina means raven," I whispered out loud to myself.

"What?" Levi whispered back.

"Corivina means raven," the king replied. He continued eating as if he wasn't shattering everyone's mind with this information. He blew out a breath. "Yeah, it does."

Everyone took a moment to let that settle in. My mother was his emblem. They weren't just lovers. You don't just make a past lover your emblem for nothing.

"She was supposed to be my queen," he whispered almost to himself.

"Markos, shut up," my mother snapped.

The king's jaw ticked. He set down his fork and looked at my mother. "You think we will be able to keep that a secret? They are mates, Cor. That means *this* is *forever*. We will do this every sabbat, maybe even their birthdays and their children's birthdays. For now, every sabbat, you will sit at this table. Eight days every year. Eventually, it would come out. I don't see why not now."

"I thought it was never to be discussed," she gritted through her teeth.

"The details, no, but the fact that we were in love and that you were to be my queen. That probably should be said." He glanced at my father.

My father was rigid as he ate. I don't think I have ever seen him so tense. He had his soldier's face on, but his eyes were swirling with an emotion I had never seen in my father's warm blue eyes—rage. Burning rage. He continued to eat, not speaking as the soldier he was. I could tell that he had no idea of this information; he had been married to my mother for almost two hundred years and he had no idea his wife was supposed to be married to the Unseelie King. It didn't explain his rage though, it went deeper than just finding out your wife was promised to another. I could see my father's beast pawing to get out and tear into someone, but he kept it in check.

I personally was reeling. My mother and Levi's father were lovers, more than that. I turned to Levi who seemed not to be affected by the information. He didn't care. It didn't really affect us; nothing would come in between us. Not even a lover's quarrel between our parents. Still, this was huge, like ground-breaking, and he didn't even seem to care.

My mother didn't reply to the king, instead turning to her food to hide from everyone's subjective stares. I tried to scratch myself again and she glanced at the action. "Marie, can I speak to you in the hall?"

Reflexively, I put down my silverware and got up. Levi immediately grabbed my wrist in alarm.

I cupped his face. "My mother would never hurt me, and I would never leave you. There are guards outside as well, they will make sure nothing happens to your mate." I smiled.

He turned to my mother, then. "I don't give a fuck if you're her mother. If you hurt her, I'll kill you."

I turned his face back to mine before my mother could reply. "You will not do that if you want me to be happy. I will never be happy again if you killed her. Even if she hurt me, I would still want her alive. She is on the never kill list—her, my father, and Kolvin." I glanced at Kolvin, whose honey-green eyes flashed with pain. "They are my family. I don't want them dead."

Levi kissed me, then. "Okay, but I will torture them if they hurt you. Non-negotiable."

I laughed, resting my forehead on his, our little bubble forming around us making the outer world disappear. "Okay, but only physical pain. You can't torture them for hurting my feelings."

He smirked. "I said Non-negotiable, did I not?"

I whispered low in his ear so others wouldn't hear. "I will bite you in a very sensitive area if you do that, and I will bite hard this time."

"You just giving me incentive to torture them, mate," he said.

"Marie," my mother spoke, popping our bubble.

I kissed Levi once more. "For eternity."

*"For eternity."*

I turned and walked to her. She had her arms crossed over her blue dress that made her skin shimmer perfectly and a scowl plastered on her face.

We walked out into the hall and a little bit away from the guards until I turned to her and started speaking. "Why didn't you tell me that you were the king's female?" It was out of character for me to interrogate her, but I was fed up with the distance she put between us.

"It was none of your business, Marie."

I rolled my eyes. "He is the father of my mate, mother. You should have told me. If you would have told me, I would have understood why you were acting weird, instead of thinking you hate me and crying in the shower every day."

She looked off to the side instead of answering. These past few months, my mother's detached persona started crumbling, and I could see that me pushing this right now would crack her armor and cause a flood to flow.

I decided to change the subject. "Mother, did you bring the necklace? I need it back."

A muscle in her jaw twitched, and for a moment, she just kept looking out the windows lining the hall that showed off the winter night. Her hard black eyes found mine and it gutted me to see her like this. She was a rock, but something was ramming into her, wearing her down.

She reached into her pocket and handed me the ruby and steel necklace.

"Thank you," I whispered.

She studied me for a moment. "Why do you smell like that?" Her voice was soft and non-accusatory.

I squirmed. "Like what?"

"Marie, don't play dumb with me. Are you pregnant?" Her black eyes peered into my soul for the truth.

"No."

"Then why do you smell like that? You smell like him, overtly so."

I scratched myself and looked down. "We just have a lot of sex," I mumbled.

"You didn't smell like that last time, this is different."

I scratched myself again.

"Why do you keep scratching yourself?"

"The dress is itchy." I fidgeted.

My mother looked at me. I could tell she knew I was lying. She had those mother powers, and she just fucking knew. "Take me to the nearest bathroom."

A tightness started to crawl up my center at her words. I turned and walked to the nearest bathroom. When we entered, she locked the door. She turned to me, her eyes churning with suppressed emotion.

"Take off your dress," she demanded.

"Mother—"

"Marie, do not argue with me."

I stared at her for a moment, not moving. I could have denied her request, but she was my mother. She had a will of steel, and she wouldn't let me get away with this.

I reached behind my neck and started to unzip my dress. I only got so far and then I had to turn to have her finish.

Her warm fingers found the zipper and I felt them tremble as she continued to slowly reveal my body to her. There were only a few marks visible from the back, the one in the middle being the only prominent one. When she was done, she let the dress pool on the ground, and I heard her slightly gasp.

I covered my breasts and turned to her. "Mother."

There were tears lining her eyes as she took my marks in, pain etching into her features.

"Mother, it's—"

"Did he do these all at the same time?" she breathed.

I nodded. "But—"

"Did you black out?" Her voice trembled slightly.

I looked down at my body. "No."

"No, but what?" she supplied, knowing there was more.

"The venom," I hesitated. "The venom paralyzed me. I couldn't tell him to stop."

She covered her mouth as she studied my body again before her eyes connected to mine. "Did you want this?"

I didn't speak, not able to lie when she looked at me like that.

"Marie, answer me. Did he ask you before he did this?"

"No," I whispered.

A tear fell down her cheek and she wiped it away furiously. Her nostrils flared and her face masked with rage.

Then she turned abruptly and stormed toward the door.

"Mother, wait, I—" She was out of the room already, and I was left standing there naked.

# FIFTY-THREE

## Corivina
## 19 years ago.

Coffee-black eyes.

Beautiful coffee-black eyes.

I had never seen something as beautiful as the little babe that I held in my arms. She was so perfect. Caramel skin and a tuft of brown curly hair on her head. A slight gold shimmer that I'm sure would shine brighter as she grew, and black nails that would grow into little claws.

I ran my fingers across her beautiful little pointed ears, and she blinked at me before she smiled.

My babe.

My beautiful babe.

I breathed in her scent. *Daisies.*

She smelled of fresh daisies.

My little beautiful babe, who smells of fresh flowers.

Her coffee-black eyes followed me lazily. She was just born an hour ago. After she fed from me, she stayed silent, watching me with those sweet eyes. They aren't Maurice's, they are mine. I don't know how I could tell, but I could.

They were mine before everything, before all of this.

*Marie.*

It sounded like Maurice. And it was a human name. I thought it was a good way to honor him for giving me this gift.

Because that's what she was, a gift, a beautiful little flower.

Pure and beautiful and mine.

I had never felt love like this.

Never. Not with Markos, not with Darius, not with Maurice. *Never.*

She is my everything, my world, my life, my only reason to live.

The pain of the last two hundred and four years had all been worth it for her. So that I could birth her. She was worth all of it.

She cooed ever so slightly, and I smiled back at her.

Her eyes were so big in her tiny little head.

I felt my broken, disheveled heart repairing just looking within them. It was repairing for her, so that I could be there for her.

I would always be there for her.

To protect her.

To love her.

I would always be her friend to confide in, but I would still be the mother who built her up to be strong.

I would tend to her like the herbs in my shop. I will water her regularly and trim her down when necessary for new and better growth.

"Hi," I whispered to her. "I am Corivina, your mother." I nudged my nose to hers, and she smiled again—a sweet, pure little smile.

"I will love no one more than I love you, I promise."

"I will never harm you and I will always make sure you're happy."

I stared deep into those beautiful coffee-black eyes. "And I will never, *never* let anyone hurt you, my flower, I promise."

I kissed her tiny little head again and spent the rest of the day staring into those coffee-black eyes until she grew too tired to keep them open.

Then I just held her in my arms.

# FIFTY-FOUR

## MARIE

*I* scrambled to get back in my dress, only able to zip it up halfway as I ran toward my mother. I caught her as she entered the dining room, rage seeping from her pores, penetrating the air as she walked directly toward Levi.

I quickly glanced at my father, still uncomfortable and tense from the king's earlier claim. Then my eyes were back at my mother who stopped right behind Levi's chair.

She pulled him by his collar out of the chair which clattered to the floor. My mother's claws seeped into his neck, causing blood to leak out.

Everything in me raged, but I was frozen, caught between my love for my mother and my need to protect my mate. I would kill my mother just for laying a finger on Levi. The mating bond demanded it of me, and it would destroy me to do so. She was my mother, my rock, my soil.

Levi straightened, glaring at my mother. He took a second to look at me, silently telling me he was okay, then he looked back at my mother. "If you wanted me to get up, you could have just asked," he grumbled as if she was not a threat.

She slapped him, making me jerk, my body squeezing uncomfortably, my mind whizzing with indecision.

"Don't *ever* touch my daughter again," she hissed.

Levi eyed me, then looked at my mother, confused. "She is my mate. I'll touch her all I like."

My mother scoffed. "No, you fucking won't. You will not abuse my daughter any longer."

Levi looked really confused at her remark. I could see panic flooding through his eyes. He again glanced at me with unanswered questions churning in his irises before he looked back at my mother. "I would never hurt her."

My mother's brows smashed together on her forehead. "She showed me the marks. Did you bite her a thousand times? She told me you didn't even ask before you did it. You paralyzed her in the process. And you fucking stand here, looking me right in the eyes and say you'd never hurt her."

Levi tensed and his nostrils flared.

My mother snorted. "You're just like your father."

"Corivina," the king gritted through his teeth.

"I don't give a *fuck* about our deal, Markos. I would rather die than let someone of your blood touch my daughter."

My brows furrowed. She made a deal with the king?

The king walked over to her, stepping between her and Levi. "They are mates, my love," he whispered but the room was dead silent so everyone could hear.

"We are not lovers anymore, Markos."

Levi walked over to me and wrapped his arm around my waist. He noticed my dress was undone and he zipped it up before meeting my eyes. They were sparked with panicked rage. I wanted to apologize for showing my mother but now was not the time.

"That was not my choice." The king trailed a finger down her face.

My mother batted away the king's hand. "Not your choice? It was *your* choice."

The king stepped closer to her. "I asked you to be my queen."

"After you did what you did," she snapped.

"Yes, my love, but I didn't mean to do that."

My mother laughed while more tears spilled down her cheeks. "You didn't mean to do that."

He wiped my mother's tears away. "I love you," he whispered. "I always have, always will."

She didn't move from his touch. She looked comfortable with the king. Anyone can see it in their body language; they did love each other, deeply.

My mother removed his hands from her face. "I don't love you." She looked at my father who was just staring at her, hurt mixed with rage simmering in his eyes.

The king's demeanor changed as he glanced in my father's direction. "Yes, the Seelie trash that you chose over me, but you didn't love him enough to have his babe? You had some human's babe. When you should have had mine."

Something in my mother changed as she took in the king's new demeanor. She tensed and her spine straightened; the rage that was directed at Levi before coming back tenfold. "I'm glad I didn't have your child, Markos. I'm glad that I cut that thing out of me."

Everyone, except my mother and the king, sucked in a breath.

*I'm glad I didn't have your child, Markos. I'm glad that I cut that thing out of me.*

The king was frozen as he looked deeply within my mother's eyes, probably replaying those words over and over in his head. "What are you saying?" His voice was calm but deadly and sent shivers up my spine. Levi pulled me tighter to him, anticipating a threat.

My mother looked away, wiping more tears from her face.

The king's voice grew in volume when he spoke again. "Corivina, *what the fuck* are you saying?"

"I was," she said, barely above a whisper. Her face was covered in tears but also filled with a rage that could burn down a whole village.

The king stepped closer to her, his face inches from hers. "You were what?"

My mother took a breath through her nose. "I was pregnant."

Within seconds, the king grabbed her by the neck and pinned her against the wall. My father and I rushed toward him, but the king threw up a barrier made of shadow. The shadows swirled and smoked, making them barely visible.

"You had my child in your womb, and you got rid of it!" the king screamed.

My mother didn't answer, clawing at the king's hand.

"ANSWER ME!"

"Yes," she choked out.

The king's hand, pulsing with black veins, pushed down harder on my mother's throat, causing her to start making incoherent sounds.

"You fucking bitch."

There was an unsettled buzzing within my body, and I was scrambling, feeling lost as I watched the king begin to crush my mother's throat. She squirmed to get away from his hold, but she was no match against him. He was going to kill her, and I was going to have to stand here and watch her die.

My father, Kolvin, and his father were just as panicked. They were all throwing their light magic at the barrier. The magic would sizzle but did nothing. It was useless that they were even trying. It was the winter solstice and the middle of the night—two times when the Unseelie were more powerful.

I looked at Levi who had followed me to the barrier. "Do something!" I screamed, tears flooding my eyes.

He opened his mouth, but nothing came out. His eyes moved toward his father, zeroing on the onyx crown, his brow furrowing, perplexed.

In that moment, it was like I could read Levi's mind as I remembered a crucial fact about kings. Kings pass down their magic to their heirs, making them extraordinarily powerful. It was why no one could challenge the king, or kill the king outright, the magic from their ancestors kept them powerful and seated on the throne. It was unnatural to horde magic like that, but everything the fae did went against nature. The only person who could actually take the Unseelie King in a fair fight would be the Seelie King.

Levi would inherit that power when he ascended to the throne. It was why Levi needed to have an heir if he wanted to forgo the duties of being king. If the current king died, it would go to whoever his heir was. Levi. But now Levi wasn't powerful enough.

*Power.* My hand drifted toward the siphon in my pocket. This was the Queen's Necklace. The power it held wouldn't fully match the king, but it was made so the queen was powerful enough to protect herself from threats.

I could feel it pulsing in my pocket. I pulled it out and looked through the barrier at the king. I didn't know what I was doing, all I knew was I couldn't lose my mother.

Channel then blast—that's what Levi said.

I drew on my magic. Black blood began to pump through my veins and spiral up my arms. I looked at the king and shot my shadows out.

I wasn't trying to hurt him or my mother. I just wanted to distract him so I could interject and end this disaster.

My shadows blasted through the barrier and went straight for the king. Without looking away from my mother, the king stopped my shadows from attacking him, holding them suspended in the air for a brief second. The ball of shadow, no bigger than my head, built in capacity as he added his magic to the mix, his angry eyes not straying from my mother. He pushed them back to where they came from with more force than I could have ever mustered.

Time slowed as I watched the shadows come toward me. My entire short life flashed before my eyes. I knew I was going to die when the shadows reached their destination. I took one last breath and closed my eyes, unable to do anything within the second it took for the shadows to travel from the king to me.

Then I felt someone push me out of the way, and I hit the floor.

# FIFTY-FIVE

## MARIE

*I* sat up quickly, holding my head from the pain I'd received from the fall before looking over to who had pushed me out of the way.

Levi laid on the floor. Motionless.

My heart paused, and I screamed loud enough to break my own eardrums as I realized what had happened.

He saved me—of course he would.

I scrambled over toward his body and shook him, tears running down my face. I could still feel him. He was alive.

"Levi!"

He blinked slowly, his blue-black eyes meeting mine, and I knew then his body was failing. I could feel the pain that racked through him as my hand touched the skin on his face. He couldn't breathe. He couldn't fucking breathe.

"Help him!" I screamed, looking at the room around me. They all stood frozen. The king had let go of my mother to see what he had done, but no one else moved.

"Please! Help him!" I cried.

They all knew what I didn't want to admit. I could feel it. Our hearts were slowing, and he was unable to breathe. None of them were healers and they couldn't get a healer in time to save him. He was dying.

I looked into those midnight blue-black eyes. "Levi, *please*," I cried. "Please don't. For eternity, you promised me. You said for eternity. *Please*."

He tried to speak, but he couldn't. He just wheezed, his eyes, eyes that were like home for my soul, stared into me saying the words he couldn't speak.

I felt our hearts slowing more.

Thump... Thump... Thump...

"No," I whispered.

Thump......... Thump.........

"No," I pleaded with those eyes.

Thump.........

Pain, fully blistering, unimaginable pain shot through me as my heart squeezed within my chest and stopped with his. I cried out in agony as I watched those midnight eyes turn cold, never to hold stars again.

His soul left his body and wrapped around mine for one blissful second, then he was gone, and my heart continued to beat alone.

Everything within me died.

I wasn't splintered.

I wasn't shattered.

I wasn't ruptured.

I wasn't broken.

I was destroyed.

Nothing could put me back together again. Nothing.

I looked down into my mate's lifeless stare. The room was deadly quiet since I stopped crying.

Frantically, I started searching his body for what I knew was on his person.

I pulled a dagger out of his belt loop and stared at it for a moment before turning it toward me, raising it—

The knife was snatched out of my hand, and I screamed.

I reached for the knife, not caring who was in front of me, or for their rose scent. I would kill them to get back to that knife. I needed to be with my mate. I rushed toward them when someone grabbed me from behind. They were stronger than me and their warm vanilla scent permeated my nose as I thrashed to get away from them.

"No! No! No! No! No! No!" I screamed, shaking my head back and forth.

I screamed and screamed, unable to get away from their grasp.

Tears clouded my vision as I screamed and thrashed, feeling my disheveled, destroyed heart squeeze painfully at having to live another second on in this world without my mate.

I felt someone's hand come around my face and whisper, "Flower," brokenly. I jerked away from their hold, cutting my face on their clawed tipped fingers.

I kept trying to get free, thrashing and screaming, wishing they would just let me die and go to him. I needed to be with him.

For eternity.

For eternity.

For eternity.

For eternity.

For eternity.

*For eternity.*

But it had been minutes without him, minutes of our eternity that we were separate, and I was lost from him.

I blinked furiously to clear the tears as I looked over at his dead lifeless body.

He was gone.
My friend.
My lover.
My male.
My husband.
My mate...
My everything was gone, and I was still here.

# EPILOGUE

## Corivina
### A Week after the Winter Solstice.

*I* stared at cold black eyes.

Not mine. Hers.

My flower, who I promised to protect, had wilted.

*One who will break you, one who will heal you, one whom you will destroy.*

If I could bring that witch back to life and kill her again, I fucking would. I knew when I saw Marie almost kill herself, she was the one I destroyed. Not Maurice. Marie.

That's what she was, destroyed. There was no better word for it.

I watched her lie on her bed, looking out the window. I doubted she even cared what was happening. She stopped crying after that silver brand was placed on her arm. She stopped talking too. Stopped eating, stopped living. Now all she did was lie in bed watching the clouds pass.

Darius came in the door, stealing my attention. It was time to feed her. He didn't look at me as he entered. He barely spoke to me after the meeting. He was angry that I had never told him about Markos and that this was all my fault.

He didn't say that last part, but I could see it in his eyes. They had changed too. They were once warm. Now they were burning with unreleased rage. He was angry with Markos; he was angry with me and I knew he was angry with himself too.

We couldn't talk about it though, there were only two of us and we had to watch her. There wasn't any time for us to talk. The brand kept her from harming herself, but there was always a loophole in fae deals, so we had to stay vigilant.

He walked over to the side of the bed that Marie was lying on and trailed a finger down her face. She didn't respond, nor did she acknowledge his presence.

He took her arm and lifted her sleeve to reveal her skin, still covered in marks. His veins started to shine with gold blood and then he placed his hand on her to feed her.

We were Seelie and we bred life. I wasn't super skilled with magic, but Darius was. He knew a way to feed her with just magic alone.

He said he would teach me, but we didn't have the time at the moment. We needed to make sure she stayed alive.

Not only because we loved her and wanted her to live but because the Seelie King required it. By fae law, she was the Unseelie heir now that her mate had died. Until Markos birthed another child, she would remain his heir and would ascend to the throne if something happened to him.

I didn't want her to become queen unless that was what she truly wanted, but at the moment all she wanted was death. She didn't want to live, and it tore me apart to see her like this. She was destroyed. *I destroyed her.*

I got up from the chair I was sitting in and went to the bathroom to look into my cold black eyes that now matched hers. I wanted to break this fucking mirror.

I didn't fucking do this, he did.

The prophecy started with him.

He was the one to break me and he was the one who killed her mate.

He ruined me, then he destroyed her. *My flower* who I vowed to protect.

Now I was going to kill him. He deserved to die for destroying my daughter, the love of my fucking life.

I didn't know how I was going to do it, but I would. I didn't care if I had to cause a fucking war to do so. I wouldn't stop until his blood was on my hands, until his blue-black eyes no longer housed a soul. Markos would die, and nothing would stop me from making that happen.

Nothing.

## THE END, FOR NOW.
## Yes, there will be a HEA at the end of the trilogy.

Book 2 of

# FAE OF THE SUN AND MOON

## coming Summer 2023

For updates, sneak peaks, bonus scenes and all things Jewel Jeffers: linktr.ee/jeweljeffers

# ACKNOWLEDGEMENTS

I think I should start this out by acknowledging the people who even allowed me to write this book during my down times at work, my bosses, Hannah, and Brittany. If I didn't have the time to work on *Blood So Black* at work, I wouldn't have written it at all. Honestly, my favorite place to write is in that gray chair in the corner of our lobby. One of my favorite scenes was created there, chapter twenty-three. I remember that scene was just supposed to be a boring scene where Levi and Marie were to bond during one of their study sessions but then I was like *"Why don't we stop and do something else?"* It was a cold winter night as I wrote that and I think it was snowing, but I'm not really sure because as I wrote that scene a magical feeling settled over me and probably distorted my reality at that moment and that's all thanks to you guys. If I was never allowed to write there, that scene would have never happened, and I am so beyond thankful for that. You guys are the best bosses I have ever had, thank you.

Thanks to the people who beta read my book, no matter if you enjoyed it or hated it, finished it, or only read the first three chapters, you helped to add something to this story and I'm forever grateful. Special thanks to Heather, you were there for a lot of my ramblings of the book, even though I practically forced you to listen when I stayed after work during your shift and talked about it. Thanks for being there and reading it.

Zainab, I am a girl who believes everything happens for a reason and following your intuition. When picking out editors for this book I had a gut feeling I should go with you and I'm so glad I did. Not only did I gain an editor I gained a friend, and I'm so happy that I have you on my team. You are truly the best, can't wait for more adventures with you. I flove you.

Thank you to Chloe and Alexis, you two are the only people who I kept as friends after high school and have been there for me in many ways before I wrote this book. Both of you guys have in some way steered me in this direction and I'm so grateful to have you guys in my path. Also, thank you

## BLOOD SO BLACK

for cheering me on every week as I wrote the story. We may not be as close as we once were because adult life is driving us in different directions, but I know no matter where I am, if I truly need you, you'll be there. So, thank you, I loves you lots.

My most special thank you goes to my most favorite person in the world, Vanessa. You're kind of my best friend even if you are my cousin, and you're the only person I know who loves smutty books as much as I do. You supported me the most during this journey so thank you for being a *good girl*. I know that you were having a hard time at the end of me writing this book and weren't able to be there for me as much, but I hoped that you didn't worry about that and I'm so grateful that you are better, and you will forever be the most important person to me. (Until I get a person with a D and/or have kids.)

Lastly, me. Thank you, Jewel Jeffers. Writing this book was hard. It was fun and exciting at times, but I went through a lot of shit personally and at the end of the day you were the one to get me through it. Sometimes it was the book itself that had me keep pushing, but it was you who wrote five days a week, it was you who rested when you needed rest and it was you who wrote when you needed to write. It was you who saved all your money for this book, rarely buying stuff for yourself so you could make this a physical thing. It was you who formed the plot, who created the world, who found the beta readers, hired the editor and cover designer. It was you who held true to the story and didn't let the opinions of others fully over crowd the story but let go of things that weren't needed in this book.

I'm so proud of you.

Even though all these people listed above were there, for the most part you were alone, and at times you felt so alone you'd cry about it for hours, but you kept going. Thank you for trying. Thank you for being there for me. Thank you for believing, it's crazy how much you believe in us. Sometimes I think hope is a bad thing but no matter how negative I am, you still hold out hope that things will be alright. I hope this is the beginning of something great. I know that a part of you thinks this book sucks and no one's going to like it and the writing style is too simple, but you've already grown as a writer to see that this isn't the best thing out there. But remember this book was never meant to be the best, it was never meant to be more than a place for you to live in and thank you for creating it because I absolutely love it here. I love my people, Corivina, Levi, Darius and Marie and I love you, thank you.